Occam's Razor

A Bill Evers Novel

I0679261

Occam's Razor
A Bill Evers Novel

Howard Upton

Library of Congress Cataloging-in-Publication Data
Upton, Howard, 1969-
Occam's Razor, 2nd publication

ISBN – 978-1-946811-00-4

1. Action/Adventure 2. Suspense Thriller 3. Military Fiction 4. Martial Arts.

Still Water Literary, LLC ™

Dedication

This book is dedicated to the outstanding men and women of the United States military who put their lives on the line every day to protect the freedoms the rest of us hold dear to our own hearts. You are the world's finest, bravest, and most courageous soldiers.

I would also like to dedicate this book to my son Brady. You have always been a pillar of light and goodness. I love you, son.

Lastly, to Cathy. Your high energy, undying love, and encouragement are what push me forward. I love you.

Acknowledgements

The amount of time spent writing a full-length novel is trivial compared to the time some of my most trusted readers spent reading through various drafts, providing feedback (sometimes to the point of brutality), and offering suggestions to make the book better and more potent. I value each of them immensely, and their perspectives are always taken to heart when I begin the editing process.

I sincerely appreciate the feedback provided by Loranda Buoy. You are a lady I admire tremendously, and your opinions and suggestions were very significant during the re-writing/editing process. LeRoy is smiling down at you right now!

Vaquita Rodgers's encouragement excited me as much as anyone who read this book. I very much appreciate what you brought to this book, your outlook on Bill Evers, and your consistently positive approach to life in general. You rock!

Randy Brown, author and friend, you gave me valuable feedback regarding dialogue and it did not fall on deaf ears or blind eyes. Your style, grace, and friendly method when critiquing my work made me smile.

Courtney, my eldest. Your feedback was great, honest, and brutal — just like you. I would not have you any other way. I love you so much and am so proud of the young lady you have become.

Tracey Sanders, once again your passionate approach to literature and editing was spot on. The time we spent going back and forth in emails and on the phone only made this story that much stronger. Thank you so much for what you do!

Dr. Bohdi Sanders, the gratitude I feel regarding your tireless work in bringing these words to life cannot be expressed in words. Your critical eye and (sometimes) hardcore feedback are invaluable to a writer still working to find his way through this thing we call *The Craft*.

Lastly, to you my faithful readers, you are the best, and I can't begin to say thank you for your patience, encouragement, positive energy, and prayers. A writer's shelf-life is short without readers — you are solely responsible for this book's creation. My undying gratitude is given to you.

What Readers Are Saying About *Occam's Razor*

Difficult to put down!

Howard Upton has outdone himself with his latest novel. Spanning the world, in settings as diverse as the novels characters, this current-affairs like, fast-paced, gripping mystery will more than hold the readers' attention. It is, in fact, difficult to put down once started. I highly recommend *Occam's Razor*.

Colonel Roy J. Hobbs, US Air Force Retired
President, Sekai Dentokan Bugei Renmei, Inc.

A Spine-Chilling, Fast-Paced Thriller!

Howard Upton's second Bill Evers novel is spine-chilling! Not only is this book a fast-paced page-turner, but the line between conspiracy theories, fantasy and reality is intertwined in such a way that the reader can actually see this story being on the headline news. That is what really makes this book both entertaining and horrifying at the same time.

As with Upton's first book, *Occam's Razor* spans the globe and interweaves martial arts, covert operations, military adventure, conspiracy theory, fantasy, and magic, all into to one incredibly terrifying story. You *will definitely* be thankful for our dedicated warriors after reading this one!

Bill Evers is America's James Bond, but with more down-to-earth reality. This book addresses the issue of PTSD in a way that you rarely see in an action/adventure novel. *Occam's Razor* has something for everyone; there is even a touch of deadly romance strategically placed throughout the hard-hitting action.

If you are interested in martial arts, military action novels, adventure novels, conspiracy theories, or just plain like nail-biting, page-turning books that you can't put down, you will enjoy *Occam's Razor*. I highly recommend *Occam's Razor*!

Bohdi Sanders, Ph.D.

Bill Evers Dossier

Name: William Samuel Evers

Aliases: Bill, Will, Buck

D.O.B.: November 2, 1973

Sex: M   Hair: BR   Eyes: BR

Marital status: S

Last known address:	1220 Hidden Cove Rd, Oxford, AL
Military service:	4th Ranger Battalion
Commendations:	Reconnaissance and Surveillance Leaders Course, 1st in class Selected to Ranger sniper school, top 3 percentile
Theater of war:	(Iraq) Mosul, Fallujah, and Najaf (Afghanistan) Kabul, Kandahar
Paramilitary:	Contractual-Liberia, Sudan, Uganda Unconfirmed: Columbia, Peru
Additional training:	High ranks in both judo and karate. Hand-to hand assessment-lethal

Occam's Razor
A Bill Evers Novel

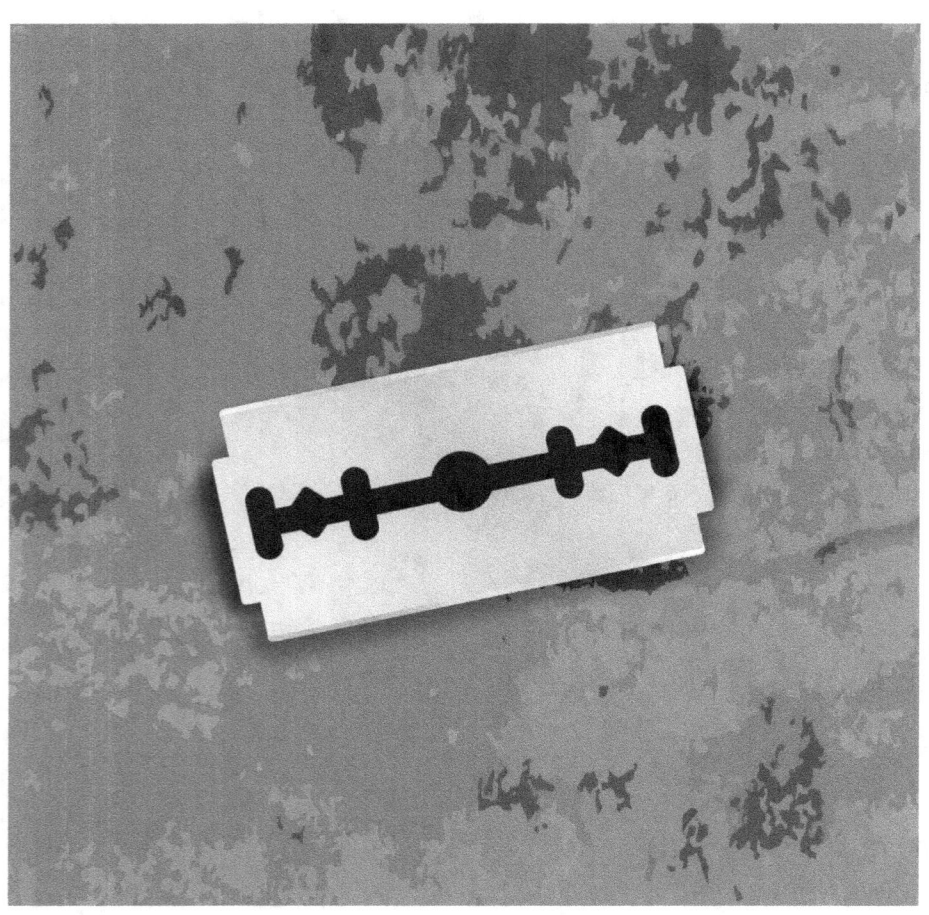

Howard Upton

Part I

We are on the verge of a global transformation.
All we need is the right major crisis and the
nations will accept the New World Order.
~ David Rockefeller ~

We must move as quickly as possible to a one-world
government, one-world religion, under a one-world leader.
~ Robert Mueller ~
(Former Assistant Attorney General of the United Nations)

Imagine there's no countries.
It isn't hard to do.
Nothing to kill or die for.
And no religion too.
Imagine all the people,
living life in peace.
~ John Lennon ~

The Grove Luxury Estate
Watford, United Kingdom
7:15 PM

The members, all two hundred thirty-two of them, were focused on the man at the lectern. His hair was meticulously combed back and styling gel carefully applied to hold it in place. More gray than brown distinguished itself creating the appearance of age and wisdom. His skin was still smooth, most likely due to expensive face creams and strategic plastic surgery. The dark blue Brioni suit he was wearing was chic, exquisitely groomed, and worth more money than many people would make in a single year. Japanese made Tenda eye-glasses framed his chiseled face, the titanium metal used in them light and never short on style.

His sharp English accent cascaded over the assembly. Before he offered his short opening speech, he stood and gazed over the ensemble of the world's elite. His hesitation in speaking was a measured bit of theatrics, but he knew the potential sway it would afford him had a tremendous upside.

Familiar faces stared up at him, many nodding in agreement. Fellow Englishman Randy Fitzgerald, Jr., whose global diamond mining operations in Africa had made him one of the richest men in the world, listened intently. Saudi Sheik Abd-El-Kadir smiled as he fumbled with the solid gold watch hanging from his wrist. It was rumored that Abd-El-Kadir's net worth was well north of one hundred billion U.S. dollars. Other such luminaries were in attendance, as well as various country heads of state.

"We are all acutely aware of the impact of global climate change, famine, and disease, and their relative influences on mankind as a whole. Gone are the days that one country can influence and reduce causation brought upon us by continued industrialization. We are truly a global village, and with that mantle comes ownership and stewardship of our Earthly environs. At the very least, we must take aim at the purveyors of disinformation and environmental disharmony. No longer can we turn a blind eye to the injustices brought upon our children by those who simply desire additional profit and creature comforts.

"At no time in human history has the prospective for its demise been more at hand. We are a species like no other. Our inherent cannibalistic propensities and inability to curb our reproductive cravings has endangered the planet to the point of total annihilation. People steal our planet's natural assets today without thought nor care for tomorrow. How can we look at one another and not be ashamed?

"Now, my esteemed colleagues, is the time to take a stand. We, with a unified voice, can slowly turn back the hands of time, lowering pollutants in our air, reducing toxic emissions that affect our ability to breathe, eliminate dependence on antiquated methods of transportation, and leverage our will against those who rob our planet of its wonderful resources. Collectively, we are the most influential, and if I may be so bold, the most powerful group of human beings ever to sit together in one room. The dynamics at work here, over the next two-and-a-half days, should not be lost on you.

"I beseech you to consider libelous and untrustworthy media resources that have nothing more than their own self-interests at heart. They are the worst kind of enemy. I beg you to pressure those individuals seeking to invade a country whose defenses are no better than a child's play-house, desiring nothing more than the country's natural resources, to change their minds. Each of us can affect change by withholding our generous funds that so many of us gladly hand out in hopes that we might somehow help a starving child or bring water to a parched settlement. I challenge every member of this prestigious organization to follow my lead by cutting off contributions to politicians and special interest groups. Money is power, and we have that power.

"Alone, few of us have a reach beyond our own limited legislative and judicial elements of government, but together we can shape and mold a world that will have at its very center, prosperity, food, water, and general sustenance for each occupant. We, my friends, have at our disposal unlimited capital that will help pave a future that many have dreamt of and prayed for. The leverage we have in our own country's media and government is incredible and should be expounded upon to the point that our collective desire will be felt. We shall not rest until we eliminate the old, outdated means of life and bring about a course correction that will forever alter humanity in such a way that there are no more wars, petty squabbling over what isn't really ours anyway, and the ability to kill without forethought. I hope you will each stand with me in this endeavor."

Several individuals jumped to their feet and shouted their approval. The rest of the room followed suit, standing and cheering in agreement. The speaker smiled and lifted a hand in feigned humility. After several moments of thunderous applause and calls for more, he moved to the microphone and spoke.

"Now," he started, "I would like to introduce our first speaker, Dr. Anthony Little, the noted and illustrious United States Surgeon General!"

Applause erupted around the room as the attendants rose to their feet when Simon Trowton, the man who delivered the opening speech and introduced Dr. Little, nodded his head and raised a hand in appreciation. Several extended anxious hands in hopes of making contact with the articulate speaker. Others patted him on the back and shouted exultations about his wonderful opening speech.

Trowton pressed through the envious throng of people, shaking hands and smiling along the way. A tall, thin black man walked toward him, others around him understanding his relative level of importance and stepping aside as he made his way forward. Many stopped to marvel at him, a few gasps escaping their mouths, his presence strong and compelling. His infectious smile, tried, practiced and perfected over the previous years, shone brilliantly, compliments of numerous rounds of bleach whitener all on the taxpayer's dime. He offered his hand to Trowton, placing his left hand on the man's back.

"Well said, well said, Simon. I would love to have some time alone with you to understand your ideas regarding the change you spoke of. Could we arrange a meeting?"

"I will check my schedule, Mr. President. I'm certain that my calendar isn't so full that it would prevent me from sitting with an affluent, influential individual such as yourself," Trowton replied with his own bright smile.

The two men shared a laugh, each knowing full well if the President of the United States desired a meeting, a meeting would be had. Secretly, however, Trowton knew the President, while exceptionally powerful, was nothing more than a puppet. It was the individuals handling and pulling his strings with whom he wanted to confer.

Trowton continued making his way through the mass of glad-handers and applause. A tall, athletic looking man with close-cropped blonde hair, also attired in an expensive suit, awaited him by the back door. He placed his hand on the man's back and directed him through a pair of thick wooden doors.

They stepped into the open atrium, richly designed with soft curtains and perfectly placed seventeenth century murals depicting angelic scenes and gloriously lush landscapes. Plush furniture was strategically positioned, offering little anonymity, but plenty of space for patrons who might desire a private word or two. Dark blue carpet muffled footsteps while completing the delicate ambiance.

The pair continued walking toward a darker corner of the large room, away from the double doors that opened from the banquet hall and away from anyone who might wander into the area in search of a restroom. Trowton turned and faced the man as he reached inside his jacket and produced a manila envelope.

"Jannick, inside this envelope are twelve separate invitations addressed to some very important people. You will deliver each invitation to the person whose name appears on it, and you must do so quietly and discreetly. Understood?"

"Understood, Mr. Trowton. May I be so bold as to ask what they are invited to attend?"

A slight glower appeared on Trowton's face, but just as quickly as it materialized he composed himself. Not a man who enjoyed being questioned by anyone, he lifted his chin and offered a silent response, his answer blatantly obvious, even as his features smoothed.

Jannick nodded, acknowledging Trowton's contempt for his question. He turned and walked back to the venue, stopping long enough to open one of the large doors and quietly slip back inside.

Trowton wandered to one of the posh chairs and took a seat. His mind spun with possibilities as his heart began to race at the thought of his plan taking shape. Naturally, he knew the most difficult segment was about to begin; convincing twelve of the most powerful men in the world to help bring about the Earth solution would require extreme leverage on his part, but he was prepared to use whatever means he had at his disposal to push his blueprint for the future of mankind to fruition.

He pulled a cell phone from his pocket and touched a one-word name on the screen, "Abaddon." The ring on the other end had with it a distinct buzz, as it always did whenever he made this call. Often, he wondered what caused the annoying sound, but eventually chalked it up to a poor connection, although the poor connection only happened when he called this particular number.

Three rings…a fourth…a fifth…and on the sixth ring he heard a click and the distinct voice of his handler, who he preferred to think of as his boss, only because being "handled" seemed too demeaning.

"It is done?" a demand more than a question.

"The invitations will be delivered tonight, after the meeting and presentations have concluded, sir," he replied as his pulse quickened and the familiar queasy feeling returned, the same queasiness he got each time he heard that dark voice on the other end.

"Invitations. How trite, my young apprentice. A more accurate description would be 'life contract,' I believe. Whatever you call them, Mr. Trowton, you best not fail me lest you be prepared for pain beyond imagination. That is, tremendous pain before your final breath."

Trowton swallowed hard and his heart rate kicked up several notches, as did his respiration. He felt a trickle of sweat fall from the back of his neck and down his spine until his undershirt pulled it away from his skin. With a bony finger and thumb, he pinched the bridge of his nose in a feeble attempt to reduce the pressure now hammering away just behind his eyes. For a brief second he considered the peacefulness death would bring him, but just as quickly pushed the thought from his mind.

"I can *hear* your thoughts, Mr. Trowton. Believe me, death would not afford you even a momentary respite from the pain and anguish I would inflict upon you and your family."

Trowton gawked at his phone, amazed that the slithering voice on the other end could possibly "know" what he was thinking. He considered the possibility that his handler had someone watching him, but that didn't explain how the man could read his mind.

He sat there for a few seconds with the phone pressed against his ear, his rapid breathing growing to the point of hyper-ventilating. Words were lost on him; his mind raced, yet his motor skills were essentially shut down. Very few times in his life had he been so scared that he found himself without the ability to speak.

An audible chuckle came from the other end. "Be sure to see this through, my son."

Trowton was relieved when he heard the click on the other end. The silence surrounding him was as warming as a blanket on a cold winter's night. He allowed himself a prolonged sigh of relief, a minor expanse of tension momentarily leaving his body affording him a respite from the stress of the call.

His thoughts drifted back in time, six months earlier to be precise. A random call on his cell phone, one that he assumed was a wrong number, but one he felt compelled to answer started the ball rolling. Trowton heard a voice on the other end, one that appeared slippery and dark to him; vaguely his mind processed the emotions the voice invoked. He felt marked, and somehow damaged.

"Do not hang up. You and I have never met, but I understand you have a strong desire to save mankind from itself, yes?"

"Who the hell is this," Trowton demanded?

"Who I am is irrelevant at this point and time. What *is* important is our mutual desire to change the human impact man has on an unwitting world. As I've come to understand it, you and I share some ideas better discussed in person. I suggest a meeting at a time and place of your choosing. However, in my opinion, the sooner we meet the better."

Trowton felt himself quickly confused and equally paranoid. Who could have possibly known his thoughts about containing the virus known as "mankind?" He had not shared his plans with anyone and his mind suddenly dashed to memories of reading Orwell's *1984. Has technology pushed us over the edge so that we're finally forced to succumb to the thought police?*

"Look, I don't know who this is, and I have no idea what you're talking about, but this conversation is finished," he responded, but for some reason could not bring himself to hang up the phone.

"Yes, Mr. Trowton, I do understand your hesitation and concern, but I assure you that I am a man of principle and have a strong belief in an orderly civilization."

"How do you know my name and how did you get my personal cell number!" he demanded.

"I will answer everything for you in time, Mr. Trowton, but only if you agree to meet with me first."

And so it was that he had agreed to meet the man who would forever change his life. They met at the very upscale Mari Vanna Restaurant in Knightsbridge, London just before sunset. When Trowton first entered the restaurant, his eyes were immediately drawn to a vibrant presence, and *he simply knew* the voice on the phone belonged to the man who emitted it.

Trowton walked over to greet him, and the man offered a curt nod of his head in response. The two sat down at their table without speaking, each man instead choosing to peruse the menu. Trowton's business dealings with powerful men and women had taught him to maintain a pokerface at all times when engaged in transactions.

After a couple of minutes Trowton's visitor put the menu down and folded his hands on the table and stared at him as though he was to be the main course. He could feel the top of his head burning even though he was intently studying his menu. Trowton raised his head to see the man staring at him, as though he was attempting to both read and assess his worthiness. For a reason unclear to him, he could feel sweat beading on his forehead and his palms were suddenly clammy. Unconsciously, he placed his hands on his thighs and rubbed nervously.

"I'm afraid I still don't know your name, Mr…," Trowton began.

"You do not know my name because I haven't given it to you yet, Simon," the man smiled.

Nerves shot, Trowton reached for the glass of water their waitress provided when they sat down. His respiration quickened and his hands shook while holding the glass. Although the man had given him no reason to be uncomfortable or nervous, Simon was sensitive enough to pick up the energy given off by those around him, and the man seated across from him had the air of someone who existed in a realm where words like "malevolent" and "wicked" were terms of endearment.

"Please, Simon, calm yourself. It is obvious I make you uneasy, but we have come together to talk and discuss things of great importance. You may call me Abaddon," the man replied.

Trowton nodded his head, a loud ringing in his ears nearly blocking all the sound around him.

"A-A-Abaddon? I don't think I've heard that name before. What is its origin?" Trowton managed.

Abaddon rolled his eyes and raised his hands to his chest, palms down, a movement that was intended to demonstrate dominance.

"The origin of my name is irrelevant, Simon, but rest assured it is a very ancient family name given to me by my father," Abaddon said, his voice firm.

Trowton stared at Abaddon, his chest rising and falling quickly. Abaddon's gaze was neutral, calm, and probing. Neither men spoke for two full minutes until Abaddon broke the silence by first offering up an audible sigh.

"Okay, Simon, I realize we are meeting for the first time, and chit-chat is essential to businessmen prior to business discussions. Without going into great detail, my name has its origins in the Hebrew vernacular, and let's just say that my father is particular to the Jewish people. Now, shall we order?" Abaddon finished.

Again, Trowton nodded his head, acquiescing to Abaddon's wishes and picked up his menu. The two once again sat in silence, Trowton reading the food selection and Abaddon studying him as though *he* was on the menu.

Their setting was one suggested by Trowton, as it was one of his favorite places. Usually, it was very crowded, which made him feel better about meeting a stranger who made him feel so uneasy. This day was no different, and he was thankful to have other people seated near them.

The food was the finest Russian cuisine and a décor that screamed love to Mother Russia. Russian made dolls and literature adorned shelves throughout the seating area. Beautifully handmade wooden tables sat at intimate intervals to other diners. Lush chairs and comfortable couches sat adjacent to the tables, creating a feeling of home and grandeur.

In spite of his nerves, he was famished. Trowton ordered a delicious serving of Siberian Pelmini, Russian dumplings filled with onions, lamb, and mushrooms, and a succulently sweet glass of Moscato d'Asti. Abaddon preferred not to eat, but sipped on a glass of Tormaresca, a nice Italian chardonnay instead.

"So, Mr...Abaddon, I fail to understand why you insisted that we meet."

A greasy smile spread over the man's face. His blonde hair was slicked back and his ice-blue eyes pierced Trowton's from behind squared spectacles. Abaddon sported a navy blue herring-bone suit that he wore without a tie and the top button left open. The suit accentuated a slender but obviously muscular frame, the frame of someone who paid special attention to his body and what went into it. Trowton noticed something odd about the man's facial features, but couldn't quite figure out what the oddity was.

Trowton's eyes fell to Abaddon's hand, which quietly thrummed a black, ragged cover encasing a well-used and handled book. It took him just a second to process what the book was, the King James's version of *The Holy Bible*. He watched as Abaddon picked up the Book and opened it toward the back.

"I prefer this abridged version of The Word, Mr. Trowton," he all but whispered. "The good king pared down the repetitious verses the Catholics prefer, as a result of the Council of Nicaea, but it's mostly the same."

Trowton's eyes fell to the opened book and saw the dog-eared pages. He noticed an underlined passage, Chapter one, verse three.

Blessed is he that readeth, and they that hear the words of this prophecy, and keep those things that are written therein: for the time is at hand.

"Yes, Mr. Trowton. The Book of the Revelation is the only book in The Bible that promises its reader a blessing for having read it and remaining beholden to its words. I read it often," Abaddon hissed.

"I'm afraid I don't believe anything written in that ancient book, Mr. Abaddon. It's largely inaccurate prose, a poor record of historical accounts, and serves as little more than a means to control an uneducated public," Trowton replied as he put the glass of Moscato to his lips.

"And that's where you and other academics get it wrong, sir. Make no mistake, this dusty book was written by those who experienced the very events described within it. No matter your nebulous opinion to the contrary, this Book is inspired and is mostly correct, with the exception of the ending. John's dream and prophetic Revelation are nothing more than an attempt at a happy ending for those who would deny the truth, Mr. Trowton," replied Abaddon.

He continued, "As an example, 'The Devil who had led them astray was thrown into the pool of fire and sulfur, where the beast and the false prophet were. There they will be tormented day and night forever and ever.'

"Tell me, Mr. Trowton, how do you presume to believe the God of gods would banish his most treasonous of angels to a lake of fire, a burning bastion of pain and torment beyond human imagination then assume throwing him into that same lake would somehow torture him for an eternity? If that lake were to become the Fallen's domain, don't you believe that God would have made the angel impervious to it? Does that make sense to you, sir?" the man finished cryptically.

"Well, Mr. Abaddon, I suppose you base your opinion of the subject on those things you experienced and studied, but that doesn't sway me from what I know to be the honest truth. I'm a humanist, a man who believes in the larger goodness of mankind. I want nothing more than for people to care for both each other and the Earth on which they walk," Trowton snapped.

"That, you pompous little bastard, is why you and those who think like you, lack direction in your tiny, inconsequential lives. I'll not sit here and allow you to simply brush aside everything I know to be factual and true. Do not dismiss me like some lunatic standing on a street corner screaming, 'The end is near,' or some other such nonsense," Abaddon fired back, his face stern and voice steady.

Trowton gulped and choked on the air he was breathing. For a few seconds he was unable to stop coughing and their waitress stopped to ask if he was okay. He waved her away, his face still red from the momentary lack of oxygen.

Abaddon spun the stem of his wine glass in his hand, his fingernails carefully manicured. "Mr. Trowton, you will come to know me as a man who is brutally honest, to the point of discomfort with the individual with whom I converse. With that, I want to be completely honest with you—together we are going to change the human landscape, but you must understand, your participation will be worth much to you, both financially and physically."

"Pardon me for being so forward, Mr. Abaddon, but what *the fuck* are you talking about?"

"Everything will be revealed to you soon enough, Mr. Trowton. In the meantime, there are a number of people you associate with that must be persuaded to join us. How you devise the plan to ascertain our goal is up to you," Abaddon hissed.

"And what is our 'goal,' Mr. Abaddon? Your cryptic speech is wearing thin on me, and I'm afraid I have other appointments to keep," he replied, a wisp of courage seeping into his chest.

Abaddon's forehead creased slightly and his ice-blue eyes seemed to...redden. "Let me assure you, Mr. Trowton, I'll not tolerate any insolence in our association. You'll be rewarded handsomely for your participation, but should you choose the alternative to our relationship, I fear your time spent among the living shall be sufficiently condensed. Are we clear?" He leaned forward on his elbows and stared directly into Trowton's eyes.

Something in Abbadon's stare told him the man was dangerous, or perhaps evil was the word he was looking for. *No*, he thought, *this individual is beyond evil*. He took a sip of his Moscato d'Asti and swallowed hard. Something electric emanated from the man, something that wouldn't allow him to break the eye-lock on him. He felt as though his soul was being raped and there was nothing he could do to stop it, succumbing to him was inevitable.

Trowton was first invited to a Bilderberg meeting twelve years earlier. He was enamored at the discussion, all of it kept private and unreleased to an uneducated and unknowing public. But what began as intriguing debate and ideas to help better mankind and take care of a planet in peril soon devolved into empty rhetoric, cocktail parties, and mindless hobnobbing among the world's wealthiest.

He became disillusioned after engaging former French President Lionel Jospin. The man was obviously an idealist, but he laughed when Trowton asked how the organization could make a more powerful statement to the world to curtail the drain on natural resources and curb the growing warming of the planet.

"Ah, Simon, how I long to be young once again, and be filled with fire and passion as you so obviously are. You must understand that the majority of wars waged in our world are orchestrated by our group. We attempt to distract a global populace while we quietly work to further our agenda through the media that many of our members own and support financially. You see? We have a plan and a course of action, but we cannot make obvious moves less the people turn on us. Would you prefer to make a flamboyant declaration, only to be drawn and quartered by those you are attempting to protect? This is why we work covertly, my friend. Manipulation of the global markets, wars, and media are just a few of the things we do in an attempt to stave off a certain man-made annihilation."

He measured Jospin's words carefully before responding. "So, in essence, you believe we should push our agenda from the quiet halls of luxury hotels and chateaus, all the while keeping ourselves from the line of fire? Don't you find that thought process a little self-aggrandizing and cowardly?"

The French President's expression changed, his face reddened and eyes narrowed. "Do not mock me, young man. I've lived on this Earth long enough to understand the mindset of mankind. I have a firm grasp on the faulty idea of American exceptionalism, European arrogance, and global Chinese domination. Change cannot be affected in loud explosions, but by more subtle nuances that bring about change in the universal mindset. Do you understand me?" His French accent grew deeper and thicker as the ire in his voice rose.

Trowton dropped his eyes and awkwardly shuffled his feet. He wanted to engage this powerful man in further debate, but he quickly realized his mistake in challenging him without concrete evidence to support his position. This was a mistake he would never make again, and one he marked up to youthful inexperience and his own ideological faith.

"My apologies, Mr. President, I should have chosen my words more carefully. I did not mean to insinuate that you were cowardly or in any way incapable. My zeal for aiding and assisting our fine organization to further our global agenda sometimes clouds my judgment," he responded with as much sincerity as he could muster.

The Frenchman composed himself, while unconsciously straightening his suit. He stuck his chin out and summarily dismissed the insolent young man with whom he had been speaking by turning and walking away.

Trowton rubbed his eyes and focused on the present. His eyes darted around the atrium and locked on a man who was eying him curiously from across the grand room. The sight of the man simultaneously confused and angered him. Trowton had been concentrating on his phone call so much that he had forgotten to check his surroundings to insure no one was listening to his conversation. He assessed the situation quickly and knew there was no way the stranger could have overheard his discussion because of the distance between them, and because he had kept his voice low. Still, he glowered at the interloper who immediately recognized his situation, turned, and exited the room.

Trowton took a deep breath and exhaled slowly. The wheels were in motion and the plan in place to make the world a more hospitable place, and to assure its resources were left to the next generation. His thoughts lifted a little of the heavy burden he had felt while on the phone with Abaddon and a tight smile formed at the corners of his mouth.

Birmingham Judo Club
Birmingham, Alabama, USA
5:41 PM

The two men grasped each other's lapel and sleeve just behind an elbow. Their feet shuffled about the dark blue mat in search of an angle and an opening. They could feel the other's leverage and weight as each man dropped his hips and centered himself to avoid being thrown. Their white uniforms were soaked in sweat and their tattered black belts told even the most novice of watchers of the years both had spent perfecting their technique, balance, and fighting spirit.

The men were roughly the same height and weight, but one appeared considerably more muscular than the other. His brown hair was longer than it had ever been, all one length with strands that appeared to tickle his shoulders, was wet and stuck to his face and neck. William Evers, Bill to those who knew him, bore a contrasting look of both extreme concentration and hyper-relaxation.

By contrast, Evers's opponent had thicker legs and a gut that protruded over his ragged black belt. Despite his outward appearance, his command of the tatami, or judo mat, was obvious to even a casual observer. His sense of balance was incredible and his quickness masked to the uninitiated.

As each attempted a throw, the other would counter. After two minutes of entering, feinting, and trying to out-leverage the other, an opportunity to suck his opponent in and hopefully gain the advantage reared itself. Evers's back foot slid up and behind his lead foot, while his lead foot began to move inside his opponent's lead leg. Ouchi gari, or great inside reap, was perfect if an opponent's hips were slightly behind and his weight moderately draped over his heels. He pulled down on the man's lapel and turned his hand into the man's sleeve, lifting his elbow and pulling his weight toward the leg he was attempting to reap, but his opponent felt the weight transition and quickly countered by centering himself and pulling his lead leg back. The brief second it took Evers's opponent to react to Evers's ouchi gari was all he needed to snap his hips and turn his back to him, throwing his own lead leg to the outside of the man, reaping his leg and executing a near perfect harai goshi.

In the instant his opponent realized his mistake he was airborne. Evers's hand dropped from the lapel and wrapped itself behind the man's waist. He centered himself below the man's hips while his back remained momentarily upright and in contact with his torso.

The throw was fast and hard, but years of ukemi, or break-falling, allowed the receiver of his throw to at least fall gracefully and without injury. Evers rode the man's body to the mat, falling into a side control that neutralized his challenger's movement. His opponent acknowledged his defeat by tapping Evers on the back.

He released the man and both stood bowing to one another before beginning the process again. For an hour they trained—sometimes Evers won a match, other times his opponent. No matter the outcome, they would rise, bow, and start again, the respect and admiration they felt for each other apparent.

The mat quickly became wet from perspiration and they would pause long enough to mop up the dampness to avoid a potential slip or accidental fall. Some of the lower ranking students stopped training to watch the two senior yudansha, or black belts, work on their techniques.

At last they stopped and bowed deeply to one another, their training finished. Evers slapped his training partner on the back and smiled.

"Your technique is excellent as always, Sammy, and your uchi mata is even better than the last time we trained together. You've been practicing secretly haven't you?" he asked with a wink.

Sam belted out a hearty laugh, his belly shaking in the process of doing so. "I have to practice twice as much when you're not here just to keep up, Bill!"

"That was a great workout, Sam. It always feels good to come down here and train with y'all. Want to shower up and grab a beer?"

"Man, I'd love a nice cold one after all that randori," Sam replied using the Japanese term for free-sparring.

As the two men walked to the locker room, the other students returned to their practice. Body upon body was sent flying through the air, and as with Evers and Sam, they helped one another up, bowed and began the process again. The students being thrown would slap the mat as hard as possible in order to reduce the impact of their bodies crashing to the floor, all of them inspired by the two seniors walking off the mat.

Evers paused for a moment to watch the youngsters practicing their judo, and recalled when he first began to train in the gentle art as an immature twelve year old. His teacher was a former Marine sergeant, Brad Timil who, like so many martial arts teachers before him, learned his art while stationed in Japan. He brought it back to the States and taught just like a person would expect a former Marine to teach—hard and without compassion or empathy.

Evers's father was a former Marine, and loved the fact that a Marine Corp sergeant was teaching the class. Young Bill had developed quite an attitude, as well as a bad temper, and his Thomas, his father, could think of no better way of instilling discipline in his son than signing him up for a militaristic art taught by a former military man. He hoped Timil could help curb some of Bill's rambunctiousness.

After learning some basic break falling techniques, Evers was personally introduced to ippon seoi nage, one of the basic and most powerful throws in the judo curriculum. Never one to warn a student what was about to happen, Timil demonstrated the technique on Evers, who was momentarily mystified at being launched into orbit. So bewildered was he, in fact, that he forgot to break his fall when he hit the mat.

Air rushed from his lungs as he landed flat on his back, and his head hit with a solid thud into the mat, his eyesight dimming and narrowing as a result of the impact. Before going completely numb, he was aware that his legs had slammed haphazardly to the floor and lay sprawling in a most unflattering manner.

He awoke sitting upright and propped against a wall. Each breath he took was an exercise in pain, and for a moment he thought every one of his ribs were broken. Timil and five other students stood over him wondering if he was alive, Timil's expression blank. A few moments passed and Evers stood shaking his head, trying to remove some of the cobwebs and fuzziness that had formed.

"You alright, son?" asked Timil.

"Yes sir, it just hurts to breath."

Timil grunted his understanding and turned to the other students. "Back to work...let's go!"

"It wasn't your fault, sensei. I just didn't break my fall like I was supposed to," Evers said almost apologetically.

Timil stopped and stared at Evers, one corner of his mouth turned upward into a sneer. "You goddam right it wasn't my fault, son. I taught you how to fall, it's up to you to apply it. Hell, I don't even understand what it is you're trying to say to me."

Evers let his eyes drop to the floor. He was confused by his teacher's reaction to his act of contrition and kindness. A tear welled up and ran down one cheek as he swiftly wiped a sweaty sleeve across his face. A quick sniffle escaped him, but unfortunately for him Timil heard it.

"Are you crying, son? Does it hurt that bad or did I hurt your damned feelings?"

"No sir. I was just saying it wasn't your fault. I didn't want you to feel bad about me getting hurt."

A smirk turned Timil's lips slightly upward. Evers thought it looked quite unnatural on the man, as his face was usually stern and his voice loud. The large instructor walked back to Evers and squatted down in front of him.

"Let me tell you something, boy. I don't have the time or the patience for whimpering and crying in my dojo. I know it doesn't seem like it right now, but in a few short years, you're going to be a man. You might as well start practicing to be one now, so stop your damned sniveling, shake the nonsense from your head, and get back on the mat and train. You understand?"

Another tear rolled down his face as he nodded his understanding. Evers didn't know it then but the decision he would make to remain in judo class would pave the way to what he would later become—a hardened soldier with some incredible hand-to-hand skills. For a moment he considered taking his judogi off, dropping it on the mat, and walking away, but he knew he could never do that. He wouldn't be able to face his mother and father, let alone look at himself in the mirror. Even at twelve years old, his resolve was such that he wanted to prove to Timil he would be the best judo-ka to ever train in his dojo. As a matter of course, he relished the thought of facing his teacher on the mat one day and throwing him in osoto gari or kata garuma.

Evers paused before he walked to the locker room to shower and get ready for that beer with Sam. Mounted above the door was a quote he knew all too well.

By what I did yesterday, I win today. Such is the virtue of practice.

A bead of sweat dripped from his brow and fell to the floor. He nodded his agreement at the large banner before walking to the locker room.

An hour later the two men walked into Zydeco's pub off 15th street. Evers chose the place for its laid back atmosphere and penchant for local blues music. He had discovered the place years earlier during his infrequent trips to Birmingham for work or to train at the judo club. The cloth awnings, three green and two blue, hung over the bar's windows. Plastic patio furniture sat outside for those parishioners wishing to eat and drink away from those crowding the stage to listen to the band.

The late afternoon sun was blocked by the heavily tinted windows. A simple wooden door opened into the expanse of the tavern. Cold air hit them in the face, a welcome reprieve from the brutal heat of the Alabama summer.

The absence of daylight and the soft neon glow of various signs created a cozy feeling inside. A large bar proudly displayed numerous liquors and several craft beers on tap. The usual night crowd had not yet begun piling into the place—only four other people were seated at two tables close to the stage.

Evers and Sam sat on stools at the bar. Evers ordered one of his favorite beers, a Chicago brewed 312 Urban Wheat, while Sam asked the bartender to pour him a Dogfish Head India Brown Ale. Evers sipped the 312 while Sam savored his by smelling the hops and malt the beer offered.

"You're just going to sit there and sniff that thing, huh?" Evers laughed.

"A beer like this is meant to be caressed, Bill. In fact, I would go so far as to say this particular brew deserves a significant amount of affection and adoration before drinking it. I like to meditate on a good beer before I drink it," Sam replied.

Evers shook his head and laughed again. "I've missed hanging out with you, Sam. It's been too long."

"The training was good tonight, Grasshopper. We've missed you around the dojo. The young kids love to watch two old guys like us go at it," Sam quipped.

Evers took another pull from his beer and said, "The training was enjoyable..I've missed it."

Sam had trained at the dojo for almost as long as Evers. The two hit it off immediately, throwing each other around four nights a week for five years. After every training session, the two boys would hang around the dojo discussing girls, school, and judo, their three favorite subjects.

"Speaking of missing," Sam said as he finally took a long, slow sip of his Ale, "where have you been? I know you travel to Birmingham periodically for work, but it's been quite some time since we last saw you."

Evers mind flashed to the time he had recently spent in Mexico and China chasing after an ancient cartouche that held the power to bring to life the Terracotta Warriors, as well as chasing the man wanting to control the army in order to sell it to the highest bidder—a former CIA and American military entrepreneur, Dan Dugan. His partner, Buddy Smith had shot Dugan in the leg while they were in Xi'an, China. He and Evers left Dugan for the Chinese military when they exited the country; they had not heard anything about the man since.

Since his return to the States, with a large cash windfall in hand courtesy of Uncle Sam after their run-in with Dugan, Evers spent most of his time on his property in Oxford, Alabama hunting and fishing. The money was tucked safely away in hidden off-shore accounts, just in case the United States government ever decided they wanted it back.

"I had to travel outside the country for a while, Sammy. It wasn't fun being away, but it was work related and I needed the money. I'm back now though, and hope to get over here to train a little more often," Evers finished.

"Work related? Where did you go? What kind of work did you do overseas?"

"I flew around, made a lot of good friends, spent time as a man-whore…you know, overseas work," Evers replied.

Sam looked at his judo partner, a man he barely knew outside the dojo, and smiled. "You're an interesting man, Bill Evers, but if you don't want to talk about your work I understand."

Evers shook his head signaling both his appreciation and the end of the topic. In no way did he want his name tied to murders in Mexico, nor did he want to be linked to the disappearance of Dan Dugan.

The two continued to drink, ordering a second and third round while they romanticized about the traditional martial arts in a way that only people who have decades of training under their belt can do. Each generation talks about how much harder the training was when they were coming up through the ranks, but the truth is, training is only as tough as the instructor makes it, and as rough as the student perceives it.

Their conversation drifted into other things like Sam's wife and children and how proud he was of his boys. He couldn't talk them into joining the dojo, but he wouldn't give up hope. Evers listened intently and asked questions at just the right time so as to avoid questions about his lack of family and loved ones.

An hour-and-a-half passed and a few customers came and went. The bartender turned on the flat screen television that hung above the bar, but kept the volume muted. The bright light of the television caught Evers's eye and when he looked up at it he noticed that the local news station was reporting on some breaking news. Although there was no sound, Evers could see the scrolling news ticker moving across the bottom of the screen.

"Over fourteen hundred in West Africa reported killed by the world's deadliest outbreak of the Ebola virus. Reports have surfaced detailing the total annihilation of an entire village." The report continued to show pictures of infected Africans in Liberia, their emaciated bodies bloodied and twisted.

His thoughts went immediately to the times he and Buddy Smith had spent in Africa. The villages they had stormed, the people they had killed, and the unforgettable stain his actions had left on his soul. Most of his time was spent in Muslim populated areas hunting down suspected terrorists, but there was some R&R time in Nigeria, one of several countries commonly referred to as West Africa.

Evers was vaguely aware that Sam was still talking to him as he concentrated on the macabre scenes on display an ocean away. Crying mothers, fathers, and children mourned the deaths of loved ones, their despair and pain manifested in tears and the contorted looks on their faces. He wanted to feel something for them, to share in their agony, but something inside him blocked any emotion. The hurt and pain he had experienced as a war-time soldier and as a mercenary prevented from feeling anything as he watched the broadcast. His mind would only allow him to wonder "how" something like Ebola could be so rapidly spread from human to human.

The virus was present in Africa when he was there working as a mercenary—everyone he worked with was aware of it and the plethora of other viruses and bad actors that lay hidden within the jungles and deserts of the continent. The CDC and WHO told the world that Ebola was spread through human-to-human contact with infected persons. Contact with infected blood and human secretions were the only way to catch the virus, or at least that's what the soldiers were told. Evers always had his doubts about the veracity of the claim; both medical think tanks were inclined to blur the truth in order to keep the world's population calm.

He knew it wasn't wholly impossible that an entire village could be eradicated by a disease that could be transmitted through direct contact with infected victims, although highly unlikely. Given the rapid pace the disease had set in Liberia, he suspected transmission to be easier than either the CDC or WHO were willing to admit.

Sam stopped talking when he saw Evers focused on the television. He watched the same scrolling ticker across the bottom of the screen and was stunned by what he read.

"Holy shit. An entire village was wiped out by Ebola? Imagine what would happen if someone infected wound up traveling to the U.S.," Sam stammered.

Evers took another long drink of his beer. "Yeah, just imagine."

Alexandria, Virginia, USA
4:12 AM

Bloodshot eyes focused on the computer screen. Those same eyes scanned the top secret information he received shortly after a phone call from an Agency insider. His shaky hand reached for the tumbler of Scotch sitting on a coaster next to his laptop computer.

As he read through the classified electronic document he felt his stomach lurch. Digestive acid and smoky liquor lurched from his belly to his throat. With effort, he managed to force the disgusting blend back down as he continued to read.

Outside his apartment he could hear the sound of police sirens wailing, and he thought with some irony about the insignificance of a police force paid to serve and protect, when in reality they were nothing more than window dressing used to keep a burgeoning population under control. A warm summer breeze blew through his open window causing the dusty curtains to move and dance in its wake.

Buddy Smith eased back in his recliner and took a deep breath. The rolling he felt a few moments earlier in his guts had passed but the storm brewing in his brain raged on. A shaky hand felt inside his shirt pocket and found the Cuban Cohiba he placed there earlier that day. On the small table next to his chair he grabbed the cigar cutter and masterfully trimmed the end. The blue flame from his lighter reached the end of the cigar as he puffed, the brown tobacco brought to life in a red-orange glow. Sweet smoke cascaded over his face and head but he barely noticed. His eyes darted back to the computer screen.

...*two test vials of airborne Ebola virus stolen from the World Health Organization's vault. Also, discovered was a missing vial of SARS from the Center of Disease Control vault in Atlanta. Escalation of violence in various regions appears orchestrated, as over ten-thousand children have been murdered in Syria alone. Coordinated efforts in Somalia, Uganda, Mexico, Honduras, Guatemala, and regions of South America provide further evidence...*

Buddy closed the laptop and placed it on the table next to his chair. He inhaled the cigar deeply, his thoughts far away. Outside he could hear children playing in his apartment parking lot as dusk began turning to night. He overheard a mother telling her son to "play nice or he wouldn't have any friends."

A sad smirk crossed his face. "Lady," he thought to himself, "you have no fucking idea how true your statement is."

He sipped on his Scotch and felt the warm glow the alcohol provided take hold of his subconscious. His forefinger and thumb pinched his nose in an effort to relieve the pressure from the headache that had begun forming an hour earlier. Without further thought he pulled his cell phone from his pocket and prepared to send a text.

"Need to see you in D.C. tomorrow." He hit the send button then puffed again on the giant Cohiba.

London, United Kingdom
7:42 AM

Simon Trowton sat in the luxury suite of his high rise office overlooking the Thames River. His grandparents had begun the company as a fashion importer, importing the best and newest clothing lines from all over the world. His father had carried on the tradition before passing the company to Simon. So adept had he become at moving new products through the customs process, driven primarily by greedy customs agents and Simon's willingness to grease their palms, that other companies began asking his advice. Rather than share his knowledge of the import process, he began a shipping company, moving any material in or out of the UK for a price. If a company needed a container to move through the customs process at a rapid rate, the shipping price was adjusted accordingly.

Coupled with his existing fashion company, Trowton had amassed a fortune second to none in the entire Kingdom. Never one to sit back and enjoy his spoils, he became a rather large contributor to various political candidates supportive of businesses, and as a result became exceedingly influential in helping shape and mold English shipping laws. Naturally, the laws he influenced were shaped such to benefit he and his company, and with the legislators in his pocket, more power and wealth followed.

He received an invitation to join a Bilderberger conference from an anonymous source. No return address and no name was assigned to the invitation; there was only his name, a date, a time, the place, and a request to keep everything secret until such time that a press release was given. Rumors of an elite, influential group of European and North American businessmen, politicians, and academics were whispered amongst the people with whom he associated, but he never dreamed of being asked to join the organization. As a matter of fact, he really had no idea of what influence this organization had, or could have, in the world of international politics or business.

Trowton attended that first meeting, a political neophyte with a lot of money and influence, but no real understanding of what the powerful elite did to drive global policy and increase wealth for their kind. In fact, the opinions and desires of the Bilderbergers moved him in such a way as to alter his perception of worldly things.

The Bilderbergers, he would learn, was an organization founded in 1954 and originally held at the Hotel De Bilderberg in the Netherlands. In that first meeting ground rules were put into place that would hold its membership to the strictest confidentiality. No one was permitted to speak about what was discussed at the meeting, which permitted its membership to talk about things deemed taboo by the vast majority of the world's populace.

Naturally, there were the usual sanctimonious discussions about feeding the world's starving people, eliminating nuclear weapons altogether, educating the masses, evolving into a non-religious conglomerate, bending the will of large corporations along with a host of other fanciful utopian ideas. Many of those ideological concepts captivated him so it was that he worked his will behind the scenes with European lawmakers in an attempt to aid the world's hungry by sending more food rations and money to the regions most in need.

He continued down that path until his meeting with Abaddon several months earlier. The initial phone call and subsequent meeting changed the arc of his involvement in the political arena. Now he found himself coercing some of his fellow elitists with promises of more power than they currently had, but some of the twelve would serve as soldiers while the others would be pawns. Choosing the twelve had proven a little tricky, but at the end of the day finding those with the least influence globally and promising them more power made the decisions easier. Trowton's sway over the Bilderbergers had grown exponentially since his inclusion, and many admired his position within the group.

He reached for his phone and dialed the number he had been given by the Saudi prince he had met with a few nights earlier. As the phone rang a continent away, Trowton stared out of his office window at the gray-drab English day as it lay down on the country like a hand attempting to suffocate a sleeping mistress threatening to share their secret. Three rings…a fourth then a voice.

"Hello?" came the thickly Arabic accent.

"You have procured the radiological devices as we discussed?" asked Trowton.

"Yes."

"And are they in position?"

"Correct," a throaty reply.

"Perfect. Detonate as planned."

The Arab clicked off without responding, but his intent was more than clear to Trowton. There was no turning back from his plan to nurse a sick world back to health. He also knew that if he failed to execute his plan, Abaddon would bring him more pain than he could endure before finally killing him.

Abaddon. Just his name struck fear in the furthest reaches of his mind and heart. Something in his raspy voice and the darkness of his eyes told him the man would not hesitate to do things to another human being that would make the cruelest of men look like a stark amateur. His mere presence made one feel as though his soul was being held prisoner, like his mind and heart were placed in a vice.

To say that Abaddon had a hold on him, in the sense that Charles Manson had a hold over his followers, was to completely misunderstand the situation. Abaddon had a physical *and* spiritual command over him. The restraint paralyzed him, forcing him to listen to what the man had to say, and he knew if he tried to explain the hold he had on him to someone they would have him committed to a local asylum.

Trowton grabbed his phone again and dialed a number. He closed his eyes and listened to the strange ring from a world away.

"Bueno?" the voice asked.

"Is the military appropriately armed and orders prepared?"

"Si, the necessary personnel know and understand their mission. They are prepared to attack."

"Give the order," Trowton commanded.

Without hesitation the voice on the other end responded. "Señor, I will deliver the orders immediately and trust that God will forgive us for doing the work he has not."

Trowton pressed the end button on the phone and exhaled audibly. "God," he thought to himself, "has forgotten us all."

The National Mall
Washington, D.C., USA
2:14 PM

Bill Evers caught the first flight out of Birmingham, Alabama's Shuttlesworth International Airport. Since their reunion several months earlier contact had been sparse. Both of the seasoned veterans understood the need to decompress after a stressful mission, and the mission that took Evers, then Buddy, to Mexico and finally to Xi'an, China was about as stressful as any mission either had ever been on.

The Boeing 747 lifted off, the pilot performing a picture perfect right turn toward the northeast. Evers was lucky to procure a ticket on one of the few direct flights from Birmingham to D.C., as only two seats remained at the time of the purchase. Several men and women wore business attire, obviously heading to D.C., or the surrounding area, on business. Two men seated at the front of the plane wore tight, close-cropped haircuts. Evers pegged them as NSA, a faction of the alphabet soup organizations whose power and prestige had grown over the past two administrations. His stomach churned at the thought that America continued down the path of Orwell's 1984 and that so many actually *believed* in the unconscionable path the country was on.

For the first two hours the plane flew with little turbulence, but a couple of bumps as they were passing through the cloud deck caused a lady to scream from the back of the plane. Evers smiled at the novice flier; he had never concerned himself with a plane crash. His father, a former Air Force aircraft mechanic once told him, "Don't worry about the plane going down, son. If it does, you won't feel a thing. In fact, you'll probably have a heart attack before impact anyway."

A quiet chuckle escaped him before he could stop it. The woman seated next to him pretended not to notice, but Evers cared little and was happy the thought of his dad, dead just over twenty years, passed through his thoughts. A hard-nosed southern man who joined the military right out of high school, his father taught him discipline with a shot of tough love. He was never one to spare the rod, but no whipping he ever received was undeserved. His father wasn't prone to violence, but he wouldn't back down from a threat. Pride and mettle were the hallmarks of the man and the only thing he was able to leave Evers when he died. Greg Evers, his father, worked himself into an early grave, stress and four packs of cigarettes a day stopping his heart in the blink of an eye.

From his father his thoughts drifted to his mother. Once his father had gotten out of the service and they moved home to Alabama, she found work in the textile industry running spinning mills at a carpet yarn facility. He remembered seeing her come home after working the graveyard shift with bloody knuckles and carpet yarn all over her clothing. She never complained about her work conditions, but he sometimes overheard her telling his father about the intense heat in the mill and the dust she was breathing.

Sadness crept over him when he thought about everything she endured to help feed her family. He silently wondered if his mother and father's struggles were what kept him from starting a family, or if his desire to fight for his country after 9/11 drove him to remain single. In any event, he had never had a serious relationship with a woman, not excluding a couple of girls in high school. Sure, he had had plenty of sex as he traveled around the world seeing strange, new places and completing dangerous missions, but one night stands had nothing to do with an emotionally committed relationship.

The pilot announced that they would be landing in fifteen minutes. Evers knew Ronald Reagan International Airport very well, having flown in and out of it numerous times. He looked out of his window as the sun set in the west. The sun shone brightly over the Washington Monument, the red flight beacon flashing on and off warning incoming flights of its height. Many suggested the obelisk was nothing more than the world's largest manmade phallic symbol, but Evers knew on good authority it was symbolic of Egypt and the Egyptian god Ra as put forth by the Free Masons who designed the nation's capital.

Fifteen minutes later the tires touched down on the runway and the plane taxied to its gate. Evers focused on his meeting with Buddy and what his old mentor so urgently needed to discuss. The timing of the text with the news report he had seen in Birmingham about the Ebola outbreak in Liberia was suspicious, but he would have to wait and see what the old man was up in arms about. A series of follow-up texts told him to meet Buddy by the Capitol's reflecting pool.

He stepped off the jet-way onto the highly polished marbled floor of Reagan International. Unlike most airports in the United States, this one was full of passengers wearing suits and formal business attire, rather than track suits and nightclub wear that one normally sees. The air was stagnant and tense. There was a sense of urgency to the entire place that slammed Evers center mass. Looks of consternation were on many of the faces as they walked down the brightly lit terminal. The general gait of those moving around him was fast and with purpose.

Evers felt out of place and was sure he stood out like a lion in a petting zoo. His stomach rolled as the taste of political disdain touched his tongue. He hated this place and everything it represented. Steeped in spineless immorality, D.C. was the capital of the United States in name only; in truth was nothing more than a kettle of self-serving idiots boiling in its own cannibalistic stew.

He slung the backpack filled with a change of clothes over one shoulder and began walking toward a sign directing him to the Metro, D.C.'s subway system. Various aromas drifted through the terminal. The smell of a Starbucks permeated the air and one of the many small restaurants selling pizza and Stromboli offered delicious aromas to hungry passengers. Evers shook his head at some people's choice of breakfast foods, but he had to admit that he had eaten much stranger foods at sunrise than those available in any airport.

A sign pointed him to an escalator leading down to the Metro line. Unlike other subways he had ridden around the world, D.C.'s Metro system was clean and secure. The absence of gang graffiti, cigarette butts, and food wrappers stood out more than the extreme cleanliness did in Evers' mind. Without lifting his head, he glanced up to see multiple security cameras pointing in every direction, which also explained the lack of graffiti.

Evers glanced around to see if anyone looked suspicious. He almost laughed at the thought when the realization that everyone in D.C. looked suspicious, ran through his mind. Well over one hundred passengers moved around the station looking for the train that would take them to their final destination.

Before meeting Buddy, he decided the need to perform a counter surveillance run would be prudent. He found the blue line boarding area and waited for the train without looking around the station. Two minutes later he heard the train approaching and took a step forward to get in line to board.

The train stopped and the doors opened, the hydraulics from them emitting a loud hiss. People piled out of the cars and headed toward the escalators that would lead to the airport's ticketing and security areas. The passengers standing on the train's platform replaced the exiting commuters and began holding hand straps and the balance poles as the doors hissed and closed behind them. People filled the available seats, a few men offering their seats to women. Evers smiled, happy to know that some semblance of chivalry still existed, and some women still appreciated the act.

Cool air drifted through the car as Evers stood close to a wall while he glanced around. Everyone appeared to be lost in their own morning thoughts, avoiding eye contact with those around them. Nothing seemed out of place.

Evers got off the train at the Pentagon City stop and moved to the back of the platform. He watched as people walked off the train and others stepped on, repeating the scene he had participated in at the airport. A few moments later the platform was mostly empty save for six other commuters waiting on trains. Evers walked to the southbound blue track, heading back toward Reagan International and waited.

The train pulled up to the platform and Evers stepped onto the second car. He was acutely aware of every passenger on the car and made mental notes about each one. A handsomely dressed black lady sat in an empty seat, her hair pulled into a stiff ponytail, as a heavyset white man in a poorly fitting blue business suit longingly eyed her. He made similar observations of the other people sitting or standing in the car; none set off his radar.

At the Crystal City stop Evers got off the train and again moved to the back of the platform and waited. None of the passengers on his car remained behind. He felt certain he wasn't being followed and began walking to the yellow line to catch the train to his destination.

Buddy asked him to meet at 11:30, which gave him a full hour to get to the meet point and scout out the area. The yellow train slowed and the doors opened. Evers remained cognizant of the passengers around him as he walked onto the train. Again, no one made him feel uneasy.

As the train began moving, he wondered what others would think about his paranoia. He brushed the thought off as he focused on the electronic Metro map on the car's sidewall. At each stop, a light would illuminate letting the passengers know where they were. The technology was simple and ingenious and, he thought to himself, so much better than New York's messy subway system.

The train made two stops before arriving at L'Enfant Plaza, the central hub where all the Metro lines met. Also present in the plaza was an underground shopping mall and food court. The entire design was spectacular, and thousands of tourists moved about the shops and food stalls indulging in the fanfare of souvenir clothing and burgers, pizza and sushi.

Before going topside, Evers walked to the shopping center and milled about, his overzealousness and paranoia still working in overdrive. Washington D.C. was the focal point and home of every American covert agency, and that fact alone made him uneasy. He stepped into a department store and took a position so he appeared to be shopping as he was facing the window. No one made a move to follow him inside the store or stop and act like they were looking at a map or some other obvious shadowing movement. Evers felt even better that he wasn't being followed, but he knew the CIA and NSA employed some damned good trackers, and if he was being followed by a team they would be even harder to spot.

He waited ten minutes, milling around the store, then walked out careful to not let his head swivel thereby drawing attention to himself. Evers walked toward another store, stopped in front of the window and used it as a mirror. No one appeared to consider his movements, but he wanted to be certain so he turned and walked back toward the department store he had just left. Instead of walking inside he stopped and knelt down just before walking in front of the entrance door and pretended to tie his shoe. Still, no one seemed to care about anything he was doing.

Satisfied that he wasn't being followed, he left the mall area and found the escalator that would take him above ground and into the heart of the lion's den. He stepped onto the Otis escalator and moved over to the right to allow those who wanted to walk the moving steps to do so. The escalator delivered him and the other riders to the top of a white marbled platform in front of several sets of glass doors.

Bright mid-morning sunlight beamed into the L'Enfant Plaza lobby reflecting off the polished walls and floors. Evers stopped walking and moved off to the side while he allowed his squinting eyes to adjust to the natural light. Men and women walked past him in search of their work or tourist destinations.

Three minutes went by and Evers stepped outside turning north on L'Enfant Plaza Road and walked toward the National Mall, which lay four city blocks from the Plaza. He walked past hundreds of people, many dressed for work, no different than the passengers on the Metro, and the others who were obviously tourists.

He turned east on Independence Avenue and walked another two blocks before turning north again on Seventh Street. Some people stopped along the way talking and snapping photos of various buildings and monuments, but most walked in the same direction as Evers on their way to the National Mall. He maintained his current pace, not walking too fast or too slow, wanting to blend in with the various groups of people.

A quick time-check told him that he had twenty minutes until he was to meet Buddy at the Capitol's reflecting pool. The spot was actually perfect for their meeting. A wide open space teeming with tourists and park security reduced the potential of being targeted by some wayward operative. The bottleneck, of course, was the transition to and from the airport, which was why he had been so careful to make sure he wasn't being followed.

He stepped onto the Mall, a massive expanse of open ground. The Washington Monument, D.C.'s tallest structure, reached toward the sun. At the west end of the Mall sat the large tribute to Abraham Lincoln; majestic and wise he sat watching over the land he both presided over and died defending. To the east stood the Capitol Building, Lady Freedom standing proudly atop the dome. It has been said that she looks east where the sun rises, bringing forth a new day and symbolically bringing forth enlightenment.

Evers suppressed a snicker at the thought of anyone in Washington D.C. being enlightened; conniving and insidious perhaps, but definitely not enlightened. He walked along the south side of the Mall, stopping just long enough to watch a group of twenty-something boys pitching a football around. Their naiveté made him smile a sad smile. Evers turned and continued walking toward the Capitol Building.

On the west side of the reflecting pool he paused and looked around. Seated on a concrete bench on the other side he found what he was looking for—an older, shaggy-haired man whose keen eyes were fixed upon his. "Damn, the old boy is still sharp," Evers thought.

Evers gave a simple nod and Buddy responded in kind. He walked around the large reflecting pool as children dangled their feet over the edge allowing the water to cool them after walking, most of them uninterested, around the Mall with their parents. Buddy followed him with his eyes without turning his head.

He sat down next to the old warrior, keeping his eyes fixed on the reflecting pool and the splashing children. The silence between the two men was strange and thick, and Evers wondered what was weighing so heavily on Buddy's mind that his mentor had not bothered to greet him upon arrival. Buddy Smith was the one man he could always count on to have a joke or make some sort of smart ass remark before they got down to business.

At long last Buddy spoke. "How're you doing, Buck?" His voice resonated its usual gravely, southern Appalachia twang.

"Well, I reckon I'm alright, Buddy. Just wondering what's got you so worked up that you wanted me to fly up here to see you on a day's notice."

"Yeah, I can see why you would be concerned, Billy. Why don't we go for a stroll around our lovely capital while we talk," Buddy replied.

The men stood and began walking west toward the Washington Monument, the Vietnam Wall and Lincoln Memorial. Evers instinctively swiveled his head right to left monitoring and checking the throngs of people strolling along the Mall grounds. He held his tongue, waiting for Buddy to begin talking.

"You should relax, Buck. There ain't nobody around here that's interested in following us or taking us out. You are on sacred ground while you're on the National Mall, old friend."

Despite Buddy's assurances, Evers remained on guard, kept his mind clear, and his hands free of their pockets. Buddy, on the other hand, walked as though he were meandering along some sandy beach, oblivious to everything and everyone around him. He seemed distant and unconcerned, almost a little despondent. Evers assumed Buddy knew what he was doing, but something in his face told him there was a much larger problem at hand.

Buddy took a deep breath and spoke without looking at Evers. "Can you believe this fucking place, Buck? All the money, all the power in the world, yet there are many here that are never satisfied with what we have. There are others, the ideologues, who believe they can change the world with a speech or a wave of their hand. Then there are people like us, the doers, the ones who stand knee deep in shit trying to make things tolerable."

Evers listened intently. Buddy occasionally waxed philosophical, but rarely did delve into the political underbelly of the United States. He preferred to remain on the receiving end of operations and money and leave the political rancor to those who enjoyed it. Yet, here he was talking about the very system that he enabled and benefited from; Evers found the monologue interesting.

Buddy turned his head and began coughing like he was choking on a piece of food. He reached inside a pocket and grabbed a handkerchief then placed it to his mouth. The coughing fit went on for a few more seconds as Evers watched his old friend's shoulders convulsively shake up and down.

"Are you okay?" Evers asked.

Buddy waved him off then continued, "The scary part in all this, Buck, aren't the missions you and I have gone on, or the people we've removed, or even the weird shit we've seen around the world. No, the truly frightening things are the legislators and leaders of the various countries around the world. The fact that these leaders have the ability to decide who lives and who dies should shake us all to the core, but humans everywhere turn a blind eye to their surroundings and ignore events they perceive as not directly impacting their day-to-day existence. To call them sheep is to disparage the wooly animals that provide us clothes and sustenance. These naïve masses, Buck, they're like plankton. They serve only as food and fodder for those they serve. Sometimes I wonder if everything I've done in my career, if you want to call what I do a career, has been worth it. Recently, I've been feeling as though I've wasted my entire life.

"Some really terrible shit is hitting a big fucking fan, Young Buck, and I'm worried. More than the usual crazy stuff has ignited around the globe, and if we don't do something about it soon things are going to get out of control. To be honest, Billy, it may already be too late."

He stopped talking and shook his head disapprovingly. Evers glanced over at him and noted the glazed-over look in his eyes. Buddy looked tired, sad, and for the first time...weak. A shudder ran across Evers' spine. To shake the old soldier's resolve something must be dreadfully wrong, but he would have to wait a little longer to try to figure out what was going on with him. Buddy seemed to want to talk, so Evers felt it best to let him get whatever it was off his chest.

Buddy stopped walking and turned to face Evers. "I know you saw the recent report about the Ebola outbreak in Liberia. Initial reports say there are just over twelve hundred confirmed deaths and another two hundred sick. Just so you know that's a load of shit. Our sources in the region have confirmed well over twenty thousand deaths with another fifteen thousand or so on the verge of checking out."

Evers stood there, his mouth agape. He tried to talk but the words could not escape his throat. They were stuck somewhere between thought and vocalization. A million things ran through his mind, yet he could not force his mouth to ask questions. He tried to process twenty-five thousand deaths and another fifteen thousand potential deaths on the horizon. Lastly, he wondered how the governments of Liberia and Sierra Leone had managed to keep the vast number of deaths and sicknesses quiet.

Buddy watched the wheels turning in Evers' head and nodded. "That's right, Buck. Someone is suppressing this information. The larger question is *why*."

Evers and Buddy began walking again. Evers's legs were a little shaky, but he finally managed a response. "Buddy, you're thinking this was a man-made event, huh? I can't imagine that you would be this shaken over a naturally occurring virus or disease. The reports I saw on television stated the rapid spread of the virus was concerning the CDC, but I suspect what the Center is really concerned with is that the virus is airborne, rather than passed through contact with an infected person."

"That's a very astute theory you're working with, Billy...on both accounts. No, I don't believe this outbreak was a result of some bat shitting in a bowl of cow intestines that was later eaten by a family of twelve. In fact, I know someone was involved in spreading it."

Evers cut his eyes at Buddy, "What the hell do you mean? You have evidence that someone was directly involved in the intentional spreading of this fucking virus?"

Buddy weighed his words before speaking, "Just like the Center for Disease Control, the World Health Organization keeps various pathogens and viruses stored in vaults at their headquarters in Geneva, Switzerland. Five weeks ago, someone broke in and stole two vials of the virus."

"Holy Mother of God," Evers replied.

"It gets worse, Buck. The two vials that were stolen were airborne versions of the virus. The initial virus was genetically mutated and kept on site," said Buddy, his voice grave and solemn.

"Are you fucking kidding me, Buddy? Someone thought it was a good idea to weaponize the deadliest virus in the history of mankind? What kind of sick bastard does something like that?" Evers hissed.

Buddy shook his head. "On the record, the virus was intentionally mutated for the purpose of scientific study. The thought process was the virus would naturally mutate from human secretion to airborne eventually. The WHO surmised and reported this would enable them to get ahead of the game in the world of combatting viruses."

Evers considered what he was being told. "Off the record, why was it mutated?"

"For the exact purpose you described. Weaponization. Many scientists believed that airborne Ebola would spread so rapidly that entire regions could be summarily wiped out. The theory was that once a region was obliterated, the virus would die off on its own. It appears that no one took into account the potential for health workers around the world to flock to the region to help the suffering. As a result, health workers were infected before flying home. The incubation period is approximately three weeks. Currently, we have no idea how many people may have come in contact with the infected hosts."

Evers processed what he was being told. "We have a pandemic on our hands and no idea who started it. Or do you?"

Buddy took a deep breath and slowly exhaled. "No. I have no idea who started it, but there's more, Buck. Let's find a place to sit down first."

They continued walking beyond the Washington Monument to the entrance of the relatively new World War Two Monument. The colossal fountain at the center of the Atlantic and Pacific Theater monuments spouted water into a small reflecting pool. Children and adults alike splashed about to cool themselves in the early afternoon heat.

The two found a free stone bench at the entrance of the Monument and sat down. They watched families mill around looking at the monolithic stones with individual state's names etched in each of them. In others were names of major battle sites. A few elderly men in wheelchairs and on crutches slowly made their way across the hallowed ground. Evers saw one old man wipe the back of his hand across one cheek.

Buddy began talking again, this time keeping his voice low because of the crowds of people. "The night before the vials of Ebola were stolen from the WHO vault, a vial of severe acute respiratory syndrome was stolen from the Center of Disease Control in Atlanta."

"SARS?" Evers asked.

"That's right, Young Buck. SARS. A SARS outbreak has been reported in Mexico City and another in Quito, Ecuador. Between the two metropolitan areas a total of six thousand deaths have been confirmed. The United States is working diligently to quarantine the areas and help others who may have been exposed to the virus."

Evers considered what Buddy was reporting. "By 'quarantine' you mean 'isolate' and 'keep the media at bay?'"

A smile that didn't touch Buddy's eyes appeared on his face. "There may be hope for you yet, Billy."

"So," Evers began, "two break-ins, two different extremely contagious viruses stolen and released on opposite sides of the Atlantic. The 'why's, where's, and who's need to be answered. Why would someone want to do this? Why did they pick the location, Liberia and Mexico, and who the hell would have the resources to pull something like this off?"

"Those are all good questions, Buck, but I haven't finished yet. There have been mass killings in no less than eight countries and four continents almost simultaneously. Masked behind civil war was the systematic elimination of ten thousand plus children in Syria alone. Did you hear me,

Buck? Ten thousand plus children." Buddy hung his head when he uttered those last four words.

"Okay, Buddy, I get what you're saying. There's obviously a link between the stolen Ebola and SARS vials, but to associate them with the other shit going on around the world right now is probably a stretch. I mean, craziness can go on anywhere at any given time, old friend, and you know it."

"Buck, you know I'm a fairly logical man, and I don't make jumps like this without careful thought, consideration, and actionable intelligence. Something else you need to know is that the Agency recently learned of four radiological devices that were purchased on the black market. We know that two of the devices have been transported into Delhi, India."

Evers listened to Buddy as he mapped the transport of the two radiological nukes from Pakistan into one of the most densely populated cities in the world. "You think this is all terrorist related? Obviously, the Muslims despise the Hindu's and they've been fighting over Kashmir since time began. Detonating two dirty bombs in Delhi would certainly cause massive casualties for years to come, in addition to striking fear into the heart and soul of India."

"What else?" Buddy asked, allowing Evers to reason through the situation himself.

Evers thought for a moment. "India would retaliate if they could prove which country was responsible for detonating the devices. Hell, they might not worry about hard evidence either. When they do retaliate…ah, shit. You think they'll nuke one of the Muslim countries?"

Buddy offered a half-hearted chuckle. "What do you think?"

Evers replied, "I don't think they'll have any choice. There will be such an outcry for blood from the Indian people that the government will be forced to act, and when they do there'll be no mercy."

Buddy nodded his agreement. "That's right, Buck. There will likely be a nuclear war before it's over. If India believes that Pakistan was responsible for the attack, they'll send their nukes in and Pakistan will retaliate in kind. In Delhi alone there are over sixteen million people. Millions will perish, and millions more will suffer as a result of the fallout.

"There's more, Billy. At least nine government sanctioned armies have begun mobilizing against their country's civilians. In at least six of these regions, no practical reason for doing so has been discovered, and none of the countries involved have admitted to military mobilization, but our intelligence says otherwise."

Evers took a deep breath and made a mental note that the two men had done quite a bit of heavy breathing during their conversation. "I still don't see the link, Buddy. Like I said, crazy shit goes on in the world all the time, and we don't always have an explanation for it."

Buddy stood up and paced back and forth in front of Evers. His face, despite its haggard appearance, was one of deep thought and experience. Evers realized how much respect he had for the old man's intellect and reasoning skills, although he wasn't yet convinced that all of the specific world events Buddy had outlined were somehow interconnected.

"I haven't connected all the dots yet, Buck, but I know these are not just random events. Typically, if the shit blows up in some third world country, you can trace it back to a civilian insurrection or a power grab by a military leader. If Al Qaida were going to detonate a fucking dirty nuke in India, our intelligence would have grabbed some sort of chatter floating around on line or across radio frequencies.

"And that's the problem we're facing, Billy. No one...not one fucking person has owned up to any of the events I've told you about. Can you imagine spreading Ebola and SARS without a motive or at least a ransom? To be so evil that you could spread viruses like that after stealing them from the vaults of the two biggest disease combatants in the world is preposterous.

"So, there's definitely a link to all the horseshit going on and we need to figure it out," he finished.

"How do you propose we figure all this out, Buddy? If our own intelligence services are stumped, how are we going to put the pieces together?" Evers asked.

"Have you ever heard of Occam's Razor, Buck?" Buddy asked.

Evers looked up as though searching for the answer to Buddy's question. He searched his memory banks for anything resembling Occam's Razor but came up with nothing.

"No, Buddy, I don't reckon I have," he responded.

"William of Occam was a medieval English friar, philosopher, and logician. He formulated a theory that when faced with complex hypotheses or problems, the answer will lie with the simplest and least complex solution. That's how we're going to figure this out, Buck.

"We have to get to work immediately. If whoever has those four dirty bombs detonates even one, the world as we know it ceases to exist. The Ebola and SARS will have to be left to the world's medical experts, but I know when we find whoever is behind the theft of the bombs, we'll also discover who spread the viruses and ordered the slaughter of tens of thousands of innocents for no good reason in other parts of the world."

Evers stared at Buddy, tension tightening every muscle in his body.

Delhi, India
6:09 AM

Ahsan rose from the bed in his better-than-average hotel room and pushed back the curtains. He picked up the tightly rolled prayer rug that he carried with him at all times. Five times each day he would stop to pray to Allah and give thanks for his life, his family, and most importantly, for not being born an infidel. He stared out over the city from his fifth floor room in disgust. The smog and smells of Delhi were equally heavy. Unclean city streets were littered with paper and other debris. The dirty unbelievers of India mulled around on crowded streets speaking in a tongue that hurt his ears.

He cleared his mind and unfurled the rug, smoothing out the corners and flattening it against the floor. Ahsan stood at the small rug's edge facing the open window with his eyes shut and opened hands raised above his head. He took a couple of deep breaths then began his prayers.

"Allahu Akbar." He crossed his hands over his chest and recite the first verse of the Qur'an followed by his favorite verse, the *Surah Al-Fatir*. He raised his hands over his head a second time and repeated, "Allahu Akbar," knelt on his prayer rug and spoke three times, Subhana rabbiyal adheem."

The process was continued until he finished his evening prayers and absolved himself of the tainted environment in which he found himself. He thanked Allah for providing him the opportunity to prove his worthiness in the on-going battle to destroy everything HE found unholy.

Ahsan had been chosen for this mission by the highest supreme Mullah Tahir al Khushk, he suspected, because of the loyalty he demonstrated during the American occupation of their brother's beloved country. He had faithfully shot and beheaded several of the American *scum* whenever the opportunity presented itself, and had volunteered several times for operational battle when the tribal leaders of Afghanistan would share intelligence about approaching enemy forces.

Without question and without remorse he brought the battle to the godless American and NATO forces whenever he could. The most holy Osama bin Laden waged jihad on the United States because of their imperialistic and unholy nature. Several of his fellow Pakistani and Afghanistan brethren refused to call the country by its name, preferring instead to call it The Great Satan.

Only the land grabbing, money worshipping Jews were worse. Their stench could be smelled across all of Islam, and his dream was to kill every last one of them. To bathe in their blood would be a righteous testament to his lord, Allah. He was united with his Arabic brothers in the desire to slay every last one of the invaders and occupiers, and no amount of western intervention, money, or education would change their minds.

Having watched the Israelis unmercifully bomb the *peace-loving* people of Palestine, Lebanon, and Beirut over the course of three generations angered him beyond measure, as did the Americans with all of their technology, drones and sophisticated weaponry. And then there were the vile Indians who invaded the fertile Kashmir and claimed it as their own.

To India he had been sent to exact revenge for his people and to claim the country for Muslims everywhere, all in the name of Allah. How it was possible that the one point six billion Muslims in the world had not unified to overthrow the Zionist bastards and Christians was beyond him.

A knock came from his door and startled him from his thoughts. He rose from the bed and reached for the thirty-eight caliber handgun he had smuggled across the border. Swiftly, he moved to one side of the doorframe and called out.

"Who is it?"

A female voice responded, "Room service, sir. You ordered dinner earlier."

So consumed had he been in his evening prayers and meditation that he had forgotten about ordering food. He took a quick peek through the peep hole to insure there was only the woman with the food that awaited him in the hallway.

Ahsan opened the door and the smell of hot food immediately found his nose. Halal blessed chicken curry, rice, hot bread, and wine sat upon a cart. His eyes moved up to the beautiful lady standing in front of him. Despite her infidel status, he could not help but be aroused by her young, tender appearance and smooth brown skin. Her dark hair lay upon her shoulders and a kind smile turned the corners of her mouth toward the darkest brown eyes he had ever seen. He wondered what it would be like to taste her and know the youth she carried so well. Her bosom was not overly large, but they were supple and ripe and he imagined what her nipples would look like in his mind's eye.

"Will there be anything else, sir?" he heard her asking in English.

He saw her blood-flushed face and realized she had watched him mentally undress her right in front of her eyes. A tinge of embarrassment flooded his own face and he quickly reached into his pocket for money. He paid the bill and gave her ten rupees as a tip and a curt nod then rolled the cart into his room.

The humiliation of being caught ogling her passed within moments as he sat at the small table in his room and began eating. His phone lay on the table next to him, silently awaiting the call to take the suitcase he had brought with him to the specific location where its detonation would exact maximum casualties and instill the greatest fear.

His hand rubbed his stubbly face; he was still upset that he had needed to shave his long, thick beard before setting out for India. He knew, however, that bearded Muslim men still drew ire and suspicion, even in a country with a significant Muslim population. His hand found the glass of pink wine and raised it to his lips, asking Allah to forgive him in his moment of weakness. Drinking was strictly forbidden in the Muslim faith, but he had developed a taste for the swill when away on assignment and out of eyeshot of those who might let his superiors know about his lack of mental fortitude.

Ahsan delighted in the food and took large gulps of wine, a sweet blush that pleased his palate. His mind drifted as he ate, ghosts of his youth pounding the sides of his cranium. A father whose relentless and sometimes painful form of discipline and adherence to the Prophet's teachings helped mold and manifest him into what he would eventually become. Quite often his mother and father struggled to find enough food to feed his four brothers and one sister, but somehow they managed to survive the hardships levied upon all his people by the filthy Zionists and Christians. They would sometimes eat the food supplied by the Red Cross even though they knew the money used to purchase the supplies came from Western charitable contributions. This only furthered the hatred his father felt for the West, and that hatred was passed on to his children, but it was Ahsan who threw himself into the war against the very people his father had taught him to detest.

His wife, Umaira, wasn't a particularly nice looking woman; indeed, his marriage had been arranged when he was only twelve years old. She was, however, a very loyal and loving wife who took especially great care of their two young sons. Umaira was also very understanding about the amount of time he spent away from home, doing "God's work" as he explained it to her.

He often wondered about the differences in women's dress between Middle Eastern and western cultures. The godless westerners relished in their women showing as much skin as possible then wondering why other men lusted after their wives and daughters. Ahsan would not think twice about taking the life of a man he caught lusting after Umaira, although he doubted that would happen given her less than stellar looks.

He stared out the window at the progress this third world country was undergoing. Trash drifted down the city streets and vehicle exhaust filled the air making it virtually impossible to breathe when he was outdoors. The Indians wanted so much to be like Americans, but could not replicate the wealth the U.S. had amassed over the past hundred years. India was a country of the conquered, America a country of conquerors. Indians were largely polite and avoided confrontation, while Americans thrived upon rudeness, stress and agitation. Even still, their long-held Hindu beliefs repulsed him. He took great pride in knowing he was on the right side of history and that Allah would one day smile upon him for his courageousness and desire to spread the words of the Prophet Muhammad.

Ahsan took a few more bites of his food, chewing slowly and thoughtfully. Once again he reached for his glass of wine and chased the tasty morsels of food with the sweet blush wine. He dabbed his mouth with the cloth napkin that rested with the silverware on the tray of food, as he languished in his own thoughts. His mind continued to drift for another twenty minutes, his eyes focused on nothing in particular as he stared out his hotel window.

Finally, he finished eating, replaced his dishes on the tray that he had removed and sat on the small hotel desk before he dined. He finished off the last drop of the wine and felt his head swim ever-so-slightly. The corners of his mouth turned slightly upward forming a small smile as he enjoyed the slight buzz the wine had presented him. He placed the glass on the platter with the other dishes, picked it up and opened his door. After glancing around the hallway, he put the tray on the floor against the wall to be picked up by room service later.

He walked inside his room, reseated himself at the table and reached for one of the two hard-shelled cases that he had placed against the wall after checking into his room. His thumbs caressed the rolling numbers that made up the two locks on the top of the case. His pulse quickened at the thought of what lay inside, and his heart thudded inside his chest.

Ahsan rolled the numbers until the code was lined up on either side of the brief case. With his pinkies wrapped around each end of the case, he pushed the buttons that would relieve the spring-loaded catches. Two concurrent pops sounded in the room and he immediately began to sweat. He could feel a bead roll down his spine and stop just above his beltline to be absorbed by his undershirt.

He lifted the soft leather top and stared inside with great wonder and amazement. The compact bomb lie dormant awaiting his command to activate. He looked at the numbers on the activation keypad written in the commonly known English numerical system. One through nine, a star and pound button on either side of the zero. "Exactly like a telephone," Ahsan mused.

His right hand gently drifted over the mechanism. The stainless steel tip of the device was remarkably cold to the touch despite the room's tepid air. He imagined the destruction it would cause when he detonated it and his slight smile turned into something much more toothy and sinister.

His dark brown eyes scanned the bomb over and over, memorizing its curvature, the wiring colors and their exact locations. With his eyes closed he could picture the explosive device's every feature. He moved his hands to either side of the case and slowly ran them back and forth along its edges, the feel of the rich leather mesmerizing.

It occurred to him he was sexually aroused. His hardness pressed against his pants uncomfortably, throbbing in time with his pounding heart. One hand drifted to his crotch and pressed against his hard-on, momentarily relieving a little of the pressure he was feeling.

Ahsan stood and unbuckled his belt and removed his pants. He said a silent prayer to Allah, begging forgiveness for what he was about to do. Again he closed his eyes, but this time he imagined the beautiful young lady with the ample breasts and smooth, beautiful skin that had brought him his dinner. He stood in front of the mirror like that for ten minutes, his stiff cock in his hand, pleasuring himself until he felt the sweet release of his own sex.

Meguru
Tokyo, Japan
7:21 PM

Terou stepped off the packed train and climbed the steps out of the subway onto 3 Chome in Meguru where the ebb and flow of the crowded street was as familiar to him as an old coat. The smell of sobe noodles and bento floated on the air as people began to pile into the restaurants and nightclubs lining the strip of road. He watched as his countrymen moved at a snail's pace down the sidewalks, packed like sardines in a can. The sight made him nauseous and angry.

In the distance he found the first place he wanted to visit: a small Buddhist temple offering a quiet retreat from the throng of people outside. This was a place where people could silently pray for whatever success or healing they required. He stepped inside, bowing as he did so. Inside the breast pocket of his sports jacket rested a small bundle of incense he had brought with him. Two candles burned inside the entrance for those who wished to light their incense as they offered prayer at the altar.

Smoke gently floated over his head and to the ceiling, the building's quiet air conditioning return system pulling the smoke and air through its filter. Terou bowed at the altar and placed the incense in one of the ash bowls placed by one of the priests overseeing the temple. He said a silent prayer to his ancestors, then to the Buddha. His prayer was a mixture of the Japanese national religion, Shinto, and Buddhism—such was the way of many Japanese who chose to interweave the two.

He took a seat in one of the pews. Only a handful of parishioners were in the temple with him; most were crowded into the stores and clubs just outside. Terou sat in silence with his head bowed. He thought about his own family and how they would not approve of his actions despite the noble nature and courage he would demonstrate.

Mr. Trowton's speech given at their last closed door meeting was so completely accurate that only now could he see the truth behind it. His entire life had been spent walking the streets of Tokyo, riding the cramped trains and other mass transit systems offered by the government, breathing the heavily polluted air, all while working his way up the corporate ladder eventually landing an exceptional CEO position with one of the leading technology companies in all of Asia. Dai Nippon Kuki Kussaku Industries lead the charge in developing and perfecting hydro-pneumatic extraction and imaging, used exclusively in offshore oil and natural gas drilling.

After being invited to a Bilderberger meeting four years prior, a tremendous honor for a non-American or European, he realized he, and the company he lead, was responsible and complicit in furthering the pollution of the seas and skies. He could not, in good faith, continue down a path that would merely reward those in the here and now, while damning the next generation to a life of filth and starvation.

Instinctively, he reached into his pants pocket and felt the small, round glass tube he had been given two weeks prior. His instructions were very specific, and he had agreed immediately when Trowton asked for his assistance. Never one to waver, Terou Hamashita made up his mind to rid the world of the disease that had plagued humanity for decades, ever since the advent of modern medicine. He reasoned that if some of the greatest minds in the world died, the next generation would be forced to try and pick up the previous generation's scientific work, subsequently taking smaller steps and slowing the rapid spread of medicine. Terou understood that the longer a scientist lived, the greater and more in depth his research would grow. He also knew that an aging human species would further strain the natural resources of the planet, while simultaneously choking it with dirty air and filthy oceans.

Meguru sat a few comfortable kilometers inland from Tokyo Bay in the heart of Tokyo proper. The neighborhood was home to many high rise office buildings teeming with some of the city's wealthiest individuals. Suited *sararimen*, as they were called, occupied offices and cubicles, each carrying leather-bound attaché cases, some much more expensive than others, but all looking very professional and neat.

The restaurants and temple served those needing physical and spiritual replenishment on a daily basis, and the bars and strip clubs that sat adjacent to the offices allowed them time alone or with their mistresses before returning to their hum-drum home lives. It was there that they would spend money and eat the foods their wives refused to cook for them, as well as indulging many of their sexual fantasies. And it was this place that Terou decided to oblige Trowton and his own beliefs in bettering mankind.

He located a public benjo, or restroom, and stepped inside. His eyes did a quick search of the men's room and located an unoccupied stall. Terou latched the door then reached inside his pocket and retrieved the vial that had changed hands several times since being stolen from the CDC in the United States. He withdrew a capped syringe, removed the safety cap, and plunged it into the small glass vial, pulling up on the plunger to withdraw ten cc's of the clear liquid.

The three inch syringe was now an elongated six inches with the plunger fully retracted. He made a fist and placed his thumb over the plunger as he examined the liquid contents. Carefully, he removed the cap and glanced at his fisted hand again. The needle was barely noticeable.

He opened the stall door and stepped into the open men's room. A couple of other men were relieving themselves in the urinal trough that hung along the wall. Terou let his eyes fall to the floor as he walked outside, dropping the syringe cap as he stepped onto the bustling sidewalk.

A small group of young hipsters made their way to one of the local clubs. Terou fell in line behind them, careful to remain a step away. A young girl, no more than eighteen years old, told her friends she wanted to check out one of the local bands playing at Lounge Neo. Neo was a new club and featured hot new acts that attracted the younger crowd. Many of the bands were steeped in techno-jazz and hip-hop, a sound that was mostly indigenous to Japan but beginning to catch fire across most of Asia.

The group turned a corner at an intersection and proceeded talking about the band and the good time they would have at the club. Terou stayed a close step behind but managed to remain nonchalant in demeanor, appearance, and gait. On two different occasions the youngsters paused long enough for one to light a cigarette. Each time Terou was forced to stop and stare into dark windows or bend to tie his shoe. He hoped the group had not discovered that he was tailing them; his mission was so close to completion.

At long last they arrived at Lounge Neo where they saw a long line outside the club's door. As the youngsters obediently fell into line, Terou made his move. He sidestepped the group as he felt his thumb press lightly against the plunger on the syringe. His right hand angled toward the girl who led her friends to the nightclub.

Terou walked briskly past the group, but as he did so he jabbed the needle into the girl's arm and depressed the plunger just slightly. The young girl cried out sharply as she rubbed the small wound. Unsure what had just happened, she lifted her hand and looked at the small hole. One of her friends remarked that something must have bitten her and her other comrades agreed.

She considered the small pin prick on her arm once more and decided that a mosquito must have bitten her. Soon the slight pain passed and the group entered the nightclub. Within three days she was running a fever of one hundred four degrees. Eight days later she was dead. In the amount of time she began showing symptoms she infected over fifty people.

Before the evening ended, Terou Hamashita infected fifteen other people.

Arlington, Virginia, USA
10:14 PM

Evers lay on his hotel room bed, his rheumy eyes staring into the distance while a news anchor talked about a new SARS outbreak in Tokyo. After he and Buddy had parted ways, he checked into a Hampton Inn in order to get a little rest. He fell asleep quickly, but his dreams swirled and took him into the darkest recesses of his mind.

Her skin was a beautiful ebony and her bright orange skirt flitted just below her knees in the warm breeze. She smiled a toothy grin at Evers who had just returned from a sniper mission deep in the jungles of Uganda. Having successfully buried a bullet between the eyes of a rogue military commander responsible for smuggling RPG's into Somalia and other questionable areas of the world, he decided that some rest and relaxation was in order and checked into a hotel in Kampala.

After checking in, Evers slept for well over twelve hours. His small team disbanded and went separate ways to avoid looking suspicious after the untimely death of their mark. He chose the Cassia Lodge and Resort, a beautiful property sitting upon a hill and overlooking Murchison Bay and the city proper. Lush and vibrant green teak trees dotted the city along with numerous pines that were non-native and frowned upon by local government.

Evers sipped waragi, or war gin as it was known locally, as he sat at a table by the pool. He wore nondescript cargo shorts and a lightweight white cotton shirt. His sunglasses concealed his face and served as a way to check his surroundings without being observed doing so.

A lovely black woman was staring at him from the pool bar. He watched as she picked up her drink and sauntered toward him, her hips swaying provocatively. Her hand lightly grazed his shoulder as she walked behind him, sensually biting her lower lip and grinning. She pulled a chair from under the umbrella covered table and sat next to him.

"This is your first visit to Kampala, my friend?"

Evers shook his head. "It is."

"You look like you could use a friend" she said matter-of-factly.

Evers smiled at the woman as he nodded his head. "I could certainly use a friend."

He gazed at her unblemished face and made note of her slightly upturned eyes and thin-bridged nose. She looked quite exotic, and her unique Ugandan accent enunciated each word wonderfully. Evers wondered why she had chosen him to talk to and wondered if she was a local prostitute. No matter her profession, it was nice to have a woman with which to converse.

"Do you have a name?" Evers asked, his southern drawl smooth and slow.

"Ritah," she replied. "My mother thought it would be elegant to add an 'h' to the end of name. I like it and find it rather unique. What do you think?" She raised an eyebrow and smiled in a way that was one part sincere, one part seduction.

"Well, Ritah with an h, I find your name very regal. Your mother is obviously a very cerebral woman."

"And what is your name, sir?" Ritah purred.

"Bill...just Bill. There's nothing regal or noble about my name, sweety."

"Bill," she began, "I prefer to call you William, if that's okay?"

"Honey, you can call me anything you would like," he said with a wink.

"You're American, yes?" she asked.

"I am American to the bone. For better or worse, I do love my country," he remarked, the alcohol beginning to loosen him up.

Ritah tilted her head slightly to one shoulder and eyed him warily. With a slight smile she said, "You Americans tend to be roguish and somewhat egotistical. At least that has been my experience."

Evers, as well traveled and versed in the perception others had of America, was still somewhat taken aback by her comment. He was no fan of his own government, most especially the current administration that promised transparency and an end to the wars begun during the previous presidency. It seemed as though the current guy sitting on the American throne was anything other than transparent, and his involvement in overthrowing leaders of sovereign countries did nothing to advance public perception of America on the global stage.

"I can understand why you say that about Americans, Ritah, but I'm not America. I love my country, but don't assume we're all loud and obnoxious assholes. On the contrary, many of us prefer to keep to ourselves and mind our own business. Our government represents us, but it is impossible to group the melting pot which is America into a single paradigm, if you understand what I'm trying to say."

She smiled her sexy smile and replied, "I think I do understand, William. Let's change the subject, okay?"

He ordered another waragi for his new friend, and the two drank and chatted for another couple hours. The alcohol made the conversation easier and Evers let slip that he was in Uganda on a clandestine mission. Ritah didn't react to his admission and he was happy for it. He assumed she wouldn't understand his vague reference about his job anyway, so the oversight could be forgiven. Still, he knew he had to be careful in his dialogue and actions, especially since he was still in the country in which he just put a bullet into a man's head.

Ritah stood and reached for Evers' hand, urging him to follow her. The couple walked slowly past the pool stopping long enough to gaze at the bay and the city that lay below them. Evers put his hand on the back of her neck drawing her face to his. He could smell the sweet scent of her light perfume and the feel of exquisitely smooth skin caused him to harden. Ritah allowed her hand to brush against his erection while offering him a wry smile. She winked at him and began pulling his hand again, leading him toward the Lodge and her room.

She withdrew her room key from the small handbag she was carrying and inserted it into the card slot. As she did, Evers spun her toward him and pushed his face into hers again. His tongue traced the line of her mouth then slowly entered her parted lips. After a few moments of passionate kissing, she pushed him away and inserted the card into the key slot again. The familiar clank of the lock disengaging sounded and she depressed the handle and opened the door.

As the two walked past the closing door Ritah turned and threw her arms around Evers, standing on her tip-toes as she kissed him deeply. He allowed one hand to touch her breasts, exploring the outside of her blouse. Her erect nipples pushed through her bra as he began unbuttoning her top. She reached for the button on his shorts and deftly unfastened it then moved her hand to the zipper in one steady motion, her soft lips never leaving his.

His pants fell to his ankles while he struggled to slip out of his sandals. He almost tripped and fell on her, but regained his balance at the last second. For a second time Ritah laughed at him. Evers couldn't help but laugh too.

The bulge in his underwear strained against the cotton as her hand slid over the elastic band and found his hardness, squeezing and stroking like a woman with experience. Evers moved a hand under her skirt and caressed the moist panties that were clinging to her body. With one thumb he hooked the top of her panties and slid them off. They smoothly fell to the floor as Ritah graciously stepped over them, not at all like Evers's struggle with his sandals and shorts.

He pushed her blouse over her shoulders and watched it hit the floor, falling next to her panties. With one hand he managed to unlatch her bra, her large, dark breasts jumping toward him. He kissed her again then pushed her back on the bed, his mouth and tongue lavishing her neck and slowly making his way to her hardened nipples. His tongue darted over one, then the other, his saliva making both shine in the soft lamp-light of the room.

She moaned then pulled him up and stuck her tongue in his mouth as she grabbed his erection and guided him inside her. Her back arched and he buried himself completely inside her. Ritah wrapped one leg around him and placed both hands on his ass willing him deeper with each thrust. Another moan began to form in her throat, but by the time it made it to her lips a pleasurable scream escaped. Evers felt her grow wetter and knew she had cum, his own orgasm on the verge. Not wanting the moment to end, he pulled out long enough to dull the sensation, but she quickly grabbed him and slid him back inside her.

"I need you to cum inside me, William," she pleaded as she looked directly into his eyes. Her expression pushed him over the edge and with one final thrust he came. His body tensed and his back arched as he moaned. Evers lay on top of her for a few moments more, the two kissing, his hand wrapped around the small of her back.

Sweat covered them both as he rolled over to his side of the bed. Ritah placed one hand on his slick chest and lightly stroked.

"That was nice, William. Rest for a while and perhaps we'll have a repeat performance," she teased.

Ritah rolled off the bed and walked to the bathroom. He was entranced with the litheness her body exuded. Her lean frame was muscular, but very feminine. His eyes began to close, exhaustion overtaking his body.

The tension he had been dealing with since completing his mission was no longer present in his body. He breathed deeply and felt the muscles in his legs, back, and chest loosen. It had been some time since he had enjoyed the pleasures of a beautiful woman and his mind and body savored the moment.

From somewhere far away, Evers heard footfalls as Ritah walked to the bathroom. A few seconds later the toilet flushed and the sound of water poured into the bathroom sink as she washed her hands. She opened the bathroom door and light slipped into the darkened room.

Evers opened his eyes slightly, his eyelashes still touching and watched in horror as Ritah pulled a large knife from her purse and heaved it over her shoulder. An immediate adrenaline dump dropped into his gut as he raised his arm in a traditional karate upper block. The knife tore into his forearm, a deep gash that began bleeding almost immediately.

"You fucking Americans!" she bellowed. "You come here and kill my people, you killed my mother and father, and you killed one of my brothers. Now it's your turn, asshole!"

She slashed again, this time raking the knife across his chest. Evers grabbed her wrist with both of his hands while kicking the side of her leg. The impact was significant, but her muscular body absorbed the blow better than he anticipated. She jerked her trapped arm back but he held tight.

Evers placed his thumb directly behind the hand holding the knife as he trapped her wrist with his other hand. He pulled her knife wielding hand to him while he simultaneously rotated her wrist away from her body, executing a perfect kote gaeshi technique—a maneuver taught early in his karate training.

Ritah's body spun with the throw as Evers maintained control of her hand. He quickly jumped out of the bed. Had there been spectators present, their two naked bodies, his bleeding arm, and the knife she wielded would have made it appear that the couple was engaged in some sadistic sexual game.

She winced in pain, but still attempted to punch him in the balls with her free hand. Fully alert now, Evers twisted harder on her wrist causing her to cry out. His eyes, now fully focused, pierced into her.

"What the hell is wrong with you, you crazy bitch?" Evers gasped, fighting hard to slow his breathing.

"I recognized you as an American. Your arrogance and desire to bring harm to my people was written on your face. It sickened me to lay with you, but I prayed to Allah for forgiveness and the will to run my knife through your neck!" she screamed.

Evers wanted to argue with her, to reason with her in some way or fashion, but he realized she was right—at least on a level he knew he couldn't articulate. Her perception of Americans was one of invaders, not liberators. She believed the American military and American contractors served no purpose other than imperialism and destruction, and to some degree she was correct.

The problem, however, was the real imperialistic nature her religion perpetuated and all the hate and harm it caused in the world. Truth be known, those at the top of the Muslim hierarchy didn't give a shit about Muhammad, Islam, or Allah. What they cared about was power, money, and control.

"Ritah, I need you to calm down," Evers replied, his voice level.

"Fuck you!" she screamed again.

He tweaked a little harder on her wrist, her face contorting in the tell-tale sign of pain and extreme discomfort.

"Who are you working for?" he asked.

"I work for no one but the people of Uganda," she spat.

Evers had been around long enough to know that few people operated independently. In fact, he suspected that she was on someone's payroll and was paid to seek out and kill Americans, no matter their place in society or business affiliation. He glared at her, holding her wrist in a tight lock, his face calm, attempting to force more information from her without speaking.

She obviously had undergone some training. Despite the pain he inflicted and the stony look on his face, she revealed nothing. He grabbed the knife hilt and forced it from her hand with some effort, yet her contorted face revealed no additional information. With a flick of his own wrist he threw the knife across the room as blood cascaded down his forearm.

With his free hand he seized her throat and applied pressure. "I'm going to ask you one more time. Who are you working for?"

Ritah gasped and coughed as he squeezed her trachea. She squirmed in his firm grip, but the years of judo, grabbing uniforms and throwing people, *made his hands and arms strong. She pushed a raspy breath through her teeth while she continued to struggle for breath.*

"I already told you," she wheezed. "I work for Uganda and I've killed lots of Americans just like you several times."

Evers released his hold on her throat, but continued controlling her wrist. Her free hand shot to her throat and began furiously rubbing it as though she was trying to coax air into her lungs by waving it down her windpipe. She attempted to pull free of the hold he had on her wrist, but doing so only made him crank on it a little harder.

Ritah cried out in pain, but managed to shoot a fast punch to Evers's balls. Instinctively, he released his hold on her to reach for his groin. Doubled over in agony, he saw her bolt across the room and bend for something.

His mind processed what was happening in a split second as a fresh dump of adrenaline shot through his veins. She spun and lunged toward him, the blade of the knife protruding from her hand like a large, razor sharp tooth about to devour its evening meal. He stepped inside her forward thrust and deflected her hand away with an open hand block. With his injured arm he performed an open hand strike using the knife edge of his hand. A loud "thwump" erupted as his hand struck the temporal lobe on the side of her head. Ritah dropped to her knees, stunned by the powerful blow. Her eyes glazed over as she struggled with losing consciousness.

Without a second thought, Evers stepped behind her, wrapping an arm around her neck and closing off blood from both the carotid arteries that traveled directly to the brain. He didn't use much pressure, choosing instead to ease her into a painless and struggle free death.

In thirty seconds her eyes were closed and her breathing slow. He continued applying the choke and within a minute and a half she was officially brain dead. Evers held the choke for another two minutes just to be certain of death.

He laid her on the floor and quickly grabbed his clothes and dressed. It was only a matter of time that the adrenaline surging through his body would dissipate and a serious case of the shakes would begin. This happened every time he killed someone, and to prevent being noticed he needed to get somewhere without people until it passed.

Evers checked the room to make sure he didn't leave anything behind then quietly walked out without giving Ritah a second glance. He wasn't in any danger of her being discovered by housekeeping until the morning, so he made his way to his room until he could calm down and think appropriately.

He withdrew his room key and opened the door. A quick glance around his room made him feel reasonably sure he was alone. However, given his encounter with Ritah, he decided it would serve him well to perform a thorough check. He cleared the bathroom before opening the closet. No one lingered in either place. Next, he checked under the bed then carefully withdrew the curtains.

As the adrenaline slowed, his hands and legs began to shake uncontrollably. He lay down on his bed and stared at the ceiling trying to calm his mind and body.

Evers's years in the field made him fully aware of what happens as the human body slows or stops the release of adrenaline. He could feel his heart pounding in his chest, his mind racing as it replayed the events leading up to this recent kill. His chest rose and fell as he fought to control his breathing, his teeth chattering like a wind-up toy.

After several agonizing minutes he got control of himself and began thinking about how he would leave Uganda without being detected. When Ritah's body was discovered he would be tracked down, as several witnesses saw them together at the pool. The thought of spending several agonizing months being tortured by those he had slowly been eradicating made his stomach hurt. He picked up the phone and dialed.

"Allo?" said the South African voice on the other end.

"I need a little help."

"What type of help do you require?" came the response.

Evers breathed deeply. "I need a ride out of here. You know where 'here' is, yes?"

"Of course," the voice reticent and somewhat arrogant.

Evers listened for instructions after explaining the situation, leaving out the most intimate of details. In less than an hour-and-a-half he was in the back seat of a helicopter flying south to a private air strip in Rwanda. The price for an immediate extraction was heavy, but he knew his contractor would pay the price. After all, finding good help was a difficult thing, no matter the generation.

He lay in his bed, distant memories of Ritah and the strange events that unfurled in the hours following the time they had spent together rolled through his mind. Never one to eliminate a woman or child, her ghost still haunted him despite her intent to do the same to him. She left him no choice, it was his life or hers, but listening to her gurgle as she struggled to breathe and remain conscious echoed in his mind like a tourist screaming across the Grand Canyon.

Sweat glistened on his chest as the news anchor on the television tossed to the local weather forecaster. The sheet beneath him was damp and cold, reminding him of the wet ground he had often slept upon in various jungles and forests around the world. The demons from his past still visited him, no matter the Hail Mary's, no matter the prayers to The Father, or his attempts at praying to The Buddha. Nothing helped, and he realized nothing would.

Desperation often filled his mind and he considered ending his life, but something willed him to another day.

Perhaps it was the memories of his dad telling him, "It's always better to be gazing down at the daisies than staring up at the roots. Remember that son, no matter how hard times get." He shook his head as he wondered whether his father was as wise as he once thought him to be.

From somewhere far away he heard a man telling him about a police action in Argentina. "Reports," the man began, "are that as many as six hundred civilians have been slaughtered. Unconfirmed reports estimate the real death toll to be somewhere in the neighborhood of two-thousand. At this time, no one knows why the Argentinian government turned its guns on its own people."

"What the..."

He sat upright in his bed and shook the cobwebs from his head, the memories of Ritah and his father mercifully falling away. The Argentinian army marched headlong into hundreds of protesters holding signs he couldn't decipher. What they were protesting and why the military elected to open fire on them was still a mystery to everyone, including the press reporting the story.

The video, a brief twenty seconds long, showed the soldiers on the front line level their weapons and shoot. Protesters at the front of the pack fell or doubled over as bullets riddled their bodies. Those not trained in military tactics may not have been able to pick out the simultaneous firing of rifles from multiple sources, but to Evers's trained eye, he saw coordination and planning. The slaughter he was watching was not spontaneous. In fact...

Before he could finish his thought his cell phone rang.

"Hello."

"Hey there Buck, it's me."

Evers heard Buddy's hand slide over his phone and muffled coughs erupted. The sound went on for several seconds and when he returned Evers could hear him wheezing.

"That cough sounds bad, Buddy. You should have it seen about before it gets worse."

"It's just a cold, Billy. This will pass like everything else does, but I appreciate your concern."

"I just worry about you, you old bastard, that's all. I don't mean to harp."

Buddy gave a small laugh, "Hell, Buck, I had no idea you had a heart. Shit fire, if I'd known you were so caring I would have insisted on flowers and chocolates."

A booming laugh came from deep within Evers's chest. He honestly could not remember the last time he had laughed so hard. The laughter, the light-heartedness of Buddy's response was just the thing he needed, no, just the thing he longed for in a conversation. It went on for several seconds, Evers laughing, which in turn made Buddy cackle, the hysterics of the silly remark contagious.

After some time the two men stopped laughing. Buddy cleared his throat and Evers could tell the conversation was about to turn serious. He waited for Buddy to speak, the silence growing still and slightly uncomfortable.

"Have you seen any news, Buck? The world is going crazy while the rest of us sit here with our thumbs up our asses."

"I just saw a broadcast about the Argentinian military attacking its citizens. That's really not so unusual, but the manner in which they did it made it obvious that it was coordinated and planned."

"That's right, son, it was most certainly orchestrated. Now, there are only a few people who could order their military to strike. There's that hot number the people of Argentina elected, Mrs. Kirchner, or the head of the military, General Fernando Vasquez. She appears to be much more interested in syphoning money and playing back door politics in order to get re-elected, so I doubt she had anything to do with the assault on the citizenry.

"Vasquez, on the other hand, is a revolutionary and a scholar. He's been overheard saying the world needs more government intervention and control over the free markets. He claims that too many people in the world receive a college education, thereby giving the weak an opportunity to prosper. You want to know what his solution for the poor has been, Buck? Let them starve to death.

"He has been a follower of both Marx and Darwin, believing in the ability of the powerful to reign over the weak and poor, while allowing those less fortunate to simply fade away. Helluva guy, huh?"

Evers listened to the silence that fell between them for a few seconds. "What are you suggesting? Do we travel to Argentina and attempt to meet up with this guy? I doubt he would be an easy target."

"That's exactly what I'm suggesting, Buck. The bad part in all this is I can't go and you'll have to do this one completely solo. Our government, the CIA included, refuses to intervene in Argentina's politics. They have their hands full right now trying to assure America that Ebola won't be spreading between its borders despite that poor bastard who just died in Dallas. The truth is, our military and government are afraid of what might happen in our own streets should an outbreak become reality," Buddy finished.

"You think our own servicemen and women will turn their guns on its people?" Evers asked, his tone rhetorical.

Buddy stared blankly at his living room wall and nodded his head. "Fucking A right I think they will, Buck. We've seen army's do it before. The Germans, the Russians, the Chinese. Each soldier, when asked, simply replied that he was following orders. These boys running around with high powered, fully automatic rifles understand one thing—following orders. If they are told to fire upon their fellow Americans, they'll do so without much thought or regret. It's what they're trained to do."

Evers nodded to no one in particular even though he already knew what Buddy said to be true. He remembered what it was like to be a young soldier, full of piss and vinegar and no idea about how the world really worked. God, country, and the United States Army were all he knew, and by God, he would have killed anyone who dared slander his country or army's name. If the order came down, he would have shot his best friend, that's how serious and inexperienced he was in the uniform.

"Buck, we have to cut the head off of the snake. That's the only way we can stop this global human purge," Buddy said.

"You think General Vasquez is heading all this activity up?"

"Hell no I don't think he's heading it up. I think he's a pawn in a horrific game of chess! What I know is he can help us find the snake. That's the key…finding the snake then decapitating it."

"I guess I'm going to Argentina then," Evers responded.

Part II

Something told me it was over
When I saw you and her walking
Something deep in my soul said cry, girl
When I saw you walking away that day.
~ Etta James ~

Deep into that darkness
peering, long I stood there,
wondering, fearing,
doubting, dreaming dreams
no mortal ever dared to
dream before.
~ Edgar Allan Poe ~

They shall hunger no more,
Neither thirst anymore;
Neither shall the sun light on them,
Nor any heat.
~ The Revelation 7:16 ~

Blood oozed from the eye sockets of a man lying on stale sheets. His nurses had stopped changing his sheets after he shit so much that it dripped over the side to the floor. When he vomited, the projectile stream of mostly digested food splattered off his leg and onto the doctor treating him.

Dr. Dafora looked in horror at the scratch on his bicep he had received the day before while trimming hedges in his backyard. His eyes moved from his arm to those of his patient whose toothy grin seemed painted by Botticelli with Dante's approval.

The patient smiled his bloody smile despite the inordinate pain he felt in his own stomach and bowels. A certain satisfaction arose in him as he realized the good doctor would soon understand his fate. Mucus ran from his nose down one cheek but he didn't seem to care. Who would really care about a little snot after shitting himself and blowing chunks?

Dafora moved quickly to the one sink available in the quarantined room. He smoothed antibacterial soap across the open wound then flushed it with cool potable water. The logical side of his mind warned him that he was infected and would be subjected to a horrendous death in less than three weeks, while the irrational side told him everything would be okay.

As he stumbled out of the patient's room a nurse looked at him, one brow raised as though she were asking what was wrong. He attempted a reassuring smile as he took a deep breath in hope of controlling the nervous shakes that were quickly beginning to show. The tremors in his hands and shaking knees began to overtake his body as he struggled to walk back to his office.

With tremendous effort he seated himself at his desk. Both hands pressed against his bloodshot eyes, the result of a sixteen hour shift treating those overcome with the Ebola virus. Despite what he had read and learned, he chose not to wear the long plastic hazmat sleeves or face shield prescribed by the leading health organizations of the world. For whatever reason he didn't want his patients to feel less than human, nor did he think the hazmat suit was conducive to a positive mental state when trying to stave off the organ eating virus. Now he was going to pay for his compassion with his life.

Once the realization of what had just transpired set in, Dr. Dafora considered his alternatives, ride it out and see if he was truly infected with the virus or end his life now. He thought about his wife and children, how they would miss him if he was gone. That said, he knew he couldn't go home for fear of infecting them all.

Conversely, he and his staff were a mere handful of medical practitioners capable of staving off the growing epidemic overtaking West Africa. Yes, the Americans and Europeans had finally joined in the fight, but only after some of their own became infected. Still, their involvement in his own continent was limited to academic study rather than actionable practices that would help contain and eliminate the horrendous virus.

In his own mind he reasoned through the possibilities of being infected. Without a doubt, his patient was consumed by the virus, its own replication eating away at his liver, kidneys, and soft tissues. The risk level of being infected was very high, but as with most humans, fear of the unknown, or in this case the known, made a person think irrationally.

He calmed down and convinced himself he was okay, rose from his desk and went back to work. With the patience of a saint, Dafora continued working with infected men and women, conversing light heartedly with his nurses and fellow doctors, finally going home to his wife and children. He kissed each child before going to bed, he and his wife made love before he dozed off.

It was his inability to accept the severity of the situation that led to his staff and family's demise over the next month and a half...

London, United Kingdom
12:09 PM

Trowton paced across the expensive Turkish rug in the living room of his penthouse apartment. He paused long enough to wipe perspiration from his forehead and nudge his glasses closer to his eyes. Frustrated, he threw the damp handkerchief on his coffee table where his cell phone lay dormant.

Things were not happening quickly enough for him, although news agencies were reporting unconfirmed escalations in the number of deaths across Africa and Japan. Recently, SARS had migrated into Okinawa, as well as being repatriated into China. Two unconfirmed cases were being investigated in Los Angeles, as recent travelers returned from Asia.

Coupled with the introduction of Ebola into the United States and Europe, Trowton knew the WHO and CDC would be working overtime to contain the viruses while also researching possible cures. The two viruses were on track to wreak havoc on the populations of both regions, but they weren't moving as rapidly as he had hoped due in large part to the various countries' attempts to contain them and his underestimation of their respective response times to the diseases.

His contact in India would help move the process along, but his grand vision would never be realized unless he could speed up the global death rate. Although war would be realized in the region and death tremendously robust, something else would have to be done. Then there was Abaddon.

He couldn't understand what his new boss's fixation on global depopulation was, but he struck more than fear in his heart whenever they spoke. Abaddon's infiltration into his life was invasive, powerful, and…if he was being honest, *evil*. There, he thought it, he accepted it, and he knew he was right. Abaddon was evil personified and had a hold on him he couldn't explain. Never one to fear death, something about the man changed that for him.

Trowton stopped what he was doing and his eyes glazed over. He had a mental image of his prone body lying in a tight fitting coffin, one of his many designer suits thrown on him by a hasty mortician. His face was pasty, the heavy makeup giving him that strange blurred look that people struggled to accept while viewing a loved one in their final repose. The bony fingers of both hands were crossed over his flat belly and his eyelids covered eyes that appeared hollow and sunken in his skull.

From somewhere outside his casket he could hear people murmuring, their discussion muffled but happy. Happy? Who is happy about a funeral, especially when you're standing next to an open coffin with a man's corpse inside it? And why wasn't there any sobbing? He could hear no one mourning his loss, and if his heart was still beating, it would have sped up as his ire increased.

Just above him he could see a person, a man in a dark, herringbone suit, the strange features of the man's face more than familiar. The same greasy smile he had upon his face when they met at the restaurant revealed yellowing, jagged teeth, a detail he had missed at their first meeting. For a moment he considered the paradox of those apparently unhealthy teeth and the fit body surrounding them. He wondered if the man suffered from halitosis, his breath smelling like a cross between warm fish and some rotten vegetable.

Why is this guy greeting my mourners and how did I die? The questions continued to pile into his dead brain, his still hand wanting nothing more than to pinch the bridge of his nose. Another person, a lady who worked for him, walked to the casket to peer inside. She didn't look sad, nor did she appear to have any remorse for the loss of her boss. He wanted to reach out and slap her, to tell her she *owed* him a couple of tears, *or at least a goddam sad face!*

Bridgette. I think her name is Bridgette. Everything began to get hazy, his memory, his vision, even his hearing. *If I'm dead, why the fuck do I still have my senses?* His thoughts seemed to transmit directly to Abaddon.

That greasy smile turned toward him, his lips parting even farther until Trowton could have sworn he saw the man's rotting wisdom teeth. Even through his passing vision, the slick hair and hard features were unmistakable. *And those teeth! Jesus Christ. Where did he get those teeth?*

The confusion started to leave him, his senses finally dulling, but still there was *that* man and *that* smile. Calmness began to overtake him even though he was vaguely aware of the herringbone suited man standing vigil over his lifeless body. Worry and fear were floating away like a cloud drifting on an easy summer breeze.

Abaddon leaned over his chest, seeming to smell him, his face mere inches from his torso. His face found its way directly above Trowton's and suddenly that fear, that inescapable hold he had over him seized his unbeating heart and mind. Something began to tug at him, inside him, deep within that area of the mind and soul that contained his human life force.

Abaddon's mouth opened revealing more than his jagged yellow teeth. At the top of his throat, scarred and pitted tonsils flexed in-and-out, in-and-out, as the man's respiration increased. There was excitement on his face and Trowton could smell his tainted breath. He had guessed right for the most part, most especially about the warm fish, but there was another blended rottenness that poured over his own nostrils. The odor was reminiscent of a garbage dumpster found behind an unctuous restaurant serving week old fruit and month old unrefrigerated meats. He half expected a stray cat to fly from behind his tongue, its angered and surprised face pissed because its meal was interrupted.

As the towering man continued to breathe inward, he could feel his life force, hell, his soul, being sucked from his very existence. Pieces of his spiritual self were ripped and spewed from his nose and into the man's gaping mouth.

The sensation wasn't exactly painful, but it certainly wasn't a cause for celebration either. He realized that this man, this person, this being, was eating him. He was being devoured by that very thing he was never sure existed. Now, in the final seconds of his own actuality did he cognitively understand how wrong he was.

Remnants of the man he had been flew into Abaddon's mouth. A satisfying chomp of his teeth was the only thing anyone near him would have heard. But no one was standing near the man, as only a handful had showed up to pay their last respects and discuss the day's happenings at the office.

Trowton shook his head, awakening from the nightmare he was having. The man in the herringbone suit frightened him not only in his head, but somewhere deep inside his very being. As the vision cleared, he felt himself begin to shake. Fear gripped him, wrapping its invisible fingers around his heart and squeezing, releasing, squeezing, releasing.

He struggled to slow his breathing before he hyperventilated, reasoning with himself as he did so.

"Get it together, Simon. You're allowing this man to control you when he's not even around," he said aloud. Deep down, however, he knew the man's hold on him was almost complete. Although he couldn't explain what the hold was or how he maintained it, he was cognizant of the unending and far-reaching grip the man had on his spirit. Slowly, his quivering knees began to steady and his trembling jaw tightened.

He exhaled, his breath loud and raspy, like that of an old man who long ago had stopped inhaling cigarettes, but whose lungs were forever damaged by the tar-filled smoke that filled them time and again. Trowton turned on his television and tuned into the BBC. More reports were detailing the shocking and abrupt breakout of SARS in a growing population of Japanese youth. There appeared to be a common link in their whereabouts—a nightclub strip in a Tokyo suburb. Since the multiple diagnoses, several others had been quarantined and hospitalized with SARS like symptoms. Fear and panic were spreading through the metropolitan area like speeding cars over the Autobahn.

New cases were now being reported in Hong Kong, Manila, and Hanoi. Dozens of deaths, the news anchor said, were causing other countries to stop flights from the affected areas. "There is a growing fear that the decision to cease flights in and out of the Asian countries with confirmed cases of SARS had been made too late," the man in the poorly fitted suit stated.

"New cases have also been reported in some of America's largest cities, including New York, Dallas, Los Angeles, and Atlanta. The American government has yet to halt international flights for travelers coming from affected countries, although several other governments are no longer accepting American passengers into their airports. It is being told that The President of the United States is very upset with the decision many of his allies made and has vowed to respond to each in due time."

Another empty threat by an empty suit, Trowton mused. The reporter began updating his viewers on the slower, but just as deadly spread of the SARS virus through Latin America. "Numerous deaths have been attributed to the outbreak, but confirmation of the number of victims has been difficult to ascertain at this time, as many Latin American governments are hesitant to reveal them to the press."

What the reporter didn't say, or had not quite understood yet, was that the two viruses were on a collision course in the United States. There was no doubt that the American medical establishment would be overcome with the two deadly diseases, and many from the medical community would contract one of the diseases and eventually perish. Such was the beauty of mass transit and unprotected borders.

It was also apparent that the Ebola strain unleashed in Africa would find its way quickly to Europe, Russia, and the Middle East. Trowton continued to think about how he could speed up the process, knowing it was his destiny to purge the planet's gluttonous hominids from its face before the medical community could find a cure for each disease.

He reached for the phone and dialed the number he had previously memorized. One ring then another, and finally a voice.

"Yes."

Trowton hesitated for a few seconds, his heart thudding in his chest. The rhythm of its beat hard and steady. His lips parted and dried saliva stuck to them both, creating a white string that snapped and whipped inside his mouth.

"Detonate."

Buenos Aires, Argentina
3:10 PM

Evers stepped out of the Ministro Pistarini Airport with his backpack slung over one shoulder while dragging a small roller board behind him. Before leaving Virginia he had stopped by a local Spy Store and purchased a pair of stylish sunglasses with a microscopic built-in camera pointed directly behind him. The rear view image was transmitted into his right lens at an incredible resolution. When he first tried them on he got nauseous until his brain adjusted to his left eye looking forward and his right eye watching what was happening behind him.

Always vigilant, and hyper-paranoid, Evers hailed a cab, while watching those pedestrians just to his six o'clock, which would take him to his hotel until he could get his bearings. After a few long moments, the world's most familiar yellow car, a cab, stopped and its driver jumped out to help Evers with his bags. Reluctantly, he handed both to the driver despite his desire to keep the backpack in his possession.

He instructed the driver to take him to the Hotel Sofitel, a beautiful and high priced hotel that he had found online. The hotel would also permit him to play the powerful American businessman role that he hoped to portray. He glanced down at his new sports jacket and Italian made woven loafers he purchased before leaving. Although the backpack might appear to the casual onlooker to be something far removed from a powerful businessman's personal attire, he had traveled enough to know that their use was growing exponentially and was now accepted as something more than an elementary school child's book bag. In fact, with the jacket, slacks, and shoes he was sporting, he thought the look might land him a photo op in GQ Magazine. The idea almost made him laugh and his mind flashed to Buddy and what the old operator would think if he presented him with a personally autographed copy of his first photo shoot in the world's premier men's fashion magazine.

Prior to unbuckling his seatbelt on the plane, Evers reminded himself that he was a high stakes, exceptionally rich and powerful businessman. His gait and air had to give off a certain cockiness and assuredness that he made million dollar decisions every day of his life, and because he seldom made poor decisions, he was prosperous.

He paid the driver the fare and took a moment to look around at his surroundings. No one seemed out of sorts. The Hotel Sofitel was intended as a posh hotel setting in the heart of Buenos Aires, and it appeared, at least from the outside, to live up to its billing.

A magnificent structure, Sofitel stood proudly just off Buenos Aires's shore; a gorgeous crescendo in the heart of other enormous buildings.

Businessmen and women, all smartly attired, talked about the day's events without giving Evers an afterthought. One corner of his mouth curled into a smirk as he realized his disguise was utterly perfect.

Even the hazy afternoon heat and smog seemed to stray from that area of downtown, as a light breeze from the Atlantic helped move clouds to the southwest while allowing a brilliant South American sun to beat down on those who dared challenge its heat and destructive gaze. Flags draped lazily, moving ever-so-slightly as the light wind blew between the monolithic buildings. Satisfied he wasn't being followed, Evers grabbed his bags and made his way inside the hotel.

The guest entrance was a tawdry display of everything wealth and power represented. The floors, walls, and columns were brazenly polished; each made of matching stone, polished so that the entire structure gave off a light tan watery hue. Ornate lighting hung majestically from the exceptionally high ceiling, illuminating each corner as though it was being displayed in a museum.

At the left rear of the grand entrance was a restaurant and bar filled to capacity, the talk and laughter reverberating against the stone tiled structure. Bell hops and other hotel staff wandered the area asking newly arrived travelers if they needed help with bags or directions to their rooms.

Evers removed his sunglasses and placed them in his shirt pocket as he looked around the lobby. No one set his hackles on end, although a couple of young ladies gave him a little more than a passing glance and smile. His ego in check, he made his way to the desk and checked into the room he had reserved before leaving Virginia.

His room was on the fifteenth floor, which, he was told, would afford him a spectacular view of the Atlantic should he choose to rise early enough to see the sunrise. Evers smiled his appreciation, reached for his room key and turned toward the elevator.

Walking through the hotel, in the lobby, and down the hallway to his room, Evers kept his eyes down to avoid looking directly into any camera that might be used to identify him. Despite using his real name and passport, not giving the authorities reason to suspect him for what he had planned was tantamount to his survival and completion of the mission.

Once he reached his room he slid the key as quietly as possible in the automated door lock assembly. The dead bolt thudded into the unlock position and the small led light illuminated green indicating the door was open. Evers stepped inside but kept his back to the wall as he reached for the light switch before the door closed all the way. Swiftly, he moved through the bathroom, closet, living room area and bedroom searching for anyone who might be awaiting his arrival.

Assured he was alone, he placed his bags on the floor and pulled the disposable phone he purchased in one of the airport shops from his jacket pocket while he stuffed a piece of tissue into the door peephole. He searched for the capital building's address, reasonably certain that General Vasquez would frequent it. A broad smile lit up his face when Google Maps revealed the capital was only a couple of blocks away from the Sofitel.

On a whim, he searched for the general's home address but came up short. "Oh well, it was worth a shot," he murmured.

He glanced at the hotel clock and saw that it was just after four o'clock in the afternoon. His stomach growled reminding him that he had not eaten since his connecting flight in Houston. Thankfully, he slept the majority of the second leg, but the long flight had officially caught up with him.

Evers stepped into one of the luxurious hotel restaurants and ordered some local fare. His empanadas were fresh and delicious, and the beer he chased them with, cold and refreshing. Sleepiness began creeping its way into his body, but he had one more stop before retiring for the night.

He crossed the street and walked into a local department store, picked out clothes that he both liked and knew were of local flavor then purchased them, four days worth. November marked mid-fall in the United States, and colder weather would be prevalent, but in the Southern Hemisphere spring was abundant. Warm temperatures meant light, cotton pants and shirts with a light jacket to combat any cool breeze that might find its way to bare skin. Evers was careful to pick out neutral colored clothing; he didn't want anything flamboyant or memorable.

Evers felt his eyelids beginning to close like slow moving garage doors, so he crossed the street and walked back to the hotel, his gait still that of a powerful business man who decided to do a little shopping before the evening officially began. His eyes swept back and forth, watching for anyone suspicious who might have an interest in his coming to Argentina. He stopped just outside the entrance door to Sofitel and made a casual hundred and eighty degree turn while scanning the various windows of the numerous high rise buildings around him. Just another tourist taking in his surroundings, he allowed his vision to skim over the area, up and down, side to side. Nothing made his hackles rise as he made a show of stretching his back and moving his head from shoulder to shoulder, presumably to crack his neck.

Bag in hand, he made his way to his room, put the clothes away and pulled the disposable phone out again. He typed in the Argentinian capital's address and used Google Earth to get an idea on the lay of the land. He mentally processed the many familiar looking buildings as his eyelids continued to droop over bloodshot eyes.

A large white building with a massive dome atop it, a spire at its peak attempting to pierce the clouds above it, Buenos Aires's capital looked almost identical to the United States Capital building. Not far away stood an impressive obelisk, reminiscent of the D.C.'s Washington Monument. The last thing he did before falling asleep was shake his head at a country whose sole desire was to copy his own. *If only they knew what I know*, he thought.

Sleep came quickly and the nightmares shortly after…

Delhi, India
6:04 AM

Ahsan rose early and recited his morning prayers, but were he being truthful with himself, he would have admitted that his mind wasn't on Allah. Rather, he could not stop thinking about his mission and how his actions would forever change the world, much like those faithful soldiers sent by Imam bin Laden in 2001. He said a silent prayer that he might sit next to Usama when his time was at hand. There was no doubt in his mind their conversations would be plentiful and enjoyable.

He showered, careful not to use the soap provided by the hotel. It was no secret to Muslims everywhere that Zionists were responsible for putting unclean fat from animals in soap in order to defile and make impure the children of Allah. His face grew hot as his ire rose through his body at the thought of the malcontent's atrocities on his people.

Once dressed, Ahsan picked up the two cases containing the devices he was assured would help bring about the beginning of the New Islamic State, a name he helped coin on a lonely mountain in Afghanistan as he and some of his fellow soldiers talked about the positive influence they were having in the Middle East, and walked down the hall toward the hotel elevators. The doors of the elevator opened revealing an older Indian woman and a Caucasian man standing in an ornate and extremely clean wooden box. Mirrors on each side of the elevator made the small compartment feel bigger than it was.

The man and woman paid him little attention, as passengers on an elevator are wont to do, which was fortunate for Ahsan. Sweat began beading on his forehead and in the middle of his back, brought on not by the heat but by the sudden onset of nerves as a result of his plans. He struggled to maintain audible control of his breathing as his heart beat a thunderous symphony of bass strikes.

A loud "ding" alerted the trio that the elevator was stopping. Ahsan looked up at the control panel that revealed they would stop on the sixth floor, presumably to pick up another passenger. Anxiety was beginning to set in to the point that he began fidgeting. He closed his eyes and told himself to relax, as an Indian man joined their party.

No one knows what I have in the cases, nor do they know what I am about to do, he thought.

Still, with each passing second of inactivity, he became more anxious. The woman looked up at him in time to see his eyes darting around the elevator like a child would watch a fly buzz around its head. She quickly looked away to avoid making eye contact with the man. *The crazy man*, she would later think.

From his peripheral he caught the woman staring at him again before tearing her eyes away.

"What?" he demanded.

"Nothing, sir…it's just that, well, you look a little distressed, that's all," she managed, her accent Australian.

"I'm fine, just mind your own business, please," he replied, a little more forcefully than he intended.

A feint scowl touched the woman's eyes, but she smoothed her expression quickly. "No worries, sir," she said as she took a half-step away from the sweaty Middle Easterner. The other two men acted as though they had neither heard nor seen anything, obviously afraid to intervene.

Not a moment too soon, the elevator stopped and offered its riders another ding, announcing its arrival in the lobby. As the doors separated, Ahsan bolted from the confined space heading directly to the parking deck and his rental car. The three other passengers watched him as he walked hastily across the lobby, each wondering what could possibly be wrong with the man.

He popped the trunk on his small rental car and placed the two cases inside, the sweat dripping from his face and nose as he did so. Once inside the car he sat motionless for a few moments, his arms shaking and his breathing heavy and labored. His mind told him he was close to hyperventilation, but his nervous system refused to cooperate with him. A fresh load of adrenaline dumped into his system and his heartbeat kicked up a few more notches. Both legs began shaking uncontrollably and his brain could focus on nothing but the explosives and his imminent death.

Some far-away, distant realm of consciousness rushed to the front of his troubled mind and suddenly he felt ashamed. Despite his previous battlefield experience, no matter the number of prayers he had offered to Allah, something gripped his essence and wouldn't release it. He was suddenly fearful of death, and deep down he wondered if he should inflict casualties on so many innocent people even though the Prophet explained that they were infidels and inferior in every way.

Another thought raced through his mind asking him what kind of man would become so scared in the final moments before he was to sacrifice everything in the name of Allah and Islam. Churning within his own psyche he felt a battle waging between his two inner halves, each armed with logic and a will to prevail. He felt imaginary blows being traded and his head pulsed with every fist exchanged.

At long last his legs stopped shaking and the sweat began to dry on his face and torso. He lessened the grip he had on the steering wheel so that blood could once again flow through his hands and fingers. For several minutes he rested his head against the headrest on his seat, feeling his heart rate decreasing a little at a time. He wondered how close he had come to cardiac arrest or a nervous breakdown. Meanwhile, in the back of his mind he could hear a voice calling to him, "It is time! Do not be afraid. Allah has commanded your service and you must obey."

He pictured an otherworldly Ahsan, a large, bloody knife in one hand and the severed head of a man in the other. A body lay upon the ground, his blood spilled into a large pool, legs crumpled at a strange angle. The face of the severed head contained within it a look of terror and pity, an interesting paradox for a man who had just been killed.

For several seconds, Ahsan allowed his mind's eye to drift across the macabre scene, taking note of his own brown body and the steady hand wielding the knife. He could see dark clouds passing overhead and the massive Ismoil Somoni Peak, one of Afghanistan's glorious mountains, standing proudly behind him. Beautiful white snow lay across the mountain, while fog and clouds circled about it like a playful animal begging for its owner's attention.

His gaze moved back to the severed head as a realization dawned on him: the head was his! One half of him had won the debate and the other would never live to argue again. For a few passing seconds he wondered which half won, then, as his hand reached for the ignition, an understanding sank into him.

The car's engine came to life and he dropped the transmission into reverse. Ahsan took another deep breath before easing the car out of the parking garage. As he pulled onto the highway he wondered how history would view his actions.

"Regardless of the history books," he said aloud, "Allah will view me with favor."

Arlington, Virginia
10:00 AM

Buddy sat in his car and watched as a small flock of ducks swam across the pond directly in front of him. His mind raced with thoughts of Ebola, SARS, mass government sanctioned killings of civilians, and potential nuclear explosions. He wondered how Evers was making out in Argentina; he had not heard from him since he left Virginia a few days earlier.

Things were not adding up, and despite his research the current global deluge, while appearing random from the outside, reeked of dark, backroom organization. What confused him, and the few CIA contacts he asked to help him with his research, were the countries and regions that were involved. Everyone was struggling to connect the dots and most were reluctant to admit there really was a connection.

"Come on, Buddy, think," he said to himself. "Who would want such chaos on a global scale? The Iranians? ISIS? Al Qaida? North Korea? Maybe the Russians were making another play for additional land and wanted to create a diversion before making a move."

While plausible, none of those possibilities seemed likely. The only country capable of pulling off mass anarchy on a global scale was the good ole U.S. of A., and he was certain they weren't directly involved. Still, he knew his government was not above genocide if it would procure another country's natural resources or further its own international agenda. But what was going on now did not appear to have American fingerprints on it. Still, he could not rule out some rogue Washington D.C. intervention that was furthering what was amounting to a twenty-first century plague.

He glanced at a young couple walking toward him, arm-in-arm, across a paved trail. They stopped to watch the ducks swim lazily across the pond, each duck taking turns diving in search of food. The young lady put her head on her man's shoulder and smiled. Buddy, never a romantic, felt a longing in his own heart as he watched the scene transpire.

He wondered what it would have been like to have a woman to come home to every night, a hot meal prepared, plates and table settings awaiting his return from the office. Of course, he didn't really have an office, he worked in the shadows doing things that young couples couldn't even fathom. They would probably sneer at him, maybe even loathe his existence if they knew half of what he had done in his lifetime. From the outside, they would have every right to hate him for his past transgressions, but it was the clandestine work he had been involved in that afforded them the opportunity to watch a few ducks swim on a pond without worrying about some errant asshole putting a bullet in each of their heads.

"Fuck them," he muttered.

Buddy shook his head and attempted to refocus on the dilemma at hand. *Who would do this?* The question continued swirling in his head. He told Evers to spend his energy in Argentina and allow the CDC and WHO to focus on the Ebola and SARS outbreaks, but the reality of the situation was that whole villages and communities would likely need to be quarantined or potentially eliminated. It was a disturbing thought, but it was probably the only true way to fence off further transmission of the deadly viruses. He made a mental note to have that discussion with his CIA contacts.

Who stands to gain and what is the net return for extermination on a global level? Natural resources? Land? The questions buzzed like a swarm of flies in his head but left no answer in their wake. In some instances the questions fit the area, but in others not so much. Liberia had at its disposal oil, diamonds, and timber, while Sierra Leone was replete with diamonds and gold. Japan offered next to nothing in the way of natural resources. Gas and oil were present in Argentina, but not to the extent that the United States had in reserve. Mexico was another country whose petroleum production was significant, this Buddy knew.

In several of those countries oil could be identified as a resource any nation in the world would want or need. Still, oil wasn't a common denominator across each country's list of natural resources. *Plus*, he thought, *OPEC and the U.S. have been lying to the world for forty years about their own oil reserves.* Each country had more than enough unrefined petroleum to meet global demands for generations to come, but false fear started at the government level and latched onto by left-wing anarchists helped to keep prices artificially inflated. Oil manufacturers, refiners, Saudi Sheiks, and numerous de facto governments, including the United States, reaped the financial windfall the hysterics helped cultivate.

Buddy snorted. "Those tree hugging bastards have no idea how much money they cost everyone in the world when they buy into the lies and half-truths spewed by the ones they think protect them."

Forcing his mind back to the task at hand, it became clear that there was no definitive connection inasmuch as natural resources were concerned. "If not for a country's resources, who would be interested in wiping out its population," Buddy asked himself?

He rubbed his chin then scratched his head. He could feel the frustration rising from his chest to his face until he began pounding on his steering wheel. His hand slammed down again and again and again, each time the rim of the steering wheel bending a little more, and each time the heel of his hand growing redder and redder.

"Son-of-a-bitch!" he screamed.

He smacked the side of the wheel then drove his fist into the leather seat of his car. A coughing fit suddenly hit him, brought on by his loud outburst.

Like the good man he was he covered his mouth, the tickle in his chest growing ever more annoying despite his fitful coughing. He felt phlegm hit his cupped hand so he reached for his handkerchief with the other.

The coughing began to reside as he went to wipe his hand. His eyes caught the large splatter of blood that had begun to drip down the inside of his palm. He coughed a couple more times as he slowly wiped away the crimson liquid. The taste of iron was rich in his mouth. He dabbed the rag over his lips, some new spots appearing on it as he did so.

"Fuck me," he said quietly. "Fuck me."

Buenos Aires, Argentina
5:05 AM

The sun had not yet peaked over the Atlantic as the night sky's red glow hung like an umbrella over the city's skyline. Evers stood at his window in his underwear staring out at the lights from the skyscrapers and other buildings adjacent to his own. Far below him he could barely make out the sounds of car engines as the South American metropolis began to wake.

On the streets around the city, protests were forming; their marchers demanding answers for mass deaths and missing citizens. From what he had seen and heard on the news, the protesters were mostly peaceful, but as with any gathering of large sums of people, the opportunity for chaos to erupt was imminent. He knew his time in Argentina was limited, despite the lack of intelligible information.

"Fucking, Buddy. I still don't know why I listen to him," he said under his breath.

His nightmares were becoming a distant memory, their net effect beginning to show on his haggard face. He was in need of a shower and a shave and his reflection revealed the scars on his chest and legs, physical memories of a couple of ferocious battles in Kabul many years earlier. Evers filled his lungs with a deep breath then stepped away from the window. He opened his backpack, picked out a t-shirt and a pair of sweatpants, slipped on his sneakers and headed to the hotel gym.

Evers stretched his legs, hips, shoulders and neck, taking an especially long time to warm up his calves properly. He hopped on one of the treadmills, hit the green button, and began jogging. Running at a nice pace, he surpassed the five kilometer mark, sweat beginning to drip from his forehead, arms, and chest. After bumping up the RPM's on the treadmill's control panel, his legs pumped faster and his breathing intensified. At the ten kilometer mark he slowed the speed to a brisk walk. He walked that way for ten more minutes while he got his breathing and heart rate under control.

After cooling down he stretched out again. His hips were very flexible and pushing his body into the full splits was relatively easy to do, especially after a warm-up jog like he had just finished on the treadmill. He assumed a few yoga positions he had learned from his judo instructor who thoroughly believed in isometric isolation of muscle groups as a method of strengthening joints, something very important in a sport that involved throwing opponents, as well as getting thrown himself.

Next, he did several sets of pushups, changing the type of pushup with each set of thirty. He began with the standard military position, changed to one handed, and finally did a handstand against the wall where he performed reverse pushups. Veins bulged from his muscular arms and sweat rolled from his stomach to his chest, finally finding refuge in a puddle on the floor beneath him. He walked a step away from the wall on his hands then knocked out five more handstand pushups without any support before allowing his feet to come back to Earth.

Evers allowed himself a few seconds to catch his breath and for the blood to settle from his face back to where it belonged. He made large circular motions with his arms, assuring his shoulder joints were loose and not still rigid after the incredible strain he put them through a few seconds earlier. His head tilted to each shoulder, cracking the vertebrae and also loosening the muscles around them.

He moved a few items out of the way to create more floor space for himself. His eyes were closed for a few seconds as he visualized his karate kata, his opponents, and the rhythm of the techniques. He opened his stance, his feet even with his shoulders and brought his tight fists to his hips. Silently, he mouthed the name of the kata, *shihohai*, in the traditional manner of all Japanese karate-ka.

His right foot snapped to his left knee as he pivoted ninety degrees to the left and slammed a right punch into the air. His kiai wasn't vocalized to avoid waking any guests. He repeated this technique three more times, rotating ninety degrees each time until he was facing the same direction from which he began. In his mind he visualized an opponent attacking him from his immediate right. His left hand shout out, pretending to grab just behind his attacker's head. He moved his right foot behind his left and snapped a vertical back-fist into his would be attacker's nose.

Another guest, towel around his neck and dressed for his morning workout, began to open the door but stopped short when he saw a man standing rigid in a strange position, his hair pasted to his head, wet with sweat, and a fierceness on his face that looked both primal and savage. He withdrew his hand from the doorknob and watched with a morbid curiosity for several minutes as the man punched, kicked, and blocked his way through what was obviously a pre-determined grouping of techniques.

Evers's chest heaved up and down from exertion. His hips drove his movements and created the power from which his technique flowed. He finished one kata then moved immediately into the next. His techniques were lightning fast and, despite training alone, seemed to punch and dismantle the imaginary person in front or behind him.

After some time Evers finished his workout. His shirt was soaked, and his limbs red, the blood pumping through them at a ferocious rate. He cut his eyes at the window of the small workout center and saw the man watching him. The man dropped his eyes, embarrassed at having been caught watching another person working out.

Evers dabbed the sweat from his face and walked out the door into the hallway.

"I apologize, señor. Your movements looked like magic. I did not mean to stare," said the man who had been watching him.

"No worries," Evers murmured. He walked past the man, his eyes looking down, not wanting the man to remember him, although he knew that possibility was out of the question.

Evers hopped on the elevator and rode it up to his floor. He glanced left then right before turning toward his room. After showering and a change into the new clothes he purchased, he rode the elevator to the lobby and crossed the street to a small diner he noticed the night before.

It was still relatively early and he needed to kill some time, so he elected to eat breakfast and sip on hot coffee. Fifteen minutes later he made his way back to the lobby and outside where the next phase of his mission would begin.

He was aware that his destination lay just over a half mile away from his hotel, but he planned on taking a couple of detours in order to siphon any would be trail that he might have picked up since his arrival. His hyper-paranoia was working overtime, but self-preservation often dictated an excessive level of caution be taken even when he was relatively certain no one knew of his presence in an area. Good counter surveillance had saved his life on more than one occasion so he figured today should be no different than any other day.

After walking to the back of the hotel and exiting through a rear entrance to the hotel, Evers turned left onto Suipacha Street, a busy road even for a metropolitan downtown area. Numerous people crowded the sidewalk on either side of the roadway, some seemingly out shopping and others heading to meetings. It was still early enough for breakfast but late enough that lunch cuisines were being prepared. Evers could smell the mixture of both as he walked.

He crossed over a busy intersection on Juncal turning left again, stopping for a few seconds to prop against a wall and look at a street map he had picked up at the hotel. The map also provided enough cover for him to check his surroundings for anyone who might have been following him. When a couple of moments passed he folded the map and put it in his hip pocket. He continued walking down Juncal then made a hard right down a wide backstreet that wove between parked cars, trash dumpsters, and delivery trucks.

Evers stopped cold in his tracks and made a sudden one hundred eighty degree turn in an effort to catch anyone closing the distance on him. No one struck him as dangerous or remotely threatening, which only served to make him feel slightly more comfortable than he had been before leaving his room.

Remaining focused, he continued down the alleyway, returning the way he originally came until he emerged on Juncal again.

He turned right on Esmeralda and walked south to Marcelo T. de Alvear. Evers looked left and saw a large park where several locals appeared to gather and enjoy the day's sun. He thought it might serve as the downtown park area much like Central Park does in New York City. Several young men played soccer while their girlfriends lay on blankets either soaking up sun or under tree limbs that provided heavy shade around the grounds.

A lone bench at the rear of the park sat unused. Evers walked to it and sat as though he was more than familiar with the park and bench. He sat facing the direction from which he had walked, allowing him to see if anyone was walking up from behind. Again, he saw no one that looked suspicious or set his hackles on end.

For almost an hour he sat in the park watching the young men play soccer and their ladies lie about on the grass. He forced himself to not look at his watch; doing so would give someone the impression he was late for something or expecting someone, and would only create more opportunity for someone to remember him.

Tracking a target or performing reconnaissance required patience and the correct temperament. Simply running to the prospective target's home, place of work, or frequented hang-outs was very amateurish and most often lead to the tracker's ultimate death. Evers understood that concept, and casually remembered lying in the same spot in the bush for three consecutive days, while waiting to take out a subject.

He was equipped with adult diapers at the time, worn so he wouldn't miss an opportunity to plant the Ugandan should he show himself. The only time he moved was to have a bowel movement, and even then it was quick, his prone body with ass cheeks centered directly over a hole he dug. He would finish his business then bury the evidence before the smell traveled any distance. Wiping wasn't an option, and he knew he stank to hell and back, but being covered in dirt and the surrounding vegetation helped him blend with the environment.

On the third day Joseph Okello stepped from a small cottage. Intelligence reports placed him at that small shack and an apartment building in Kampala. In both instances it was believed he was attempting to acquire heroin that he would later trade for a small nuclear device to be fitted on the tip of an RPG. Statements from captured associates of his claimed he wanted to shoot down an international domestic flight from the country's capital heading to Paris.

Okello stopped just in front of the cottage door and shook hands with another man, Okello's skin a dark black, the result of generations spent roaming the land beneath the fierce African sun. Evers watched him through his powerful rifle scope, his crosshairs overlapping his target's left eye. He thought about how white his eyes appeared to be, alert and attentive. The man's smile was inexplicably that of a natural leader, charismatic and charming. He appeared at ease in conversation, his dark shirt flapping in the hot summer breeze.

Okello extended his hand to shake with the other man, a deal presumably made, a small attaché case in his left. Evers watched him nod his head vigorously while in conversation with the man he probably had made the drug deal with, and thought he could faintly hear Okello laughing, even from a thousand yards out. He turned toward his jeep and took a step.

The hole in his forehead appeared before the crack of his weapon was heard by the man Okello had just shaken hands with. Blood trickled between the man's eyes and Evers watched in fascination as confusion crossed the man's face followed by stark recognition. Evers quickly re-chambered the next round, sliding the bolt back and forth, seeding the next round in the barrel.

Before the other man could run for cover, Evers squeezed the trigger and planted a round just above his ear. Brain matter and pieces of skull sprayed the door and wall behind him. The man fell forward, his body draped over Okello's as though the two were forlorn lovers napping in the afternoon sun. Evers was struck at the ironic scene—two men entwined like lovers; both involved in atrocities, or would be atrocities, to be committed globally.

Evers lowered his weapon and head at the same time, easing both down in case someone was watching in the distance. He had seen a few people come and go over the past few days, but no one new had shown up the day Okello was leaving. Assuming no one else was there was one thing, but being certain of it was something altogether different. He was taught to always err on the side of caution, to take his time, breathe deeply, and remain focused on executing the mission and getting out undetected.

Cautiously, Evers began his slow turn, belly-crawling through thickets of vegetation he couldn't identify and through grass almost as tall as he was. An incredible mountain range loomed just behind him, its peaks covered in snow. He moved slowly for just over a day-and-a-half, his Ghillie made from the grasses and scrub he was crawling through.

He found his way to the LZ, or landing zone, where a Blackhawk helicopter swooped in to pick him up. He couldn't recall a time he had been happier to see one of those choppers with its sound suppression systems in full-auto. It made a quiet 'whoop-whoop,' rather than the typically loud sound rotor blades made on a standard military chopper.

He eased himself back on the floor of the helicopter, securely fastened in the back and fell fast asleep, stress and adrenaline finally taking a toll on his body and mind. When he awoke, he was lying in a military issued cot, the previous days and nights nothing but a distant recollection.

Evers allowed the memory to drift like a piece of paper stirred by an early morning wind. He glanced around the park, saw the young men still playing soccer and their girls still browning their already golden bodies. From a nearby road he could hear the morning traffic continue to buzz through the city center, some drivers blowing their horns in a fit of road rage.

"There are pissed off people everywhere, I reckon," Evers chuckled to himself.

He cleared his head, rose from his seat and took off on the remaining five-and-a-half block walk then hailed a cab. Evers's eyes flashed around the large area just before leaving, saw no one that gave off a dangerous vibe so he walked south on Florida Avenue. Twenty minutes later he flagged another cab and hopped in.

The car smelled of sweat, unclean leather and incense. His driver had the passenger side window all the way down, but even the outside air couldn't push the musty smell from the interior. Evers looked down at his shoes as he told the driver to drive him to the corner of Cine Teatro Opera and Carlos Pelligrini Avenida. Not making eye contact would make the man's memory of him less reliable should authorities question him later.

Evers exited the car after what seemed like forever, the mixture of odors playing heavily on his olfactory senses. He paid the fare and stepped onto the sidewalk and began walking toward the Obelisco Center Suites. Carefully, he watched as his cab driver and his disgusting car pulled onto the road and headed in the opposite direction.

For another hour he continued the SDR until he arrived at the Hotel Chile in one last cab. He looked around carefully before getting out of the car, his paranoia kicked up a notch.

He paid this cabby, thankful that his car had not smelled like sweaty ass infused with cheap incense then began walking toward the entrance of the hotel. His destination only a few more city blocks from his current location, Evers elected to walk the rest, careful to stop suddenly and look at himself in a window as he scanned those behind him. Still, he had not flushed anyone into the open and was relatively certain that he wasn't being followed.

Avenue de Mayo veered northwest and intersected with Avenue Rivadavia, which continued due west on the city's street grid. He turned left and walked down Callao Avenue where he saw the dome of the Congressional building looming over an expanse of concrete and greenery. As he closed on the massive structure he was struck at the similarities between it and the United States Congressional building.

Its copper dome had long since turned green, but the color did little to distract from the splendor and grandeur of the white stone structure. The Plaza de los dos Congresos sat by itself in a massive park replete with beautiful trees and shrubbery. Evers was struck by the lack of obvious security, despite the hundred or so peaceful protestors marching in front of the building. Only a handful of guards, armed with pistols and nothing more, stood on top of the stairs blocking the front entrance. He felt certain the protestors were aware that if they chose to charge the front door that the guards were probably under strict orders to shoot first and ask questions later. A threat like that had a way of subduing even the most uncivil of civil unrests.

He knew the likelihood of an incredibly large number of cameras being present was considerably high, so keeping his head down and sunglasses on to shade his features was important. The peaceful mob, he realized, was a fortunate distraction for those controlling the cameras. His standing back and observing would not attract any worthwhile attention because security would be too focused on everyone else.

A large circular drive wound its way up to the building where a swing gate crossed over the entrance to an underground garage. Even though he was there on a scouting mission, Evers decided to find a bench in the park fifty or so yards away from the complex and protestors and watch cars come and go. He doubted his impromptu lookout would yield much in the way of results; hell, he didn't even know if General Vasquez was in the country, although he suspected he was given all the civil unrest.

A few cars came and went, but none of the passengers appeared to be the General. He spent a significant portion of his flight from Virginia studying a picture of the man he downloaded to his smart phone and was beyond assured he could pick him out of a crowd with little problem.

Chants from the crowd rolled over the street and the park. He watched as they marched in circles holding signs demanding answers about the dead and missing. A distant ghost whispered in his ear that these people should be thankful for their lack of knowledge. Evers agreed with the voice he had grown accustomed to hearing in his own head.

A strange movement caught his eye as the cross arm from the garage rose. Loud jeers rose from the crowd when a large limousine with lightly tinted windows pushed forward. Rocks flew toward the windows that glibly deflected them as though the rocks were made of paper. "Bulletproof, obviously," Evers said to no one in particular.

He slid forward on his bench and squinted. Sure enough, in the backseat sat General Vasquez. "Goddam, it's really him," he murmured. He watched as the car drove west then made a sudden right at the first intersection. Evers impulsively checked his watch and noted that it was 3:45PM.

He stood and stretched as he turned his back from the direction Vasquez's car had driven. His eyes gazed over the protesters before checking the sunglasses' rear view for anyone who may have noticed him. No one seemed to take any interest in a guy standing and stretching and looking around the congressional building with minimal interest.

Evers forced himself to wait a few minutes before leaving. His mind raced with possibilities. *Was Vasquez a creature of habit, or did he arrive and leave the office at different times? Was he in the office most days, or did I catch a lucky break?*

He walked south two blocks before turning left. At a corner he hailed a cab and slid into the backseat.

"Pistarini aeropuerto, por favor," Evers told the cab driver. The driver nodded his understanding and drove to the airport, weaving in and out of heavy traffic. Evers paid little attention to the immediate threat posed by the cabbie's manic attempt to negotiate oncoming cars and trucks, focusing instead on Vasquez's appearance.

The short distance of the drive played no bearing on the amount of time it took them to arrive at their destination. Almost an hour passed from the time he jumped in the cab until he arrived at the airport. He paid the fare and walked directly into the departing flights area. Glancing quickly to the left and right, he found an escalator and rode it to the baggage claim and rental car level.

Evers rented a mid-sized sedan, as well as a GPS system. He found the silver Toyota Camry in the designated parking spot, hopped in, and navigated his way back to his hotel. Only after walking into the lobby did he realize how hungry he was, so he made his way to the hotel restaurant and ordered some food.

While he waited on his supper, he sipped on an eighteen year old Macallan Highland Scotch. The cost of the drink was outlandish, but the whiskey's fruit and ginger flavors, coupled with the traditional hint of wood smoke settled his mind and emotions. He ran a hand through his thick brown hair and sighed.

As early thoughts of a plan began swirling in his mind, Evers took another long sip of the Macallan, savoring the taste before swallowing.

Delhi, India
Sector 24, 10:46 AM

Ahsan had planned this part of his trip ever since Allah called him to action. He drove past Indira Gandhi International Airport over the Delhi-Ajmer Expressway. The traffic was unbelievable; never in his life had he seen so many cars, people on motorcycles, bicycles, and on foot. Taxis passed him by as though they owned the road, their exhaust blowing black plumes of smoke into the dirtiest air on the planet. Toxic fumes found their way into his car and he began coughing. The smell of diesel and leaded fuel made his stomach lurch and his head throb.

A brown-white cloud hung all around him, and his visibility was limited to no more than a block at a time. The overcrowded streets and sidewalks swarmed with human bodies, each Ahsan found to be more disgusting than the next. Men, women, and children of India — to him they were no different than the many stray dogs that occupied the same filthy sidewalks and streets.

Packed neighborhood after packed neighborhood slowly passed by his car window. Dark skinned men and women, all dressed similarly, some with red dots between their eyes, the women with their hair braided and hanging limply down the middle of their backs, walked with purpose and intent. To where Ahsan did not know, nor did he particularly care.

The traffic congestion and polluted air were almost more than Ahsan could stand. He reminded himself of his mission, of his desire to do Allah's bidding. To pass more time, he allowed his mind to wander to his hotel and the young lady who had brought him his food. At once he could feel himself getting excited and silently wished he had spoken kindly to her and taken her for his own, even for one night.

"Allah would have understood my needs, as he does all men," he reminded himself.

Perhaps on a subconscious level he realized he had entered Sector 24, his destination. While studying maps of Delhi, Ahsan quickly realized that entire neighborhoods and towns, or suburbs, were divided into sectors. It made navigating a little easier when the driver saw that he was moving from one sector into another.

He eased his car through the traffic and found what he was looking for. A massive expanse of a building, which seemed to sprawl to the four corners of the earth sat just to his left. Its multi-storied façade emblazoned with several retail store logos. The Ambience Mall was one of the largest of its kind in all of India and on this particular day, as it was most days, the parking lot was jammed with cars. He imagined the inside would be crawling with the disgusting citizens of India, the unbelievers, and the filth-ridden infidels of the country.

Ahsan found a parking spot some distance from the mall entrance, parked, then got out and popped the trunk. His head snapped around looking for anyone who might be watching him. Not seeing anyone paying attention to him, he reached inside and removed one of the attaché cases and walked back to the driver's seat closing the door behind him. He placed it on the passenger's floor, pushing it up the slope directly under the dash and out of sight from anybody that happened to look inside the car. Lastly, he draped a light jacket over the case.

After inspecting his work and feeling reasonably certain his brief case was securely out of sight, he stepped out of the car, locking the door as he did so. He headed to the entrance in order to perform some reconnaissance work, and decide on the best place by which to execute his plan. His freshly shaved face felt strange to him, and the clothes he had purchased in order to blend in felt rough and loose, but he knew he must make small sacrifices in order to carry out his objective.

The automatic doors slid open and he walked inside. The cool air washed over his body and the smells of every mall in the world rushed through his nostrils. From every direction the smell of fried food, new clothes and perspiring people hit him. His every sense was on high alert, and he could feel his heart beginning to race again.

He checked around the entrance foyer and was slightly amazed that no mall security was searching bags carried by those walking into the building. Ahsan knew it was not uncommon in stores around the world for security guards and metal detectors to be placed in order to stifle potential attacks. He was greatly relieved to find this to be an obstacle he would not have to overcome.

Laughter and the reverberations of kids screaming echoed off the vast walls of the mall. Escalators and elevators carried consumers up and down from store to store. His eyes scanned the long aisles teeming with people wandering in and out of stores. Some stopped at kiosks in the middle of the aisle to peruse items sold at the mobile stores.

Ahsan spent another thirty minutes wandering around the mall, stepping in and out of stores as though he was in search of some much needed clothing, shoes, or a book. He made note of where mass throngs of people gathered, primarily in the food court and in the kid's area. Small rides and playsets were in place to give parents a much needed break from children intent on driving them crazy while they attempted to shop.

He turned and walked back toward the entrance, sure to keep his head low and eyes down. Again, he could feel his pulse quicken and heart pounding in his chest. Sweat began forming under his arms, on his brow and in the small of his back. He fought to control his breathing as he made his way outside, across the parking lot, and to his car.

His butt slid across the small driver's seat as he scanned the area, assuring no passersby, patrolling law enforcement or security officer was around. His hand groped for the case, shifted the row of numbers on the tumbler to the code that would allow him to unlock it, then flipped the latches with his thumbs. He stared at a series of lights atop a metal container, a small, thick acrylic window showing a murky, greenish liquid inside. Lining the inside of the case was C-4 explosives with quarter inch ball bearings pushed inside the pliable material. Beneath the container housing the liquid, Ahsan knew there was another pile of the explosive laced with even more ball bearings. Numerous wires ran in different directions, including leads to the explosives, but his eyes fell upon a small module sitting silently atop the container awaiting its command.

Ahsan depressed the power button on his cell phone and watched as the small LED screen shined, several icons illuminating on the small glass window. Next, he reached inside the case and pressed a little button on the module. A series of blue lights came to life, all in a line and glowing in order, one lighting up for a second before the next one in line began doing the same.

He picked up his phone and enabled the blue tooth capability in the settings and waited a few seconds for his phone to detect the module inside the case. His eyes watched intently as words, all in English, appeared: *Bluetooth connected to device.* Ahsan's heart notched up another gear and he briefly thought it might leap right out of his chest. With shaky hands he carefully closed the case, dropped the two clasps into place, and rolled the tumbler, locking it once again.

The case rested in his lap as he placed his hands on the steering wheel. His head fell back upon the headrest where he closed his eyes and breathed deeply attempting to slow his heart rate. He felt for his keys inside his pocket, grabbed them and started the engine allowing the air conditioner to work its magic on his overheated body. Although no visible security had been present inside the mall, he didn't want to appear suspicious and give someone time to alert the authorities, especially while he was carrying an attaché case filled with the surprise he was about to give India.

He waited fifteen minutes before shutting off the car's engine. The sun was sitting directly atop him, the shadows around him short and without purpose. More vehicles prowled through the lot, their drivers looking for spots in which to park. He watched as many people walked from the mall toward their own cars, but it seemed that for every one person who left five more took their place.

The place was crawling with men, women, and children, but in Ahsan's mind they were nothing more than vermin—vermin that was worthy of only one thing: extermination. He took a deep breath, mopped his forehead with his shirt sleeve, and stepped outside the car, brief case in hand.

He stepped quickly, despite telling himself not to do so, and made his way back inside the mall. The cool air being pumped through the building hit him just as it had the previous time he entered. The same noises and smells assaulted him again, but his mind barely registered them. This time he stopped for a few seconds and scanned the area, once again finding the food court. The area still teemed with people vying for the different foods offered, most at exorbitant prices. He was thankful to find one store that offered Halal meats, all of it prayed over at the time it was slaughtered in the manner The Prophet had outlined.

He chewed his food without thought, paying no attention to the flavors or texture of that which crossed his tongue. All around him there was movement, talking, laughter, and smiling. The over indulgences of the country's wealthy permeated the floors and walls, as did their blasphemous religious beliefs. Hindu gods with multiple arms were nothing more than heretical and their followers deserved to die. Perhaps they would find out in the afterlife how wrong they had been and be subjected to unimaginable pain and torment, or maybe Allah would condemn them directly to hell where they would burn for an eternity for their sacrilege. Either way, they would come to understand their foolhardy belief in gods that didn't exist was unforgivably wrong.

That thought alone brought a peace to Ahsan that he had not felt in a considerable time. In the back of his mind a remnant of pity had been clawing at him, telling him that his actions were not honorable, nor would they be condoned by Allah, but the teachings were clear and his understanding was now resolute. Only during his morning prayers, when the sun rose over the land and cleansed the dirty night of the things that occurred in the shadows did he feel sure about his mission. Shortly after completing his prayers, however, something would creep into his psyche...doubt, fear, and sympathy for those he killed in the name of God and God's armies.

But now he suddenly felt a calmness, an overwhelming sense of rightness. A smile crept across his face and he impulsively felt for the case that rested at his feet. The solidity of the handle offered him a sense of assuredness about what he was set to do. The mission was bigger than him, larger than Al Qaida, ISIS, the Taliban or any of the other armies sworn to defend the laws of God and The Prophet.

He stood and dumped the trash from his tray in the can closest to his table. With a slight flick of his wrist, he tossed the tray into the stack begun by other parishioners of the food court. His eyes darted around the area one more time before he turned and walked back the way he had come, leaving the brief case on the floor where it had rested while he dined.

Ahsan hurried down the wide floor, dodging men and women along the way. His sense of resolve and calm had waned and he realized his respiration and pulse were quickening once again. Sweat formed on his face and ran down his nose. Adrenaline caused him to look distraught and panicked, and the people he passed took note of his erratic behavior. Behind him he thought he heard someone calling for him.

"Sirrah! Sirrah!" the voice called.

Ahsan's feet came to a halt and he turned to see a young man, maybe twenty-five, chasing after him. In the man's right hand was his attaché case!

Without thinking about what he was doing, Ahsan turned toward the exit and began running, his eyes wide. People stopped walking and watched him as he ran by, thinking that he was probably a common thief and running from the police or some store security personnel. One man attempted to intercept him, but Ahsan feigned a step to his left, the man taking the bait. He didn't slow down as he slammed a fist into the man's throat, rupturing his trachea. The Samaritan dropped to his knees as he clutched his throat, his airway blocked and his vision already becoming tunneled. He struggled for breath that wouldn't enter his lungs and clawed at his own neck in a feeble attempt to cling to life. The last thing he saw was a group of people standing over him screaming and yelling for help that never came.

Ahsan reached for his phone as he ran. The young man who had been chasing him stopped when he saw what he did to the individual attempting to block him and dropped the case on the floor in disgust and shock. With great effort Ahsan touched the icons on the screen, the one in particular he needed was shaped as a star inside a crescent, an ancient symbol of Islam.

His finger touched the screen, missing the icon as he ran. Just ahead of him he saw the doors from which he had entered, tucked the phone into a pocket and ran as hard as he could until he reached them. With a firm push one door flew open, the early afternoon air hitting him squarely in the face and chest. A car blew its horn when he dashed in front of it, narrowly missing an outstretched leg. From inside he could hear the sound of a woman screaming at him in the native Hindu tongue. He was relatively certain she wasn't bidding him a pleasant day.

Ahsan fished the keys from his pocket and depressed the unlock button. He heard the lock chirp about fifteen feet to his right, turned and ran toward the car. He flung the door open and jumped inside, his head and eyes darting about the parking lot in search of anyone still in pursuit.

Only a few moments earlier did he believe his heart rate could climb no higher, but his chest felt as though it would explode at any second. His hand fumbled for his phone, found the power key and touched it. The screen lit up and the same green icon he attempted to touch a short time earlier appeared. His finger moved toward the screen and the crescent-starred icon that seemed as though it stared at him in some strange and alien defiance.

From his left he heard a man scream. His head swiveled in the direction of the voice and he saw a small group of men running toward him. His eyes were wide and his pupils dilated so much so that anyone looking him in the face would have thought his eyes were purely black. With unbelievable speed he snapped his head back to his phone's screen and with one trembling finger touched the green icon.

London, United Kingdom
8:12 PM

Trowton passed his time waiting by his telephone and staring at his television in his living room. News reports from the BBC said the spread of SARS and Ebola were rapid and devastating. Every continent was impacted by one or both viruses. Their rapid spread was creating mass hysteria in several countries. Food and water shortages began occurring in several areas. The idiotic American preppers were buying caches of various commodities, ammunition, firearms, and gasoline en masse. As anticipated, international news outlets fueled the fire by falsely claiming higher fatality rates and misconstrued ways of contracting the diseases.

All of this had put his mind temporarily at ease. He was sure that looting and killing would begin as the viruses continued spreading. Trowton often remarked that the human psyche inevitably resorted to murder and mayhem anytime mankind faced any sort of potential catastrophic event. Fighting death with death was one element of this trait he found simultaneously perplexing and reassuring. He could always count on human beings to react like lemmings falling off a cliff.

Abaddon had not contacted him in a few days, which also gave him a reprieve from the stresses he was enduring. The biggest relief had come by way of seeing his plan come together. So many moving pieces gave way to more than simple consternation; on the contrary, there were several times he wished for strong drugs and a quiet hospital bed. Now, he watched as the world burned and his objectives moved closer to attainment.

He reached for the wireless mouse sitting next to the large monitor atop his desk and shuffled it around until the black screen came to life. In the top-center of the screen was a rolling counter. New numbers to the far right continued to climb—approximately ten clicks every two seconds. A greasy smile crossed his face while his wire-rimmed glasses sat at the end of his nose.

Trowton read the number aloud, "Twelve million four hundred thirty-two thousand estimated deceased."

A great sigh rolled over his lips. For the first time in days he felt his appetite returning and a sense of normalcy creeping into his psyche. Everything was happening as it should, and despite his initial fears of failure he knew deep within his own soul he was making the world a better place.

To no one in particular he said, "This overcrowded world, slowly starving itself, suffocating under its own carbon releases, parching itself while polluting its own rivers and streams will someday thank me."

A distant voice screamed out to him from deep within his own head. "You're a monster! How is it possible that you believe killing millions of innocent people is somehow okay? You are no better than Hitler, Stalin, Mao, or bin Laden!"

Trowton scowled at the voice. He shook his head, trying to force whoever, or whatever, from saying it again. The voice rescinded into the dark cavern of his mind from whence it was born not to be heard from again, at least for a time. Trowton was happy that he silenced it, even temporarily. More and more frequently he had begun hearing this strange person speaking to him at the most inopportune times.

"I'm nothing like any of those people," he seethed. "Their actions were based upon world domination, fueled by a desire for raw power, greed, and a sense of entitlement. I have no such desires. I merely want our planet to exist, its people and nature in harmony, rather than the current state of mankind beating nature to death. Numerous warnings have been given, yet inaction has furthered the demise of Earth. No longer will I stand idly by and watch the deniers have their way. After years of begging and pleading with the elites, I've come to realize they are nothing more than sources of self-righteous hot air. Perhaps if I stood them all in front of a windmill farm they could help create enough energy to light all of London."

He stood again, straightened his suit and tie and began pacing his apartment. As with everything, timing was of the essence and this part of his plan was no different. He considered the mass deaths now occurring and the media's attention in each area of the world. News from India had been largely quiet, and his contact silent for over twenty-four hours. He suspected news, good or bad, would be heard soon enough from that region of the world.

Trowton walked to the large set of French doors just beyond his dining area and stared down at the sprawling mass of a city, the Thames winding through it at a snail's pace. Cars and buses passed over bridges and avenues, their numbers more than the stars. At least he knew the stars were there, although seeing them was problematic. The light pollution and smog from the city blocked the night sky, something else that infuriated him beyond belief. He watched as planes seemingly stacked atop one another flew into London's Heathrow International Airport, further polluting the skies and air.

His mouth was agape, even though none of this was new to him, and his mind amazed that the Earth had survived as long as it had despite man's constant attempts at murdering it. He pulled a handkerchief from his breast pocket and mopped his forehead and mouth before returning it. That same hair-raising smile pushed across his face as he walked toward his desk again, the wheels in his brain turning rapidly.

With a little effort he pushed thoughts of pollution and Earth-murder from his mind and turned back to the task at hand. The ticker on his monitor continued to stream; the estimated death toll continuing to climb globally. Even the assaults on the people in South America were going better than expected. The United States and its allies could not send troops to every region of the globe and expect to be of any help. All of the "natural" catastrophes and military action were occupying the attention of governments everywhere, but no one had developed a plan to combat them all. This was the simple brilliance of his plan.

Now it was time to release the next phase, furthering the fear and mass casualties needed to even the odds for the world's possible survival, even if the odds would be evened for a short time. *Hopefully*, he thought, *someone else would take up the cause after he was gone*. The truth of the matter was that he was under no illusion he would survive to see his plan through to completion, although he said a periodic prayer to any god that might be listening for his own survival.

And then there was his new partnership with that bastard Abaddon who interjected his own corrupt ideology into the mix. Try as he might, Trowton could not remove himself from the man, nor could he ignore his orders. Each time they spoke, it seemed Abaddon wanted more death and destruction, rather than the arbitrary population reduction for which he planned.

No matter how much he attempted to rid his thoughts of the man, the stain of his memory could never be erased. The threats he had made during that first meeting were real, Trowton simply *knew* it to be true. Despite not being religious, he feared what this person was capable of, both in the here and now, as well as the beyond. Yes, he was coming to realize there may be something other than the short time spent walking on the Earth, although he had no concept of what that "something" might be.

A shiver ran over his spine and he reached for the handkerchief again. He could feel the sweat once more forming on his face, visions of that evil grin and hate-filled eyes resonating within him. A deep breath and long, heavy exhale helped settle his nerves only slightly, but it was enough to steady his hand as it reached for his desk phone.

On a small, spiral bound notebook sitting beside the phone were a series of phone numbers, each with its own unique international exchange followed by the digits that would allow him to speak directly with those engaged in his plot. One finger dragged down the page until it found the number it was seeking. He clenched his jaws in defiance of everything he had been taught about the "goodness" of man. All the history they taught to him had been written by winners of wars and conquerors of lands, and he knew it was nothing more than half-truths and lies.

With his free hand he depressed the speaker button and listened as the familiar dial tone hummed from the phone. Several rings later a distant voice answered, the accent distinctly French.

"Oui. Please speak."

Trowton smiled at the Frenchman's polite greeting. "It's me. St. Laurent is the target. Initiate the attack."

A few seconds of silence passed, neither man saying anything, the only sound their breathing.

"As you command, monsieur. I will commence with the attack plan as we discussed," the voice on the other end answered.

Trowton clicked off the call as he nodded his head approvingly.

"Chaos shall bring about order to an otherwise unruly world," he mused.

Buenos Aires, Argentina
5:33 AM

Evers sat bolt upright in his bed. Sweat rolled down his chest like a salty mountain stream. His breathing was rapid, his chest heaving to fill his lungs with air. He instinctively grabbed the sheet with both hands, balling it up between his fingers, as his eyes darted around the darkened room.

Visions of U.S. soldiers with limbs blown or shot off, headless torsos, and innards ripped from their stomachs filled his brain. Distant screams from other fallen comrades echoed in his ears and mind. Tears welled up in his eyes and quietly began rolling down his face. He could feel his blood racing through veins and arteries as though in a race for its own existence, pumped rapidly by a heart that felt like a sledgehammer against his sternum.

He rubbed at his bloodshot eyes and tried to clear his head. The dreams that used to fade as soon as he woke had been working their way into his waking hours, their stain remaining with him sometimes for hours. With a trembling hand he reached for the glass of water he left on the nightstand before he fell asleep the previous night. He gulped, droplets missing his mouth and falling down his chin to his naked chest.

Evers sat in his bed for half an hour pulling himself together. The sweat began to cool and eventually dry on his body, but his sheets would remain soaked for some time. Ghosts from foreign lands and distant times floated about his room. The smell of cordite, mixed with C4 and human blood, seemed fresh in his nose and bitter on his tongue. He could have sworn that he was still on the field of battle, guns blazing, friends screaming in agony, and an unrelenting enemy trained and hardened in the mountains and plains of Afghanistan.

As the sun peaked over the Argentinian skyline and into his room, he managed to shake the memories from his head, but the pain, grief, and anger remained. Somehow, he felt like the emotions allowed him more focus on the mission at hand. From some far-away place he could hear a voice, Private William Hutchings, telling him that they were going to "get those cocksuckers, every last one of them." Despite having watched Hutchings die a slow, pain-filled death after one bullet pierced his side and entered a lung, and another blew off half his neck, Evers could hear his sputtering cries for revenge. To his dying breath, Hutch, as he was known to everyone in the unit, was a diehard Army man. He was also one hell of a shot, and fell just short of qualifying as a Ranger because his temper often got the best of him.

"Punch one goddam master sergeant and get branded a loose cannon. Fuck 'em all, I always say!" Hutch would laugh himself into hysterics after saying that, but he didn't talk about the specifics involved in his violent disobedience. No one in the unit doubted Hutch's tenacity and penchants for violence. Hell, he thrived on it. Evers recalled a time when his buddy drank eight beers then invited anyone in the camp to kick his ass…if they could, and if they were willing to put up fifty bucks.

Several men lined up to take his bet, some of the battle-tested special forces types such as SEALs, Delta, and Green Berets were a few that wanted to shut him up. But Hutch was having none of it. His ability to delve out pain and discomfort with his fists was seconded only by his ability to knock a pimple off a rat's ass at three hundred meters with a .50 cal Barrett rifle, one of the heaviest sniper rifles out there, but certainly one of the most accurate.

They gathered outside, just a short distance from the mess hall, which stood at the outer perimeter of the camp. There was no wind or sound, just the buzz of overhead lights powered by generators. Several infantrymen circled the area making an impromptu fighting ring.

First up was Chad Truit, a loudmouth E-6 with more piss than vinegar. He put his hands up in a traditional boxing fashion, but Hutch bobbed and weaved, avoiding every jab or hook. Two minutes after they had squared off, Truit's chest was heaving while Hutch remained calm and collected. He managed his breathing not unlike an alligator would while resting on the bottom of a pond. His fighting style was unorthodox and awkward, his hands sometimes at his sides and sometimes off to the sides like a 1980's Russian boxer. His feet, however, were always directly under him, never stretched more than they should be, and never, ever so close together that he could easily be knocked off balance, or worse.

Hutch threw a right cross, connecting with Truit's jaw, right on the hinge. A loud popping sound was followed by a crunch as he immediately followed up with a straight left to Truit's nose, affectionately known as the snot locker. Blood poured from the ruptured appendage, as Truit struggled to catch his breath. His nasal passages were fully blocked so he opened his mouth to catch his breath. When he did, Hutch unleashed the next flurry of punches, knocking two teeth out and breaking two others. His limp body hit the deck, a small plume of dust and sand scattering in the nearby air.

An Army medic ran to Truit's aid while the rest of the men cheered or booed depending upon who they had wagered for or against. Hutch popped his neck and motioned to another man who had been standing nearby, bare chested and sweating slightly from his warm up exercises and the stifling night air.

Someone yelled, "Kick his ass, Hano," obviously directed at the half-naked man now bouncing up and down as he stared at Hutch.

A thick Cajun accent swept from Hano's mouth, "Oh, I'ma keek his ass real good. I'ma chew dat muddafucka up, eat half-a his ass, den shit it right here in front of his stupid looking buddies."

Hutch laughed out loud. "Come get some, coon ass. It's been awhile since I've had a scrap with a Louisiana boy."

Hano dropped his chin and raised his fists in a classic boxing stance. Hutch's hands were again raised next to his head, his entire torso and face exposed. He winked at Hano, a mocking gesture that sometimes made a man so angry he would forget himself and fly directly into a rage. This time was no different.

The Cajun bared his teeth and charged his opponent. Just before Hano reached him, Hutch sidestepped and buried a fist into the man's ribcage. The sound of skin on skin was loud, and it's one that is unlike any other sound in the world. Everyone watching the two men brawl made a loud, "Oooooh!" There was no doubt the impact hurt Hano, especially when he staggered and grabbed for the side that had been hit.

Hutch seized the moment when Hano's guard was down and jumped high into the air, slamming a second fist into the side of the man's face. Hano dropped immediately to the ground, his head slamming into the dirt, and a snorting sound forcing its way from his lungs, the sound men make when they've been knocked unconscious and the human brain is trying to recover from being shut down.

Money changed hands and Hutch claimed his share. As he turned to leave he saw Evers watching him. "What are you looking at? You want some too, or do you think I'm cute?" he taunted.

Evers shrugged his shoulder and offered a half-grin. "Neither."

Hutch nodded his head and said, "Yeah, that's what I thought. None of you pussies can hang with me anyway."

Evers, young and full of testosterone, had not yet learned the art of leaving well enough alone.

He cocked his head to one side and said in his southern drawl, "What I meant was I don't think you're cute, and if you were offering up a sexual favor I wasn't interested. If you're looking for another sparring partner though, I might just be your man."

Hutch's mouth opened but no words came out. He couldn't believe this little bastard was talking to him like that after watching him take two guys out in a matter of seconds.

"You talk a lot. Why don't you shut the fuck up and get over here?"

Evers took his shirt off and moved his shoulders up and down, much like Hutch did earlier, then moved his head from side to side popping the vertebrae. He threw four or five slow jabs to start warming his joints up, and made a point of performing a couple of squats with his hands directly out in front as Hutch watched.

Even as a young man, Evers was muscular. His six foot frame carried two-hundred twenty pounds effortlessly. Arms bulged with the look of weight training and a lot of calisthenics, and abs that all beach goers would envy.

"Are we going to fight or are you going to amaze us all with your River Dance skills?"

"Oh, we're going to fight. I have two hundred dollars in my pocket that says I take you out. How does that sound?"

Hutch laughed again and nodded at one of his buddies, acknowledging that the bet would be covered. Quickly the crowd circled the two men as Hutch assumed his unorthodox fighting stance. Evers remained relaxed, his stance slightly open and his hands raised to chest level with his palms facing forward. He turned as Hutchings slowly circled him, Hutch looking for an opening, Evers waiting patiently for his attacker to move.

Without warning, Hutch jabbed catching Evers squarely on a cheekbone. The sting of the punch caused him momentarily to see stars. He was struck at how quick his adversary was, despite the strangeness of his fighting stance. Evers shook his head and focused on the man's midsection, his peripheral vision seeing his hands and feet.

Hutch shifted his weight on his forward leg and threw another jab at Evers's face, this time narrowly missing as Evers moved his head out of the way. He didn't waste any time with a follow-up punch, throwing a right cross at Evers, but Bill watched Hutch transfer his weight on his lead leg a second time.

Instead of ducking or weaving, Evers stepped inside the attack, seizing Hutch's punching arm while Evers wrapped his free arm behind the man's waist. In one deft motion, Hutch went flying into the air, crashing to the ground a split second later. Evers didn't miss a beat, jumping on his opponent's chest even as Hutch struggled to regain his breath. Punch after punch rained down on Hutch's face and upper torso, the impact of the next worse than the one just prior.

Evers was impressed by the man's bravado and ability to remain awake, even though he was hitting him with everything he had. Hutch was unable to defend himself adequately though, and his friends soon stepped in to break up the melee.

Hutch wobbled to his feet, his face a bloody mess, his chest heaving, and his eyes glassy. Evers slipped his shirt back on, turned to Hutch and smiled at him, a little machismo of his own shining through. Hutch spoke to him, but what he said was a little unexpected.

"Goddam, boy," Hutch began, "that was a pretty good whooping you put on me. I'm not used to that. You're alright in my book."

Evers dropped his eyes and shook his head, accepting the compliment like a man is supposed to, without words and with much dignity and honor. He walked over to Hutch and extended a hand. Hutch grabbed it and shook it, and from that moment on, they were inseparable. Inseparable, that is, until Hutch died in Evers's arms.

And there they were, Hutch lying in his arms, bleeding out like some wild game hunted for the shear sport. He listened as the dying man's lung collapsed and the bullet wound sucked air into its opening. The side of his neck gaped open like a small cave, the muscles within contracting and relaxing as he struggled to breathe. Hutch grasped Evers's arm and managed one final wish.

"Kill all those raghead motherfuckers, Billy. All of 'em."

The smell of gunpowder sat heavy in the air, and the hot, dusty land continued to bake in the afternoon sun. Hutch's iron rich blood soaked through his BDU's and onto Evers's hands. The odor was unmistakable and the sound of death reverberated all around the two men.

Then, just like that, he was gone. No more smart ass remarks, no more breathing, and no more heartbeat. Private William Hutchings's body lay limply in Bill Evers's arms and everything the man had, or would ever have, was gone. The reality of the situation would not hit Evers until much later; at that moment he felt nothing but anger. He allowed Hutch's lifeless body to slide off his lap while he reached for his rifle and stood upright.

In less than a second he spotted two AQI's, Al Qaeda in Iraq, and bore down on them, caring nothing for his own personal safety or for the mission at hand. In his head and heart there was only hatred for the men who had taken one of his closest friends, and his response was to make their families and friends feel the exact same way.

Revenge was such a meaningless word compared to the way he felt at that time. When the first bullet entered the first AQI's head and continued on, slamming into the wall behind him and knocking a chunk of it to the ground, Evers grinned. He grinned like Satan willed him to take that life and enjoy every second of it, and that is what he did—he enjoyed it.

The second AQI target watched as his friend's head exploded into a red and grey geyser. For a split second he hesitated before raising his own rifle in Evers's direction, finding the lone American soldier standing over the two foot wall on the roof of the building. Unfortunately for the Al Qaeda operative it was too late. Evers beaded down on his chest and squeezed the trigger on his rifle.

The report cracked and echoed through the valley of buildings surrounding the combatants. Evers watched as the bullet entered the man's sternum and a small stream of blood issued from the entry wound. Still, the man stood, partly in shock but mostly because he, too, was a battle hardened warrior.

That evil grin wrapped itself around Evers's face again as the crosshairs from his scope found the man's nose. Once more he squeezed the trigger and watched as a cavernous opening was created where the man's face once was.

Without any thought he trained the rifle to other rooftops and open windows in search of another life to take. On that day, the enemy should have been happy that a smiling Bill Evers had found no other soul on which to feast.

Evers continued to sit in his bed and hold his head. More than anything he wanted to wipe out the memories of friends and fellow soldiers being taken from him too soon. He wanted to undo the pain he helped delve out to some during his time as a mercenary. From somewhere deep in his own gut he wanted to scream for the nightmares to leave him alone and allow him to live his life as he chose to live it. But those dreams, he realized long ago, were a part of who he was and who he would always be.

As the sun continued to rise and shine into his hotel room, the hope and promise of a new day meant little to him. All over the world pain and suffering continued to rage like a fire burning out of control. He never thought of himself as a superhero or savior, just a man who wanted to right some of the wrongs he felt like he had committed.

He shuffled across his hotel floor, grabbed the empty coffee pot and spent the next few minutes making a hot concoction of java. At least a freshly brewed cup would make him feel human again. He waited as the water heated inside the maker and dripped brown, liquid heaven into the recycled paper cup provided by the hotel.

As he sipped it, the dreams and memories began to fall to the back of his mind, never completely gone, but far enough away to allow him to breathe easier. He pushed away everything else and began putting together the actions he would take during the day. Seeing if Vasquez would show himself for a second time in as many days would be the catalyst for creating a true plan.

Evers drank his coffee and rode the elevator to the hotel lobby. He stopped long enough to eat from the buffet the hotel restaurant provided to its guests. Not surprisingly, the food was excellent. Fresh fruits, eggs, and salmon were available, as was a cook who would prepare omelets and waffles to order. Orange juice was squeezed as patrons waited. He wondered why Americans didn't revolt and demand all of their hotels provide this service, although he already knew the answer—money.

He ate, left a nice tip on the table and walked to the parking garage where he found his rental car. The key slipped into the ignition, Evers started the engine and drove back to the Capital building, careful to switch back a few times while watching for anyone who might be following him. After an hour of driving, he found a parking area close to the park where he could leave the car without worry of it being towed.

For an hour he sat in the park watching the protestors gather and grow even more anxious. News and rumors of additional civilian murders at the hands of the Argentinian military were being reported. Several rumors swirled about that included deaths in the thousands. Evers was hearing chants of an uprising, which he felt would be a huge mistake given the lack of arms the populace had been denied by the government. It seemed to him that an uprising would merely give the military leaders a reason to kill more of their own, despite the fact that he couldn't figure out why they were killing to begin with.

The more people that showed up for the rally, the more that would begin to take notice of a man sitting idly by on a bench. He saw a couple of men look at him inquisitively, wondering why and how he could just sit there while thousands of their own people were being slaughtered at the hands of a perverse government. It was then that Evers decided he had outstayed his welcome and retreated to his car.

Although it was a little further away from the capital, his vantage point was still very good. He could watch cars come and go, and was still capable of identifying passengers so long as the windows weren't tinted. His sunglasses gave him the luxury of seeing anyone who might try to sneak up behind him, so his anxiety level was considerably lower than it was while sitting in the park, exposed to God knew what.

But with the good comes the bad. Now he was stuck in a car, immobile and at the mercy of anyone who did manage to approach him, most especially if they happened to have an illegal firearm. Not that a firearm being illegal would matter if he was shot through the head, but the word "illegal" stuck in his head like a bad lyric in an overplayed song.

Staking out an area in a car was much more difficult for Evers than was trailing a target through a jungle or desert. Sitting around on a stakeout allows an individual's mind to drift and lose focus. That, in Evers's mind, was why most cops failed to apprehend a criminal early on when watching criminals from their car.

To help him keep his mind clear, he plugged his iPod into a port made available on his rental car's dashboard. Before he left the States, Buddy had turned him on to an up and coming two person band.

"What the hell are they called?" he thought. He focused on the band's name as he fumbled with his iPod. "Ah, now I remember. *Smooth Hound Smith* is what they're called. I like their sound, but I would never admit to Buddy that he was right about them," he grinned.

I know it's been so long
Looking for a fight
I don't want to be alone
I get low, all the time
You know (get low) you're always on my mind

Sure am fine in that dress
The way you fix your hair

Man is staring at me
And I don't even care

I know it's been so long
As if I think you mind
I don't want to be alone
Get low! Get low!
All the time

Evers bobbed his head slightly to the beat of the song, even though he knew that he might draw some attention.

"Fuck it. This is some good goddam music," he said aloud, channeling his best gravely Buddy Smith voice.

The man and woman duet, Zack Smith and Caitlin Doyle, cranked out the eerie tune as Evers focused his every effort on watching the capital building. He forced himself to stop bobbing his head while the music spoke to him in a cryptic, but meaningful way.

For hours Evers sat and watched the building for any movement. He saw a few cars come and go, but none that he recognized as being the same as the one he saw the previous day. If he had been a praying man, he would have prayed that Vasquez be that creature of habit he hoped he was. So much so that he would come and go in the same car, daring anyone of the protestors to approach him.

Yes, that felt right. Vasquez seemed the arrogant type to him, and just one to hope that some wayward fool would attempt an attack on him so he could give the order to shoot, or better yet, do the shooting himself. That thought helped him remain focused on the mission. He checked his watch—3:38PM.

He leaned forward, his eyes hard and determined, focused on the garage and lift gate that stood at its entrance. A few minutes later he watched as the gate rose and the nose of a car inched its way forward. Many of the protesters moved toward the car and just as quickly pushed back.

Evers felt his heart rate kick up several beats. His eyes squinted in a reflexive manner, willing them to see even more clearly than they already were, in spite of his perfect vision. The crowd continued to push away from the car, clearing a path for its driver and...its passenger!

"Fuck, it's him," he breathed.

His hand instinctively reached for the shift lever and put the car in drive. He eased forward slowly so as not to alert the driver that he was being followed. Evers maintained a comfortable distance of five car lengths behind Vasquez to completely avoid notice. He also drove in the right lane while Vasquez's driver insisted on driving in the left.

The car made a left at a traffic light and Evers eased into the same lane so he could also turn. He watched as Vasquez's car slowly navigated the road, careful not to speed or do anything that would bring notice to the vehicle. At a massive brownstone building the driver turned the car into a parking garage directly beneath it. Evers slowed down just enough to watch the driver and its passenger disappear.

He drove another two blocks, found a place to park and got out, checking his surroundings for anything or anyone suspicious, walking back toward the brownstone and Vasquez. All of his senses were operating in hyper-drive, every sound, cough, or aroma getting his immediate attention. Being this close to his target offered no room for sloppiness or mistakes. Either of those things would certainly lead to an untimely death, or worse, a failed mission.

As he neared the building he instinctively checked for video surveillance cameras both on the building proper and on the surrounding structures and light poles. Evers did not notice any and with great care approached the front door. Before he reached for it, he noticed the board of push-buttons with names next to them.

"A call box," he thought.

If there was a call box mounted to the outside wall that meant the door was locked. His only option would be to enter the garage on foot—an altogether dangerous proposition and one that he was not particularly excited to take. He looked at the garage opening and noticed a man-door next to it, presumably put in for those who walked from their apartment to local markets or jobs that didn't require personal transit.

The likelihood of a camera being mounted inside the garage was considerably higher, given the globalization of technology and serious crime. He pulled his sunglasses from his shirt pocket and put them on. Immediately, he was able to see one hundred eighty degrees to his rear. A few more steps and he was at the door.

With a slight tug he pulled it open and stepped inside keeping his head low in case a camera was mounted in the nearby vicinity. The garage was notably darker than it had been outside, and unfortunately for Evers, he was forced to remove his sunglasses so he could see. Still, it took a few seconds for his eyes to fully adjust.

Once his eyesight had grown used to the darker surroundings, he promptly set out in search of Vasquez's car, careful to remain in the shadows. Within half a minute he spotted it on the far side of the garage, a head noticeable inside behind the wheel. Evers thought for a moment.

"What would a prestigious military general be doing in a brownstone apartment this close to the capital building? Is he meeting with an informant? Is he planning another attack on the people of Argentina? Perhaps he has to speak privately with someone regarding a coup against the current government."

None of those possibilities seemed logical to Evers. As a general, he would have others doing his dirty work, especially doing things like meeting with informants, no matter how important they might be. He would not need to meet remotely to plan another attack on his fellow countrymen, so that idea wasn't plausible. The coup d'état was distinctly possible and reasonable. Men like Vasquez were never happy until they were in complete control, their fingertips dripping with power.

But even that didn't quite feel right. Vasquez was highly respected by both the Argentinian president, and until recently, by the people of his country. Evers suspected that had he wished it, Vasquez could have easily been elected president without having to overthrow the reigning leader and creating even more turmoil in a country that constantly walked the razor's edge of economic and political stability.

No, none of those things seemed right to Evers. That left one plausible explanation in his mind—a woman. Vasquez must have a mistress who lived in the brownstone. The small amount of research he had done on the man stated that he was married with one child, a teenage daughter. A woman would explain the consistency of his timely departures from the capital. She got off work and he needed to be able to see her and still get home at a decent hour without raising suspicions of his infidelities.

Satisfied that he had come to the correct conclusion about Vasquez, he quickly glanced around the garage looking for cameras. He noted one pointed back toward the entrance and at him. Fortunately, Evers had kept his head down, which would make it difficult for anyone to properly identify him on the camera's video feed. He had also stayed as close to the shadows as possible making identification even more difficult, and most likely impossible.

Evers's only chance to get at Vasquez would be in the garage since he did not know which apartment the general had escaped to. This limited what he would have to do in order to have a serious conversation with the man about his worldly transgressions. Rapid fire thoughts came to mind and Evers carefully crossed the garage to Vasquez's car, and an unsuspecting driver.

Before the driver could spot Evers, he ducked low behind other cars and slowly made his way across the garage. Evers was certain the driver had made this trip numerous times, had sat in the same spot bored out of his mind while his boss waxed his carrot upstairs. Repetition spawned boredom and boredom gave birth to inattentiveness.

And there he was, his head leaned back on his seat's headrest, his eyes closed and his breathing slow and steady. Evers continued his slow and meticulous approach toward the driver's side door. Squatting low he reached to the side view mirror and with his index finger pushed it upward, moving it out of the driver's line of sight.

Evers raised his body up slightly and peered at the driver and the door. The window was rolled part-way down, no more than three inches to allow some air to enter the car. With his left hand he reached for the door lever and eased it up, his body just behind the door now. He felt the tension in the latch as he raised the lever further until the pressure on it was such that it would have to be popped, which would wake his newly acquired target. No matter—he didn't intend on his actions taking more than a couple of seconds.

He popped the unlocked latch on the car door and opened it quickly. The driver, confused and disoriented snapped his head to the left just in time to see Evers reach in and grab him by his jacket's lapel and yank him from his seat. He tumbled to the garage's concrete floor, and as he did so, Evers grabbed his other lapel with his free hand, rolled on top of his chest and pulled the driver's head toward him, about eight inches from the floor.

To his credit the driver reached for Evers's hands and tried to yank them free, but the effort was in vain. The strange man accosting him had seeded his thumbs deeply into his jacket's lapels, his wrists crossed forming an X. In one swift motion Evers slammed the driver's head to the floor knocking him unconscious, but not hard enough to split his scalp open.

The driver, now out cold, lay limply as Evers moved his chest close to the man's own, simultaneously pulling his hands and the man's lapels in a circular motion across his throat. The choke, nami juji jime in Japanese, was intended to suffocate an opponent by cutting the blood supply off from both carotid arteries. Evers held the choke, counting to sixty as he looked about the garage for anyone returning from a day of shopping. What a shock a person would have if they were to wander upon a man squeezing the life from another.

Fortunately for Evers no one came. He released his hold on the driver and took a deep breath. His heart pounded as adrenaline coursed through his body. He placed two fingers over one carotid and felt for a pulse—nothing.

Scanning the area again for cameras and seeing none, he dragged the dead man's heavy body back into the car, quietly closing the door behind him as he did so. The next part of his impromptu plan included stripping the driver as fast as he could of his uniform and putting it on his own body. Evers worked fervently, his hands and body not yet shaking from a loss of adrenaline. He kept his mind focused on Vasquez and the next part of his plan as he undressed the driver.

The driver was a little smaller than Evers and squeezing into his clothes required removing his own shirt and pants first. Even still, he was forced to suck his stomach in order to button the pants. He had to keep his own shoes on because the dead man's feet were so much smaller than his own. *No matter*, he thought, *Vasquez won't have enough time to notice my shoes.*

After a long four minutes Evers was fully dressed and looking the part of chauffeur, complete with the man's hat on his head. At least in the dark garage he looked the part. He glanced over in the passenger side floorboard at the dead driver and shook his head.

"The poor bastard had no idea why he was attacked or who was doing it. I just hope to God he doesn't decide to visit me in my dreams."

He took a deep breath and placed both hands on the steering wheel. He figured Vasquez had been in the apartment just over thirty minutes. If he was a regular office guy, he would need to be finishing his business shortly so he could resume his role as husband and father.

Almost on cue he watched as the General pushed open a door leading from a stairwell into the garage. Evers noted that the man had a sense of mental alertness as he checked his right and left for assailants. He also took notice of the handgun on Vasquez's right hip. Evers couldn't tell if it was strapped into the holster or not. Not that it mattered at this point, as he was far too involved in his plan to pull back now.

The general put his head down and walked toward the car, Evers waiting patiently before he stepped out to open the door for him. *Breathe*, he told himself. *Stay calm and focused Billy and this will all be over in a few minutes.*

Fifteen feet, ten feet, five feet. Evers reached for the door handle while pulling his hat low to hide his face. He opened his door and stepped out, turning his back on Vasquez as he opened the door just behind the driver's seat. From the corner of his eye he saw the General give him a quick nod of appreciation.

Evers moved around the door in one fast step. He slammed his left forearm into the back of Vasquez's neck as he grabbed the pistol from the man's hip with his right hand. *Thank God it's not strapped in*, Evers thought.

The General grunted with the force of the attack, but in spite of his age, all his strength had not yet left his body. He recovered faster than Evers thought possible and began trying to roll toward the backrest to eliminate the possibility of his attacker having his back. "Smart man," Evers said to himself. The problem for Vasquez was not his lack of desire, but Evers's incredible training regimen. In one swift motion he drew the General's gun and slammed the heel of the grip into the man's cheekbone. He howled in agony.

Evers pulled the slide back and chambered a round in the military issued .45 caliber pistol and aimed it directly at Vasquez's nose. Both men were breathing hard, Vasquez after being attacked and Evers after having attacked a second man in less than ten minutes. Something in the floorboard caught Evers's eye and he reached for it as he kept the pistol leveled on Vasquez's face.

"A sure enough fucking-A Cuban Cohiba cigar?" he asked the General. He shoved it into his own shirt pocket before returning his gaze back to his prisoner. Vasquez looked past the weapon and stared directly into Evers's eyes.

"American? Fuck the United States!" he spat.

Evers whipped him across the face again with the pistol as he brought his hand down over the man's mouth before he could scream again.

"Let me explain something to you, General. You are in no position to be insulting someone else's country. In fact, I would be willing to wager that you aren't in any position to say another goddam word unless you are spoken to first, are we clear?"

Vasquez sneered at Evers, "You won't shoot me. The gun's report is too loud and you will be heard, hunted down, and captured within minutes. My men will have your balls cut off and stuffed in your arrogant American mouth before sundown."

Evers offered the man a smirk. "You may be right, General, so let's solve that problem right now."

He slammed the gun's barrel into Vasquez's mouth, shattering several teeth as he did so. As the man began to scream, Evers jammed a knee into his solar plexus as he steadied himself with his other foot on the floor of the car. The man's inability to fill his lungs with air curbed his pain filled yell.

Evers began speaking again. "With the barrel of this pistol shoved into your big mouth, the report will be muffled. It's like shoving a potato over the barrel when a silencer isn't available, General. I've had to do that before too. I would also like to be very clear with you, this isn't the first time I've shoved a pistol into a man's mouth in order to silence a round. I have no qualms pulling this fucking trigger right now and putting you out of your misery, you disgusting excuse for a human being.

"Now, if you have any desire to remain above ground, you'll do exactly what I tell you to do. You'll answer every damned question I ask or your life will be over in an instant. This is your decision to make, so if you are in the market to die alone, in the backseat of a car, parked in the garage of your mistress's apartment, just say so and I'll pull this goddam trigger right now."

Vasquez's eyes widened showing the full brown circles of his irises. His face twitched with fear and as he stared into Evers's eyes he knew the man wasn't bluffing. Those eyes were filled with hatred and vengeance, and he had no doubt that, should he give one iota of resistance or show the slightest amount of rebellion his last thought would be to question why he had not simply listened to the man.

He watched as a bead of sweat rolled down his attacker's face and dripped onto his pressed uniform. The thought that this insolent American trash could overcome him and hold him hostage with his own gun infuriated him beyond belief. There was little he could do with that emotion, at least for the time being. As he had been told, if he cooperated he would live, and that meant he could exact his vengeance once the maniac was gone.

Evers watched the man's features with great interest. He thought he understood everything that was running through his mind; the despair, the anger, the hatred, and the hope to be released if things went well. In his own gut he felt nothing but disgust for the man whose mouth he was now forcing a pistol into.

"Why, General? Why did you order the death of thousands of your fellow countrymen? What sane man does that?" Evers's brows were almost touching, the intensity evident in both his voice and on his face. He eased the gun from Vasquez's mouth and watched as the man turned his head and spit pieces of teeth onto the car's floor.

Blood cascaded in small streams down the creases of the man's face. As Evers watched him feel the inside of his mouth with his tongue, assessing the damaged he had inflicted, he estimated Vasquez to be fifty or fifty-five. He wondered what he had done or whose ass he had kissed to have been promoted so highly in the Argentinian army. Although not unprecedented for someone his age to achieve very high military status, Evers had never heard of the man until recently.

Doesn't matter. This son-of-a-bitch is going to talk to me or he's going to die.

"Don't make me ask you a second time, General. Why did you order the death of so many innocent people?" Evers pressed the pistol to the side of the man's neck, more so for effect than anything else.

Vasquez took a deep breath before exhaling. Evers could smell plasma and wine as his breath drifted across his nose, no doubt wine consumed as he undressed upstairs with his whore. The General licked his lips and sputtered.

"I was recruited by a man while traveling overseas to help control the world's population. I have no evidence to the contrary, but I'm certain I'm not the only one. You must understand that I take no pleasure in having innocent men, women and children removed from this life, but our world lacks the sustenance to support the burgeoning growth rate," he finished.

Calmness came over him, much as it did when a man confessed all his murderous sins to a priest in a confessional. There was a sense of relief, as a pressure valve on a steam cooker would give a pot full of boiling vegetables. Vasquez felt as though the weight of the world had been lifted from his shoulders, but on his face and in his eyes no remorse was present.

Evers stared at him in disbelief. Over the years he had read about a fringe movement, perpetuated by bantering from a few scientists that the world was overpopulated and needed to be brought under control. Even though he had seen and experienced so much in his life, not once did he stop to consider that a person would act upon the theory of overpopulation by systematic elimination.

Coupled with radical fringe groups like PETA and Green Peace, suddenly the world becomes unstable and anarchy rules. For a brief second Evers wondered if all his work, everything he did in the shadows, was worth it. Was he merely delaying the inevitable? Would the crazies eventually win the day? It surely looked to be the case at that moment, as he stared a monster in the eyes. The psycho who currently was sucking wind through shattered teeth was solely responsible for the death of hundreds or perhaps thousands of his fellow countrymen.

"You fucking monster," Evers began, "do you even have a speck of decency in your body? You kill on a whim then run over here to satisfy your sexual needs without so much as a thought for the families left in your godforsaken wake?"

He slammed the barrel back into Vasquez's mouth and sneered at him. "I ought to do you right here, right now. I can't imagine anyone would really miss you, you sick bastard. Of all the things I've done in my life, of all the people I've taken from this world, not once have I considered it an act of morality. You sit in judgment of people just trying to make a go at life, not harming anyone, not trying to kill or overthrow a government, seize power unjustly, or murder without cause. These are people trying to get by and raise their families, go to work and do the best they can, and somehow you think taking them out of this world is bettering it, you sanctimonious motherfucker!"

Evers hand was shaking with the anger he was feeling. His thumb drew back the hammer on the pistol and he adjusted his body so he would have better leverage on the weapon. He saw the terror run across Vasquez's face as he coughed and sputtered emitting spittle and blood that shot out of his mouth and landed on his hand.

Evers calmed himself and reached for the icy cold tendrils of the killer to overtake him. "You have one last chance to tell me who asked you to commit these murders. If you don't answer me I'll continue my investigation and eventually find him. Regardless, you'll be dead and that suits me just fine. Do you understand what I'm telling you?"

Vasquez shook his head as tears began streaming down the sides of his face. Fear gripped him even after his confession. He thought about his own family, and Maria, his girlfriend who lived upstairs. He loved them all and had acted out of compassion for his planet, for the human race, and even though this strange man thought and felt otherwise it was the truth.

He attempted to say something but the pistol's barrel muffled and tangled his speech. Evers withdrew the weapon to give Vasquez another opportunity to speak. He nodded his head in a silent order for the General to begin.

"Trowton," he slobbered. "The man's name is Trowton, he's British and lives in London, I think."

"You better not be lying to me, you sick son-of-a-bitch," Evers warned.

"I'm not. I swear to you I'm not lying," Vasquez replied.

Evers stared into the man's frightened eyes and shook his head. "Yeah, I believe you…I think you're telling me the truth."

Vasquez closed his eyes and sighed heavily. His relief was momentarily lived, however. Evers slammed the gun one more time into his mouth and pulled the trigger.

St. Laurent, France
8:18 AM

Khaled sat in the cockpit of the Cessna 750 and stared at the control panel. For years he had made a terrific living flying his private jet all over Europe and the Middle East for wealthy French businessmen. He originally planned on flying the large commercial planes for one of the major airline companies, but found that he enjoyed the smaller crafts and working independently as opposed to operating on a large company's schedule.

His family had moved from Tehran after the Ayatollah seized power in the late 70's, not because they feared for their lives, but because they feared for their personal economic state. His father had always prayed as the Quran ordered and took his family to the local mosque with great regularity. The family settled on being Muslims who embraced their faith, but loved the financial opportunity the west offered. That, plus the fortune his family had amassed in the Iranian oil fields, as his father led the government controlled National Iranian Oil Company, or NIOC as the Brits and Americans called it, was being seized by the newly crowned spiritual leader of Iran.

Khaled was afforded the opportunity to attend some of the best schools in Europe and earn an education that he could not possibly receive in his homeland, and for that he thanked Allah. Little in the way of global news affected him as he spent so many of his waking hours in the air moving about from airport to airport. He did, however, watch in morbid fascination as the second commercial airliner hit the World Trade Center in New York City, and later watched the towers fall in a massive mushroom cloud of concrete and dust. When reports began surfacing that Osama bin Laden was responsible for the planning and carrying out of the attack, he wondered what would prompt a man born into the money of a rich Saudi family to commit such an atrocity against thousands of innocent people.

When he was idle in a foreign country or town, he found solace in his Quran and told himself that he would attempt to be as devout as his father had been in both prayer and attending Mosque. That desire led him to a small Mosque in Paris where the practice of Islam was embraced and viewed with admiration. A young and fiery Imam preached sermons directly from the Quran, explaining to his followers that The Prophet demanded fealty and subservience to Allah.

It was there that Khaled first learned of the invasion of westerners into his homeland of Iran and their exploration of oil fields. They demanded oil rights be given to them, and while the British and Americans prospered so many of his own countrymen and women suffered. The Imam explained that this had happened time and again in other Middle Eastern countries and each time the infidels robbed the Muslim countries of the beautiful and precious resources while their brothers and sisters were forced to fight for the scraps that were left behind.

Khaled had learned from his father that the Brits were the ones who discovered oil in his country and shared that newfound wealth with the people of Iran, but the things the Imam explained seemed much more historically accurate, or at least his words were stated with a considerable amount more conviction than those his father spoke so long ago. It was there that he learned, at least in a much more cerebral sense, what awaited him in Heaven, most especially if he lived his life according to the will of Allah and followed the teachings of The Prophet.

After several visits to the Mosque he felt pity for his European friends and thought back to some of the scorn that many of the whites he lived around wrought on those dissimilar to themselves. It was not his nature to become angered, but anger and hate is what he began to feel after listening to the Imam preach for over a year. He and others just like him would sometimes drink coffee or tea afterward and share their own experiences growing up in a country filled with aristocratic hypocrisy. The only contempt they shared with their French counterparts was their hatred of the Jewish filth that invaded the banks and businesses all over the world.

The Imam continued to preach about the unholy alliance the West had formed with the illegal land-grabbing Jews and supported them in their fight against the rightful owners of Israel. Slowly but surely did Khaled's opinion about Europe and America begin to transform and become clearer. He focused on the words of the Imam and listened with more intent when he met with his fellow Muslims before deciding that should he be called to jihad he would do his part to appease The Prophet Muhammad, *allahu akbar.*

After running through the pre-flight checklist, Khaled reached for the engine ignition switch and listened as the plane came to life. The plane's jets roared as fuel coursed through their lines and fed their insatiable lust for more. He made a few more checks before grabbing the throttle and easing it forward.

As the plane rolled onto the runway he could hear the tower radioing that he was clear for takeoff. The flight plan he turned in three days earlier detailed a path to Lyon, France. Times, altitude and the exact path to the destination airport were all detailed according to French regulations. Everything was in order as the engines roared again, this time with even more fuel as the Cessna bounded over the blacktop. He pulled the throttle toward him and the nose of the small passenger jet lifted, the inertia forcing his head to his seat.

He glanced at the copy of his flight plan lying in the empty co-pilot's seat next to him. The regulation requiring a co-pilot, he knew, was not mandatory if his license was top-notch, which it was, and he was not carrying any passengers, and he was not. The flight plan mapped out a pretty straight shot to his penned destination.

His Cessna rose to an altitude of ten thousand feet as he looked immediately to his right, seeing the massive structure he knew was there. The flared end and billowing cloud of steam flowing from its top let him know the nuclear facility was in full operation that day. He eased the throttle forward and leveled the nose of the plane. A voice came over his headset telling him in English to continue to climb, that he did not have authority to fly at that altitude.

Ignoring the order, Khaled continued on his path for another moment before gently turning the plane to his right. He could hear the voice from the air traffic control tower ask him if he was having problems with the plane, or if there was some sort of medical emergency causing him to deviate from his flight path. The pilot grabbed his headset and threw it to the floor under the empty co-pilot's seat as he continued to bank to the right.

His plane, now lined up with the nuclear stack, jetted forward as he increased the throttle. The twin Rolls Royce engines screamed as the plane flew at almost six hundred miles per hour. Khaled pushed the nose of the plane downward, and from his headset he could hear voices screaming at him although he could not understand what they were saying. No doubt they were ordering him to resume his original course or return to his origination point even though he had no plans to do either.

As the plane descended it hit some turbulence, which caused the wings to bounce wildly. A veteran of many hours of flight time, no amount of wind disturbance caused Khaled alarm. He continued on his course, the nose of the plane now pointed directly at the middle of the nuclear stack.

The plane plummeted downward and from the cockpit Khaled could see several people scrambling to get away from the nuclear plant. He began his prayers as his heart raced and sweat poured over his body. In just a little time he would be in the presence of Allah and be given the wonderful virgins promised to him by The Prophet.

Sunlight gleamed through the cockpit window and Khaled took note of the glorious blue sky. No cloud was on the immediate horizon and in his mind he could hear his praises being sung by his Imam and all his fellow Muslims throughout the Middle East and around the world. He would be glorified like the wonderful martyrs before him, just like those who flew those planes into the American buildings, and the recent shooters in his own France. Yes! He would most certainly be remembered for his actions in helping to remove so many infidels in Europe.

Alarms sounded around the St. Laurent nuclear facility. Inside, engineers worked feverishly to shut down the reactor, no matter the futile nature of their actions. The cooling fan speeds were increased to reduce the heat on the fuel rods and nuclear material being generated to help power homes and businesses throughout France, as well as surrounding countries.

He watched from his plane as a few cowards made it to their cars and began speeding away from his approach. *No matter, they will die later, as will their co-workers and their families.* Khaled took a deep breath and closed his eyes, saying one last prayer to Allah before his plane made impact.

Khaled's Cessna 750 struck the stack just below its middle. The plane pierced the incredibly thick wall rather easily given its speed and weight. Within a second after impact the plane exploded, its fire laden shell hitting the far wall then falling over seventy five feet into the stack's nuclear well.

The secondary explosion sent an incredible plume of smoke and steam into the blue French sky. Light winds began pushing it eastward. Screams of agony and fear permeated the area as new explosions and flames jettisoned from the destroyed stack. Loud sirens pierced the countryside and an alert system began announcing the radioactive cloud and wind direction to locals.

Hazardous material teams suited up in fire stations from as far away as two hundred miles, Japan's Fukushima fresh on their minds. Police mobilized, attempting to set up a perimeter to keep television and radio crews away from the site, while France's Directorate General of Civil Aviation ordered all aircraft grounded in the country and also declared French airspace off-limits to flights from other countries.

Several thousand metric tons of radioactivity dispersed into the air as hot nuclear material and waste began burning at thousands of degrees centigrade. It was too soon for authorities to begin measuring the radioactive Becquerel level, but early estimates placed the disaster at five times worse than that of Chernobyl.

Delhi, India
11:21 AM

Doors and windows were the first things to blow out of Ambience Mall. Next a large section of wall on the eastern side of the building, followed by a section of roof that was catapulted straight into the air. Lastly, bodies and body parts flew from the building's new openings in almost comical fashion. Men, women and children alike screamed in unison as flame and parts of the mall structure pierced their bodies, in some cases amputating appendages, and in others creating a macabre scene of death and destruction like no horror movie could ever hope to accomplish.

Smoke and cinder block lay strewn across the parking lot; Ahsan was lying prone next to a small yellow car. The percussion from the explosion sent him flying and for a few brief seconds he assumed he was dead. His ears rang and his senses were not yet functional. He had a brief sensation of cordite mixed with food, all atop a cacophony of human misery. As it turned out, his sensation was correct.

Ahsan gathered himself, feeling his arms and legs for anything missing or destroyed. His pants were torn and he could feel abrasions on both knees and one elbow, and perhaps on his face, but of that he wasn't certain. He felt for his car keys but they were missing, probably knocked from his pocket during the explosion. His cell phone was also nowhere to be found, which concerned him more than the missing car keys.

On hands and sore, bloodied knees, he scrambled around in search of his phone, the physical evidence contained inside it needed to not only try him for the death and destruction of hundreds, but also the next phone number needed to detonate the other device. As he combed the parking lot, trying in vain to remember the direction from which he had run, he saw a set of keys, a rental tag still hanging from them. He stood and limped toward them, stepping over the body of a young mother and her barely breathing daughter.

Ahsan gave the woman and child little more than a cursory glance as he bent to pick up his keys. Beneath the car next to his keys a glint of something glass caught his eye. As fate would have it he reached for and found his cell phone, the display monitor cracked but functional.

From a distance he could hear the sirens of police cars and ambulances, but still he smiled.

"Allah has blessed me today with this phone and with the ability to continue with his plan to eradicate these infidels," he said aloud.

As he began the search for his rental car, he wondered how much radiation from the dirty bomb would now be in the air, and how, if he were to live for some time yet, it would affect him as he aged. He knew a little about the adverse health reactions to those whose bodies were exposed to high levels of radiation, specifically after the Americans bombed Hiroshima and Nagasaki, as well as those hate-filled Russians who succumbed to their poorly built reactor many years ago, but beyond that he understood little.

Police cars screeched into the parking lot as several mall-goers still limped and crawled from the rubble. Ahsan watched as law enforcement set up a perimeter around the immense parking lot. There was little doubt that India's military would also be showing up in short order to assess the damage and cause of the explosion. Hope of him finding his rental car and escaping quickly diminished.

He watched as injured and uninjured people attempted to dig through remnants of walls in search of missing loved ones. Wails of agony and despair filled the air, but none of it seemed to faze Ahsan. His next target, Indira Gandhi International Airport was now unreachable. He was suddenly overcome with a sense of failure, despite his earlier glee of having survived the blast and recovering his keys and phone.

Despondent and indifferent, Ahsan sat down in the parking lot and watched the recovery effort. No one yet realized the explosion was merely a release agent; the spent nuclear fuel would be the true killer. Years from now, this region would still reel from the onset of radioactive material in the ground, water, walls, and air. Generations of these filthy Indian unbelievers would reap the harvest of what Ahsan planted. Some, still, would be left infertile with tumors and cancers growing in their bodies, and those who were fortunate enough to conceive a child would watch in horror at the physically and mentally deformed fruits of their loins joined them in the world.

At least that was a small victory for the man who would bring Islam and Sharia Law to the rest of the world. The uneducated miscreants would learn that this was only the beginning of Allah's reigning supremacy. There would be others, Ahsan was sure, that would follow in his footsteps. Many young followers were anxious to do Allah's work as portrayed by The Prophet Muhammad.

And so he sat and watched and listened to the melee all around, when it suddenly dawned on him that his work was not yet finished. He looked down at his phone then jangled his keys in one hand, turned and began searching for his rental car again.

The people running in the haze of the attack were still in shock, and as police arrived they focused on setting up check-in stations and trying to segregate the wounded from everyone else. Ahsan tried to not limp as he walked, hoping to avoid attention or recognition from anyone who might have seen him inside the mall. He knew the likelihood of anyone that close to the attaché case surviving when it detonated was more than minimal.

Still, avoiding attention at such a crucial time was tantamount to carrying out his newly formed plan. He ducked slightly as a helicopter whooshed by apparently carrying first responders and required medical instruments. A small grin crossed his face at the prospect of the new arrivers being contaminated with the radioactive fallout, but he forced himself to remain focused on his new mission.

Ahsan walked, stopping long enough to right himself against a parked car until he finally spotted his own. Once again, he fished his keys from his pocket and opened the trunk where the second attaché case lay hidden from view. He noticed only in passing that his rental was covered with a fine layer of dust residue from the explosion.

He walked to the driver's side door and pressed the unlock button before sliding onto his seat. The weather was tepid but not overbearing, but he began sweating profusely once again. Just as the last time, his heart was pounding and he could hear his pulse in his head. His palms glistened with wetness as he rolled the tumbler on the case.

The code properly entered, Ahsan depressed the two buttons on either side of the case's face and watched as the latches popped. Inside, lay a second bomb, assembled exactly the same as its predecessor. The glowing lights and numerous wires running to and from the C-4 explosive were intimidating enough, but the large vial of spent Uranium caused him to take a deep breath.

He dug for his phone and unlocked it using the pre-set security PIN. The phone face sprang to life beneath its cracked exterior revealing a series of icons as familiar to Ahsan as the hair on his own arm. He reset the Bluetooth connection and waited a few seconds to see if the bomb and phone would link up. Like magic the words reappeared on the screen—*Bluetooth connected to device.*

Ahsan exhaled deeply, simultaneously happy that his phone's Bluetooth capabilities had not been damaged in the explosion and that the bomb did not detonate as he stared at it. He closed the top of the case and refastened the latches, locking both by rolling the tumbler numbers one more time. Carefully, he placed the case in the passenger's seat then looked around for anyone who might be watching him. No one looked out of place, insofar as people running about a chaotic scene would look out of place.

For a final time, Ahsan bowed his head and prayed a long prayer to Allah, thanking him for the opportunity to serve him and for the resiliency to create a new plan, however less resourceful it was from the original. He meditated in silent prayer for several minutes finishing with a forceful, "Allahu Akbar."

One hand on the steering wheel, he reached forward and placed the key in the ignition starting the engine and turning the cool air conditioning on full blast. He relished in the cool air that wafted across his face and chest, and for the first time in a long time, felt at peace. With his right hand he dropped the car into reverse and eased out of his parking place. His was not the only car attempting to leave, but was certainly one of the few.

He watched as police turned drivers around at a checkpoint set up at a mall exit. Ahsan assumed that each exit was similarly blocked, which was fine with him. There were a large number of medical personnel stationed with the police officers and behind them a large crowd of onlookers had gathered to watch despite the police efforts to keep them at bay.

Five more ambulances turned into the parking lot, all lined up at the police checkpoint. Each waited for clearance from the law enforcement officials before driving into the lot in search of empty areas far enough away from the building to assure their personal safety, but close enough that the wounded would not have to be transferred for a prolonged period of time.

In a flash of brilliance, Ahsan pointed his car directly at the lineup of police and ambulances. As he crept along, he picked the attaché case up and placed it on the floorboard behind his seat. With his right hand he reached for his phone and depressed the button that brought the display screen to life. The green icon lit up as he moved his thumb over the screen. His foot pushed on the car's accelerator moving him at a high rate of speed, especially given his locale and the current apocalyptic scene surrounding him.

One officer noticed his car moving toward them, his eyes suddenly large with the imminent danger it represented. He looked inside the window to find a dark, clean shaven man with Middle Eastern features who wore a western Polo shirt, rather than the typical round-faced Indian dressed in a dashiki. His hand dropped to his holster searching for his sidearm.

Ahsan understood completely what was about to happen. In an instant he watched as the nasty Hindu police officer groped for his puny pistol strapped to his holster. Still saying his prayers, he mashed the accelerator to the floor pushing the rental's tachometer needle into the red zone. He listened as the engine raced with the influx of fresh gasoline being flushed through the fuel injector, and watched as the police officer began screaming for assistance.

Other law enforcement and ambulance drivers turned their heads to see what the commotion was about, but it was too late. The officer managed to draw his weapon, level it, and squeeze off one round that struck Ahsan center mass through the windshield. The bullet's velocity was slowed enough by the car's window to keep the nine millimeter round from exiting his back, lodging itself just to the right of his heart.

Ahsan struggled to remain conscious and draw breath as one of his lungs collapsed. Five meters from the line of first responders he glanced at his phone and allowed his thumb one final touch on its screen. For only a split second did he see the tiny green icon turn red.

The attaché case exploded as the signal from the phone reached the wireless detonation device. C-4 and ball-bearings were launched in all directions, but the most important ones penetrated the car's fuel tank causing a second explosion. Ahsan's rental car became a one ton grenade, metal fragments from its exterior deployed in every direction. Many of the pieces found flesh as one large, sharp piece from a door soared through the air at unbelievable speeds and through an ambulance window. The razor sharp edge sliced through the driver's skull at an almost perfect parallel plane to the road's surface. His brain was neatly severed two inches from the top exposing gray matter that looked like slimy, dark packaging popcorn.

Force from the explosion sent the cop who shot Ahsan backwards where he landed in a heap fifteen meters away. Fire and shear heat burned through his uniform, his face and all of his exposed skin. The coroner would later determine that he died instantly, but that was far from the truth. He lay there in agony for several seconds, the shock of the situation and the severing of many nerve endings creating pain beyond anything he had ever felt in his life. So much was the pain that mercifully his brain shut down his nerve center until it could figure out how to cope with the intensity of its body's injuries. His internal injuries were not on the same playing field as his brain and began shutting down one-by-one a few seconds after his brain.

Two other cars next to the rental exploded in fireballs that arced some thirty feet into the air. Gasoline and the stench of burning metal and fiberglass filled the air. Clouds of black and white smoke drifted upward and outward from the three vehicles carrying with them radioactive material. Ahsan could not have planned this second detonation any better.

Even though the initial blast in the mall would wreak havoc on surrounding communities for some time to follow, the second explosion released the radioactive material into the air at a resounding rate. No one from local law enforcement would think to test the air quality for at least twenty-four hours, their thoughts more on the stereotypical terrorist act of killing several and scaring many.

Ambulances and other police officers continued to file in to help the fallen. All were on high alert now, as they had no way of knowing whether the murderer acted alone, in tandem or as a group. Other malls around the city were contacted and ordered to clear them of patrons immediately. Gandhi International Airport stopped incoming and outbound flights, evacuated the airport and began searching every piece of luggage for anything that could explode.

Within thirty minutes cell phone footage of the explosion was splashed across the internet, as some spectator close enough to the event captured the blast. It was later that the individual responsible for uploading the footage would become mysteriously ill and die. The radiation poisoning he suffered from was almost incalculable.

Arlington, Virginia
7:41 AM

Buddy watched the morning news, his jaw slack and his face contorted. He could not believe what he was seeing. It was as though the entire world had unexpectedly begun to devour itself like some vulgar virus attacking an unhealthy body. He took a deep breath and heard the unavoidable wheezing.

He looked away from the television at an old photograph hung on the wall. In it, he and four of his old Army buddies stood, each with an arm draped around the other, all in desert battle dress uniforms. Buddy was the oldest of the group, but only by a few years over that of Tommy Cline. TC, as he was known to everyone in the unit, was a good man, a man with nerves of steel and a true passion for all forms of blues music. Buddy smiled as he remembered his friend playing harmonica and singing in a small band he and a few other soldiers put together at Camp Blackfoot in Iraq.

After moving back into civilian life, TC got a job driving big rigs over the road and they lost touch with one another. Buddy received a call two months earlier that his friend had been in an horrific crash and was burned alive. Rarely was he saddened at the loss of life, but TC's passing hit him hard and made him think of his own mortality.

His eyes shifted to the handkerchief sitting on the armrest of his recliner. It was splattered with his own blood after a recent coughing fit. Buddy shook his head at the sight, reached for a Cohiba, and lit it. Not to be outdone by any physical ailment, he inhaled deeply and grinned at one of his personal vices he enjoyed so much.

He turned his attention back to the news and was mortified at the two explosions in Delhi. Video of dead women and children being pulled from the carnage was indescribable. Large columns of smoke could be seen churning into the sky, reminiscent of the massive stacks of smoke filtering out of the World Trade Center on 9-11.

The cameraman panned to his right to show what was left of several vehicles that exploded in what was described as a suicide bombing. Buddy watched as policemen and medics rushed to the aid of other police and ambulance drivers that were targeted in the attack. No further attacks had been noted at that time, and the talking head news anchors felt confident that this had been a planned detonation by a sleeper cell jihadist.

Another breaking report from France indicated a plane had hit a nuclear facility and radioactive material was blowing across parts of Europe. Men in hazmat suits carefully surrounded the perimeter of the nuclear site as fire and smoke continued to spill from the craggy top of the stack that remained after the plane smashed into it. An aerial shot of the carnage showed the tail of a Cessna inside the remnants of the stack.

Buddy squinted his eyes as the television broadcaster detailed the crash in what was certainly a planned attack. He inhaled the Cohiba again and blew a smoke cloud into his apartment's airy living room. His eyes drifted to the floor and his mind whirled in thought, the 'why's', 'how's, and 'who' playing out in a silent song.

His cell began ringing, one of those pre-programmed tones offered by the cell phone manufacturer that sounded horrendous and continued to be set as a tone by those who didn't understand the technology. Buddy had no idea how to download a better ringtone and settled on a strange melody that he never heard until someone first called him.

"Smith," he answered.

"Hey," Evers's familiar voice said.

"How's it going down there?" Buddy asked.

"You know, the usual. People, places, sightseeing and learning. Are you using the e-mail account I told you to set up?" Evers asked.

"Yes sir I am," Buddy responded. "I'm assuming it will be coming special delivery, huh?"

Cryptically, Evers replied, "My location is the word. Look, I know you said you couldn't do much for me down here, but things are getting hot. I'm going to lay low for a couple of days then I've got to get out of here. My staying here for a while may require a little intervention on your side of the Rio Grande."

"Understood," Buddy said. "I'll check it now. Stay safe and I'll be in touch."

He clicked off his phone, got up from his seat and walked the ten paces to his laptop computer. Reluctantly, he placed his reading glasses on the end of his nose and peered at his keyboard as he entered the url in his internet search bar. Buddy watched as the homepage of ProtonMail opened, prompting him for his username and password.

Evers, he knew, had recently stopped using the anonymous bulletin boards that could be run using encryption software. He believed government agencies, specifically the NSA's data-mining program, could zero in on a message and decrypt it within seconds if needed. Not one to let a little thing like federal spying slow him down, Buck discovered this new technology and told Buddy about it.

Once he entered the requested data, a second box asked him to confirm the encryption data. A Swiss based company, ProtonMail was developed to keep the U.S. and European governments from eavesdropping on private e-mails sent and received by those wishing to protect their privacy, a necessity born of the Edward Snowden admissions. A simple encryption password was all that was needed to send and receive secretive messages from one party to another, especially if one party was capable of accessing a generic online e-mail account. ProtonMail user-to-user interface was automatically encrypted, but Evers insisted on using the encrypted feature button offered on the ProtonMail toolbar.

"I love that paranoid fucker," Buddy mused as he entered "Argentina" into the encryption field.

As his inbox loaded Buddy wondered what Young Buck had found and what he could do to help him given the political climate at the moment. A few seconds passed and he had the answer to the first part of his question.

He read what Evers left in the body of the message; a simple sentence asking him to research a name, a name that meant nothing to him, nor rang any bells.

He grabbed up his cell phone again and scrolled through his contact list until one name in particular was highlighted. His finger touched the name then he brought the phone to his ear as it began ringing.

"CIA, Davis," a voice responded on the other end.

"Are we secure?" Buddy asked.

"As secure as two people can be when one person is calling from a cell phone," Davis warned, referring to Buddy's incessant use of his mobile device.

"We need to meet. The usual place?" Buddy requested.

"Give me half an hour," Davis replied.

Buddy hung up the phone and walked to his room to put on a clean pair of jeans and a stylish pullover shirt that he picked up at a department store on the "fifty-percent off" rack. He brushed through his long hair as he looked at himself in the mirror. Even though he brushed and combed rigorously, the hair on his head refused to cooperate. He shrugged his shoulders, grabbed his favorite University of Georgia ball cap, and pushed it on top of his head.

"Best goddam comb man ever made was the ball cap," he mumbled.

In a flash he brushed his teeth then headed out the door to a Dunkin Donuts that was just over two miles from his place. He enjoyed the coffee and donuts there and the background noise made speaking in public better if one were trying to avoid being overheard. Buddy sat there for fifteen minutes when he saw a familiar face walk in.

Allen Davis was your typical late thirties, fit Generation Y'er. He had the look of a wannabe fashion model that missed out on the youthful opportunities of his early twenties, but still longed for the opportunity to see his face in a magazine so he worked feverishly on his physique. His suit was tailor cut but not exactly flattering. The dark gray hung a little strangely from his muscular shoulders, a sure sign it was purchased during a buy one-get one sale at Joseph A. Bank.

Davis nodded at Buddy who sat casually at a table away from the line and the cash register. His placement in the restaurant, Davis knew, was tactical and done out of habit. He had full view of the store, sat far enough away from the throng of customers who came and went, so as to avoid being overheard, and could watch everyone as they came and went. Davis was familiar with Buddy's background and knew he was not a man to be crossed. His confirmed kill list was probably longer than any he had seen in his time at the Agency, and he was certain that Smith would have no qualms in adding him to it if the need should present itself.

Mocha latte in hand, Davis turned and walked to Buddy's table and sat down. He watched as the seasoned veteran killer sipped coffee that had steam rolling from its cup like a volcano on the verge of eruption. He wondered how Smith could do that without wincing.

"So, what did you drag me down to this fine five-star dining experience for, Buddy?" sarcasm dripping from Davis's question.

"Don't knock the Dunkin. These dot heads have figured out what a good cup of coffee should taste like, son. You should remember that," he replied.

Davis rolled his eyes and chose to ignore the salacious racial insult rather than engage Buddy in a discussion of tolerance and global harmony. Besides, given his past transgressions he doubted anything he could say would change his opinion on...anything. He figured it was better to let Smith speak freely, without any moral recourse than tempt the ire of a man responsible for killing well over one hundred human beings in his lifetime.

Buddy began, "What are you analyzing pukes at the Agency doing about this global shit storm? The fucking world is burning and it looks like you and your boys are sitting around the office with your tally whackers in your hands. Your president refuses to acknowledge terrorist activity for what it is and no one challenges him to the contrary. So, help me understand what you sick bastards are planning to do about all this anarchy, Allen."

"Is this why you brought me down here, Buddy? You felt the need to chastise me and berate the very people who feed you? I think your priorities are a little screwy," Davis responded.

"Don't be a fucking drama queen, Allen. I'm asking you serious questions. What is the Agency doing about this stuff?" Buddy demanded.

"Even if I could tell you what we were doing, and I'm not at liberty to discuss jack-shit, I wouldn't tell you, you old goat. You are a bitter SOB, Buddy Smith," Davis fired back.

Buddy nodded his head and took a long sip of his coffee. The steam rolling from the corners of his mouth, the three day old beard stubble, and Buddy's long, greasy hair that lay lifeless on his stout shoulders reminded Davis of a grizzled dragon. *Any minute now this bastard will start breathing fire and burn this whole damned coffee shop to the ground.*

Smith sat the cup down on the table and leaned forward. "Let me tell you something you little bastard, I know how this world turns and understand the geopolitical lay of the land. Now you and I have developed a working relationship, and I think you're a pretty good kid, but that arrogant attitude of yours is beginning to rub me the wrong way. Keep in mind I still have connections in your building, and there's a few outstanding favors I've yet to cash in, but if I need to call in the favor mobile, I'll do it and you're just as likely to find yourself out of a job. I've been one of those dark shadows doing the Agency's dirty work since before you were shitting yellow, boy. Are we clear?"

Davis was visibly shaken by Buddy's threat even though his face revealed little. A slight tremor of his hand, a few beads of sweat on his upper lip and a subconscious insistence to lick his lips was enough body language to let Smith know his message was made clear.

"Look, Buddy," Davis said, his voice strong despite his case of nerves, "all indications are rebellious pockets of insurrection are popping up around the globe in response to the growing global economic downturn. At this point, that's all we really know. The Ebola and SARS outbreaks are still running rampant and both viruses are depleting many of our resources. We still haven't tracked down the thieves and at this time have no clear knowledge of who could have been responsible for their release, or why for that matter."

"What are the connections between the virus outbreaks, the attacks in India and France, and the mass killings in South America?" Buddy asked as quietly as possible.

Davis pushed his brows together and responded, "I'm telling you the truth when I say the Agency doesn't believe there's a connection. The viruses, yes, the attacks in France and India, maybe, but the rest is happenstance."

"Happenstance?!" Buddy exclaimed.

A few people in line turned to see what the yelling was about. Buddy glared at each of them, it seemed, at the same time. Something on his face told the Dunkin Donut patrons to mind their own business, and that's exactly what they did. Each of them turned to and faced the front almost simultaneously. That event did not pass Davis by and he made a mental note of what just occurred.

"Calm down, Buddy. You're smarter than shouting in a public place," Davis warned.

"Don't tell me to calm down. People are dying, the world is on fire, and you pencil dicks are sitting around praying the problem just goes away. Well, I've got news for you—the problem never just 'goes away.' Problems get fixed by men like me. Now I suggest you fuckers start working on the obvious and start trying to figure out the link between all these circumstances," Buddy growled.

Davis studied Buddy's face and wondered at the deep concern written on it. Something about it looked familiar and the analyst in him put the pieces together in a few seconds.

"You son-of-a-bitch, Buddy Smith. Are you conducting your own black op? Do you have someone out there working your personal angle? If you do, you ignorant fool, you'll hang for treason or spend the rest of your miserable life in Leavenworth," Davis said, no longer caring about Buddy's background and former bravado.

"What if I am? Are you going to tell someone? Would you risk involving yourself in my public defamation just to satisfy some bizarre sense of patriotism you may be feeling, or would you do it in hopes of some mediocre promotion? Lest I remind you, we've worked together on a number of clandestine operations, and just to make you wonder, I might have recorded those missions in a certain encrypted software package set to disperse itself to every global news agency in the civilized world should I not periodically log into the system.

"Naturally, a man my age and in my condition may not remember if what I just told you is true or not—things sometimes get blurry in my head," Buddy drawled.

"What is it you want from me, Buddy? Yes, we've worked together on a number of operations, but the CIA isn't your personal fucking information repository. So, if you think you have a ton of leverage on me, then it's time you go ahead and use it because I'm already tired of you thinking you can blackmail whenever the need arises," Davis hissed. His own face now contorted into that of a man who just found out his wife was having an affair.

Buddy eased back in his seat, momentarily detaching from the conversation, a psychological ploy used to suck an adversary back in who might think he had the upper hand in an interrogation, and he had no doubt that Davis now thought he had the high road. *Time to change tactics.*

He took a deep breath and composed himself. "Listen, Allen, I just need some information beyond the normal horseshit I can find on the Internet about a specific person. I have no idea who this guy is, but I suspect you can find out much more than I will be able to ascertain. Whatever I learn after you help me out I will share with you. Can we at least agree upon that?"

Buddy watched Davis's features soften slightly and figured he had possibly de-escalated the discussion. He watched as Allen drew the mocha latte to his mouth and drank. There was something about his masculine temper and effeminate drink that struck Smith as funny and it took some effort to keep from smiling.

Calmer but just as stern Davis asked, "What's the name?"

"Trowton, Simon Trowton, apparently a British subject who is somehow mixed up in all this stuff," Buddy answered.

"Simon Trowton the shipping mogul?" Davis asked.

"I have no idea, Allen," he responded in a fatherly voice. "I've never heard of this guy and don't know what his involvement is in this mess."

A knowing half-smile crossed Davis's face as he replied, "I seriously doubt Simon Trowton is involved in any sort of global genocidal activities, Buddy. From what I know about this guy, he spends his time watching the world markets, worrying about ways to import and export items into countries that are otherwise off limits to many, and hob-knobbing with elites. The tabloids say he is quite the playboy, and apparently doesn't mind showing up at different events with a different young lady on his arm each time he makes a public appearance. Somehow I don't see him fitting the mold of mass murderer," he finished.

"Regardless, I would appreciate if you could do a little research for me. Find out if he's taken an interest in WMD's or arms shipments. His role as shipping mogul would seem to fit in this case, don't you think? He would certainly have the means to move this stuff around if he needed to."

"Not one government agency has contacted us to request assistance in tracking down someone that may have smuggled arms into their country, Buddy," Davis patronized.

"But we do know that both SARS and the Ebola samples were stolen at almost identical intervals. Attacks and mass murders around the globe begin popping up everywhere and you boys are sitting in Langley fiddling each other's doo-dahs. I happen to think you're smarter than that, Allen, and have to wonder what the White House and State Department have to do with the current lack of intelligence and ability in your agency," Buddy speculated.

Davis took a deep breath and exhaled audibly. "Listen, Buddy, our hands are tied. This administration thinks that downplaying a situation, no matter how grand it is on the *fuck me scale* will help quiet things down. It's all political and never action oriented. The State Department follows suit because most of them fear for their jobs. If they cross the White House's media lines, they will be on the street looking for gainful employment in no time flat."

"In all my years on this planet, Allen, I have never seen such a politically motivated, downright useless bunch of vaginas in charge of the greatest nation on Earth as I have now. I can't even fathom that inaction in times of international crisis is tolerated from the top military brass. What the hell is going on with them? I know a lot of those men and understand that being in their position and being told to be pussies is mutually exclusive," Buddy demanded.

Davis rose from his seat and looked down at Buddy. "I understand your concern and I hope you appreciate the precarious position I'm in at the moment. Give me some time to do a little research regarding Mr. Trowton's involvement, or lack thereof, in the current crises. As much as you piss me off, Buddy, I can usually count on your intuition, so I'll take this seriously."

Buddy reached for Davis's hand and shook it. "That's all I could ever hope for, Allen, and I do sincerely thank you for your efforts."

Davis turned and walked out of the coffee shop to his car where Buddy watched him drive away. "You probably put a considerable number of years back on your life by agreeing to help me too you ungrateful little bastard," he muttered.

London, United Kingdom
12:09 PM

The buzzer notifying Trowton that someone was there to see him whirred on and off at least eight times. As annoying as the sound was, Trowton found it even more irritating that someone could be so rude that they would continue to push the button numerous times without giving the homeowner an opportunity to answer first. He made his way to the intercom and depressed the "talk" button.

"Yes?" he bellowed.

"I would like to come up for a visit," came an ominous reply.

"Oh fuck…fuck…fuck!" Trowton said aloud without depressing the talk button. His heart immediately started pounding in his chest and his hands and face began sweating.

"To what do I owe this surprise visit, Mr. Abaddon," he managed.

"Just ring me in, Simon," Abaddon replied without hesitation.

Trowton stood there, his head resting against the wall next to the intercom. He mopped his head with the sleeve of his long t-shirt before raising a shaky hand to the button that would allow his visitor to enter the building. His finger reached the button and pressed it, another buzzing sound coming through the intercom system notifying the visitor that the door was now unlocked.

He waited by the door for the strange man who maintained a hold over him. Try as he might, he could not explain the fear he felt when he was in Abaddon's presence, and no matter what he told himself when he was away from the man, he could not defy him.

Heavy footsteps just beyond his threshold told him his visitor had arrived. Rather than open the door, however, he waited for Abaddon to knock, wanting so much to at least give a perception of confidence, no matter how false it might be. He stood staring at the door waiting for a knock…

From the other side he heard, "I can see you standing there, Simon. Open the door, now."

Trowton's eyes grew large and he thought he would vomit right there on his living room floor. He scratched his head and rubbed his chin, two nervous ticks he had picked up at some point in his life. Slowly, he clambered for the door and turned the knob.

Abaddon walked in and faced him. "We have more work to do and you must execute it much faster. There is little time to waste."

"M-m-m-ore w-w-w-ork?" Trowton sputtered.

"Yes, you sniveling little worm, more work. I want you to locate a fully armed nuclear weapon and prepare to drop it on Manhattan, New York. On the black market, I have learned, there has been made available a Russian version of the United States W-88 nuclear warhead. The four hundred seventy-five kiloton warhead is perfect for our plans, Simon. It is located in a quiet bunker Cyprus at the Port of Larnaca. A man of your knowledge would have little problem procuring and transporting it just off the coast of New York where it is to be launched.

"I dream of a strike on the new Freedom Tower. Wouldn't that be grand?" Abaddon marveled.

Trowton sputtered, unable to put a coherent sentence together. *This has nothing to do with my plans. Random attacks for the sake of mass casualties and terror have nothing to do with thinning the herd, although he'll probably argue that it does.*

After several attempts he managed, "I'm sorry, Mr. Abaddon, but detonating a nuclear warhead to knock down a building makes no sense. My position has been purely scientific in nature, and yes, I agree that killing millions of humans in one strike serves the purpose on the whole, but I do not find it conducive to human sustainability. New York is, after all, a bastion of knowledge and other like-minded individuals who strive to bring about betterment to the human condition."

Abaddon took four steps toward Trowton, covering a distance of ten feet faster than anyone or anything he had ever seen. The man's eyes and face were afire. Literally, Trowton watched as Abaddon's irises darkened, turning an amazing red. He almost fainted at the sight.

Abaddon's nostrils flared and he bared his teeth. The smell of rotten flesh flowed from his mouth to Trowton's nose. His stomach convulsed and he thought he would vomit on the man's shoes.

"You weak, perverted excuse of a man," Abaddon growled. "Even now you don't understand what it means to remove the wretched. I've watched you for a long time, sanctimonious and habitually elite. In your mind only those you deem worthy should live, while the rest of mankind should be removed. The reality is…none of you deserve to live on this Earth. Chaos and destruction pave the path forward!"

Trowton's eyes widened, as the previous few moments played over and over in his head. He was a man of science, choosing to live in the moment while understanding his past. Everything science proclaimed about the damage man caused on this planet he absorbed and regurgitated to anyone that would listen. Global warming, ozone depletion, fracking in the United States, over population, pollution, the incessant deforestation around the world, and the killing of life in our oceans were topics he would interject any time the opportunity presented itself. Through political maneuvering he not only became a member of the Bilderbergers, but a leader amongst other like-minded men and women.

Now he stood face to face with a maniac, a man who did not share his dream and mission of population control. No, this man thrived on chaos and anarchy. But to what end? Something about him brought fear at the most primal of levels, but there were other things that tickled his mind, that defied logic. His words bemoaned attack and death, but for no other reason than that.

Trowton shifted his eyes up and met Abaddon's gaze. It is said that the eyes are the gateway to a man's soul, and in those eyes Trowton saw nothing but pain, emptiness and hate. He watched as the man raised a hand, his bony fingers long and extended. His palm was pasty and lacked the creases every living person has on their hands. The entire surface was as smooth as glass.

In one deft motion Abaddon brought his hand down, landing it precisely against Trowton's face. The smack of skin on skin and bone on bone was distinct, and the force of the blow dropped its target to his knees. Stars exploded in Trowton's head and the light from his room all at once became dim. He had been struck before, but never with that much force.

He shook his head and began to rise, but his visitor raised a foot and smashed it against his head, flattening him to the floor and sending a cheekbone directly into the tile. Trowton could feel the sticky warmth of his own blood pouring from a gash on his face and rolled over on his back gasping for air.

Abaddon watched him writhe about as he walked to the kitchen sink and poured himself a glass of water. He drank, allowing a considerable amount to dribble down his chin, splashing off his chest and to the floor. With the back of his hand he wiped the remnants from his face, walked to a chair and sat down. A few feet away Trowton still lay on the floor groaning in pain.

"Get up. I don't have all day to fuck around with you," Abaddon demanded.

Not wanting to disobey an order and risk another beating, Trowton rolled over and came to his feet. He placed the back of one hand against his cheek then looked at the smudge of blood left behind. Once again, he shook his head then stretched his neck as he tried to get a sense of what just transpired.

"Sit," another command.

Trowton did as he was told, but the confused look on his face stood only to irritate Abaddon.

"Don't attempt to play the victim with me, you weasel. Innocent looks upon your face serve no purpose. You've begun something you don't quite understand, but in due time what you have put into motion will become quite clear. In the interim, I am leaving with you a name and a phone number. This is the information you will need to make the nuclear purchase. You are to have it transferred by cargo ship through the Straits of Gibraltar then onto the island of Madeira. There it will be moved to another cargo ship, the Maersk California, where it will await my orders.

"I assume you know how to move the warhead without interference from those who desire to thwart such missions, yes?" Abaddon asked.

Trowton shook his head affirmatively as he continued holding his hand against his swelling face. He began to say something, but the words were low and ineffectual.

"Don't be so foppish, Simon—it's so unbecoming of a man who desires to bring science and civility to an otherwise uncivilized world," he laughed aloud. "If you have something to say or ask, then spit it out!"

He sucked wind into his lungs and mustered a last ounce of courage. "I have never wanted to deplete the planet of its entire population, or create such chaos that mankind couldn't recover. My plans have been to simply curb the population growth and perpetuate that which binds us all—science.

Religion and populist opinion have driven policy and madness for several hundred years, Mr. Abaddon, and I don't see why you are intent on adding to it. In fact, I don't really know who you are," he finished.

Abaddon studied Trowton for almost a full minute before speaking. "That is true, Simon, you really don't know me at all. I know you fear me, however, and I can assure you that your fear is not unfounded. Right now, who I am doesn't matter, although I suspect you'll figure it all out before everything is said and done, but you are correct in your assumption that I thrive in the realm of chaos and anarchy. Each of those things are my personal domain, and both have created great men and women over the course of human history.

"Although you may think attacking the Freedom Tower with an incredibly powerful nuclear warhead is a tad over the top, don't you also find it somehow ironic that a weapon made by Americans to destroy a certain number of mankind shall be put to the test in America's most snake-infested city? It's a cesspool, Simon, and you'll be doing the world a grand service by helping to destroy it.

"The blast radius will be almost four point eight kilometers, or three miles if you prefer to measure using dead king's digits and appendages. After the buildings fall and the initial shock settles, we will get to watch a mushroom cloud that will kiss the upper reaches of the atmosphere. The fallout will cover much of the eastern seaboard before it drifts out to sea and turns toward Europe.

"You see? My vision is much greater than yours. The world will lose a considerable number of its human inhabitants and I will be a very happy individual," he smiled as he stressed the last word.

Trowton walked to one of his nearby chairs and sat down, his mouth open and slack. Words scrambled around inside his brain and refused to be formed in his mouth. Rarely would he be caught at a lack for words, but what he just heard prevented him from reacting cerebrally. Abaddon wanted nothing more than death and destruction for the purpose of his own enjoyment and pleasure. There was no reason for his wanton desire to bring death to people other than his personal satisfaction. He watched as his visitor continued smiling, as though he was reading his mind. Something inside him wanted to scream, to fall to the floor in a ball crying and begging for forgiveness. But who would he beg?

"And if I refuse?" Trowton asked, the weakness of his words making them sound like a piece of thread used to replace a guitar string.

Abaddon tilted his head, that strange and ugly grin somehow seeming out of place on his face. He opened his mouth to speak and for the briefest of seconds Trowton would have sworn all his teeth were filed to sharp points. He was reminded of the pointy tops of a picket fence, the difference being the lack of whiteness of the man's teeth. Trowton thought he could vaguely smell a hint of rotting flesh coming from his mouth and his stomach began lurching again.

"Refuse? I have no reason to believe you will refuse me, Simon. In fact, my only concern is that you will fail me. I find your lack of spine disgusting and unwillingness to recognize your own pitiful weakness unsettling. How you've lived with yourself all these years is a mystery. Fortunately, you'll have one last opportunity to prove me wrong by making sure that that warhead is on that ship. There's no need in my reminding you of the pure anguish you will feel at my hands should you not come through."

Trowton bowed his head in a final act of defeat and submission. Whatever it was that Abaddon held on him, on his spirit, the man's will beckoned him to comply, and comply he did. He waited for his visitor to begin some cliché laugh, mocking him for his weakness, assuring his neighbors would learn of the softness that permeated his body, but that moment never came.

Abaddon rose, looked Trowton over, that same grin the only display of emotion on the man's face, turned and let himself out the door. For over twenty minutes Trowton sat there staring at the door, awaiting the man's return to do God knew what to him.

God? What God? There is no one but me and my choices.

He considered the irony of Christianity and free will with that of his own self-imposed religion. *The Church of Simon.* The decisions he had made, the back door politics and maneuvering—all of it had led to this moment in time, and now he would reap what he had sown.

Reap.

He opened his mouth and screamed.

Buenos Aires, Argentina
8:19 PM

Evers drove Vasquez's car until he found an abandoned factory with a warehouse just to its side. The buildings sat lifeless in a neighborhood not unlike tens of thousands he had seen all around the world. Aging and sometimes dilapidated, homes were built adjacent to the factories, its workers happy to be so close to their places of employment, and only a short walk from the bedroom to the factory floor. Back home in Alabama, he reminisced, these places were called mill villages, the homes built around the textile mills that either no longer stood or remain abandoned.

He scouted the area as he drove by and saw that it was gated, but the lock had long since been removed. No light shown from the buildings; the only remaining security was a street light draped unremarkably over the entrance and a sidewalk passing along its front. Yellow light cascaded overhead, its illumination somehow both soft and harsh.

Taking a chance on being seen, he turned the car around and parked just prior to the driveway, got out, and walked to the gate. He glanced around to see if anyone happened to be outside, something that would prove problematic if he were discovered and pushed it open, the bottom links dragging and scraping across the old asphalt.

He walked back to the car, his gait long and quick, hopped in and eased through the opening. He stopped long enough to push the gate back to the closed position, then drove to the warehouse with his headlights off. The stillness of the night and the dread lying over the neighborhood gave Evers the feeling that even if he were seen no one would care or report him. Still, it was in his best interest to remain alert in case some bored policeman rolled through the area as he was finishing his business with the now deceased General Vasquez and his driver.

At the warehouse he discovered the door to be padlocked, examined the hasp and took another quick glance around as he moved to unlock the car's trunk. He moved the faux floor that hid the car's spare tire and the tire tool he needed. Grabbing it and swiftly moving back to the warehouse door, he placed its flat end at the bottom edge of the hasp and worked it until the aluminum of the large drive through door began to fold inward. The gap between the door and hasp gave Evers all the room he needed to apply some pressure and strip away the rusted screws holding the two together. The screws dropped to the ground and Evers pulled the door open.

Once inside, he assessed the damage he had inflicted upon his victims. The driver lay crumpled in the passenger floorboard where Evers had carefully placed him. He certainly wanted to avoid passing another driver who might glimpse at a dead man riding shotgun. Vasquez's lifeless body was unceremoniously draped over the transmission hump in the back floorboard, brains and blood pooling beneath a head with a massive exit wound. In the heat of the moment, Evers did not consider any damage that he could cause the car by shooting Vasquez the way he did, but the gods of good fortune were smiling on him that day as he found no damage or leaking fluid leaking on the garage floor.

For the briefest of time, Evers reflected on his handiwork and was not dismayed by the lack of compassion or empathy he felt for the deaths of either men. *It's all part of the job and never personal. Men in positions and roles like theirs should be conscious of their surroundings at all times, aware of the people in their immediate vicinity, and cognizant of bottlenecks, literally and figuratively, that could lead to a hasty termination of life. Instead, they move about because of their elite titles given to them by some other haughty person, feeling as though they are untouchable. For men like these, especially Vasquez, his ego overrode common sense. Fuck him, he deserved to die.*

It was sometimes like that for Evers, the rationalization, the reasoning, and personal validation of being judge, jury and executioner. He supposed, not incorrectly, that most people reasoned things in their own minds to ease the burden of guilt they felt. The Bernie Madoff's of the world, responsible for stealing millions of dollars through his Ponzi scheme, probably rationalized his actions in his own head as justifiable and worthy, even though in the darkest recesses of his mind he knew what he was doing was wrong. Legislators and presidents who played with soldier's lives during wartime to further a political agenda, he knew, would do the same thing.

And here he was, allowing the same self-serving justification to run through his own brain, even though he understood what kind of monster Vasquez had been and the violent crimes he committed against humanity. The burden of death was final and rested heavily upon the shoulders of the one who would levy it. Evers resigned himself to carrying that albatross and moved on with the business at hand.

He took his time wiping down the entire car, the steering wheel, the leather seats, the door handle, the trunk and tire tool. After removing the driver's clothes, he folded them and stuffed them under one arm, planning to dump them in a garbage can some distance from his current position. He used one end of the pants to open warehouse door, careful to wipe any surface down on both sides that he touched when opening and closing earlier.

Evers walked in the shadows back to the gate, not unaware of the metaphor between the darkness and his own life. He opened the gate only far enough to allow himself to squeeze through, and for a final time returned it to its resting place. A final glance in either direction told him no one was watching or paying attention and nothing seemed out of place. There were no people, young or old, gathered at street corners to pass the time. There was only silence around the neighborhood that rested in the silhouette of the old factory.

He walked north, careful not to rush, maintaining a normal gait as that of someone out for an evening stroll, despite the emptiness of his surroundings and lack of other pedestrian traffic. Evers made several turns through back alleys and down side streets, using his own counter surveillance skills to try to flush anyone out that could be following him. There was little doubt in his mind that he was alone, but the completion of the previous job had his senses working overtime and his paranoia at more than moderate levels.

Forty-five minutes of turns, stops, and continuous walking made him relax a little. People in his line of work did not remain in it for long without a heightened sense of mistrust, of this he knew. Now he found himself in a busier part of the city, nightclubs and young party-goers out for an evening of drinks and laughter. He watched one couple walking on the sidewalk adjacent to him, the young man's hand wrapped tightly around the waist of a beautiful lady. She smiled as he talked then laughed when he said something funny.

Evers felt a little sad as he watched the scene, his own inability to have a substantial relationship brought on by the line of work he found himself embroiled in. No matter how much he wanted it, something inside him reminded him that he would be putting an innocent in harm's way. He pulled his jacket tighter, the brisk fall air of the Southern Hemisphere biting into him and raised his hand in the universal signal of cab hailing.

He asked his driver to give him a tour of the downtown area, which allowed him to check the side view mirrors to cars that might be following. The cabbie, looking rather bored at the night's prospects, was more than happy to drive a passenger around, showing off his home town and watching the fare continue to tick up and up on the digital odometer mounted to the dashboard.

They swerved in and out of traffic, the driver calm and professional when it came to dodging and avoiding collisions. Evers acknowledged each point of interest the cabbie pointed out, Evers was happy his command of the Spanish language was substantial. He continued checking the car's mirrors for anything that looked suspicious, but nothing caused him alarm.

Satisfied they weren't being tailed, he had the driver stop several blocks from the Sofitel. He paid the fare and gave the driver a considerable tip for taking the time to show him around the city. Evers cut through a few back alleys and doubled back four times completing a very good surveillance detection run. Once inside, he went directly to his room and packed his few belongings then jumped on one of the several hotel elevators to return to the lobby.

"Yes sir, may I help you?" the receptionist asked.

"Checking out a little early," Evers responded, keeping his head tilted down and not making eye contact.

"We're sorry to see you leave early. Was there anything we could have done better, Mr. Evers?"

"No," he said, looking up, not wanting to act suspicious, "everything was wonderful. I finished my work early and get to go home a little faster. I'm anxious to get back to my wife," he lied.

"I understand, sir. Safe travels," she smiled as the printer spit out his receipt.

He smiled, grabbed his bag and walked out of the lobby heading due west away from the downtown area. Earlier, while riding in the cab, he noticed an area with several indistinct, nameless hotels, standing as they do for patrons wishing to meet a hooker or girlfriend for a few hours of fun and excitement. Those same businessmen who venture downtown to work most likely spent time in these same hotels, renowned for their lack of pizazz and ability to maintain the anonymity their patrons needed when hiding an illicit affair from an unknowing, or uncaring, wife.

The late fall air blew over him, sending a chill up his spine. The black wool overcoat he wore helped to deflect the bitterness of the night, but even its tightly woven fibers struggled to keep all of the wind from his body. He reached for his coat collar and flipped it over his neck, the collar provided a little relief from the cold air traveling through him and also served to better hide his identity.

Evers traced his earlier steps and found one such place, its office light the only indicator that it was open. He walked inside, paid cash for the room—no questions, no answers, and no forms to complete, just the way he liked it. He entered the room, searching it quickly, not expecting to find anyone or anything awaiting him. Once he put his clothes away, he decided it was time to get out for a while.

Probably not the smartest thing to do, what with your recent activity, but what the hell? A drink would do me good, as would just being around people, even if I don't interact with anyone. He was familiar with the psychological desire to be around people after taking a human life, and no matter how hard he fought the need, invariably he gave in and wound up sitting in a park, walking through a mall, or in this case, hanging out in a bar.

He remembered the rental car he left behind and decided right then would be the best time to retrieve it. Leaving it behind after Vasquez and his driver disappeared would not be wise, and he felt certain that the authorities had already been made aware that he was missing. Evers felt certain that Vasquez would have been very discreet about his rendezvous point with his mistress, but running a good surveillance detection route of the area would be pertinent.

He hailed another cab and had the driver drop him off four blocks from his car. Evers paid his driver the fare before heading off in the opposite direction of the brownstone apartment complex, watching and looking for ambush and surveillance spots—those spots he would have used if he was secretly looking for someone or following them. He made numerous turns and switchbacks in an effort to draw out anyone who might have followed him or might be following him now.

Evers considered the possibility that a multi-person team could be set up in hopes of finding a suspect in the disappearance of the General. His SDR spiraled inward toward the parking lot where he left his car, careful to avoid the brownstone completely. No one set off his radar and he was certain that he wasn't being followed. He found his car and spent almost an hour driving, turning and switching back in order to flush out anyone following him. Satisfied there was no one on his tail, he found a public parking lot three blocks from his hotel and parked.

Time for that drink, and the pleasure of just being around a few people.

Evers walked several blocks in search of a place in which he would feel comfortable. The usual loud thumping techno-music and Latin American dance music permeated the air when he would walk by. He was under no illusion that a decent night club, without the twenty-something crowd as the target audience would be difficult to find, unless he decided to go to a hotel bar. That, of course, was out of the question.

He checked into a low profile hotel because he did not want his face detected on a surveillance camera, the possibility of which was almost certain if he patronized a bar such as that. So he continued his search until he spotted a place a little more than two-and-a-half kilometers from his hotel. He noted the cars parked outside: nice but not extravagant, modern but not regal, and all removed from the younger generation that frequents clubs the world over.

As he approached La Trastienda a familiar sound filled his ears. A small smile touched his face as the sounds of Lurie Bell, a famous Chicago blues man, scored the frets of his guitar backed by a local Argentinian band. Evers had read that the different forms of American blues were slowly filtering through Argentina, and as with many countries around the globe, anything from the United States would be embraced.

Evers watched as men and women entered and left the club, each dressed in business casual attire and all appearing to be in their forties and fifties. Men wore stylish black or khaki slacks and button down shirts, while many of the ladies were comfortable in their hip hugging straight black skirts and various blouses. He was happy that he had changed into his own black slacks and light blue Oxford shirt before leaving. Blending and remaining unseen as he indulged in a little Buenos Aires nightlife would help put his mind at ease.

Cabs and cars swept by as he walked to the door. The sights and smells of man-made urbanism were in full swing. Food, fumes, stale beer, and raw sewage mixed to form what Evers came to understand as the scent of humanity. The aroma was never pleasant, but in a strange and affectionate way not unwelcomed to those who appreciated some of the finer things that a large metropolis had to offer.

The place had the feel of an early twentieth century speakeasy without the relative anonymity that such a place would offer its patrons. On the contrary, the low ceilings spread over significant floor space, tables lining its walls and opened in the middle for those who desired to dance. The bar sat just inside the entrance, forcing the patrons to wait for their waiters and waitresses to bring them their drinks, and alleviating the usual crowding around the bar that invariably occurred as the thirst for alcohol became more prolific as the night waned into later hours.

He was pleased to see that the entire bar was free of cigarette smoke, a thing that kept him from frequenting many nightclubs in other parts of the world, as he made his way to an open table in the back of the bar. He found a small table with two chairs that no one was seated in and pulled the one facing the entrance out so he could sit down.

Lurie belted out the haunting lyrics of "Smokin' Dynamite" as his fingers worked the frets of his electric Gibson. The raw power and energy of the song hit Evers in a visceral way, Lurie singing about the plight of the poor man. Indeed, Evers had seen poor the world over, the real poor, not what American's referred to as destitute. People living in make-shift shanties or sleeping on the ground, rummaging through garbage cans to not only feed themselves, but their starving families were the definition of poor. And while he understood the plight of a rich country like the United States having some who would qualify as "poor," the fact was that assistance in some form was available to those who wanted or needed it. That wasn't so in most countries, and even though Evers spent his life in the shadows, battling that which many chose not to, he still had a soft spot for those who were without.

For just over an hour he listened to the gutsy Chicago style blues while he sipped on a wonderful Macallan twelve year old Scotch. The rest of the crowd engaged and swaying to the music like only Latinos will do. Music seemed to flow through them, permeate them, and even guide them. It was interesting for Evers to watch their interaction with the band and the riffs they played.

He was amazed at the lack of obnoxious conversation that typically accompanies live performances in nightclubs. Once people begin talking and drinking, they feel the need to scream over the top of the band in an effort to be heard. Evers found this to be rude and annoying, and in his younger days he would walk to the table and ask them to hold it down. If the testosterone amped up and one of the loud talkers decided to challenge Evers, the outcome was always the same—pain and blood.

These days, by both necessity and driven by an acquired wisdom, he tried to ignore others and focus directly on the band. As he got older it became easier to do, and he was elated on this night to not have to worry about such things. He listened closely as Lurie finished his set with "Sweet Home Chicago." That song always made him smile, but on this night made him a little homesick.

From the corner of his eye he could see someone staring at him. In that sixth sense that warriors develop over time, he could also feel it, like someone burning a hole in the side of his head. He was careful not to swing his head around too fast to see who it was, choosing instead to scan the room to see if anyone looked out of place, might be blocking the exit or working in tandem with whoever was staring at him. His sweeping gaze looked nonchalant, just a lone man looking about a bar in order to see if he might recognize anyone there. No one caused his hackles to rise.

Finally, his eyes fell on the person creating that burning sensation inside, the one staring at him. She was dark-skinned with lithe legs and arms that were simultaneously feminine and muscular. Her eyes were so dark that Evers wondered if they were brown or black, the low lighting not helping him decide. The royal blue Michael Kors sarong skirt she wore was split well beyond decency, drawing even more attention to it as she sat with her legs crossed. The ensemble was complimented by a low cut purple blouse that fit her waist exactly right and showed off her ample breasts. Her hair was pulled into a bun that accentuated her long neck and supple shoulders.

Evers offered her a smile and a tip of his head. She turned to the bar and grabbed her cocktail and jacket, spun around on the barstool and uncrossed her legs. She stood and began walking toward him, and for a brief second he wondered if she was a high priced hooker looking to strike a business proposition with one of the few single men in the joint.

She walked with purpose, her hips swaying and breasts straining against the buttons of her blouse, everything about her beautiful and seductive. *Easy, Billy. You don't know if you're being set up. Remember that girl in Uganda that nearly cut your head off.*

He looked up from his seat and studied her closely. Unless she was hiding something up her sarong, he did not think she was capable of hiding a gun. A knife was a different story, so he told himself to keep an eye on her hands.

"Hola, senor," she smiled.

"Hola, he replied.

"You are American?" she asked in moderately accented English.

"Is it that obvious?" he smirked, a little dismayed that she had picked up on his nationality so quickly.

"Not so much, but I've never seen you here before, and you looked very pleased to be listening to American blues," she replied.

She's very astute and probably a prostitute as I assumed. That may not be a bad thing, as she won't pry too deeply into my personal life if I'm paying her as an escort.

"Please have a seat," Evers offered. "Your drink is close to empty, may I get you another?"

"That's very kind of you. Why don't you order me one of what you are having?" her lovely white teeth gleaming in the subdued lighting.

Evers raised his hand and waved their waitress to his table. "Two Macallan twelves, please," he asked in Spanish.

The lady raised a brow and smiled at him. "Your pronunciation is very good. Where did you learn to speak Spanish?"

"I travel a lot. It's a necessity of sorts, although many people speak English. Sometimes, however, I find that speaking a native tongue puts the listener at rest," Evers explained, hoping that his intentional vagueness would not be explored too much further.

Her smile was flirtatious. "What is your name?"

Damn. Here comes the first lie I have to tell.

"Randy," he said, using the first simple name that came to mind. He looked into her dark eyes then finished, "Brown. Randy Brown."

Jesus Christ, am I an idiot. Why do I put myself in these situations?

"Randy is a nice name. I'm Emilia Suarez and am very pleased to meet you." She continued, "I hope you forgive my forwardness, but I couldn't help noticing you were here alone and thought you might enjoy some company. Sitting in the back of a room and listening to music from your own country when you are traveling makes some people both happy...and sad."

She's good. Careful, Billy, don't let yourself get sucked into something you don't understand.

"You're right, Emilia. Listening to music originating from home can make a person nostalgic and possibly a little sad, but fortunately, I'm just enjoying it for what it is," he smiled.

"I see, and I don't mean to offend, Randy, the expression on your face told a different story. Where are you from in America?" she asked, quickly changing the subject.

Evers recognized her polite gesture in doing so.

Lie number two coming up.

"North Carolina," he replied, knowing he could not hide his Alabama accent, but doubting she detect the dialectic differences that only southerners understood.

"Ah, I hear it is beautiful there. I read a lot about the United States and have visited New York on three occasions. I presume you have visited that wonderful city?" she asked.

His mind drifted to the many times he had found himself wandering the streets of New York City's west side. He had a love-hate relationship with the city and its inhabitants. On the one hand its history and massive expanse of sky scrapers were things he enjoyed. Architecture was a passion for him, and there were few places in the world that offered as much as New York. On the other hand, there were the boisterous New Yorkers, always on the defensive, never making eye contact with anyone, and living their lives within themselves. He found this trait, native and intuitive to those who lived there, peculiar. A city with eight million inhabitants and some of the loneliest people on the planet was a thing he could not process, and he would often wonder why anyone wanted to remain there.

Evers thought New York's vibe was the draw for most people. It is a city always alive and awake, and it is a place of constant motion. Perhaps, he sometimes thought, that was what he found discerning about it...the forever movement of people. It went on day and night, with no end in sight. Other cities rested when the sun dropped behind their skylines, but not New York. It was, he realized, the perpetual insomniac.

"Yes, I've been to New York many times," he shared without going into detail. It was obvious to him that she was enamored with the city, and he thought it better to keep the conversation focused on her, rather than him.

"I think Broadway is my favorite. I love going to see plays there. The actors are amazing and the crowds so supportive. I also enjoy the energy of Times Square and the insanity of it all. There are so many nationalities represented in one small place. The city is so large and so small at the same time. I'm mesmerized by it," she finished.

Evers watched as she spoke, taking note of the way her mouth formed the words and the way she rolled her r when she said 'mesmerized.'

He smiled as she spoke but finally interjected, "Emilia, you are a dazzling, beautiful and articulate woman. I guess I'm just a little confused about why you decided to come talk to me. I mean, with all the men here in Buenos Aires, you're here with me. Don't get me wrong, I'm flattered and am enjoying our conversation, but I felt the need to ask."

She laughed, her head tilted back as she did so. Evers watched her, enjoying her laughter and carefree spirit. He noticed her red lipstick and how it was perfectly applied to her lovely lips. She continued to chuckle for a few more seconds, picked up her drink and sipped.

"Mmmmm...I love the spices and hint of oak in this Macallan. It was a very nice choice. Now, why did I join you here? Haven't we already discussed that? You looked like you could use some company so I asked to sit with you. Is more reason needed?" she asked.

Evers looked away, searching for the right words. "Emilia, it's just that...I mean, I'm not exactly supermodel material, you know? You could be with any man here, or anywhere for that matter, so I'm just trying to figure out why you picked me."

"Ah, Mr. Brown, you do not strike me as the insecure type. No, in fact, your outward appearance is very strong and commanding. And there's something else about you that I find intriguing," she paused then began again. "Perhaps it's that you give off a sense of danger. I doubt that many men here would think about challenging you to a fight for any reason, and while that trait will scare away some women, I find it truly rare in men and am very attracted to it."

Evers felt his face flush and thanked God for the dim lights. He watched her raise the glass to her mouth, her lips forming around its edge, and sip the Scotch. Everything about her posture, the way she held her drink and her ability to express herself with body language told Evers there had been training, perhaps an etiquette class?

He smiled at her, "Well, I guess that clears that up, huh?"

They both laughed again.

"I realize in the U.S. women are expected to be demure and wait for the man to begin the interaction, but here in Argentina we encourage self-expression and sexuality, but in a tasteful manner, you understand." She sipped the whiskey again, closing her eyes as she did so, savoring it as it dripped down her throat.

They sat there for another hour and a half, Evers mainly listening while Emilia enjoyed questioning him about the United States, most especially concerning its major metropolitan cities. She focused intently as he described Seattle, the three large California cities, Boston, Atlanta, Chicago and Dallas. When he spoke of Dallas her interest was piqued.

"Tell me of the cowboys there. Do they walk around with their guns on their hip and big hats on their heads like our cowboys in the countryside in Argentina?" she smiled, her question and tone serious.

It was Evers's turn to laugh.

Emilia looked at him, a tinge of hurt on her face as well as a modicum of embarrassment. "I apologize, I didn't mean to say something stupid. Please forgive me."

Evers composed himself then did something he had not done in a long time; he reached across the table and clasped his hands over one of hers. In an instant he realized what he had done, realized his mistake, but it was too late.

The warmth and smoothness of her hand was the first things he noticed. The second was her refusal to pull away from his grasp. Lastly, she stopped talking and stared into his eyes. With one thumb he caressed the top of her hand, unwilling and not wanting to stop.

This is a huge mistake, Billy. You need to be thinking about getting out of the country, rather than how you are going to conquer this here fine young vixen. Come to think of it, she may be the one who conquers you.

"You didn't say anything stupid, Emilia," he smiled. "A lot of people believe Texans walk around just as you described, and to be honest, there are some that do. The truth is most Texans are just normal people with regular jobs, living in nice homes and carrying on with their lives. They are, though, very proud of their home state, possibly more so than most other Americans."

He watched as the redness left her face and her shoulders relaxed while he explained to her about people from Texas. She continued on for another twenty minutes asking about other areas of the United States, remarking several times about the size of the country. She was amazed that Americans felt like they needed that much space in which to survive, and Evers had a difficult time trying to express to her why his fellow countrymen and women felt the way they did about the place. In fact, he had never given her question any thought and was quite perplexed when he attempted to answer.

"I don't know how to answer that, Emilia. We're Americans—that's the best I can do," he laughed.

She laughed along with him then raised her glass and finished her Macallan. Evers grabbed his tumbler and followed suit. Emilia stood without speaking and draped her jacket over her shoulders. "I have enjoyed our conversation, Randy, but think it is time for me to go home. This fine Scotch has made me very light-headed and I'm afraid if I stay here much longer I may not leave at all."

Evers smiled as he stood and looked into her eyes. Her dark, flawless skin and gorgeous eyes were accentuated by her drunkenness, which he found to be both cute and seductive. One perfectly tanned leg crept from the slit in her sarong and he felt a stirring down below that was certain to cause him much more embarrassment than Emilia's question about Texas caused her.

"Emilia, we've both had quite a bit to drink. I don't think I could live with myself if I allowed you to go home alone and something was to happen to you. Would you mind if I escorted you to your door," he asked, both hopeful and, he would later admit, bashful.

"Mr. Randy, if I did not know better, I would think you are trying to find out where I live so you could stalk and harass me," she giggled.

A half-grin etched on his face, he replied, "That's exactly what I have in mind."

"In that case I must insist that you walk me home. I don't live too far from here," she said as she offered him a hand to hold.

They stepped outside in the brisk night air. He pulled the collar of his coat up and she looped one arm through his and eased closer. The sensation of having a beautiful woman walking arm-in-arm with him, as well as the generous quantity of Scotch he had consumed, made Evers feel like a nervous teenager.

Don't lose your head, Billy. Be vigilant.

He scanned the area directly in front and casually glanced to his left. As they passed a storefront with a large paned window he stopped and turned toward it, Emilia still hanging onto his arm.

"Aren't we a handsome couple?" he asked as he glanced to their rear.

"Yes we are, Randy, but if you don't get me home soon, you will be alone again because I will die from this cold," she laughed.

They walked the few blocks to Emilia's apartment, Evers's nonchalantly scanning each side of the street as they walked. He hoped that she did not notice his persistent level of alertness and security consciousness, but if she did he would explain that he was still a little uncomfortable in a foreign country.

The cold kept her head tucked into her coat and if she did notice his paranoia she did not mention it. She stopped at the bottom of some steps and turned to face him.

"Well, this is my apartment," she said a little sheepishly.

"It looks like a nice neighborhood," he replied with little conviction in his voice.

"You seem a little nervous, Randy. Do I frighten you?" she asked wryly.

He laughed. "No, you don't frighten me, Emilia. It's just that it's been a long time since I've spent time with a woman. You have no idea how much I've enjoyed our conversation tonight."

She looked into his eyes, her own pupils dilated from alcohol, and if Evers's instincts were correct, a tinge of excitement. Emilia smiled at him then wrapped both arms around him, laying her head on his chest, nuzzling against him. He thought he heard her purr.

"I think you should come inside," she whispered.

Evers considered his situation for a moment. He had just killed the head of the Argentinian military, and most probably the heir apparent to the presidency. Things were going to be hot as the search for the General intensified. Should he have left the country the same day as Vasquez's departure from this world he would have looked suspicious. *Waiting another day would not hurt and the chances of them discovering the bodies so soon were remote. What the hell, I was planning on spending another night in Argentina anyway, so I might as well do it with a lovely woman.*

Neither of them spoke as they walked to the top of the steps, Emilia pulling a set of keys from her purse. As she fumbled to unlock the door, Evers scanned the area one more time. Her lack of security consciousness and the uneasiness he felt as they stood outside, exposed to anyone who might suspect him of assassinating General Vasquez, made him exhale loudly when he heard the key push the tumbler inside the doorknob.

A rush of warm air swept over the couple as they stepped across the threshold into the apartment. Evers was happy to have the door between them and the street and similarly awestruck to be in the apartment of such a gloriously beautiful woman. Emilia draped her arms over his shoulders and moved her mouth to his.

Their tongues met and flicked about the other's mouth, exploring and tasting. Evers pressed her against the wall, her head bumping a painting hanging in the hallway next to the front door. Her scent, the light perfume he could not place and the smell of her hair was driving him crazy, not to mention the taste of the Macallan on her tongue.

She pulled away from him long enough to unbuckle his belt and unbutton his pants. He was embarrassed by the massive hard-on that fell from his underwear as she pulled them down, although he had already explained that it had been a considerable time since he had been with another woman. Her dress brushed up against him, the sensation driving him wild.

Evers pushed her away long enough to step out of his pants. The thought of being ambushed with his pants around his ankles was more than his mind could overcome, despite his horniness and the knowledge of what was to come. After he stepped out of his pants she moved to him, her face planted firmly on his and her hand stroking him. A groan escaped and he could not tell if it was from him or her.

He began to undress her, pushing her coat off her shoulders and hearing it land in a heap on the floor. Her dress zipped in the back, a small hook and latch keeping the neckline from releasing. She laughed as he struggled with the dress.

Goddam it, it's easier to kill grown men than it is to undress a woman.

He watched as she reached behind her head and unlatched the hook. Evers felt her dress give way to gravity as he eased it off her shoulders. Her bra latched in the front, and thankfully he had no problems with it. The black thong she was wearing rolled down her brown thighs and over her perfectly shaped calves finding the floor in their wake.

Evers wanted to turn her around right there, but she grabbed his hand and led him to the living room. He was amazed by the grandeur of the room, the artwork and simplicity of the area. The couch, two chairs and flat screen television were very modern, and the lamp décor, both obviously Tiffany designs, were elegant and sophisticated. Her couch was a Calvin Klein sectional—simple and luxurious. Obviously, her tastes were intriguing and upscale.

She pushed him back onto the couch, his back pressing against the cool upholstery. She straddled him, reaching down and guiding him inside her. He watched as her hair fell beside her face and her breasts began bobbing up and down. Her breathing intensified as did his, both their hips meeting the other in time.

Evers closed his eyes as he attempted to control himself, not wanting to lose it just yet. Emilia continued to ride him, her moans and breathing growing louder. He flipped her over, easing her down on the couch without pulling out. Her wetness saturated him and the smell of their sweat and sex combined to create an aroma he had not sensed in a long time.

Emilia pushed her hips toward him, her legs wrapped behind his own as she began to moan even louder. For a moment he wondered if her neighbors would hear them, but quickly pushed the thought from his mind. He felt her tighten as she came and watched as her eyes rolled to the back of her head. Her mouth opened and she breathed a satisfactory sigh.

She grabbed his head again and pulled his face to hers as he continued to thrust in and out. Her tongue shot into his mouth, aggressively seeking and searching. Her smell and the excitement of the moment could no longer contain him. He arched his back and came inside her, her hands moving to the small of his back and pulling him further inside and her legs squeezing against his ass.

Evers rolled off the top of her and collapsed to the floor. Emilia began laughing as she propped herself on her side and looked down at him. It was her turn to watch him as his chest heaved up and down, his nostrils flaring while they attempted to suck enough air in to replete his respiratory system.

Sweat rolled along the contours of his body, his fit abdomen gasping for air and his heart pounding in his chest. He smiled at Emilia, grabbed her arm and pulled her onto him. She yelped as she fell into his arms, then began laughing as the two embraced.

For another hour the two made love, each time as though it was the first. Evers gave no thought to the outside world, to explosions, to mass murder, nor to disease running rampant through various countries. This night, in this moment, there was only Bill Evers and Emilia Suarez.

Evers opened his eyes and stretched. The taste of day old Scotch laid on his tongue like old moss growing at the base of a tree. He stretched then tried to focus, his head slightly pounding and his heart thudding in his chest as it attempted to purge the remaining alcohol from his body.

The room was unfamiliar to him, the dark golden colored drapes hanging over the windows, the stylish reclaimed chestnut wood of the Emmerson dresser and matching end tables next to the bed. He looked to his right and saw hints of sunlight reflecting off dark stained bamboo floors. Everything in the room screamed of a particular bravura in elegance, balance, and simplicity.

In a rush the previous night came powering back into his mind, and his head snapped to the left only to find the space next to him empty, the pillow fresh with the depression of Emilia's head. She had flipped the covers off her, leaving them neatly folded at a precise forty-five degree angle. No doubt, he thought, some strange OCD mannerism that he did not find unappealing.

Evers took a deep breath and was pleased to smell fresh food being cooked. In the distance he could hear footsteps dusting around on a floor. She's cooking breakfast. *Oh, fuck...I should have left when I had the chance.*

He got out of the bed and dressed. Immediately, for a reason known only to someone whose life had been spent in the line of fire years before, followed by a life in the shadows over the previous year, he began searching the area for anything that looked out of place or for something that could be used against him like a camera or recording device.

Damn it, Billy, she's a nice girl. Why don't you just walk in there and eat the breakfast she's obviously working hard to make you?

Evers walked into the kitchen and found Emilia standing in a short, white terrycloth robe finishing two glorious omelets, roasted potatoes, a slice of toast and freshly squeezed orange juice. His stomach rumbled, and he was reminded that the previous night he hadn't eaten, but merely indulged in both liquor and a spectacular Argentinian woman. He allowed his eyes to move from her perfect legs to the heavy display of cleavage that her robe revealed.

Emilia's face flushed when she saw Evers staring at her.

"I got up a little early and wanted to prepare breakfast for you, Randy. My apologies for my dress, but after last night I no longer felt it important to appear modest," she smiled, a little apprehension showing on her face.

"Don't blush. You are the most incredible thing I've seen in a lifetime, Emilia, and I appreciate breakfast more than you will ever know. I'm afraid I have to leave when we finish eating though," he said, ashamed and remorseful.

She looked down for a moment then looked him in the face. "I understand. Tell me, do you have a family in the United States? I mean, I get that a man who travels will sometimes look beyond his own wife and I'm not judging you if you are married, but I must know the truth," she finished.

Evers chuckled, "No, I'm not married, Emilia. It's just that my work calls me back to the States. I have many things to fulfill in order to bring a project I'm working on to completion."

He watched as she breathed a sigh of relief. Even though she tried to give him a pass for potentially being married, he realized that she was a woman of principle and did not want to be the cause for some marital angst back in the good ole U.S. of A. He wondered if she might feel the same attraction he felt, something more than just physical, but that weird chemistry thing so many psychologists talk about when two people just hit it off.

She placed their food on the table and sat across from him. He could tell she wanted to say something, but struggled with the proper words, that awkward morning after a first time sexual encounter. Evers reached across the table and squeezed her hand, offering a reassuring smile.

"Randy," she began, "I don't want you to think you are obligated to see me again. It's just that I…," she trailed off.

He winced when she called him Randy, the alias he was forced to use until he got out of the country. There was nothing more that he wanted than to tell Emilia his real name, but he knew that was impossible. In fact, he suspected an all-out search for General Vasquez was en route and his departure into Uruguay was immediate. When the authorities figured out he had not left the country in the proscribed time, they would begin to search for him; he did not want to be there when the search began.

"Obligated? I don't feel obligated, I feel like I would enjoy seeing you again," he replied. In his heart he knew he was serious, but his head told him that it would never work. *You're embroiled in some weird stuff, Billy, and you just killed an Argentinean dignitary. Plus, she thinks your name is Randy. Tell her again how you should see one another.*

She smiled at him, her teeth wonderfully straight and her gums healthy and pink. Her lips were full and ripe, her hair pulled into a ponytail. He wished he could stay with her for another day, but he knew that was not possible.

"Listen, Emilia, I have to leave today, and I realize that sounds bad after the discussion we were just having, but my work requires that I go," he said.

She looked down for a few seconds then lifted her face, sadness and beauty entwined to create an interesting and thought provoking mosaic.

"You don't owe me an explanation, Randy, only the truth. I hate to sound like the little girl who is lovesick and chases after a boy who only wanted to steal a kiss, and once the kiss has been stolen he is off to the next girl. Does that make sense?" she asked.

He ate a bite of his breakfast, loving the Latin flavors and spices she included in the omelet. He took a drink of his juice then responded to her.

"You make sense, Emilia. Like I said, I would love to see you again and it sounds as though you feel the same way. Once things settle down with work, I will call you, if you would be willing to share your number with me."

They ate in silence, Evers's mind already focusing on his escape plan from Argentina. Emilia stood and turned on a radio she kept in her kitchen that she listened to when she cooked. Warm Latin music floated from the speakers, but it was obvious neither were listening to it. A news story broke…

Evers watched Emilia's face as the news anchor reported the story. Although his Spanish was not good enough to translate everything being said, it was obvious that they were talking about the missing General Vasquez. Her mouth was slightly opened, a look of shock or despair, Evers could not tell which, then she clinched her jaw tight. She jutted her chin forward, the first look on her face replaced with a particular sternness.

"The leader of our military is missing and no one has seen him since yesterday," she said.

Evers felt a wave of uncertainty wash over him as he watched her reaction. His paranoia began creeping in and he fought to maintain a stoic look. Deep inside his chest he could feel his heart slamming his ribs.

"Maybe he decided he needed a little downtime. I'm not sure what it means for him to have disappeared for a day," Evers responded.

She stared at him for a moment before replying, "It's said that he is killing his own people, but he does it in such a way as to avoid publicity. Still, people say that he has ordered the murder of thousands of my countrymen and women. To be honest with you, it would not bother me if they found his car wrecked in some ditch and him dead in it."

His mouth twitched. *She has no idea that her wish has essentially come true.*

"Well," he began, "if he did murder all those people, perhaps karma will catch up to him."

She gave him a sad smile and continued eating her breakfast. He watched her and could tell from her body language that she liked him and wanted him to stay. How he wished he could stay with her, even for a few more days, but that possibility wasn't in the cards. Evers wondered if God truly did hate him.

When they finished eating she stood and took their plates to the sink. He walked behind her and wrapped his arms around her waist, lightly kissing the back of her neck. She leaned her head on his shoulder then turned and put her arms around his neck, pulling him close and offering a passionate kiss.

After a minute he pushed away from her and walked to the door, not stopping to look back.

Focus, Billy. You'll only put her in danger if you stay.

Evers walked eastward away from her apartment and the club, not wanting anyone to recognize him from the previous night and put his face in the same place despite the low probability. As he walked he thought about his night with Emilia. Sure the sex was great, but that part of the evening had much less meaning than did the intimacy of touching and talking. For him, that was what he missed most about not having someone in his life.

The walk helped him clear his mind. There was no doubt he would be roiled with emotion after his encounter, but the operationally trained portion of his brain knew it would eventually separate and compartmentalize the previous night. He focused on the SDR he was engaged in, his eyes sweeping back and forth until he felt Emilia's memory fade away, the previous evening quietly becoming another memory.

He hailed a cab, directing the driver to pull over in front of a random department store several blocks from his hotel. From there he conducted a thorough surveillance detection run, careful to double back several times in an effort to flush out a person, or persons, who might have developed an interest in him. He made it to the lot and spotted his car parked between two others. No one sat in either car adjacent to his own, but a group of three young men were propped against another car directly behind his and seemed to have taken an interest in him.

Evers scanned the area wondering if the three twenty-something's were working for someone or just hanging out in hopes of stirring up trouble. His instincts told him they were nothing more than thugs looking for an easy target; he hoped he wasn't going to be the one they decided to victimize today, because if they did, they were going to regret it.

The one closest to him stood with his arms crossed watching his approach. He pushed himself off the car as Evers walked across the lot toward his car. Evers remained focused on the obvious leader of the group, but kept the other two in his peripheral as well.

Under normal circumstances he would have made an effort to avoid any trouble or confrontation, but given his time sensitive situation, he altered his course and walked directly to the thug whose threatening posture seemed to falter at the sight of his "victim" moving toward him. Adrenaline hit his belly igniting a focus and ferocity that he had long since grown accustomed to when he found himself in life and death situations.

Miyamoto Musashi, Japan's most famous swordsman, wrote in his short treatise *A Book of Five Rings,* "You win battles by knowing the enemy's timing, and using a timing which the enemy does not expect." Evers had spent a considerable amount of time studying the work of Musashi, and that particular quote resonated with him like no other.

Evers grabbed the first man's jacket sleeve, the man he had come to identify as "Tough Guy," and pulled it toward his waist while simultaneously reaching under the other arm, finally rotating his hips into the man. In one felled swoop, he sent Tough Guy airborne, making sure to maintain his grip on the man's sleeve. O goshi was a basic and favorite throw he had learned many years earlier and when the man landed flat on his back, the wind driven from his lungs in one loud and audible exhale, he was happy that his old hardcore teacher had forced him to repeat it until it was perfected.

Quickly, Evers raised one size eleven foot and stomped down on top of Tough Guy's ankle. A satisfying crack rang out and the man screamed in pain. Rendering their leader ineffective, Evers turned his attention to the other two men who both stood with their mouths agape at what had just happened to their friend.

Another quote Evers always kept at the front of his mind was one written by the great Chinese general, Sun Tzu. His book *The Art of War* was required reading at all United States military colleges because of its timeless wisdom. A specific passage from the chapter about deploying a country's forces relayed to the reader that "Whilst you are unsure of victory, defend; when you are sure of victory, attack." Evers considered that passage, looked into the eyes of his two remaining adversaries, and attacked.

Evers launched himself at the second man whose eyes were wide with disbelief. In most instances, those who believe themselves to be on the offensive are shocked to find themselves fighting for their lives. Such was the case with this individual. In less time than it takes to blink, Evers grabbed him by one sleeve and one lapel and shot a *mawashi geri*, or round kick, into the outside of his thigh.

The powerful kick dropped the man to the pavement and Evers moved into position just above his face as the man grabbed his leg and rubbed, trying to ease the explosion of pain he was feeling in one small, centralized area. The shock of the kick and the enormous amount of pain he felt created the opening Evers needed. He dropped to one knee bringing a tightly clenched fist with him, smashing it into the man's jaw. Another crack and Evers knew the guy would be visiting the emergency room to have it wired shut, if he allowed him to live. The pain was such that his central nervous system shut down, the man knocked out and unaware that Evers was now moving to his other friend, the last to remain standing.

Tough Guy's third friend held both hands up in submission before turning to run. Evers was on him just as quickly as he had been the other two, and could hear the guy begin to scream, the fear and his own adrenaline creating the fight or flight syndrome warriors learn about in their first week of boot camp. Alternately, despite his speed, the adrenaline in Evers's system created a slowdown effect in his own mind. He watched his own actions appear in frames, not unlike still photos being moved horizontally in front of his eyes.

From the man's rear, Evers shot his right hand around his neck, his thumb rapidly cinching up and through his jacket's lapel. With his left, he hooked the man's own left arm in a half Nelson, exposing the carotid artery on the same side of his neck.

Evers squeezed the half-Nelson as he wrapped the lapel around the man's neck in a circular fashion, executing *kata-ha jime*, or shoulder choke. He felt the guy's body go limp, but he held the choke for a few more seconds to assure he was unconscious, finally releasing him and allowing the sleeping beauty to slide to the ground.

He turned his attention back to Tough Guy and took three long strides to reach him. The injured man writhed in agony, his ankle shattered and the pain gut-wrenching. Fear gripped him as he watched his attacker stand over him. Evers placed the ball of his foot over the man's ankle and pressed down. A fresh scream rose from his chest. In another swift move, Evers dropped a knee on the man's chest and listened as the scream stopped and the wind was driven upward and through his mouth and nose. He stood up and moved his foot back to the man's shattered ankle.

"What did you want with me?" Evers demanded.

"Nothing! I swear! We were only going to take your money, I promise, now get off my fucking leg!"

Evers pressed down harder and thought he could feel shattered pieces of bone beneath the sole of his shoe. Tough Guy's scream confirmed the sensation.

"One more time, what did you want with me?" Evers asked again.

"I already told you, just your money, that's it. Are you fucking crazy, man?" Tough Guy agonized.

Evers considered the question and briefly wondered the same thing. He pushed the question to the back of his mind and put a little more pressure on the broken ankle. Although satisfied that the three men just happened to pick on the wrong guy, he had to make a decision whether to eliminate them or let them live. Killing them would potentially draw more attention to him, attention he couldn't afford. There was also the problem and time consuming effort of disposing of three adult bodies.

On the other hand, there were three witnesses who had not only watched, but felt the wrath of an American who easily disabled and rendered them ineffectual. He weighed his options then turned his mind back to Tough Guy who was preparing to let out another agonizing scream.

"Listen to me. It's never a good idea to try to steal from another human being. Comprende? Especially a man who feels cornered—we're the most dangerous kind. If word gets back to me that you've talked to anyone about what happened here, I'll hunt you down and make sure you never attempt to rob anyone else," Evers warned.

"We won't, man, I swear. We won't say anything about you. Just please get off my fucking foot!" he begged.

"I'm going to leave now, but I want you to understand a few things first. Thirty minutes after my departure, even with that nasty injury, you're going to get pissed off and think you need to teach me a lesson by calling the authorities. In fact, your friends will take you to the hospital and while you are there you will be asked by the doctors what happened to your ankle. Like I told you a moment ago, if word gets back to me that you or your friends opened your mouth, I'll find you. And just in case you think you have an out if one of your buddies starts talking, understand that I will hold you personally responsible for their actions. Think you're in pain now? What will happen the next time I see you will make this feel like a tiny pinch on the arm, and that's what you'll feel before you take your last breath," he finished.

Tough Guy stared at Evers, and his eyes told him that he understood what he just conveyed. Evers felt reasonably sure that he was safe, at least long enough to get out of the country and to an airport. His victim looked like the pain would remind him to keep his mouth shut as well as reminding his friends to do the same.

Evers nodded at him then walked to his rental, unlocked the door and climbed inside. He watched as the two more seriously injured men rolled around on the ground while the third began to awake. An image appeared in his mind with a photo of himself and a caption below it reading "Warning: Choke Hazard." Evers laughed at the silliness of it all and hoped that Tough Guy was wrong, that he was not insane and the image was nothing more than his adrenalized central nervous system trying to downplay what had just happened.

He navigated back to Pistorini International Airport and found the rental car center. After dropping the car off, he walked toward the terminal with his bag as though he were catching a flight that day. He entered the departure area, made a few aggressive turns to check for a tail then found the escalator that took him to baggage claim. His chin was carefully tucked toward his chest so as to avoid the thousands of security cameras that were so prevalent in airports all over the world.

Once he was downstairs he walked outside and hailed a cab. He asked the driver to take him to the ferry that would get him to the Uruguayan island of Montevideo, the capital and home of their largest international airport. The ferry ride was three hours long, an almost unbearable amount of time for Evers to remain in one place without his paranoia driving him insane, but the bottleneck also yielded an advantage—anyone following him would be bound to the same boat ride, and most likely flushed into the open as a result.

The Burquebus was the independently operated ferry line that scuttled passengers from Buenos Aires to Montevideo for the equivalent of eighty-two United States dollars. Evers made the Uruguayan monetary exchange before shuffling off to purchase his ticket. His research told him that he would have to proceed through customs once he arrived in Uruguay, but his sense was the level of scrutiny would be considerably less than that of an international airport. In addition, security was typically lax on ferries, although he could not think of one good reason why. To sink a boat with a couple hundred passengers aboard would be a major scare coup for any terrorist outfit, but Evers figured a sinking vessel wasn't nearly as newsworthy as a plane flown into a skyscraper or as dramatic as a video of one man beheading another.

He boarded the gigantic vessel and sat down next to an older gentleman with a scruffy two day beard and clothes that smelled of sweat, musk, and a lack of detergent. In the very least, the odor emanating from the gentleman, he assumed, would keep curious people from eyeballing him or attempting to commit his face to memory. The heat inside the ferry intensified the man's aroma, and he noticed people walking to seats further away from their location. He knew, however, the remaining seats directly behind and adjacent to them would eventually fill, but for the time being he was content with his view of those passengers entering and being seated.

No one stepping onto the ferry made him uneasy or uncomfortable. In all his time working in the shadows, the things he learned to lean heavily upon were his instincts and ability to spot a stalker or hunter. No matter how much an individual tried to mask his identity, whether it be in the way he dressed, or talked, or even his gait, there was still that primordial aura he gave off and could never hide.

Not that it would matter whether or not someone intended him harm at that point, but he could not imagine anyone stupid enough to make an aggressive move with all the witnesses sitting around him.

His nerves momentarily settled and his anxiety lowered, he closed his eyes and rested. The long ride to Montevideo coupled with the encounter he had with the thugs in the parking lot had exhausted him, not to mention coming down off the adrenaline high.

His chest rose and fell, his breathing deep and peaceful, and his thoughts filled with images of Emilia. The ride across the La Plata inlet was smooth and uneventful. Other passengers passed the time by talking and looking out windows at the spectacular South American coastline. Several people read magazines or books, and many closed their eyes after inserting buds into their ears to listen to their favorite music.

Evers slept, his dreams, thankfully, were quiet.

Arlington, Virginia
9:09 AM

Buddy sat at his kitchen table staring out a window, lit cigar burning in an ashtray that had not been dumped and cleaned in some time. The morning sun was shining radiantly and the bright blue sky lacked clouds. Planes passed overhead leaving contrails in their wake, in search of the three major international airports around the area. Trees swayed to a cool late spring breeze pushed by a cold front attempting to gain a foothold before the summer sun usurped its frigid throne. Throughout the courtyard below, Japanese cherry trees stood in full bloom, their beauty long since prostituted and convoluted by a government and locale whose lack of understanding of Japan's love of simplicity, especially in nature, had given rise to an economic boon known as the National Cherry Blossom Festival.

The original trees were a gift from Ozaki, mayor of Tokyo, some twenty-nine years before the United States elected to drop two nuclear bombs on an already war-torn and devastated Japan. The message was clear to the rest of the world: Don't Fuck With Us. Many countries heeded that warning, while others worked covertly in hopes of gaining access to the power of the split atom. And while many other, smaller countries thumbed their collective noses at the United States, the U.S. went about its business of exploiting natural resources needed in an ever-growing and oil hungry country, rather than entering into business deals. "Sources and methods" would eventually be a catchphrase used by covert operators, and their bosses, as a way of distancing themselves psychologically from the global pain they were administering.

A couple of cardinals sang songs to would-be mates and danced about the boughs of the trees, their red bodies somehow creating the ironic appearance of matted blood on pure linen, a reminder of the nuclear atrocities committed decades earlier at the expense of people who were guilty of living in a country whose leadership had declared war against the United States.

He reached for his cigar and took a long drag, the smoke drifting to the ceiling, hitting his ceiling fan as it slowly spun, furthering the yellow tobacco stains that had begun years prior. His lungs filled with the cigar's comforting flavor before pushing it through his nose and mouth, seconds before a coughing fit struck him. He put a handkerchief to his mouth, the coughing increasing in intensity before tapering off seconds later. He glanced at the piece of cloth, blood splattered in small globs, not unlike the scene of the cardinal sitting on a limb of the cherry tree.

With one hand he placed the kerchief on the table next to him then puffed on the cigar again, careful not to inhale. He wondered how Young Buck was getting along but felt reasonably certain that he was okay, as he had received no news of his capture or death. His mind drifted between reports of death on a global scale and the gloomy stories of suicides by family members who had lost loved ones, and finally his discussion with Davis.

Something was missing, some component that Buddy had been unable to piece together and Davis either was not telling him, or did not know himself. He made a point of moving that disconcerting thought that his primary intel connection at the Farm might have misled or lied to him about what was going on; if he found out that was the case, he would deal with that later.

"Focus on what we know," he said aloud.

"Weaponized SARS and Ebola released and spreading at an alarming rate in urban areas and third world countries, a plane flown into a nuclear reactor, mass killings in Argentina…" his words drifted.

Buddy jumped when his cell phone began ringing, its sound agonizingly loud against the silence of his apartment. He looked at the number and recognized it—Virginia, local, and one he knew wasn't being tracked by some federal entity.

He clicked on but didn't say anything.

"Hey," came a voice from the other end.

"Hey," Buddy answered, responding to Davis.

"Have you heard anything out of India?"

"No, but I'm sure you're going to enlighten me," Buddy replied, his voice curt.

"There were two bombs detonated in Delhi, one inside the Ambience Mall and one in the parking lot just outside the mall itself," Davis offered.

"Nothing very unusual about that, Allen, so I'm assuming you've got something more for me," to the point again.

"Of course," Davis said, annoyance in his voice.

Buddy had to smile at the youngster's bravado. He would be a formidable ally or opponent, depending on the direction his career path took him. Buddy would have to be careful to not underestimate him going forward.

Davis paused and sighed audibly, perhaps to gather his thoughts and consider what he was about to say, but, Buddy suspected, more for dramatic effect. The move was right out of the "how to play your asset" CIA handbook, so much so that Buddy almost laughed out loud. Buddy waited the ploy out, not commenting on Davis's hesitation.

"Look, as with a lot of what I tell you, this is classified information and hasn't been released to the general public yet, although it's a matter of time until it's reported internationally," Davis said.

Buddy remained silent, not wanting to appear anxious about any new information that might help him put enough pieces together to at least form a partial picture. He was also cognizant of his breathing, controlling his respiration and pulse. Davis had given him workable intelligence in the past, much of which had helped him and some of his contracted folks finish missions and return home safely.

"Those explosions in India were radiological dispersal devices. Radiation levels are relatively low, as is expected when one of those things is detonated, but the political and economic impact globally will be significant," Davis stated.

"An RDD? A dirty bomb has finally been detonated in a populated area. Any idea about the casualty rate?" Buddy asked.

"Not yet. We suspect the total number of deaths will be comparatively low compared to, say, the attacks of 9/11, but that's not what is bothering people," Davis replied.

"People, huh? You mean agency egg heads who are worried about losing jobs because they didn't see this coming?" Buddy asked, the sarcasm thick in his voice.

"It's doubtful that anyone will lose a job in the States over this, but the Chief of Station in India could be at risk. His potential removal wouldn't really be a loss for the region and would probably suffice when the blood hungry media learns about the radiological implications. But there are others outside the agency who are gravely concerned about the economic impact the explosions will create."

Buddy did not have to think hard about who was troubled by the explosions and the proverbial subterfuge that would follow as a result. The U.S.'s economic recovery since The Great Recession had been one made up primarily of rhetoric and printed dollars not backed by anything remotely associated with something like the gold standard. What that meant was the dollar's value was based upon consumer confidence and nothing of intrinsic value.

"So, what are you thinking now, Allen?" Buddy asked, one brow raised.

"About what? Do you mean I'm convinced that the recent events around the world are somehow related? If that's your question then I have to admit that you were probably right," Davis responded.

Although it was contrary to his nature, Buddy did not dwell on Davis's admission that he was most likely correct about the mass killings and intentional viral infections. Instead the wheels in his brain turned at high speed.

"The larger question is how was it possible all of this was coordinated right under the noses of every major spy agency in the world?" Buddy asked.

"I can't speak for the other agencies…"

"I don't think you can speak for the fucking farmers either," Buddy interrupted, using the 'farm' moniker that a lot of spooks use to describe the CIA.

"Listen, I've been straight with you about what I know, Buddy," Davis stated, struggling to maintain his composure.

Buddy reached for his cigar and puffed again. "Well, that doesn't explain how a global attack could be planned and executed without someone talking. Did you ever follow up on the Trowton feller?"

"Yes, I did some research and found a few interesting tidbits of information," Davis responded, his voice considerably more measured and controlled.

Buddy moved the phone to his other ear and exhaled a cloud of smoke. Again, he did not speak, waiting instead for Davis to continue. He was sure his ability to hold his tongue spooked the young agent, which was the end result he was hoping for.

"Are you familiar with the Bilderbergers?" Davis asked.

"I've heard references and rumors, but can't say that I'm really familiar with who they are," Buddy replied.

"Not who, but *what*. The Bilderbergers are a group of the richest, most powerful and influential people in the world. World leaders, including United States presidents, current and former, come together once a year to discuss global issues like climate change, economics, disease and other topics that they perceive as critical. They earned their name because the first meeting was held at the Hotel Bilderberger in the Netherlands in 1954. Their discussions are uber-private and each member is sworn to secrecy. I mean these people are the world's elite, Buddy, and their money buys influence anywhere and anytime they decide they need to change some policy or start a war or possibly redistribute a nation's wealth. These people are the proverbial cogs that make the world turn."

"Sounds like a joyful bunch of folks to party with, Allen," Buddy said. "What do they have to do with Trowton?"

"Like I said, they are the richest, most powerful people in the world. Trowton certainly qualifies monetarily for inclusion into their exclusive fraternity, and we learned that he recently participated at a Bilderberger conference," Davis reported.

"I thought you said this was a highly secretive group. How do you know Trowton took part in this meeting?" Buddy asked.

"What's discussed inside is highly confidential, but the paparazzi stays hot on the trails of participants once they find out the location of the meeting. The meeting site changes each year and once the media learns of its location, they line up to snap pictures of the limos pulling up to the venue. Several photos were taken of Trowton as he arrived and left The Grove Estate in Waterford, England this past December," Davis explained.

"I see," Buddy responded, "but are you assuming he is mixed up with what is happening around the world right now?"

"I prefer to call it an educated guess," Davis offered.

"Yeah, you agency boys do a lot of that. So, what are you thinking?" Buddy posed.

"Sounds like we need to get to Mr. Simon Trowton and ask him nicely if he's responsible for global murder, or knows who is. It would also be beneficial if we could understand the motives behind it all," Davis said, a little too enthusiastically.

Buddy took another pull on the cigar and exhaled the smoke. He watched as the cloud inched along in a white mass then fell apart and disappeared. Long, dry ashes hung limply from the cigar's end, heavy enough to make it appear that they would fall at any moment, but short enough that Buddy knew it wasn't time to dump them. All experienced cigar smokers understood the "ash rule" and refuse to pat them into an ashtray until absolutely necessary.

He furrowed his brow then asked, "Who is 'we,' Allen? You said it a couple of times, so I'm curious about whether there's a job opportunity awaiting me."

Davis waited the obligatory five seconds before responding. Buddy suppressed a grin as he imagined Davis sitting through the interrogation and manipulation courses they taught at Langley. In his mind's eye he could see the youngster furtively taking notes, on the edge of his seat, as a non-operative instructor explained the ins and outs of the human psyche. To their credit, Buddy was well aware that such amateur tactics worked well when speaking with the uninitiated, but against a seasoned operator the attempt to make him uncomfortable was useless. He waited Davis out, his hand fingering the cigar that he had placed back in the ashtray moments earlier.

"Well, if I'm not mistaken, you already have a stake in this operation, although I am uncertain who you are employing. Our last conversation would lead me to believe you are deeply involved. Your country would appreciate any help you would give it in unraveling this mystery and bringing it to closure," Allen stated, his tone matter of fact.

This time Buddy was unable to keep the laugh inside. "My country would appreciate my help? You do realize who you are speaking with, yes? I've given more to my country than it will ever be able to repay, Davis, so let me be clear with you—if you want my help, it's going to cost Uncle Sam, and it's going to cost him a lot. Whether I have any interests beyond what you are already involved in is irrelevant. Have I asked you for updates? Sure. Do I care what you do beyond this moment? Probably not," Buddy finished, his own tone harsh, although he was far from convincing himself that he was being forthright with Davis.

Davis's youth and inexperience pervaded his offer, and Buddy's years spent dealing with both experienced and inexperienced CIA agents made the conversation easier for him, and difficult for the former. For a fleeting second Buddy actually felt sorry for the youngster, but that feeling quickly passed and his focus became even more resolved.

On the other end of the line Davis inhaled audibly then exhaled louder, the audio signal of stress and the following mental attempt to remove it from the body. Buddy could almost see Davis's lungs filling with air and his cheeks puffing outward as the air was forced from them. He pulled the cigar to his lips and took another long drag from it, the smoke filling his mouth and some of it seeping into his lungs.

"I could probably arrange something," Davis stated, attempting to sound like he was conceding the point.

"There was never any doubt in my mind that you could. You're a good man, Allen. Don't let the agency ruin that," Buddy stated, his voice conciliatory and genuine. Deep down, Buddy had developed a keen likeness for the young agent despite his inexperience. Perhaps his inexperience was what drew him to the youngster, or maybe it was his own paternal instinct, that same feeling that had interceded so long ago with Young Buck. No matter which, he felt an obligation to help forge this particular agent, to make him something his country could be proud of, even if his government might hate him for it later. Yes, it was a cruel way to look at youth, but it was the way of the world. Buddy's own manipulative mind refused to separate what was right from what would land him with a substantial payday or what might actually help mankind at some point and time during its development. *If mankind can keep from destroying itself first.*

Another deep breath and exhale. "Well, don't go getting all sexually excited about the plausibility of extorting your country, Buddy. There's some checking I will have to do and confirming that you are eligible for this op, but I feel good that I can make it happen," Davis proclaimed, his own self-importance ringing through as Buddy shook his head.

"I want to tell you something," Buddy began, "there's a guy I know, I've always called him Young Buck, but he has outgrown that nickname. He was a youthful, arrogant individual once upon a time, but he's now a seasoned human being. Maybe it's time for someone new to wear that moniker."

Davis let the slight pass by without comment. It was evident that Buddy was referring to him, although he wondered what part of their discussion had led him down that path. Regardless, he tried hard to maintain his composure and control his breathing, although he wondered if Buddy had earlier heard him exhale.

Buddy smiled at Davis's silence. He could imagine the consternation written on his face and the mental wrestling match taking place in his mind to remain quiet. It was a sign that he was maturing and trying to control his emotions. Perhaps one day his seasoning would afford him an opportunity for advancement on the Farm, but for now Buddy enjoyed having a key contact working inside who, at times, provided useful information despite not being wholly seasoned.

"Give me some time to make an inquiry. I'll try to have an answer for you today. I suspect, given the international attention these items are getting, many governments will want the problem to simply go away," Davis said.

Yeah, 'go away' so they can deny any involvement or knowledge of the security breakdowns, sitting at the same table or in the same room as a potential mass murderer and being complicit in a movement to depopulate the Earth, Buddy thought.

"Alright, Allen, I'll be here anxiously awaiting your call," Buddy's voice rife with sarcasm.

On the other end Davis actually chuckled. "You really are a cynical old bastard, Buddy."

Smith smiled and clicked off and reached for his cigar. Right then another coughing fit hit him, ashes from the cigar falling to the floor as his body convulsed. He reached for his handkerchief and held it to his mouth.

After the fit passed, he withdrew the kerchief and looked at it out of habit. He took a deep breath, thankful no new blood splatter adorned the fabric.

He sat in silence for an hour, then two, puffing his cigar and staring out the window. Birds came and went, and a cool breeze shook the limbs of the trees adorning the courtyard. He watched as a squirrel ran over the ground and up a small oak in search of a bounty not yet born from the tree. Another cigar lit and sitting idly by in the ashtray, its smoke tendrils drifting up and cascading over his torso, waited for his hand to lift it to his lips and puff it like a slow moving freight train compressing water into steam and blowing the residue skyward.

An ache throbbed deep within his chest, a pain he knew he couldn't compartmentalize in his brain or hope to self-heal after a particular length of time. He tried to ignore it, masking the pain with liquor, but recently he realized how weary he was becoming. The blood splatters were getting larger and presenting themselves much more frequently, and thoughts and memories of days past were ever present in his mind. He realized, on a subconscious level, that he was reviewing and rationalizing his life.

Karma, getting yours in the end, or whatever a person wants to call it, was never anything Buddy believed in; rather, he insisted that life was simply *there* and the removal of life was part of the equation. But now he wondered if he had been wrong all those years, and whether the ghosts he had created over a lifetime were set to torture him for an eternity. There would be no vindication for the things he had done and understood that if an eternity in Hell was awaiting him, he would have to suck it up like the good soldier he was and deal with it.

A chill ran down his back and his body quivered in response. He shook his head and chuckled nervously. Warriors, young and old, understand the psychological impact of bad news and the toll it takes on the human psyche. Sitting alone in an apartment only intensified the emotions he was feeling, but he realized the feeling would pass in time. He capitulated as the feeling of dread overtook him. His eyes closed, he imagined dark, fleshless hands grabbing his ankles and pulling him down...down...down into a murky abyss filled with things his imagination refused to acknowledge.

Faces of those whose lives he ended prior to their expiration date smiled at him, small holes in their heads and rivulets of blood leaking over noses that were rotting from the skin that struggled to keep them intact. Their gruesome smiles and strange sounds were only surpassed by what he imagined was their odor. *I can actually smell death.*

People whose names he could not recall appeared in his mind. One such memory drifted across his line of sight before turning and standing within an inch of his face. So close, in fact, that he could almost smell its decaying breath. The memory tilted its head and stared into his eyes searching for recognition, the face strangely familiar to Buddy, but one he could not recall with any level of certainty. One thing he was sure of—he owned the memory and the face belonged to someone he had removed, even if he could not recall the logistics and timing of doing so.

The thoughts paraded over his field of vision for a few minutes before fading to the back of his mind. A keen sense of relief flooded his body after the haunting visions recused themselves. His eyes dropped and he thought of Young Buck and his struggles with PTSD. He wondered if what he had just dealt with was what bothered his protégé in his sleep. He suspected it was and felt a twinge of sympathy twist and wind its way through his body.

Mercifully, his phone rang, pulling him away from his thoughts and visions of times long since passed. He looked at his cell display and saw that Davis was calling. Buddy let the phone ring two more times before picking up. There was no sense in appearing anxious, especially since he wasn't.

"Smith," he answered.

"Hey," Davis replied.

Buddy held the phone and did not speak, knowing that silence makes the other party uncomfortable and more likely to talk to fill the vocal void. He also understood that Davis had learned the technique during his on-boarding with the Christians In Action. Goading Davis was something he enjoyed, although he sensed the kid was getting better at his job and would eventually learn to control his emotions.

Davis exhaled loud enough for Buddy to realize his silence had irritated him. He smiled and considered apologizing to him for the mind game. *Fuck him—he'll figure it out one day.*

"I got an answer," Davis began.

"Okay," Buddy said.

"We'll bring you on board, but this must remain low key. Trowton needs to be questioned, but he doesn't need to know who is doing the questioning," Davis replied.

"And if he doesn't answer…" Buddy asked, his question a leading one.

"Then it's safe to assume his silence is an admission of guilt, or at least one of complicity," Davis responded.

"I'm assuming at that point you would need him rendered unable to speak should he elect to hold his tongue?" Buddy asked.

"You assume correctly, but remember, Trowton is a very powerful man and discretion is an absolute must. If you deviate from that course, the United States will deny any and all involvement with you or anyone you are working with," Davis stated, the company line officially towed.

"Aren't you the good little soldier," Buddy drawled. "Of course I know what's at stake here, Allen, and you know I take my job seriously, so there's no need to threaten an old man who has seen his country turn its back on good men in the past."

It was Davis's turn to remain silent. Buddy imagined him sitting in a chair, his face beet red as he struggled to control his breathing.

"The price is a quarter million wired to the same account as last time," Buddy said.

"Done," Davis replied as he clicked off.

Two hundred fifty-thousand United States dollars to bring about the end to random global eugenics. Only in America. Buddy shook his head, drew deeply on his cigar and opened his laptop. He almost laughed at Evers's creativity and ingenuity in finding the encrypted email server. After finding out about it he asked Davis to check into its security and had been told the CIA was working overtime trying to figure out how to decode the encryption. Thus far they had been totally unsuccessful.

"Score one for the good guys, the bad guys, and anyone else using this damned thing," he muttered.

He typed on the keyboard, sending Evers a message he hoped he would be able to retrieve soon. As tempting as it was, he knew better than to try to contact him via cell phone; he kept it turned off to avoid being tracked and only turned it on when he needed to call. All he could do now was wait.

Part III

Now if I let this dead man linger in me, I might get a little idle in my ways
So I'm going down to the Celebration River
Gonna take this dead man down to a watery grave
~ The Imperials ~

Boiling heat, summer stench, 'neath the black the sky looks dead
Call my name through the dream and I'll hear you scream again
~ Soundgarden ~

Driving faster in my car, falling farther from just what we are
Smoke a cigarette and lie some more 'cause conversations kill
Falling faster in my car.
Time to take her home her dizzy head is conscious laden
Time to take a ride and leave today no conversation
Time to take her home, her dizzy head is conscious laden
Time to wage along, to wage along, to wage along
~ Stone Temple Pilots ~

Pearls and swine bereft of me
Long and weary my road has been
I was lost in the cities, alone in the hills
No sorrow or pity for leaving, I feel

I am not your rolling wheels
I am the highway
I am not your carpet ride
I am the sky
~ Audioslave ~

London, England
10:21 PM

Trowton could not stop sweating, even after taking ice cold showers and drinking a variety of iced drinks. So nervous had he become that his teeth constantly chattered. He thought his heart would leap from his chest or simply explode—either of the two alternatives would have been acceptable to him.

Within him, there seemed to be an ever present feeling of foulness gliding through his veins. The feeling made him feel helpless and vulnerable, sick and despondent, and he longed for a quick death but lacked the guts to take his own life. He felt weak and ineffectual, consumed over the past several days with images of hideous beings whose eyes glowed red as he lay in his bed. Sleep avoided him, and he tried to convince himself the images were not real, could not possibly be anything more than his own imagination running wild through a mind that had consistently served him well his entire life.

His visitor, Abaddon, had been in constant contact since his order to move the nuke, and despite his inclination to the contrary, Trowton could not refuse the man. As it was, since Abaddon's more frequent visits, the coincidence of his greasy feeling and inability to sleep seemed, to him at least, to be related. There was no evidence to support his theory, but then what evidence beyond what he knew already did he really need?

He looked in his bathroom mirror and was shocked at what he saw. His cheeks were sunken, his face emaciated, and what had been a bountiful head of hair was now falling out in clumps. Trowton's first thought was of images he had seen of the Holocaust. Ironically, he had secretly admired Hitler's ambition to rid the world of the Jews, although Trowton's own aspirations were not so narrowly envisioned.

The discussions he had had with various academics, some of which were leading scientists in their related fields, and the significant amount of time he dedicated to studying the global impact of humans created within him a desire to curtail the imminent population growth that would destroy the Earth. Human beings, in his opinion, were like termites. They ate away at all the natural resources and cared little for the planet that gave everything they needed to survive. In the name of capitalist endeavors, they polluted the air with toxins and carbon dioxide from factories, vehicles and common household chemicals. Humans, without thought or consequence, dumped harmful chemicals into the ground and streams used for drinking water.

Yes, something had to be done to curb the planet's population growth before humans were allowed to completely destroy it. He grew weary of the uneducated masses screaming about their God who placed things on the

Earth to be used and consumed as they saw fit. How ignorant they are to believe such nonsense! And God, that imaginary father figure in the sky who watched over everyone, yet refused to intercede to protect that which he built. God they say? He knew there was no God, and the Bible was a false narrative created to control the ignorant. If only the people of the world could see the harsh truth as he had come to know and understand it.

And then came the momentum behind the idealistic nature of his plan. Seeds planted at various Bilderberger meetings, secure, private phone calls with men he could trust to not only be a part of his radical plan, but to execute each layer as they had promised to do. Lab created disease injected into those who continued to consume resources out of necessity in Africa, detonation of dirty bombs in India and a suicide mission into a nuclear factory in France. Trowton despised releasing nuclear material into the atmosphere and ground, but he knew if his plan came to fruition that the planet would eventually restore itself. And the mass killings in South America were messy and archaic, against his own moral beliefs to be honest.

Guns were tools of destruction that belonged in the past and should have faded away into distant memories like the horse drawn carriage of the nineteenth century. But alas, there were those who insisted on having, keeping and using them. Trowton knew he really shouldn't complain about the deaths caused by firearms, but he also quickly realized they were used in countless wars to control the very resources being consumed that he was trying to protect.

And now his plan was in motion. Recent reports estimated the total decimation of human beings at around three and a half million. It wasn't nearly enough, but it was a good start. If only he could rid himself of Abaddon. His stench hung around his neck like a filthy albatross, and threatened his sanity like nothing he had ever experienced.

He dressed stylishly, his shirt an earthy light brown tone and his chic Defend skinny jeans custom tailored to his thin waist. His brown Belen loafers were double-strapped and worn by only Europe's most affluent. Trowton completed the ensemble with a ball cap to hide the missing hair and to offer light disguise should some wayward gentry recognize him and attempt to rob him of his wallet.

He was so tired of being cooped up in his own place that he was willing to risk a walk into the world that he loathed. Walking helped clear his head and clarify what his next steps would be. He took the stairs down into his building's lobby and waited as the doorman pushed open the large glass door, the sights and smells of London's nighttime hitting him all at once.

In the distance he could hear the whine of a police car siren. The smell of the street was strong and pungent, a combination of tar and the incessant dampness that accompanies a British evening. Through the tree boughs wafted fishy scents from the stagnant Thames River, its waters long polluted despite tremendous efforts to correct centuries of putrid human sewage discharge and other contaminates being dumped over its banks.

Cars buzzed over the various bridges that connected the two sides of the city, their headlights diminished by the bright lights strung across the supporting cables and hung upon giant poles lining each side of the roadway. A few late night restaurants were still pedaling their wares, but the smell of food did nothing to help ease the feeling of starvation in Trowton's belly.

In a deep quadrant of his brain he understood that his starvation was a spiritual one, rather than physical. And no matter how much he tried reasoning that spirituality was for the ignorant, something gnawed at his mind. He could visualize three gnashes over the grey matter that was his brain, blood weeping from the wounds and dripping to the base of his skull. A shudder ran over his body as he attempted to push the thought away.

He began sorting through the two biggest problems he was faced with: moving a nuclear warhead across international waters, and the man who held an icy grip on his soul. First, the warhead. As directed, he had procured an armed missile on the black market, using layers between him and the Russian willing to sell it. Next, he hired someone to eliminate the thread of people leading back to him after the purchase was complete. Getting the shipment to port through Cyprus had been much less complicated, and moving the container over open waters even less so.

Still, even with his plans to reduce the world's population by at least twenty-five percent, the thought of detonating a fully armed nuclear warhead made his stomach roll. Perhaps it was because there was some strange sense of responsibility he felt toward his fellow humans, or maybe it was because he did not want to contribute further to an already polluted and contaminated planet. He could not be certain what was driving the remorse he was feeling. Then suddenly it hit him and he was forced to admit the reason for his hesitation: he would bear direct responsibility for the detonation.

Yes, it was true that his plans were being doled out by those with whom he had collaborated, but his hands were not covered in blood, at least not directly. This was different, though. Now he was the person executing the purchase, movement and ultimate detonation of a WMD over the heart of a city already rocked by two planes slamming into its mammoth Towers.

To make matters worse, he would bear direct responsibility for not only polluting the air, but the ocean and some rivers as well. That ran counter to everything he believed in, but mostly it was the human annihilation he would delve out that ate away at his insides like a ravenous parasite coursing through his intestines. Then there was that greasy feeling he felt comingled with his soul. It was as though his spirit was attempting to slide through him and away from his own physical self, while his mind's hands fought to contain it and keep it inside. The sensation was maddening, and he was vaguely aware that his spiritual battle was creating its own form of insanity.

Trowton stopped and considered his mental health. "Crazy people seldom realize they have teetered over the edge," he said aloud.

He shook his head then continued down the sidewalk, walking parallel to the River Thames. The cloudy night glowed red from the city's lights, just one more problem with overpopulation and mass urbanization.

Within the next three weeks the cargo ship containing the warhead and missile would arrive at the New Jersey shipping docks where it would be off-loaded and remain stored until Abaddon either took control of it, or gave him specific orders on detonation. There was still time to resolve the problem, but he had to think and act with haste.

Just as urgent was his relationship with the man that had control over his mind and spirit. So strange had the procession of events been with Abaddon that Trowton had never requested his contact information, but simply complied with his every demand, no rebuttal and no questions asked. How it was possible that a renowned businessman and very intelligent person like himself could so freely give himself over like that both perplexed and scared him.

Not knowing where the man resided was problem number one. If he could not find him, he certainly could not have him removed. For a few seconds he wondered if it was conceivable to have the man eliminated. Abaddon's hold on him was deep and complex, so much so that Trowton felt it was supernatural.

He considered his different meetings with Abaddon, the logical part of his mind finally overtaking the fear and irrational aspects of his psyche. They had first met at a restaurant, then later at his apartment. Each time he was drinking something.

"Could that bastard be poisoning me, or dropping something into my drink that would almost force me to comply with his wishes?" he asked himself. "The plausibility of him being within reach of my drink each time we met was substantial, and I have little doubt that he would go to such measures to have his way with someone."

He continued thinking about the Abaddon situation. The only piece of the puzzle he had not put together in his mind yet was the thought control the man had over him when he called on his phone. There was little doubt in his mind that the evil man had most likely given him enough of the poison that the residual effects were carried over for several days. Trowton told himself he would do some research on the subject when he returned home.

The reasoning and rationalizing continued for another hour, the walk making him feel so much better that he actually smiled for the first time in weeks. He stuffed his hands in his tight pockets, taking time to look around. The oft traveled ports and cities that he visited did little to please him more than his own. London was a fabulous place, just overcrowded and stealing resources at an alarming rate. Naturally, Londoners did not consume the

Earth's resources like the filthy Americans, but that was only because their land mass was considerably smaller.

The same thoughts continued buzzing around in his head as he walked further and further from his apartment. He considered diverting the shipment to another port and selling the missile back to the Russians. Even if he lost money in the deal, he felt as though there would be some recompense for his stained soul.

"Soul. I'm not a religious man, and can't fathom why I continue thinking about my soul being greasy or stained. What the fuck is wrong with me? Have I allowed Abaddon to consume so much of me that I've convinced myself that I'm damned for an eternity?" He said to no one in particular.

"I think you know the answer to your question already," came a voice from behind.

Trowton almost jumped through his skin, subsequently tripping on his own feet and stumbling as he turned to see from where the voice had come. Standing there on the dimly lit sidewalk was the man he had been thinking about for over an hour.

"How the fuck did you find me," Trowton screamed!

"I suggest lowering your voice, Simon, lest you test my pleasant disposition. After all, you've called my name numerous times in the last two hours. I could only presume you needed to speak with me," Abaddon chided.

"I wasn't calling you," Trowton choked from a constricted throat, his heart already hammering in his chest and the adrenaline surging through his body. He was prepared to run for his life, but what remained of his common sense told him to stand down and pay attention. Some vague awareness recalled the conversation he was having with himself about his drink being poisoned. Confusion ran through his mind like a strong wind through a massive canyon.

Abaddon watched Trowton's face with a certain amusement. Trowton had a sinking feeling that his thoughts were not only being controlled, but read. His face twisted as the mental anguish further seized his emotions.

Without hesitation, Abaddon spoke to him.

"We have a new problem."

Trowton's teeth chattered, "What problem? Our plans have been executed flawlessly."

Abaddon's lip snarled, "You fool. Did you really believe that instituting a plan like yours could be conducted without suspicion or some form of outside intervention?"

"I...I...I don't understand. I have been very careful to keep the communication trail back to me at a minimum," he pleaded.

"Yes, but it would appear that under duress, even those you believed to be most loyal or highly trained will give up the most secretive of information," Abaddon hissed.

"But who? I have heard from few since the plan's implementation," Trowton responded, his British accent stately despite his fear.

"It would seem that a certain military general has given up your name and now the Americans are aware of your potential involvement in this global plan of genocide," Abaddon replied, a wry, strange smile on his face.

"Vasquez? Vasquez gave me up? To whom? Why would he do such a thing? He was deeply involved in the movement and directly responsible for the thinning in Argentina, and he was well protected by the president. I don't understand," Trowton said, the pitch in his voice rising with each question.

Abaddon raised one hand to silence Trowton. "I'm afraid humans are frail creatures and will provide any information asked of them if under distress or discomfort. The fine general was obviously made to talk on less than voluntary terms."

Trowton raised an inquisitive brow. "How do you know this?"

"I know a great many things," Abaddon replied, the menace in his voice was a veiled threat on his tongue.

Another chill ran through Trowton as another police siren blared in the not-so-far distance.

"So he was captured? By whom?" Trowton asked, his voice shaky.

"Now, that is a wonderful question, Simon, and much more worthy of your analytical mind. We must get to the root cause of a problem before we are able to correct it, wouldn't you say?" Abaddon asked, his tone rich with sarcasm.

He continued, "Apparently, General Vasquez was prone to lunchtime rendezvous with a particular young lady with whom he had met several months ago. As luck would have it, a particular individual picked up on his rather animalistic ritual and awaited his return to his car. It was there that he was interrogated and shot. His brains, what few the idiot had, were littered about the back seat. A truly gruesome site as word would have it."

Trowton choked again and his pulse quickened to the point of making his fingers throb with each beat of his heart. His legs wobbled and his knees began to buckle. Abaddon watched him with mild interest.

"Pull yourself together Simon. There is no time for squeamishness. If you are to continue carrying out our plans, you must prepare yourself. Vasquez was a weak-minded old man, blinded by a false sense of security and power. You would do well to learn from the mistake you made in trusting someone like him."

"What do we do?" Trowton asked. "If the Americans know that I have been leading the movement, they will come after me before my work is completed."

"My sources tell me that only a handful of Americans are aware of your involvement, and the one who would act upon the General's information is being dealt with as we speak. It is critical that you not waver on the warhead being moved into the New York City harbor, Simon, elsewise I will be unable to protect you any longer."

"Protect me? What do you mean? How have you been protecting me?" he spluttered.

"Are you really so naïve as to believe that you have conducted this operation alone without assistance from those who want to see it through? Why do you think I contacted you to begin with, Simon? I have been keeping watch over you since our first meeting. Do not disappoint me by thinking of not completing this mission again. If you do, the next time we meet," he stepped face to face with Trowton, "will not be pleasant."

Montevideo, Uruguay
2:14 PM

Evers sat in a seat by his gate at Carrasco International Airport, his eyes still heavy after the trip across the bay. Once he reached Montevideo, he sought out an internet café in Ciudad Vieja, the Old City, to check his secured email. A message from Buddy was awaiting him.

We have a strong lead on someone involved in creating this shit storm. Need you to contact me asap. Hope all has gone well with you. Reports about a certain missing someone have been floating all over the net for a couple of days now. Lots of conspiracy theory but nothing factual or concrete. Let me know when you receive this and when we can speak.

Evers left a brief note saying he was fine and that he would be contacting him soon before closing the browser and purging the computer's url cache. Out of habit he wiped the keyboard with the sleeve of his shirt, his paranoia raging full steam ahead.

It had been a while since he had eaten so he found a sidewalk café selling pan-fried cakes called torta frita. The inside of the delicacy was doughy and sweet; his stomach thanked him by growling as he stuffed the torta in his mouth. There was a newspaper stand next to the torta cart with a picture of the General on the cover. His marginal Spanish allowed him to get the gist of the article which stated Vasquez was still missing and the search intensified. No arrests had been made but a couple of suspects were thought to have been involved in his disappearance.

Evers scanned the area for anyone he thought looked out of place or suspicious. Again, nothing caused him any alarm, but he was thankful his excessive paranoia ate at him to impulsively look around an area for anyone wishing to do him harm. He also enjoyed the architecture of the old buildings that stood before him. Many had been built in the early nineteenth century and were marvelously preserved.

The street smelled of history and crawled with locals and tourists alike, most with cameras hanging from their necks or cell phones pointed at a beautiful cathedral or nestled just above a plate of the local cuisine where the pictures would find their way to the internet at a later time.

He purchased another torta then hailed a cab to the airport. Evers doubted they had any suspects yet but were hoping to frighten someone into doing something stupid and irrational, thereby flushing himself into the open. His experience kept him calm and cool on the ride to Carrasco, but he knew that security would potentially be tighter than usual.

After paying the cab driver the fare, he picked up his bag and stepped to the sidewalk. Security seemed normal and he did not get the sense that anyone was on alert. Still, he knew he would have to be careful because he was certain the Argentinians would have contacted their neighbor to be on the lookout for anyone who might have had anything to do with the disappearance of their military leader. He almost laughed at that thought. *What would someone doing harm to another person look like? Would he look like me or that guy standing over there at a kiosk?* His eyes drifted over an obvious business traveler attempting to print his boarding pass.

He purchased a round trip ticket from Montevideo to New Jersey's Newark Liberty Airport. Buying a one way ticket was a sure way to draw attention to one's self and attention was something he did not want or need. In addition, traveling into the New York City metro area was a common occurrence at airports the world over, so his purchase would not draw unwanted interest.

Evers watched the local news on one of the television sets mounted from the ceiling at his gate. An international news correspondent was reporting breaking news that General Vasquez and his driver had been discovered assassinated at an abandoned warehouse in Buenos Aires. No details were currently available at the time detailing the cause of death, but some reports indicated that at least one of the two men had been shot in the head.

He felt his heart rate ramp up a few notches, but gave no outward indication of the anxiety he was feeling. There would not be a sense of well-being until his feet were firmly planted in the United States, far from the reach of the Argentinian government. He suspected, however, that the Argentinian president would use the double homicide as a political ploy, releasing rumors and making ambiguous statements about the potential involvement by some of her enemies. However, if there was evidence revealed that a U.S. citizen was involved, all bets were off. He was sure that he had sufficiently cleaned the crime scene, removing fingerprints or any possible footprint, but modern DNA testing could possibly detect some unfamiliar hair or skin residue unlike any that would normally be present in the car. Tracking him down would require significant effort, though, which was why he would only feel relief when he was back on sovereign soil.

When the gate attendant at long last announced boarding for his flight, he was relieved to see no law enforcement had moved into the area, either discreetly or to make the passengers visibly uncomfortable. He gathered his belongings and found his seat, his face stoic and reserved. Evers settled in for the long flight to Newark as the other passengers continued to pile onto the plane like cattle headed to slaughter.

The total flight time was just over fourteen and a half hours, plenty of time to rest. Evers said a silent thank you to the air gods for a flight with little turbulence and few children screaming at the top of their lungs. A lady sitting adjacent to him attempted to strike up a conversation, but when Evers appeared uninterested she closed her eyes and drifted off to sleep.

He managed to sleep the majority of the flight, unable to remember any dreams and no one around him looking as though they overheard him talking or thrashing about. He awoke when he heard the landing gear engage during the plane's final decent into New Jersey and cracked his neck while he looked around the cabin. A man, sitting across the aisle and two seats behind was leaned back in his seat staring blankly at the headrest in front of him.

The man was caucasian, in his mid to late thirties. His short brown hair, what was left of it, was receding deeply creating a rounded point in the middle of his forehead. He wore squared framed glasses, which created the appearance of hardline facial features. Evers wondered if the glasses were prescription or designed to change his face's look. His nondescript navy blue North Face lay neatly in his lap atop a pair of pressed khaki Chino pants. The light blue Ludlow shirt he wore sat casually with the top two buttons opened. His entire ensemble gave the impression of a youthful traveler out seeing the world.

But Evers detected something that those sitting around him obviously did not. Certain people give off particular vibes—people are generally wary of street thugs intent on doing harm, although they can't explain why they feel a certain way about the individuals they are trying to avoid. Others, still, mask themselves in costume and blend with locals, their dress, gait, even their diet will change in an effort to meld with those around them, although they have zero interest in becoming part and parcel with the locals. These are the operators, or CIA spooks who roam the world, and they are truly professional in their area of expertise.

Some spend a lifetime devoted to spying and gathering intel, while others are field agents specializing in the taking of human life. Many of these men and women are proven snipers, capable of spending countless hours lying prone, one eye focused on a high powered scope waiting for their victim to show himself. Then there are those whose abilities are developed to capture or kill a suspect at close range, with weapons, both concealed and those that are opportunistic in nature, or with bare hands.

Many of these seasoned operators have an ability to become "un-seen." They are the chameleons of the underworld, the shadows that move silently, unnoticed by everyone around them. If a person were to ask them how they are able to walk around unnoticed they would talk to them about Zen, inner-focus, and lack of thought.

Ex-spooks, former CIA operators working independently of the government and without the constraints of rules are the most treacherous. It is true that government field agents get away with a tremendous amount of murder covered up with money, lies and disinformation, but even those individuals work within the confines of rules and guidelines. The independents work on their own terms, for negotiated rates, and care little for government or political affiliations. They are the soulless, the rogue, and the freelancers. Evers knew this type all too well, and wondered if he fit the mold. It would be something he would have to consider at a later time.

In the meantime these people, Evers knew, were the really dangerous ones. They could slice a person's throat and eviscerate him before a sound could escape, and well before the predator was ever noticed. The man staring at the headrest was such a man, and he wondered how he had missed him earlier. Further, he wondered how he had tracked him to Argentina and who he was working for.

I'll have to think all that through later.

Only another operator, a man or woman who moves in and out of the shadows could pick up the slight sense of danger such a person exudes. The vibe is buried inside the person, painted over like a da Vinci canvas, coated until the first layer hides well below the surface. His mind is always aloof, never intent on the task at hand until the opportunity presents itself, that way another individual could not "pick-up" on his thoughts.

Evers's eyes passed over the man without stopping. He did not want to give any indication that he had spotted him and realized who he was, or at least *what* he was. His hand reached for the magazine in the seatback pocket and he flipped through it, trying to keep his own mind off the man seated behind him. There was no way the man would make a move on the plane; too many witnesses and the possibility of a flight marshal nullified any potential strike. Besides, this type worked alone and unnoticed, never in the open.

He closed his eyes thinking back to one of the lessons Buddy had taught him when they were trudging through the jungles of east Africa. They had been hired by a third party they were both sure had been licensed by the CIA to seek out a warlord intent on overthrowing the government at the time, a government friendly to U.S. interests and needs. The third party served as an intermediary that offered the United States government insulation and denial if they were captured or killed. "Just a couple of free-lancers trying to make money from some other government or special interest" would be the Company line.

Smith signaled for Evers to stop walking. Their trek had taken them almost four miles through dense jungle brush and some of the nastiest insects in the world. Mosquitos attacked them from all angles and did not seem to mind the camouflaged BDU's they wore to help blend with their green and brown surroundings.

The always present mustiness that pervaded the heavy foliage became heavier when Buddy's hand thrust in the air. His other senses immediately kicked up several notches and the familiar feeling of adrenaline dumped into his stomach and was promptly processed through his heart and into his extremities. He was keenly aware of birds and other animals moving in his peripheral vision, but struggled to see what Buddy had spotted directly in front of them.

He watched as Smith squatted and examined something in total silence. Watching the man make an assessment was like watching a long-time surgeon looking over an MRI as he sought to find what ailed a patient. Smith was a master tracker and could do so in total silence. He would glare at Evers if his respiration was high enough to be heard, and the man's hearing was top notch.

A few seconds passed and he finally realized a freshly broken branch from some small vegetation was what his mentor was examining. "It's fresh," Smith mouthed.

They had been tracking a man accused of assassinating a Ugandan business executive. The executive was believed to be the chief financier behind a quiet crusade to crush a rebellion intent on removing the current president of the country, a regime the executive had apparently prospered under. Through third and fourth party intermediaries, the two Americans were hired to find and eliminate the murderer, a man named Odongo Nakibuuka.

It was rumored that Nakibuuka spent a significant amount of his time sojourning through the Ugandan bush, and after several discreet inquiries, they were able to ascertain his commonly used entry point. The methods he used to kill the executive were unknown to Evers and Smith, and how it was determined he committed the act not disclosed to either of them. Generally, neither concerned themselves with the means and methods used by the individual they were hired to find, that is unless their means and methods made them a much harder target.

The two men continued on for another ten minutes, and again Buddy raised his hand and immediately dropped to one knee making himself small and harder to see in the thick jungle greenery.

When Smith had instructed him to halt, Evers assumed a crouching position just as his mentor. Smith signaled to him that he could see one person directly ahead and to move into position alongside him. Briefly, Evers marveled at a soldier's ability to "talk" with only his hands and to be understood by those around him.

Evers belly crawled into position next to Smith and rose to one knee. He glanced around their surroundings and checked one time behind them to assure no one was stalking the stalkers. Feeling better that they were not being followed he tracked Buddy's gaze straight ahead.

In a clearing about one hundred meters away they watched as a thin black man stood shirtless with his arms raised skyward. A strange looking necklace with what looked like teeth adorned his neck. His mouth moved in silent prayer as his eyes rolled to the back of his head. Sweat poured over his bare chest and dripped from his forehead and nose.

The two men watched him, fascinated by the intensity of the man's prayers. Evers scowled and looked at Buddy, shaking his head as he did so as if to ask, "Why the fuck is he in the middle of the jungle doing this?"

Smith shrugged his shoulders, the look on his own face as perplexed as Evers's. The men continued to watch the mysterious acts of chanting, prayers, and occasional genuflection to no one or thing in particular. Evers began to raise his rifle for the shot, but Smith placed his hand over the barrel and pushed it down.

He placed a finger over his lips in the universal sign to "remain silent" then made a quick circular motion in the air with one finger indicating the possibility of others who might come running to see who was shooting whom. Evers nodded once indicating he understood, and then turned his eyes back to Nakibuuka.

The man began to sway then progress into a strange dance, his body and head oscillating in ways that made the spectators wonder if he possessed a skeletal system. His torso writhed like a snake as he stepped, one knee impossibly high in the air, the other foot, it seemed, barely in contact with the ground.

Evers rubbed his eyes to make sure what he was seeing was real when out of nowhere a smoke ring appeared around Nakibuuka. Behind him Evers thought he could see small flames that were not there only seconds beforehand. The chanting grew louder and the dancing more violent, his body contorting in inhuman directions. The cloud of smoke encircling him became denser causing his voice to echo off the white walls and climbing tendrils that erupted from the ground.

Scales began to appear on his naked skin, his torso like that of a snake. His arms and legs began to retract and his head narrowed to a triangular shape. Flaring nostrils hardened and stood where the bridge of his nose once resided. The snake man fell to the ground slithering inside the smoky ring.

A loud voice boomed from nowhere and everywhere at the same time, speaking in a language Smith and Evers could not decipher. Its sound was ancient but clear, throaty, but powerful. The tone was unmistakable and burned itself into Smith and Evers's mind, and although they could not understand the words being spoken it was clear they were directed at the snake thing crawling in its wake. There was no doubt that voice and creature were also master and servant and that whatever was being spoken involved direction and commands.

Momentarily, the two American men squatted in shock struggling to believe what they were seeing and hearing. Processing an event like that was beyond the scope of the human mind, and both men fought with everything inside them to keep from being pushed over the edge mentally. Their core had been equally shaken.

Buddy shook his head, a neuro-linguistic reaction to remove what he had just seen and bring himself into a more recognizable reality. Evers blinked rapidly, his physical response similar to Smith's as he tried to wipe away what he had seen.

In the distance the smoke decreased and eventually dissipated leaving a lone, slender black man lying on the ground. Nakibuuka stood, his skin returned to normal, the sweat still covering his body. His eyes focused on the area around him and both Evers and Smith dropped silently to the ground before his field of vision crossed over them.

They each moved into heavy foliage cover when they heard the man moving toward them, presumably to return from whence he came. Evers saw a leg cross in front of his face then suddenly stop about four paces beyond his sight. His heart rate jumped into high gear and he thought for a second that the pounding against his chest wall would be so loud that Nakibuuka would hear it.

The man spun around, the grass and weeds twisting beneath his shoes. Evers could hear him breathing and sensed he was looking for something, or someone. He wondered if the man had felt their presence as he walked past them, his primal ability to pick up on a predator triggering something in the back of his brain.

He continued to spin, looking for something that might give him cause for concern. Evers fought to control his respiration so it could not be overheard. Several long seconds passed before Nakibuuka decided he was being overly paranoid and decided it was safe to leave. The two men waited another full minute before moving, rising slowly to one knee, watching their target head into the dense jungle.

Smith spoke, the voice activated communication mic hanging from his neck relayed to the wireless ear piece in Evers's ear canal.

"We still can't be sure he doesn't have a spotter or a team hanging back, although I suspect we would have been culled by now. Unless we're left with no choice, we need to take him out silently. Understand, Buck?"

"Got it," Evers replied.

Evers fell in behind Smith as the two took off in search of Nakibuuka. Once again, Evers was in awe at the level of stealth in which Buddy could move. His footsteps were totally silent and his feet seemed to glide across the jungle floor while Evers could feel his own boots occasionally pushing into the mud. Evers watched closely how his partner moved, attempting to mimic everything he did, but try as he might he would invariably feel his boot slide into the muck followed by the usual "slooooop" sound they would make as he pulled them out of the mire. Each time it happened he watched Buddy's head shake furiously as if to say, "Fucking amateur."

As they made their way quickly through the thickness of the jungle, he noted Buddy's constant data collection—bent stalks of grass here, a snapped twig there, a footprint heading in another direction. *Within twenty minutes they could hear someone directly ahead, walking alongside a fast moving stream. Whoever was there was panting from exertion; Evers had no doubt who that person was.*

They came to the edge of the tree line before it dropped away from the running creek that ran over the ground, its flowing path leading to some larger, more welcoming body of water. Small flying insects buzzed and hopped from rock to protruding rock, sometimes touching down in the stream to take an infinitesimally small drink to quench their thirst. Several gnats had taken an interest in a particular object squatted by the riverside.

Evers and Smith watched as Nakibuuka scooped water from the creek and doused his head and body. Obviously still exhausted from his recent encounter with whatever weirdness he was involved in, coupled with a serious hike to the stream, the man felt it time to catch his breath. His hands reached for another helping of water to wash over his heated body. This time Smith moved in concert with his target's movement.

Evers watched as Smith moved soundlessly behind the thin black man, Smith's eyes cast downward and not looking directly at Nakibuuka. Evers thought this approach strange and made a mental note to ask about it later. He was three meters from the man when Nakibuuka seemed to feel something about to happen and turned his head to see what was creating the uneasy feeling.

The whites of his eyes grew large and his mouth flopped open when he saw the men clad in BDU's. Evers could tell the man wanted to scream, but the adrenaline that immediately hit his blood stream constricted his vocal chords preventing any sound from escaping. His body tensed as though bracing for some sort of impact, but Buddy launched an arm out and around the man's neck, the blade of his forearm jamming into his esophagus. Unlike no choke he had seen before, Evers watched as Smith brought his other hand up to meet the one wrapped around Nakibuuka's neck, meeting palm to palm in what looked like some sort of evil method of prayer.

In a flash, Nakibuuka's hands shot to Smith's arms in an attempt to relax the pressure on his constricted airway. Buddy's head settled to the opposite side of his victim's own where he applied pressure directly against the man's jaw hinge.

Unable to move his head in either direction, nor tuck his chin to increase the potential for more air, Nakibuuka began panicking, working his hands frantically against Buddy's arms. He attempted to pull them away from his neck, his long fingernails digging into his attacker's skin.

Evers watched the struggle in morbid fascination, Nakibuuka emitting a strange gurgling sound, Smith remaining intense and spookily quiet. Buddy settled his hips pulling the man backward and pulled the top of Nakibuuka's upper-back into his own chest. The man's head pushed forward into Buddy's forearm, creating another round of intense resistance. In that same instant, Buddy pushed forward with his forearm, severing the cervical column at the base of the man's neck. Evers heard a loud crack as Buddy broke the man's neck. He released his victim and stood, observing his handy work and brushing himself off at the same time. Evers noted that Buddy was barely breathing from the struggle before casting his gaze over the broken black man whose head rested at an impossible angle.

Buddy looked up at Evers and said, "C-2 and C-3 separation always makes a nasty sound when they break away, but goddam if the result ain't the same, huh Buck?"

Evers sat down on a fallen tree, his mind reeling from everything the two men had just seen and done.

"I don't know, Buddy. I've never broken a man's neck before, and now that I've seen and heard it done, I'm not sure that I'll put it on my bucket list."

Buddy smirked at Evers's reply. "It's one helluva thing breaking a man's neck, Buck. You're about as up close and personal to him as you're going to get without an invitation to have intercourse."

"I'm not sure how you're able to joke around after what you just did," Evers said, his voice a little more stern than he intended.

"I'll tell you how I'm able to do it, son. I find a bad guy, a bad guy whose death I'm being paid to bring about, then I kill him and collect my money. The way I see it, I've done the world a favor and I'm getting paid well in the process. Besides, I'm pretty fucking good at it," he drawled. "I'll tell you one more thing too, Buck, I have no conscience and no sense of loyalty to a sumbitch I'm being paid to waste. You understand?"

Evers decided not to pursue Buddy's complete lack of compassion, but made a mental note to remember his last comment in case the time came that he found himself on the payout end of Buddy's services.

"How were you able to sneak up on him so quietly?" Evers asked. "He never heard or sensed you until the very last instant."

Buddy looked away for a second before turning his attention back to Evers. "Have you ever felt someone looking at you, Billy? Been in a room or outside, not really paying attention to your surroundings, but you feel an itch in the back of your brain and the hair standing up on your neck?"

Evers considered, "Yeah, of course. I always assumed it was my sixth sense kicking in, or something."

Buddy nodded his head and continued, "In a way it is your sixth sense. It's a survival instinct buried deep within our DNA that some call a 'gut feeling' or 'intuition.' It's what enabled some fucking sea urchin to crawl out of the ocean, develop legs and arms and eventually walk upright. It kept our ancestors from being eaten and gang raped by wild herds of tyrannosaurus rex's and shit."

Evers burst out in laughter. The past several hours came crashing down on him all at once, and Buddy's joke sounded like the funniest thing he had heard in his life. He laughed until Buddy started guffawing, both men rolling around on the ground holding their sides right next to Nakibuuka's corpse. Neither seemed to recognize the bizarre scene for what it was, nor the surreal nature of the moment. Or, it was entirely possible that neither really cared.

Buddy finally caught his breath and the two stopped laughing, the chuckles coming and going in waves until, at long last, they passed. Buddy continued his explanation without attempting another joke.

"People sense other folks looking at them, Buck. When you are stalking prey, whether it's a deer, an antelope, a gorilla, or a man, never allow your direct line of vision to fall on him, and I mean anywhere on his body. Do you understand? Look slightly away, keeping him in your peripheral vision. People don't get their hackles up when they are watched peripherally, but direct line is something completely different," he finished.

"That's why you were looking away when you walked up on him," Evers stated.

"Yep," Buddy replied.

Again, Evers changed topics. "What was that shit we saw back there, you know, when he was praying and chanting?"

"Amigo, I have no idea what the hell that was, and I don't think I want to stick around here any longer waiting to find out. Whatever or whoever was talking to him didn't appear to be someone I want to fornicate with—time to beat feet," Buddy said.

As though a movie played in his mind, the end fading to black, his memory finished with him and Buddy heading out through the dense jungle. He took a deep breath and shuddered, the voice he and his partner overheard when Nakibuuka was praying as fresh in his mind as the day he had heard it. Without looking behind he did a mental checklist of Newark International, their terminal was C., the international hub.

He knew he and his follower would both have to clear customs, but his knowledge of his tail stopped there. More problematic was whether the guy was working as a team with someone else on the flight or with someone waiting his arrival in Newark. Someone traveling with him on the plane would be relatively easy to flush out, but the latter could prove to be much more difficult.

Evers would have to worry about the tandem approach later. The first thing he needed to do was try to get the man he now identified as his secret admirer alone so he could politely question him about his intentions. There was significant difficulty in doing so and certainly could not be done in an airport with hundreds of surveillance cameras positioned at every turn.

However, outside the terminal presented opportunities that would not be offered at many other airports around the world.

The pilot landed the plane on a runway paralleling the New Jersey Turnpike, the traffic comparatively light at four-forty in the morning. Evers looked out his window and saw the familiar shipping booms looming over the New Jersey shipyards, their massive structures and steel cables standing at attention, illuminated by artificial light. They waited for barges and ships to bring containers from foreign soils to be distributed across the country's expanse.

Just beyond the shipyards the bright lights of New York City's lower west side served as both beacon and warning for newcomers intent on hitting the big time. Evers had seen firsthand how the city chewed people up and spat them on sidewalks and rat infested subterranean public transportation areas. In all the time he had spent there in his lifetime, the welcoming hostility was something he still struggled to understand. How or why people enjoyed living in a constant state of alertness was as foreign to him, he supposed, as living in the secluded outback would be for someone raised in the City.

Evers exited the plane and made his way to the customs area. Cell phone usage was prohibited and he took note of the awkward way people stood around, their minds free to roam without the distraction of text messages and social media. His admirer stood a good distance behind him, casually taking in the sights like anyone new to the New York City metro area would do. *A little too casual*, Evers thought.

His passport stamped, he walked through the largest of the three terminals, the white floors and walls reflecting the fluorescent lights. Arriving and departing passengers combed the walkways and moving sidewalks, many of the women looking as though they were dressed for a nightclub and the men appreciating their attire.

Evers made a sudden turn into the men's room. Doing so afforded him the opportunity to take a look behind him. As expected, his admirer followed behind, keeping a safe distance and walking on the other side of the walkway. The turn into the restroom would be problematic, Evers knew, for anyone following. A quick decision had to be made by the follower—move into the restroom and risk exposure, or roll the dice and hope the individual checked a bag and pick him up again at a luggage carousel.

The safe bet would be the carousel area, most especially because they had just gotten off an international flight and almost every person in the world traveling internationally does so with at least one checked bag. But if this guy was a professional as Evers suspected he was, he knew the travel habits of one accustomed to moving about in the shadows undetected, which meant minimizing time spent in any one location. Not checking a bag in that case provided the covert person less visibility and more mobility. *No*, Evers thought, *he will certainly follow me into the restroom for fear of losing me at the baggage claim area, and he would be correct in doing so since I didn't check a bag in Argentina.*

He walked to a urinal and unzipped, his eyes straight ahead. A few seconds passed before his admirer joined him at the urinal bank. Evers almost smiled at the man's predictability and reasoning; he was probably upset about having to make a pit stop, but given the length of the flight it was expected. Evers shook off then washed his hands before leaving the restroom. He knew the man would wait a few seconds before exiting, but he also understood that he could not wait very long for fear of losing him.

Evers walked past the security exit into the main foyer of the terminal and paused for a second to scan the area. He found the sign he was looking for, which pointed to an escalator leading one floor above. It also gave him a few seconds to confirm his tail was still with him.

Never one to disappoint, Mr. Admirer was there, his gait shortened and his pace slowed when he saw Evers pause momentarily. Evers continued up the escalator to the air train, standing on the platform until it showed up. When the double doors opened on one of the cars, he stepped inside, his back to the front of the car so he could watch other people, including his follower, do the same.

He watched as the man stepped inside two cars behind his. The doors closed and the trained pushed forward to one of the big parking decks then onto the airport station. As usual, the air conditioning was not working on the Airtrain, and for a moment Evers had a vision of its passengers being cooked alive like crawfish.

When they arrived at the Newark Airport Station, he found a kiosk and purchased a New Jersey Transit ticket that would take him into the New Jersey's Penn Station then on to New York's own train hub with the same, and more famous version of the namesake.

"Such creativity in naming stations between these two states," Evers muttered to himself.

He reminded himself that New Jersey, much like Philadelphia, suffered from "little brother syndrome," as they both stood in the shadow of America's greatest metropolis, so the similarity in names did not surprise him nearly as much as it might a newcomer to the area.

Mr. Admirer stayed with him, his ability to trail without being spotted growing worse, primarily because Evers was adept at flushing single followers from the shadows. Evers wanted to feel some remorse or pity for the man—obviously he had spent a lifetime perfecting whatever technique he had been taught in the school of stalking. The hard truth, however, was following a man suffering from extreme paranoia made his task arduous at best, and the man's lack of paranoia would be his undoing.

The numerous cameras, witnesses and presence of law enforcement prevented the man from making a move beyond remaining in tow with him, but the first chance the man got to drag Evers into a dark corner and do God knew what to him would be taken advantage of; of that Evers was certain.

After changing trains at New Jersey's Penn Station, Evers watched as the man following him again hopped on a car exactly two cars behind him. A small but telling habit that meant he was afraid of allowing Evers out of his sight, but still wary enough to maintain a modicum of distance. The man was cautious, but not overly so.

Several minutes later their train stopped in New York's Penn Station. Evers stepped onto the platform and followed the signs leading upstairs and into the Manhattan morning. A fresh dose of adrenaline dropped into his gut and his heart began hammering in his chest.

He stepped outside Penn Station onto an already busy West 33rd Street. Careful not to turn around to try to steal a glimpse of Mr. Admirer, Evers began walking west, periodically stopping as though to get his bearings in a city teeming with skyscrapers, locals, and tourists. To have turned and looked directly at him would have been enough to tip his follower that he knew he was there, and his admirer's lack of knowledge was his only advantage at the moment.

Evers knew the city well, having spent a considerable amount of time there in years past. Little had changed with the exception of the new Freedom Tower whose brazen position in the Financial District waved a distinct "fuck you" to anyone willing to fly a civilian aircraft into a building. Its mirrored glass reflected everything right about the United States and everything conceivably wrong about its ridiculous government, most especially the current regime of posers and power hungry charlatans.

"Focus, Billy," Evers muttered to himself as he continued west toward the Henry Hudson Parkway, an enormous white building standing silently to his left. The almost abandoned James A Farley United States Post Office once proudly delivered mail to the majority of Manhattan's residents, fully covering two city blocks on eight acres of prime New York real estate, but now provided a glimpse of times long past and technology ever present. Having once employed close to 16,000 workers, the building was a mere shell of its former self, employing around 200 now.

He stopped and peered toward the Hudson River, Hoboken, New Jersey on the far bank staring back at him. A look of confusion passed over his face, as though he had lost his way on the streets of the big city, something not abnormal for the casual tourist visiting the concrete jungle. Evers continued on before turning left on Ninth Avenue.

Mr. Admirer was keeping a safe distance behind, giving Evers a chance to duck into a Duane Reade drug store, a retail establishment found all over Manhattan. He stood at a display just inside the store and watched as his follower moved beyond the store entrance mere seconds after he had ducked inside. Evers waited a full ten seconds before stepping over the store's threshold onto the sidewalk.

Without hesitation, Evers crossed the street then turned right to continue following the man who would have preyed on him. It was ironic that the predator oftentimes becomes the prey. Evers kept his thoughts and eyes forward, remembering the lessons of the jungle. From his peripheral vision he watched as the man began to panic, suddenly realizing the person he was following had most likely ducked into some store after making the turn.

Mr. Admirer stopped and looked around, an amateurish move if ever Evers had seen one. As he walked past the man's line of sight, Evers noticed the look of anguish on his face. He was certain a thousand things were running through his mind, and if the man was the trained assassin Evers assumed he was, he would quickly realize that it was *his* life that was now in danger.

The man began backtracking as Evers continued his pace toward the next traffic light. Now at a safe distance, Evers watched him unimpeded and without worry that he would sense his eyes on his back or spot him across the street. Mr. Admirer's composure was soon a distant memory as he moved frantically up and down the sidewalk peering inside store windows in hopes that he would glimpse the man he had followed from Monte Video.

Evers watched as the man grew more frustrated, finally turning and walking back toward West 33rd. He impulsively looked left before making a right, seemingly headed back to Penn Station, which posed a problem for Evers if he was going to have a shot at questioning the man. Evers's gait changed as he attempted to remain close to his admirer without giving himself away.

As they walked back to the Penn Station, Evers's eyes shifted around for a weapon of opportunity. Not having a gun or even a knife was disconcerting, especially when one was not sure if an adversary was carrying. To assume he or she was not, was dangerous and stupid, so Evers searched for something, anything that could be used to level the playing field.

All over New York green netting and orange hazard tape warned locals and tourists alike that they were close to a construction zone. Close to one such area of netting, Evers saw what looked like a small piece of steel sticking from the ground, the earth exposed as a result of some recently removed portion of sidewalk. He bent to pick it up and was pleased to find a small steel file connected to the opposite end of the exposure. Evers pocketed the file as he continued walking.

A fresh adrenaline dump surged through his body as he watched Mr. Admirer enter Penn Station. He was careful not to close the distance any faster than his current pace for fear of being spotted in the darkened plate glass doors that lined its entrance. The man walked through an automatic door that slid on aluminum tracks. Safe to pick up his pace, Evers walked into the station stopping just long enough to allow his eyes to adjust to the dimmer light.

He gazed onto the massive expanse of floor and watched as Admirer looked around, apparently found what he was looking for and set off in its general direction. It did not take Evers long to realize that the man he was following was not heading to the New Jersey Transit or Amtrak counters; rather, he found an escalator taking him down one level. Again, Evers smiled as he realized the man was looking for the subway, which meant he would be staying locally in hopes of regaining Evers's scent.

He followed the man downstairs and watched as he purchased a subway ticket at a kiosk. The man hovered closely to the machine and, not surprisingly, inserted cash. Evers dug a five dollar bill from his own pocket and prepared to make a similar purchase. In his peripheral he watched as the man pushed through a turnstile and began walking toward the blue A-C-E line. Quickly, Evers grabbed his subway card and followed, staying a comfortable distance away from the man.

The train pulled onto the platform a few moments later. Mr. Admirer climbed onto a car, and Evers, acting as his follower had in Newark, stepped onto the car immediately behind him. The doors shut and the train began moving northward.

They passed over the Forty-second and Fiftieth Street platforms without exiting the train, but at Fifty-ninth, or Columbus Circle, Evers watched his admirer step off the train. Evers hesitated for three or four seconds to see what the man would do—the wait paid off.

The man checked left and right then walked directly to a bench and sat down. Evers was happy he hesitated before walking onto the platform as he understood exactly what the man was attempting to do. He would wait until the platform mostly or completely cleared to be sure he was not followed.

Evers had a quick decision to make: stay on the platform and act as nonchalant as possible, or move upstairs to the next platform and hope Mr. Admirer was either leaving the subway system altogether, or planning to hitch a ride on another train heading in a different direction. The third possibility was that he would wait on another A-C-E train and continue riding north. If that happened, Evers would lose him should he elect to wait it out upstairs.

He made the quick decision to flow with the crowd to the upstairs platform. A local musician was hammering away on an acoustic guitar and Evers stepped over to him, turning his body so that he was facing the musician. His position also made it possible for him to see the steps and anyone walking up them.

One minute passed then two. Evers tried listening to the man doing a fair job at impersonating James Taylor as he sang "Fire and Rain." The melody swept across the tiled floor causing several people to stop and listen.

A man and woman stood together next to Evers who was growing more impatient. At the three minute mark he started to leave, but stopped dead in his tracks when he first saw the top of a balding head followed by eyes framed with dark rectangles. Slowly he turned his head away from Mr. Admirer and smiled at the musician, although he was really smiling at his good fortune.

Evers's eyes tracked with the man as he made his way around the platform heading directly to the one train. *Well played, sir*, Evers thought. He had almost fallen for the long wait as the man watched the remaining passengers on the platform. Most likely, he had awaited the next train to make sure those lingering about got aboard and headed along their way. That is what he would have done if he had been in the man's shoes, but his impatience almost got the best of him.

He watched the man walk down the steps, again giving him ample time before following him. Before leaving the James Taylor clone, he dropped a dollar in the man's guitar case and gave him a thoughtful nod. The musician smiled at him as he continued playing and singing. Others followed Evers's lead, dropping change and bills in the case before wandering off to their next destination.

His walk down the steps would be tricky, as he would have to keep his face down to avoid eye contact with Mr. Admirer while still trying to locate him. He placed one hand on a handrail and walked at a pace keeping up with others around him. At the bottom he saw him staring at the staircase, watching those who descended them, but his gaze was one of complacency and boredom.

Too bad for you, Mr. Admirer.

Evers walked past the man, he would have referred to as "the mark" in a previous life, without making eye contact. He kept his head angled away from him and walked steadily with those around him. Once he settled behind the crowd he watched Mr. Admirer to see if there had been any recognition written on his face.

The man had either not recognized him or he owned the best poker face on the eastern seaboard. Evers stood with his back to the wall with several other passengers. He watched as several tourists read over their pocket subway maps, attempting to maneuver through New York's literal underworld. Something moved on the train tracks and he saw several rats rummaging through discarded chip bags and hot dog wrappers.

Another street musician sat against the wall playing his acoustic guitar. A young black man, his soulful voice filled the platform with the bluesy tune "Mojo Working." Several folks crowded round him as he belted out the lyrics to an old delta song.

I got my mojo working
But it just won't work on you
I got my mojo working
But it just won't work on you
I got my mojo working
But I just don't know what to do

People clapped and danced in time to the young man's song and dollars rained into his guitar case like a fast moving stream over a cliff. Each time someone would drop money in his case the musician would shout out, "thank you!" *A man with talent and business sense*, Evers thought.

The train arrived and the people piled on it like sheep being led to slaughter leaving the guitar player behind to entertain another group of sheep who would wander in at any time. The doors closed and Evers watched as Mr. Admirer stood and held onto a strap dangling from the overhead handrail. He looked as despondent as any other person riding the subway, and Evers thought he was either capable of completely and totally blending in with the crowd, or he was distraught over having lost the person he had been following for almost a whole day.

They passed over an identical path they had taken earlier, unloading at Thirty-fourth Street beneath Penn Station.

He's being careful, but he didn't notice me at Columbus Circle. That means he's either tired or lazy. No matter which, I'm going to make him understand the mistake he just made, a tiny smile appeared on Evers's face, something he was cognizant of doing more of recently.

Again, Evers waited three full seconds before exiting the train, giving Mr. Admirer time to begin the ascent up the platform. People walked up the stairs and Evers made sure he followed his prey, once more, from a safe distance. He watched as the man exited through the turnstile and entered Penn Station, the smell of food and people co-mingled into what one could only think of as New York City.

Mr. Admirer walked directly out of the station, not hesitating to check behind him. His movement suggested that he was sure he had lost Evers earlier and was intent on moving elsewhere in the City, rather than taking the train back to the airport, and he felt certain that he was not being followed in the process. Evers considered the mistake the man had made in his assumption; he wanted to make his move soon.

They walked westbound on Thirty-third; Evers was certain he knew where they were heading. A Marriot Fairfield Inn stood a block away, and it was then that he knew he had to act. That end of mid-town was unusually quiet and Evers figured most of the tourists were hanging out in Times Square, the largest New York City attraction by far.

The hotel, heralded for its lack of architectural ingenuity, stood like a box next to a wide brownstone building and a parking deck. In fact, all of the buildings on that particular side of the road were wholly uncreative and aesthetically unappealing, including the Fairfield, with its two hundred thirty-nine rooms of towering incongruous and unimaginative creativity.

Between the hotel and the parking deck Evers spotted a narrow alley. He counted only five people on his side of the walkway and picked up his pace to close the distance between the two men, his eyes maintained low and left of Mr. Admirer's feet. Evers took a deep breath, the adrenaline beginning to surge again. He reached inside his pocket and withdrew the medium sized file, the flat rough end in his palm and the pointed shaft protruding from his thumb and forefinger.

Evers began counting the distance between the two of them, the distance to the alley closing quickly.

Eight meters. Six meters. Two meters. He lifted the file even with his admirer's kidney then took three large steps in rapid succession directly toward him. With his left hand he grabbed the collar of the man's North Face jacket and simultaneously jabbed the business end of the file into his right kidney.

Evers released his collar and covered his mouth before he could scream. He twisted the steel tool clockwise, ripping flesh and organ in synch. The man struggled against the pain, but Evers arched his head and neck toward his chest in order to control him.

He did a quick check over his shoulder to see if anyone had noticed him. The beauty of New York City and many other massive metropolitan areas was the almost innate desire of its inhabitants to mind their own business. Everyone continued on their way without stopping to see what the excitement was about. Evers knew, however, that someone would most likely call NYPD, so the time he spent in one spot was crucial.

Evers pushed the man behind a parked food service truck.

"Who the fuck are you?" he asked.

The man didn't answer, only gritted his teeth. Evers pushed the file a little deeper into his tissue.

Evers considered his situation for a moment. He was dealing with a professional, someone trained to compartmentalize pain and accept an inevitable death. Without much pretense, he elected to change tactics.

"I don't know you, and I'm guessing you don't know me beyond some goddam dossier you read by some bastard who wants me dead. At the end of the day, you and I are the same and shouldn't be made or paid to track each other down. Look at us now, two men fighting for survival in a goddam New York City alleyway. Who the fuck wants to die like that, huh?" Evers reasoned.

He continued, "All you have to do is answer my questions and I'll let you go. Hell, I'll even call you an ambulance because you and I are the same kind of soldier." Purely from a psychological perspective, Evers knew that reasoning with a hostage was the surest way, beyond pain, to acquire a semblance of compatibility, in creating a connection that would lead the hostage to believe he or she would be released if they simply complied. In the mind of the hostage, he begins reasoning with himself, denying that he will die and begins telling his torturer what he wants to know. Even though the most battle hardened soldiers know better, every mind has a breaking point, but in Evers's case, he had to get his admirer to a breaking point quickly, lest he garner unwanted attention from a potential passerby or some employee bringing trash to the alleyway.

Evers turned the business end of the file and pressed his hand tighter against his mouth to muffle the inevitable scream. He moved his mouth closer to the man's ear and continued speaking.

"They can save you. There's still time for me to call for help, and the truth is, I'm tired of killing. So let's try something else. What's your name?" Evers asked.

Something as simple and undeniable as asking someone their name helps put their mind at ease. There is no sense of giving away critical information and the hope is the captor will let you go without inflicting more pain. The tactic was used the world over in interrogations, but until a man has been questioned when his life is on the line he really does not know how he will respond, despite the bravado shared at bars when speaking hypothetically with friends and colleagues.

Evers felt the man's jaws begin to move and released the firm clasp he held over the man's mouth.

"D-D-Daniel," the man replied through clenched teeth.

Good, a name, Evers thought.

"Okay, Daniel," he began, his voice calm and controlled as his eyes continued checking his perimeter, "tell me where you began following me."

The man grunted and breathed heavily through his nose as he attempted to compartmentalize the pain. Evers watched as the man looked to the left, a psychological cue that Daniel was attempting to recall a specific memory.

"Uruguay," he panted. "At the airport."

"I see," Evers replied. His admission meant he was hired, and someone had to have known he was in Montevideo. He thought he had been very careful and wondered if Emilia had sold him out to someone. If she did, he was going to make her pay, although he hoped that his assumption was not true.

Evers decided to continue asking softball questions before pressing harder.

"Did you buy your ticket at the airport or in advance?" he asked.

Again, Daniel looked left recalling an event.

"At the airport," he grunted.

"And you followed me from Monte Video to New York City. Why were you following me?"

Daniel hesitated to answer, and Evers twisted the file a little further, his hand clamped over the man's mouth to once again muffle his scream.

Again, Daniel panted hard and clenched his teeth. With great interest Evers watched the man reason his response. Telling him why he was following him would not breach the trust of his employer and would buy a little more time in hopes that someone might call the police to help him.

The man took a deep breath and once more answered through clenched teeth. "I was hired to follow you."

Now is the time to push.

"What were you going to do to me here in the City?" Evers questioned.

Daniel closed his eyes tightly and blew air out of his mouth then sucking more in through his nostrils. Evers pushed the file a little deeper into his kidney and could feel warm, sticky blood flowing over his hand. If he did not hurry up and get the information he wanted he was going to be seen by some onlooker or the guy was going to bleed out. Neither option appealed to him.

"Were you supposed to kill me?" Evers asked, his voice remaining calm, almost friendly.

Daniel nodded his head in the affirmative.

"Okay," Evers replied. "Who hired you?"

Daniel's eyes grew wide and he shook his head signaling to Evers he was not going to respond. The file was pushed another half an inch into Daniel's body causing his eyes to roll to the back of his head.

"Ah, fuck," Evers muttered as he watched the man pass out from the pain and shock. He withdrew the file and shot a glance around as he placed the file on the ground. No one was within eye shot of the pair. He placed one hand on the man's chin and the other on the back of his head. Evers rolled Daniel's chin up toward his shoulder then quickly snapped his neck as he rotated his hands, a classic break found in his Yoshukai seisan kata, as well as being taught in hand-to-hand combat in the Army.

There was little time to be upset or disappointed in the lack of information gleaned from the man, but he had learned something important—someone was on to him. He pushed the possibility and coincidence of Emilia being the common link between the two to the back of his mind. For now, he had to move and do so quickly.

He drug Daniel behind a dumpster and bent to pick up the file. Evers stuffed the tool in his pocket then noticed how bloody his hand was. He drew his shirt sleeve down further then stuffed both hands in his pockets. No other sign of blood was on his clothes or shoes.

Once again he walked into Penn Station, keeping his head low and his face away from the many cameras mounted around the enormous building and found a restroom. He walked into a stall and wiped his hands with tissue until all the damp blood was sopped up. It still looked as though he could be a hand model stand-in in a horror film so he grabbed a wad of toilet paper, and then stuffed it and his hand back into his pocket. He walked out of the stall and began searching for an available hand sink away from the eyes of men filtering in and out of the restroom.

Good fortune was smiling on Evers as a sink at the end of the wall was open with no one washing their hands for two sink spaces between. Quickly he moved to the sink and stood with his back slightly angled toward anyone who might walk next to him. He scrubbed for a good forty-five seconds until he was satisfied all the blood had been removed then pulled the wad of toilet paper from his pocket and cleaned up the sink. If anyone was watching him, they would have assumed he was just another person combing the streets and subways of New York.

Evers pitched the toilet paper into the trash bin and walked into the giant foyer then walked downstairs to the subway. He rode the one train north to the West Seventy-ninth stop, got off the train and sat down on a bench until the area cleared, similar to Daniel's movements earlier. He reminded himself to be more cautious than the late Mr. Admirer had been.

The upper west side of Manhattan was much quieter and calmer than most other areas, primarily because of the money needed to live there. Wealthy business men and women, movie stars, and athletes lived in the brownstone apartments and townhomes located next to the Hudson River, so its pricey boutiques and restaurants kept the majority of locals and tourists at bay.

Evers walked to the top of the platform and looked around, his lost tourist façade in full swing. There was no one milling about in the area so he found the southbound platform and walked downstairs. The area was hot and stuffy and stank of ages of sweaty people, alcohol, dirt and history. He let one train pass without getting on it, his paranoia working in hyper-drive. Exactly eleven minutes later a second train screeched to a halt in front of him and he got on.

Evers rode the train back to Columbus Circle, careful to look around the platform before walking to the top. No one looked or acted suspicious, but he continued his surveillance detection run by turning east and walking toward Central Park. He turned north on Central Park West and passed the gaudy Trump Tower and glimpsed at a few people practicing tai chi in the park. The massive globe statue in front of Trump's reminded passerby's of one of the world's richest men's global influence, even if that was not the original intent of the sculptor.

He continued walking north until he came to West Sixty-fifth. Evers turned left quickly, stealing a look behind him as he did so. No one made any sudden moves to catch up to him, or look his way as he made the move. He continued one block to Columbus Avenue then turned south.

The landmark he was seeking stood directly in front of him, however, he needed to make a phone call then find a store to buy some new clothes. He found a store selling disposable cell phones, walked outside and located a bench. Evers punched in the familiar number and listened to the rings before someone picked up.

"Hello," came the ruddy, deep southern drawl that often made Evers smile. It did so again.

"Hey," Evers responded.

"Goddam, Buck, it's good to hear your voice. I was getting seriously scared." *Scared* came out sounding like *skeert*.

"I'm okay. Got lots to talk to you about though. Can you meet me?" Evers inquired.

"Hell yeah, I can meet you. You in town?"

"Close. I'm in the big city. Can you come up here?"

"I hate that fucking place," Buddy complained, "but for you anything. I'll get cleaned up and hop the train. It'll take me a few hours. Where do you want to meet?"

"Take the train to Columbus Circle then call me from the southwest corner of Central Park. You can reach me on this number. See you in a while," Evers finished and clicked off, happy that Buddy did not push to meet near D.C. His warranted distrust of everything government screamed "stay away!"

Evers spent the rest of the afternoon buying some new clothes and sitting in a local club sipping on a twelve year old Cragganmore, one of his favorite Speysides, and listening to a local blues band. He did not catch the name of the band, but their sound was soulful and their music more of the delta sound.

"I reckon this is a good way to end a fucked up day," he said to himself.

New York City, New York
5:33 PM

Evers lay on a bed twenty-eight stories above the street in the Double Tree on the north end of Times Square. From his window he could see the iconic neon billboards that are so famously on display during New York's New Year celebration. Teams of tourists scoured over Broadway, dodging the thousands of yellow cabs that seemed to speed up anytime a person stepped onto a busy street.

To the south he could see the new Freedom Tower, standing proudly in Battery Park where the World Trade Center towers once loomed, each a twin, both born and destroyed together. As with most Americans, that fateful day in September stuck in his head, replayed on each anniversary when terrorists brought their hate to the country's shores. He remembered how his fellow citizens rallied around the flag and screamed for vengeance in the wake of the attack, and how quickly the stomachs of those same "patriots" soured as the war moved forward. Those who never served in a combat mission would never grasp the good that was done in the valleys and mountains of Afghanistan, nor would they appreciate the sacrifices made by his fellow service men and women.

Evers shut those memories down before the ire they stirred boiled over. He forced himself to think back to his time with Emilia then his trip into Uruguay. The only time she would have had to contact someone was the interval between leaving her apartment and the ferry ride across the inlet. It also meant she would have been a plant at the night club, something that did not fully register with him.

His arrival at the bar that night had been purely random, and although he could not remember if she had been there before him, or came in later, the prospect of her being planted there to seduce him was very remote. If she had not been a plant and did not contact someone to follow him that could mean Buddy was in on it.

Smith had double-crossed him in Mexico City as he attempted to win over Dan Dugan's trust. Dugan had been pursuing an ancient talisman that contained a spell that had some strange control over the Terracotta Warriors in Xi'an, China. He later explained that he did not intentionally double-cross him, but had to make a couple of hard decisions in his attempt to remove Dugan himself. While the whole thing seemed plausible, it did not erase the fact that Smith had put him in mortal danger, leaving him in an airplane hangar getting curb-stomped by some pissed off Mexicans with whom he had earlier had a deadly encounter.

It took some time for him to get over that episode, but he had eventually begun trusting Buddy again. Besides, Smith had little knowledge of his whereabouts in Argentina, and he certainly did not know of his escape to Montevideo. That fact mostly eliminated his old mentor from the equation, although he knew Buddy's global reach was tremendous. He saw little value in Buddy having him killed there versus anywhere else in the world.

So, if Emilia and Buddy are satisfactorily ruled out of the equation, who is left, he thought. The common connection that came up time and again was Trowton, but how could he have known where he was and what he was up to? Or perhaps Vasquez had learned of his arrival and put a tail on him, even though his SDR's had been carefully considered and executed.

"Dammit, I have no idea who put that clown on me in Uruguay, but at least I can rule out Buddy and Emilia," he muttered.

He considered this mental exercise valuable, mostly because he was at least able to rule out all but a few people in the world. Evers almost laughed at his deductive reasoning. His finger dropped to the power button cn his television's remote control and pressed it. The television slowly came to life.

Evers searched for a news station, although he understood that the majority of America's news corporations were run by special interest groups and disseminating information was left to the viewer. He hoped that the reports of the global catastrophe would not be politicized and hidden from the public, but he had his doubts.

"The United States military has deployed three thousand troops to east and west Africa to help combat and contain the spread of the deadly Ebola virus. Extensive hazmat training has been conducted with the troops prior to their departure. They have also been tasked with building temporary hospitals and morgues. The morgues will contain incinerators to aid in the disposal of infected bodies, which greatly contribute to the disease's spread," the reporter announced.

The reporter continued, "In Japan the government was quick in their response to contain the SAR's outbreak throughout Tokyo and some of the surrounding provinces. However, some 120,000 people have succumbed to the disease before the government could fully contain it. The disease is said to have spread at an accelerated rate, much faster than it had previously been transferred from human to human.

"Estimates of death rates in Africa as a result of the Ebola virus are between 250 and 400,000. This is truly an agonizing time in the history of mankind. How the diseases were spread is still being investigated by several countries.

"The devastating release of nuclear material in both France and India is still being investigated by their respective governments. The total number of deaths from both incidents is currently unknown, as neither government has offered a body count. It is presumed by many leading experts that those numbers will rise dramatically once evaluations in the surrounding areas are conducted and subsequent deaths attributed to the explosions are made.

"Rumors of civilian purging in Argentina seem to have come to a stop, as the country's military leader, General Vasquez and his driver's bodies were discovered in an abandoned warehouse. Many eyewitnesses claim that he was solely responsible for an estimated twenty-five thousand murders over the past few weeks. The Argentinian government has remained largely silent about Vasquez's murder, but has indicated they believe anti-government revolutionaries are responsible ," he finished.

"Jesus Christ, the death toll will surpass the hundred million mark if this ass clown Trowton isn't stopped," Evers said aloud.

He lay like that, lost in thought, for another half hour when he felt his disposable phone vibrate. The number was a familiar one so he picked up.

"Yep," Evers answered.

"Yep? Why is it you continue to disrespect your elders after they've spent half a goddam day coming to this god awful metropolis to see your sorry ass?" Buddy asked, although Evers sensed he might have had a crooked smile on his face.

"Where are you?" Evers asked.

"What do you mean 'where am I?' Where did you tell me to meet you? You aren't about to send me out on one of your goddam surveillance walks are you? I'm getting way too old for that shit, Buck," Buddy said, his tone serious now.

"We have to do what we have to do, my friend. I had a follower today, so I'm a little more tense than usual," Evers replied.

"Follower, huh?" Buddy asked. "Maybe he just thought you were cute. I hear tell them South American boys don't mind switch hitting, if you know what I mean," Buddy laughed.

Evers responded, his voice calm and cool, "He wasn't trying to pick me up, and he won't be trying to pick anyone up again."

Buddy was silent for a few minutes then said, "Okay. Tell me where you want me to go."

Evers mapped out a thorough SDR for Buddy, which included hailing a couple of cabs, a walk through Soho then another cab into the trendy East Village. He figured once he got there, he would contact him again. Besides, the amount of time it would take Buddy to get to the Village would give him more than ample time to run his own SDR and get there before the meet. That way he could tell if Buddy was being followed, or if he was trying to set him up. Lastly, he told the man to wear some nice clothes—nothing over the top, but business casual.

They logged off the call and began their respective runs, both men checking behind them, as well as around them, as they did so. Evers made his way to the hotel lobby, turning north on Broadway before switching back on the other side of the street, carefully watching around him for anyone who might be changing their gait to keep up with him. He walked a block and hailed a cab taking it to Thirty-first and Lexington.

Evers took a few seconds to check his surroundings, noting how much quieter the east side of Manhattan was as compared to its western counterpart. No one in the area made him uncomfortable or seemed out of place, but of course in a city where no one person ever seemed out of place, a tail could be difficult to spot.

He walked south on Lexington then turned west on Twenty-sixth keeping in the shadows of the trees lining the north end of Baruch College until he intersected with Park Avenue South. Evers crossed over the road then turned left, again checking behind, around, and across from him for anyone trying to maintain his quick pace. He found the stairs leading below ground where he would take the Six Train to Astor Place.

The train was relatively empty on that side of the City, as it usually was on the eastern side of the island. Not once did he feel uneasy by the passengers riding the train with him. Once he got off at Astor Place, he made his way top-side to East Eighth Street where he found his destination point: Tompkins Square Park.

Tompkins was famous for its previous role in "housing" a significant portion of the city's homeless in through the 80's. During the early 90's the City elected to clean the park up and make it a more appealing area for the East Village residents. As Evers approached a park entrance, he could hear local musicians playing music. Nearby, the sound of an acoustic guitar played some Marshall Tucker Band riffs, as the musician sang "Can't You See." Evers was impressed with the singer's ability to sound so much like the old southern rock band.

After spending a few moments scouting out the area, checking for obvious hiding spots and look-out points, he found a bench and made himself comfortable. He only had to wait for a few minutes until Buddy came walking toward him, his face blank and un-telling. Evers watched behind Buddy for anyone who might be tagging along for the ride, but no one was paying any attention to him.

As he approached the bench, Evers could not help but notice Buddy's face. It was washed out, white and thin. Heavy bags lay beneath his eyes, and his jowls drooped on an unshaven face. His usual long hair lay limp on the back of his neck. His shoulders sloped downward as though a heavy weight rested upon them. There was a look of tiredness that overshadowed him, as though he had been exposed to all the knowledge of the world. Evers lamented the possibility and wondered how much ugliness and darkness Buddy had seen in his lifetime.

On a positive note, he dressed appropriately as Evers had instructed. His dinner jacket was a navy blue, his off-white shirt opened at the first two buttons. His khaki pants were neatly pressed, his black shoes freshly shined. Evers was impressed.

Buddy gave Evers a nod and sat next to him on the bench. The two sat in silence for a few minutes until Buddy's gravelly voice broke it.

"You're looking good, Buck. A little tired and worse for wear, but good," he offered a tired smile.

Evers looked away before responding, "So do you, Buddy."

Buddy began laughing until one of his coughing fits set in. He covered his mouth with his handkerchief; Evers did not see any sign of blood as he had weeks earlier in Washington D.C.

"Fuck you, Young Buck. I know I look like shit. I'm forced to see myself in the mirror every morning. This is what you have to look forward to one day, son," he grinned, "getting old and haggard."

Buddy continued, "How are you resting?"

"I'm okay, Buddy," Evers lied, not wanting to have the uncomfortable discussion about the severity of his dreams with the man.

Buddy dropped his eyes and nodded in quiet understanding. He realized the topic was a sensitive one with his friend and former student and that timing with any topic was fundamental to any healthy relationship. He sensed that the timing was not right and dropped the subject.

"So, tell me what you've been up to as you've gallivanted through Latin America while the rest of the world burns. Please tell me you've stopped stroking your little wee-wee and finally hooked up with one of those fine little South American women while the rest of us heroes were doing the Lord's work," Buddy teased.

Had it not been for Buddy's constant nagging about him finding a woman, Evers would have thought he knew something about Emilia. As it stood, there should only be two people in the world who knew anything about their relationship, and Buddy was not one of them.

"That's the Buddy Smith I've come to love and cherish. Always thinking with his libido and trying to live vicariously through one of his students," Evers laughed.

"Now don't go getting all sexually interested in me, Buck. I must admit a certain level of wariness when a friend uses words like 'love' and 'cherish' in the same sentence with my name. Furthermore, if I were living vicariously through you, my dominant hand would be calloused and my DVD player worn out from playing the same old porn flicks day after day," his bellowing belly laugh extending beyond their immediate area.

Evers, sensing the time was right to leave the East Village, suggested, "I have a place I think you would enjoy. It's a little more upscale than this park and features a decent selection of single malts. The food is outstanding and the view impeccable."

Buddy leaned back on his bench and narrowed his eyes as he looked into Evers's face, "I'm intrigued, but if you're asking me out on a date, you need to know I don't swing like some of the freaks in this park. I realize you boys that spend a lot of time in the field somehow find yourselves getting a little attached to the man paying your bills," he pointed a thumb at himself, "but that's no reason to go getting all homoerotic on me," he smiled.

Evers rolled his eyes. "You are one insufferable son-of-a-bitch, Buddy Smith. Let's get out of here."

They walked back to the subway station and caught the six line north to East Forty-Second. Evers led the two men topside, each checking their surroundings impulsively. From East Forty-Second they hitched a ride with a cab to Amsterdam and Sixtieth.

Evers paid the tab as the two men stepped out of the cab toward the sidewalk. Evers knew how adamant most cabbies were about exiting their cab to the sidewalk—safety first! Both men took a moment to look around. The west side preppies were busy going on about their lives without any idea regarding what was happening in their world. Evers wondered how it would be to live in a world of naïve bliss, looked at Buddy and saw the same thought cross over his face.

"These fucking people," was all Buddy said.

"Yeah, no clue, huh?" Evers asked his rhetorical question.

A retaining wall in front of a brownstone apartment yielded a rose bush, daffodils, and a beautiful, full juniper. It also provided Buddy with a resting point, his hand holding on as his head tilted backward, lungs expanding with tremendous effort to be filled.

"Are you okay?" Evers inquired.

"I'm fine. Just let me catch my breath. Hell, I ain't the spring chicken I used to be, Buck."

Evers glanced around then focused his energy on his old teacher. For the first time since they had become reacquainted at his place in Alabama, he felt something; perhaps it was worry or sympathy for the man, but whatever it was it was flooding his system at the moment, in addition to the heightened sense of paranoia because they were forced to stop for a few minutes.

Buddy coughed a couple of times then nodded at Evers, his signal that he was ready to continue. They made a couple of quick turns and switchbacks, but finally made their way to their destination.

An unobtrusive, medium height brownstone building standing at the corner of West Sixty-Third and Broadway, the Hotel Empire was a New York City landmark. The hotel lobby was immaculately adorned, in some ways over the top with zebra print couches and cushions, and in others tasteful and exquisitely upscale. The marble floors were shined to perfection, and the wood handrail attached to a spiral staircase at the far end of the lobby exuded age and detailed artisanship.

Buddy leaned over to Evers and said, "I hope you aren't bringing me here for a sexual liaison. I thought I've been clear with you that I don't swing that way."

He knew better than to engage Buddy. To do so could start a landslide of homosexual one liners that would take them into the early morning hours. Instead, he looked at him and pointed his chin to the set of elevator doors where several people were awaiting a ride.

"Where are you taking me, Buck?" Buddy asked.

"Just wait and see you impatient old bastard," Evers snipped.

A young man in his twenties overheard the exchange and started laughing. Buddy glared at him prompting him to shut his mouth and mind his own business. Evers simply shook his head and chuckled.

They stepped onto the elevator with a small group of other people. An elegant looking young lady in a sleek black dress and matching heels pressed the button for the rooftop. Buddy elbowed Evers and raised both eyebrows at the woman. Evers rolled his eyes and shook his head again as the elevator continued on its upward climb.

After a couple of minutes and a few stops, the door opened to the rooftop lounge. Part of it was enclosed, but a door opened to the exterior of the roof where several tables and decorative couches sat, surrounded by circular tables. The lights from surrounding apartments and businesses illuminated the various buildings adjacent to the Empire. The noise of the city was far below them, a low-level hum from the streets was all that could be heard.

Important businessmen and women, and those who wanted to be seen meandered between the enclosed restaurant and outdoor area. Everyone was sharply dressed and enjoying themselves, stopping momentarily whenever the elevator door would open to check its passengers for someone else they might attempt to impress. Luckily for the two men, they were unknown and therefore lacking in interest to the patrons.

On impulse, both Evers and Buddy scanned the room for anyone who might be looking at them too long or taking a special interest in them in general. One man, sitting with an attractive blonde at a table in the back of the room, gave Evers a hard look. Evers took note and was sure to keep an eye on him while there, although the look, Evers knew, may have been more of a testosterone and alcohol induced stare, as men sometimes do when they sense someone with combat experience enters a room.

The two men walked through the restaurant toward the door leading to the outside lounge area. Evers kept his eyes forward but watched the man at the table from his peripheral. He could not feel the man watching them as they passed, which probably boded well for his ability to continue breathing in the near future. Still, Evers would watch him periodically.

Evers and Buddy found a corner table, but continued to stand for a few moments taking in the view. They both propped their elbows on the ledge and stared out over the West Side of Manhattan, both thankful to be above the crowded streets and noise. There was something serene and gentle about the mean city streets when hovering above them. In a strange way, both men appreciated the area much more from their aerial perspective.

A beautiful brunette waitress apologized for interrupting them, but asked if she could take their drink order. Before Buddy could speak up, Evers asked for two Laphroaig eighteens on the rocks. Buddy turned his head and stared at his former apprentice and smiled.

"I'll be damned. I reckon I have officially passed the torch. You are now a Jedi master, Young Buck," his voice serious.

Both men began laughing, the laughter turning to manly cackling, both struggling to catch their breath. There was something about inordinate stress and a well-timed joke that caused people to hold their sides and belly laugh until they were on the verge of passing out.

The two of them sat down as the waitress brought their drinks to them. She placed them on the table and handed them menus. Buddy gave her a warm smile and a wink, making her giggle as she walked away. They each began looking over the food selection, each finding something they wanted to eat. Evers placed the menu on the table and began to speak.

"Look, I wanted to update you…"

Buddy held up a hand silencing him. "Buck, we have all night to discuss your business down south and what I've learned while you were gone, but right now we both have a glass of liquid gold sitting in front of us. I suggest we wait a while and enjoy what the Good Lord has placed on this Earth to help us momentarily alienate ourselves from the problems we all face."

The grizzled veteran raised his glass to his nose and breathed deeply. "Buck, God is smiling down on us right this minute. If he weren't, we'd be one of the camel jockey's in the Middle East offering up a big toast to Allah and turning up a glass of goat piss."

Earthy aroma filled his nostrils, the smell of peat was warm and pleasing. He took a sip with his eyes closed tasting the peaty fields of the small island off the coast of Scotland, Atlantic sea salt resting on the sides of his tongue followed by sweet spices that slipped down his throat.

He nodded at Evers to follow suit. He lifted his own glass to his nose and took in the sweet pungency then sipped as Buddy had. "Damn, that is fine," he proclaimed.

The two men sat in silence sipping their drinks. Evers let his eyes drift over the man who had eyeballed him when he first walked in. He was fully engrossed in conversation with the young lady at his table, she smiling and blushing and he stroking her hand. *Just as I thought.*

Evers turned his attention back to Buddy who took another long sip of whiskey.

Apparently ready to discuss current and recent events, Buddy said, "The fucking world is turned upside down, Buck. I'm sure you've heard reports of the global death rate as a result of the viruses, nuclear attacks and mass slayings. I can assure you that most of the estimates are considerably south of what they should be. My sources have estimated immediate death as a result of the aforementioned at closer to two million globally."

"Holy shit. Who the hell does something like that?" Evers asked.

"I believe we both know the answer to that, but the better question is 'why,'" Buddy replied. "Before we get to that, tell me what you learned in Argentina."

Evers briefed Buddy on the events leading up to their meeting in the Village, leaving out his soiree with Emilia. If he told him about her, he would never hear the end of it. Besides, he saw little value in detailing his evening with her since he had already deduced that she was not involved in Daniel following him from Montevideo.

His interrogation of General Vasquez was of special interest to Buddy.

"So, he ratted out Simon Trowton, huh? Well, that sews that seam up. My sources are telling me that he's behind this mess. We need to get to him and find out if he can call it off and make sure we stop anything else he may have planned.

"Now, this Daniel character that followed you, that's interesting. You say you didn't have any interaction with anyone while you were in Buenos Aires or Montevideo?" Buddy inquired.

Evers felt like Buddy could see right through him, but stuck to his guns. "No, I had no interaction with anyone while there."

"That is interesting. I wonder how in the hell he picked up your trail?" Buddy mused.

It was Evers turn to ask a couple of questions. "You said 'your sources' earlier. Who are your sources? I will assume one of the alphabet soup organizations close to your home."

"You would be correct, sir, and now there's some financial gain as a result of our involvement," Buddy smiled as he raised a brow.

"When this whole thing started you said big brother wasn't going to be involved," Evers replied, his voice dripping with sarcasm.

"New estimates of two million deaths seem to have changed that, and if our suspicions are true about who is leading this anarchy, I can assure you our older sibling has a sincere interest in bringing about a quiet end to the situation. They're offering a quarter million to contract us old whores out. What do you think?" Buddy asked.

"If they really want this thing done quietly, my mind is in the half million range. There's going to be a lot of risk involved in taking out a British dignitary, especially a rich one connected to a lot of other rich dignitaries," Evers stated.

"That is a fact, Buck, that is a fact. Let me reach out and see what I can do. Perhaps I can persuade Uncle Sam that a half million dollars to keep it from getting involved in this mess is a drop in a very big fucking bucket," Buddy replied.

"If the Christians in Action are going to be involved, they should also supply a little firepower when we get there. I would feel much better with a Colt 1911 at my side or in my waistband," Evers added.

"I'm certain those arrangements can be made, Buck, but there's something I've got to tell you," Buddy said, his voice low and eyes looking down at the floor.

"What it is it?" Evers asked, his brows furrowed.

"I can't go over the pond with you. You're going to have to do this alone. I have all the faith in the world in you Young Buck, and will help any way I can from here," Buddy stated.

Evers stared at him for a few minutes, his gaze looking him up and down. For the first time he realized how thin Buddy looked. He had never been a huge man, but he was solid, his arms and legs full and muscular. Even in his later years, Buddy had always been a man to be wary of, but now he looked frail. His face, as Evers had noticed earlier, was drawn and sagging. The pastiness of his skin was even more evident in the pale outdoor light of the Hotel Empire.

"Are you sick, Buddy?" Evers asked, his own voice low and the tone serious.

"Yeah, I'm sick, but I'll still kick your ass up between your ears if you start looking at me all sad-like, you hear me?"

Evers hesitated for a few seconds before answering. "Yeah, I hear ya. So, what's wrong? You finally got a case of the incurable gonorrhea on one of your jaunts to the far East?"

Buddy laughed out loud again. "I've known you what…twenty or thirty years, and now you decide to develop a sense of humor?"

Evers laughed, but his laughter was uneasy. "You going to tell me what's ailing you?"

It was Buddy who now hesitated. He took another sip of the Laphroaig and exhaled through his nose. Evers watched as a calming look came over his old friend's face.

"Well, it started out with some pretty serious hacking and coughing, so I went to see my doctor. He took some x-rays and ran all kinds of tests. When I showed up at his office a week later he had this somber look on his face, so I knew the news wasn't going to be good. Told me I had advanced emphysema, which didn't really surprise me, what with the smoking I've done in my life and some of the god-awful shit I breathed in Over There. Both sides released some pretty harsh stuff, Buck, and those ridiculous hazmat helmets they gave us couldn't keep all of those chemicals out of our lungs.

"Anyway, the good doctor continues talking then tells me that I've got a pretty serious mass growing across both lungs and short of a double lung transplant, he didn't see much hope for me," Buddy laughed again before continuing.

"Can you imagine that? I've had women the world over tell me there ain't much hope for me. Hell, I've been hearing that for years. So, all of this bullshit has curtailed my ability to really offer you any help, at least in the physical sense," he finished.

Both men again fell into a pit of silence. Evers swallowed hard then asked, "How long?"

"That's always the question isn't it, Buck? How long do we have left? Hell, the doctor told me it could be two months or two years...he really wasn't sure. All I know is that I want to see this mission completed and figure out what's driving it. I can't imagine that this guy Trowton is working alone, and it would be interesting to find out everyone involved in his scheme, whatever that scheme is," Buddy said.

Evers nodded his head, his veneration for the man swelling. There had always been a certain reverence he felt toward the grizzled veteran, but that feeling was growing considerably at the moment. What man, when faced with death, will consider anything but his own demise? Yet here they were, talking about finishing the mission and hopefully saving a lot of people in the process. If there was a living definition of 'courage under fire,' Evers was looking it in the face.

"So that's that," Buddy said. "Let's enjoy this evening then I'll make some calls in the morning to begin working on our payday and some overseas firepower. How's that sound?"

"Good," Evers replied, his voice a little despondent. "That sounds good."

Buddy began looking around. "Now, what are the chances of us getting laid up here, or do we need to take our business elsewhere?"

For the second time that evening, both men laughed until their sides hurt. Evers ordered another round of Laphroaig as the two sat and talked about faraway places and the strange things they had seen.

JFK Airport, New York, New York
6:10 AM

Evers pinched the bridge of his nose, the coffee not yet doing its work in his caffeine deprived body. The sun began peeking over the Atlantic in its journey upward into a cloudless, blue-bold sky. Announcements from various gate attendants occasionally interrupted the dull hum of the terminal, as more and more passengers began filtering down its center walkway.

The smell of airport food drifted about, reminding him that he would soon be on a trans-Atlantic flight and subjected to the super-heated airline meals created and packaged somewhere on the southwest shores of Lake Michigan. Another hour would pass before his flight began boarding, so he rose and walked to a nearby restaurant and ordered some breakfast.

He chewed the scrambled egg burrito and sipped coffee, memories of his conversation two nights past still fresh in his mind. Evers had been the dealer of death many times in his life, and suffered greatly from his involvement, but the flood of emotions after learning of Buddy's terminal illness was weighing heavily on his mind. No one had beaten death in the history of man, but realizing someone you cared deeply for was looking at the end of his life cycle was still a difficult thing to rationalize.

The two men stayed and talked at the Hotel Empire until three in the morning, the alcohol and remembrances from a lifetime ago furthering the bond between the two. They reminisced about fallen comrades and strange, dark places hidden from sight the world over, many having succumbed to some thick jungle growth until some unsuspecting fool happened upon it.

They also discussed how much more the United States government was involved in shaping and molding lives the world over. Perhaps, they surmised, the government had always been involved in such things, but only until the Internet allowed John Q. Citizen to boast of knowledge and spread rumors at the speed of light, did D.C.'s finest creep back into the shadows and attempt more intricate, deeply rooted covert activity.

Uncle Sam's unprecedented involvement in the day-to-day life of America's working millions, all in the name of security, had provoked a backlash so substantial that many elected officials were forced to stop supporting the Patriot Act. In return, Buddy reflected, many of the alphabet soup organizations worked feverishly to circumvent the laws in order to continue spying on the very people paying their salaries.

9-11 had opened doors the government had been wanting entrance to for decades. Buddy shared some of his insight into new weapons being created, and the consistent urban warfare training conducted in U.S. cities all over the country. The government was quick to downplay the advancement in spying technology, weapons, eavesdropping, bank account monitoring, and urban training conducted by the military as something necessitated by the ever growing potential for a second terrorist attack.

Furthermore, Buddy explained that he had good information the government was now infiltrating bank accounts, domestic and foreign. There was no longer a need to invade countries for their natural resources when all you had to do was move money from their account into a secret U.S. government controlled account. Cyber warfare was the rage, and people like the two of them were soon to be things of the past.

As the Scotch flowed so did the conversation. Evers learned things about his own government and the shadow organizations that maneuvered within it. He was no adolescent mercenary, fresh off the farm or out of the military. No, he had seen more than his share of the shit, but what really turned the world was far removed from his own imagination. Control of resources, via the Interweb and other means, was so remote from his personal intellect that his head began hurting long before the alcohol depleted his system of water and added the congeners found in whiskey.

As they parted ways, Evers made Buddy promise they would remain in close contact. As usual, the old veteran's response was unique.

"Listen Buck, I sleep with my underwear on unless I'm in the company of a beautiful woman. In your case, I intend on remaining fully clothed because you're worrying over me is making me more than a little nervous. The fact that I have cancer should be enough to warn you that I won't try you in hand-to-hand combat should you become sexually aroused around me, but my preclusion to things filled with gunpowder and lead will hopefully be enough to abate your wet-ish dreams about yours truly."

Evers stared at him for a full minute. "Have you practiced that speech in the mirror back at your place, you sick old bastard?"

Buddy's head flipped backward and a roar of laughter erupted. Several people still seated at the Hotel Empire turned to see what the commotion was about, but he did not seem to care. The old man embraced Evers like he was *family*. In fact, he was pretty sure the two of them were the only family the other had.

Evers had gone back to his room and slept most of the next day, waking long enough to eat in the hotel lobby. He spent some time staring outside his hotel window into the mid-town lights, the waves of tourists rippling across the streets far below.

He rode the subway the next morning to Chinatown, mulling around Canal Street until he found what he was looking for.

Several Haitians and Nigerians had taken over a couple of blocks on the west side of Canal, peddling rip-off DVD's, designer purses, sunglasses, and watches. He found one such gentleman selling passport covers, each labeled with a different country's shield.

"Those are five dollars," he said, his voice monotone but filled with a Caribbean accent.

Evers reached inside his wallet and removed a five dollar bill, folding it lengthwise and holding it between his index and middle finger. As the man reached for the bill Evers pulled it back.

"I was hoping to find someone who could help me put something inside this passport protector," Evers said, eying the man.

"What do you want inside of it?" he questioned warily.

"What do you suppose goes inside a passport protector?" Evers asked, his head looking left and right to assure no one was listening to their conversation.

"I don't work with no cops, man. Now give me my money or put the cover down," the man warned.

"Do I look like a cop to you?" Evers demanded.

"All you white folks look like cops to me. You come around here asking to see my peddler's permit every few hours, but before you go home to your nice apartment, you make sure to stop and buy my shit. Fuck all you cops," he said, his eyes meeting Evers's.

"Look, I don't have time to dick around with you. I'm sure there are plenty of other folks out here willing to take my business, but I need some work done quickly, and I have a feeling you can make that happen. The pay is three hundred…cash. Your choice though, take it or leave it," Evers said as he straightened his back.

The man licked his lips and considered the cash amount. It would take him hours to make three hundred dollars selling the items on his table, and that was only if the tourist traffic was heavy. Vendor competition on the streets of New York was considerable, but most especially in Chinatown.

Evers watched the man mull the prospect of making three hundred dollars over in his mind.

"How do I know you ain't a cop?" the man asked, giving in to the lure of money.

Evers glared at him. "You don't, so I guess you'll have to trust me."

The man looked down for a few seconds then to a man standing a few feet away.

"Najac, come here, man."

Najac, tall and wiry, walked to the man's table as he eyed Evers suspiciously.

The two spoke a form of Pigeon English that Evers could not understand. He caught a familiar word here and there, but that was it. Najac kept looking over to him, presumably trying to size him up and determine whether or not he was a police officer. Finally, he walked to Evers and looked him in the face. Evers noticed the veins bulging from the man's thin but muscular arms.

"My friend say you need a passport. I can help you wif dat, but if I find out you a cop, I kill you dead," he warned.

Evers nodded. "Fair enough."

He followed Najac into an alley then through a door leading into the back of one of the many store front shops. Inside he saw a camera, a blue screen backdrop and a table full of paper material.

Najac motioned with his head toward the backdrop. "Move dere and I take you picture."

Evers did as he was instructed and watched as the man tinkered with the camera before snapping the photo. Afterward, he told Evers to come back in two hours to pick up his passport.

"It better look legit for three hundred bucks, my man," Evers stated, his eyes narrowed.

Najac looked up from the camera and nodded his understanding.

He made his way east on Canal then turned north, walking under the welcoming arch of Little Italy. Evers always felt like those two blocks were the happiest place in all of New York. Rarely did he see anyone frowning or upset. Most were content after finding a wonderful little restaurant in which to dine and drink beer or sip wine. It was unfortunate, Evers thought, that Chinatown was slowly creeping into and devouring this historic piece of New York.

"Progress, I reckon," he said to himself.

He sat down at a table outside a sidewalk café and ordered cannoli's and coffee. Both were the best he had had in a considerable time. The coffee was rich and hearty, the cannoli light and sweet. He watched as people milled about, checking out hawker stalls and t-shirt shops, all oblivious to what had befallen the world.

Evers was certain everyone, or most everyone, was aware of the casualties around the globe, but Americans, he knew, lived a life of comfort and disconnect. Events or calamities that occurred in other regions outside the safety of the United States borders got cursory mention on the evening news, giving way to more newsworthy items like which Hollywood starlet was recently arrested for DUI, or what team was picked to win the Super Bowl. To say that Americans lived in a vacuum was to insult vacuums.

He paid his bill then headed back into Chinatown. He found Mott Street and walked south beyond the large bend in the road to the foot of the Brooklyn Bridge. Evers walked out onto the walk path created for pedestrians not wishing to ride the train or brave the New York City traffic.

For twenty minutes he stood in the middle of the bridge taking in the sites around him. New York was a city that he both detested and loved. He hated the claustrophobic feel of Gotham, but loved the multi-cultural aspects it had to offer. Rich and poor, black, white, Asian, Indian, Middle Eastern…they all lived next to one another, most often without conflict. The place was most assuredly a melting pot, but it was also a place where dreams died, where the takers continued taking, and the leaches of society drank every ounce of blood they could get from an individual.

Evers checked his watch and headed back to the west side of Chinatown where he hoped to have a wonderfully forged passport. He considered traveling overseas under his real identity, but decided against it given what had transpired in Argentina. He thought it better to leave few clues behind should he be called to action again.

He found the man from whom he purchased the passport cover who, in turn, pointed with his chin toward a man sitting on steps outside a door entrance. Evers quickly recognized Najac who motioned to follow him down the same alley. Najac checked his surroundings, Evers presumed in search of cops, but he too took a look around to be sure he wasn't being set up for a mugging, or worse.

No one seemed to be paying them any attention as they headed off down the alley. When they were sufficiently far enough from the ultra-busy Canal Street, Najac pulled the forged passport from his hip pocket and handed it to Evers.

Evers opened the small booklet and began flipping through it, his photo and credentials perfect. The watermarks and reflective material embedded within the identification pages masterfully done.

"Sam Nelson?" Evers asked, reading the name printed on the passport. "Where did you come up with that name?"

The heavy Caribbean accented man replied, "I like dat actor Sam Elliot, and you look like a Nelson to me. I see you are happy with the work?"

"I'm more than happy with your work, Najac," Evers replied.

He reached into his front pocket and pulled out three one hundred dollar bills and handed them to the man. From his other pocket he fished another hundred and handed it to him.

"Why the extra money, man?" Najac asked.

"Three things: one, if I ever need to call on you again, I hope you'll give me some help. Two, to prove to you I'm no cop, and three, if anyone asks...well, I think you know the rest," Evers said, one brow pushed high on his head.

Najac began laughing. "Man, you right out of a bad fucking movie, but yeah, I understand and be happy to help you if you need it again. I be right here in good ole Chinatown."

Evers reached out and shook the man's hand before taking two steps backward then turning to Canal. When his feet hit the sidewalk he glanced left then right, his eyes finally landing on the man he had come to know as Passport Cover. Passport gave him a nod, which Evers returned.

He shook his head and rubbed his eyes, JFK Airport now fully awake. The gate attendant announced that they would soon begin boarding their flight for London's Heathrow International Airport in the next fifteen minutes. The usual barrage of instructions about how to line up and not breaking in line that most people largely ignored were offered. As usual, passengers began crowding the gate area.

Evers closed his eyes again and did a mental checklist of everything he would need once he landed in England. He checked his watch, stood and walked to the gate with the rest of the sheep.

Port Newark Container Terminal
Port Newark, New Jersey
11:19 PM

The massive shipping vessel arrived at the docks loaded with numerous containers. Waters from the Hudson splashed against its hull as it powered down in the dredged port area. Overhead, planes descended into the three major New York airports, the last of the evening's flights. Several cars passed by the port on the New Jersey Turnpike and US1.

Several dock workers began moving to unload the various containers. One such worker climbed a ladder to the top of the units and began attaching enormous straps through various loops. Above his head, a shipping boom stood at an angle, a massive anchor waiting to be connected to the strap. The man working the levers of the boom deftly raised the first container and placed it on the ground where the remaining shippers would be stacked.

Each of the off-loaded units was inspected for the proper shipping documents and seals affixed to their doors. This particular load was one having high tension seals applied, eighth inch metal cables laced through the doors then locked into place with a hasp containing a unique numerical identifier.

Long ago the dock workers ceased being amazed at shipping origination points, something any normal person would be infatuated in seeing. This particular vessel was loaded at a port in Cyprus, in the heart of the Mediterranean Sea and transported over the Atlantic to the United States. Cars, food and dry goods were moved like this every day and the men working at the various docks around the country were used to seeing such shipments.

The men moved methodically, like robots, each container stacked atop another until the vessel was empty. There they would stay, awaiting further shipping orders to be loaded on another vessel or to be picked up by truck and moved through some distribution channel.

One container was lost in the middle of the container mountain. Its stockpile dormant as it waited to be activated, ironically just over a mile from its intended target…

Evers exited his plane, and for the second time in a few days found himself standing in front of a customs agent answering the usual mundane questions that prevented no one from attacking or harming a country's people. The entire ruse that was airport security had not prevented an attacker intent on bringing harm to others, and the more Evers travelled the less patience he had for it.

"Welcome to London, Mr. Nelson," the agent said, his voice tired and his eyes heavy. He examined Evers's fake passport, shining a black light on the document in an attempt to spot a forgery or altering of the document.

Evers smiled at him, his face weary from travel and the time difference. "Thank you."

The standard bevy of questions were asked, "What brings you to England? How long will you be staying? Have you brought any illegal items or substances into the country with you? Are you carrying more than ten thousand United States dollars on your person?"

Evers wanted to roll his eyes after each question, but maintained the neutral look on his face and answered obediently. He watched as the agent haphazardly inspected his identification then looked over his declaration document. The agent then looked up and stared Evers in the eyes, a common practice to see if the passenger becomes agitated or nervous. Evers was neither and only wanted to get on about the business he was there to conduct.

Another minute passed slowly. Evers thought of sitting in a doctor's office and how time seemed to grind almost to a stop. The feeling was similar when dealing with customs agents.

He watched as the agent picked up his stamp and depressed it on an empty page. The agent handed the document to Evers and offered a halfhearted, "Enjoy your stay."

Evers thought to himself, *When I get back home I'm going straight to Chinatown and giving Najac a hug.*

He exited the airport terminal silently thanking himself for not checking a bag. Traveling light was a learned and practiced behavior that many less well traveled individuals lacked. In his line of work it was almost a practice of necessity. Outside, he hailed a cab and asked the driver to take him to the Marriott Hotel on Bath Road, a pricey hotel, but convenient in proximity to the airport.

The ride was short, and thankfully the driver did not want to engage in any conversation. They pulled up in front of the hotel, its large glass frontage sleek and modern. Blue LED lights illuminating the facade gave it a fresh, appealing look. He paid the driver the fare, grabbed the back pack he brought with him and walked inside.

The interior was vibrantly decorated, the colors all bright pastels. Several patrons lounged in the lobby enjoying a glass of wine and idle chit-chat. A man and woman sat at a large granite table, both handsomely dressed and presumably discussing business.

Evers checked into the hotel using the name given him in Chinatown by Najac. He had made the reservation prior to leaving for JFK, as well as stopping by a local bank to exchange a thousand dollars for British pounds. At the hotel he paid cash for his room and requested that he be placed on the first floor. He despised the bottleneck created in elevators and stairwells.

The registration clerk, a lovely young lady of about twenty-five, checked him in and was able to offer a room to accommodate his request. Evers thanked her for her help then walked in search of his room. Once inside, he inspected the bathroom, the closet, behind the curtains and under the two full sized beds.

"Better safe than sorry," he said.

He decided to shower then grab a bite to eat. Tomorrow would begin his search mission for the man he and Buddy assumed was behind the global anarchy.

Evers made his way to the hotel lobby where he ordered a nicely prepared steak and salad. He did not feel the need to go out in search of a restaurant having smelled the wonderful aroma of food being prepared on site.

After eating he located the hotel business center and logged into his ProtonMail account. Evers sent Buddy an email notifying him of his arrival and that he would check back in the following day. He knew the man would understand the intent of his message and did not add any unnecessary verbiage around his request.

Evers walked back to his room and turned on the television. The BBC was reporting an uptick in the number of deaths spreading through Africa and Asia as a result of the Ebola and SARS viruses. Evers knew the uptick was manufactured by government reporting agencies in an effort to squash an increase in public fear regarding the accelerated death rates. By reporting a slow rise in casualties, most people would feel as though the various world governments were closing in on a cure or at least containment. The dynamic of viral explosions would most likely send the whole planet into a frenzy, thereby pulling more military and police resources away from a burgeoning and systemic problem.

The news lulled his mind to fuzzy, far-away places as his eyes grew heavy. Anchor men and women reporting the news became a low hum in his head until he fell into a deep sleep.

He walked somewhere in downtown London, his eyes sweeping vertically and horizontally, attempting to seek out anyone intent on bringing him harm. The night was unusually chilly, even for London, and he wrapped his long jacket tighter to his body to prevent the cold from seeping further inside. Damp English air stuck to his face like a cold cloth dunked in frigid water.

Evers had no idea where he was going or for what, or whom, he was searching. He only knew that he must continue forward. Oddly, the streets were empty, devoid of life except for him and the sound of his own footfalls against the brick lined sidewalk. No cars passed, and stores, while flashing neon "open" signs were without anyone inside, including those who would be working.

He shivered and began to grow a little frantic. Why was he the only person on the street? The time seemed early enough, although the sun had gone down, and the store signage insinuated that others should be there with him. Ahead of him he spotted a shadow moving quickly, perpendicular to the street he was traveling.

His head instinctively shifted left and right continuing its search for anyone, or anything, thinking of attacking him. He quickened his pace to find out the source of the dark shadow that darted in front of him seconds earlier, his mind racing with possibilities. The oft created beings of his past appeared to him in his sleep and he wondered if he might be dreaming now.

Evers took a deep breath and could smell the old city. From the distant Thames he could smell the ancient river, its waters a slow moving liquid decay. The damp concrete, pavement and bricks emitted their own pungent aroma, and spices and food wafted across his nose.

"If no one is around to cook, why do I smell food? And if I'm dreaming, I could not really smell these things, so this must be real," Evers uttered.

Convinced that he was not dreaming, Evers walked to the intersection where he had seen the shadow pass. He looked to his left then turned to the right, the direction it had moved. The street was a short one, dead ending after two blocks.

A lone door stood closed, its wood painted a dark green, offset by the stream of streetlight shining upon it. At its top, an illuminated sign that read "Enter Here," beckoned. Evers frowned and looked around for any indication of another human being but found none. The door seemed to call to him, pulling him toward it. His heart began beating hard inside his chest.

He reached for the door handle and pulled—unlocked. Inside, one lone incandescent bulb shone at the top of a flight of stairs. Evers walked inside and began climbing the staircase, as quietly as possible, the wood beneath each foot moaning and creaking from his weight. Above him he heard someone shuffle across the landing.

His right hand shot inside his jacket searching for a pistol he did not have then moved inside his pants pocket for a knife. There was nothing inside his pockets, no keys, no paper, and certainly no knife. He wondered what he had been doing all day, but could not recall anything beyond his appearance on the empty London streets.

Cautiously he stepped onto the landing where he just heard the shuffling sound seconds before. To his right stood another door, this one a deep cherry stained, opened only inches. He could see nothing inside so incredibly dark was the room. His heart continued to hammer away at his sternum, the blood coursing through his body like a runaway train. Something in his head told him to stop, that he stood to gain nothing by entering the room.

But rather than trust his instincts, he reached for the door and pushed it open. The dim light from the overhead bulb did little to part the darkness of the room. Evers took one step inside, his left hand still resting on the door, the other reaching for anything that might be in his way.

Nothing impeded his movement and he continued stepping inside the room. Once he cleared the doorway he turned to look for a light switch on the wall. His hand felt around, but touched nothing except the wall itself. No light switch, no pictures hanging—nothing.

Something moved to his left! Evers's head swung in the same direction just as something seized his neck, lifting him off the floor. A vile stench of rotten meat, flesh, and fish overcame him, and he thought he would retch right on his own feet which dangled perilously three inches off the floor.

A light appeared a couple feet from Evers's face, but he struggled to determine its source as whatever had snatched him off the floor was squeezing his neck so hard that his head was tilted up in an effort to reduce the pain. Seconds passed and he saw a hand with long, sinewy fingers extending from an upturned palm. On the palm stood a flame burning like a small campfire; its flames not quite touching the skin, and the skin remaining normal and unaffected by the heat.

As the grip tightened on his neck his eyes bulged, feeling as though they would fly from their sockets. The hand wrapped around his neck and the base of his skull turned him a quarter circle. Evers looked into the eyes of his captor, a tall man whose age could not be immediately established. His hair was grey and receding, slicked back into a thin layer covering his scalp. His skin was smooth, time having not touched it, and Evers noted that he lacked even the tiniest trace of crow's feet. His eyes were coal black and in the corners were dots of red where there should have been dark pink skin, the gathering of skin forming the caruncle.

Straightaway, Evers was struck by something missing in those eyes. There was no life where life should have been teeming. The man's lips peeled back into an evil grin, and the smell of rot and decay grew stronger. His teeth were pointed and jagged, yellowed as though he smoked multiple packs of cigarettes a day chased by copious amounts of coffee.

A vague familiarity tickled Evers's brain about his captor. There was a hint in his features that made him feel as though he had seen the man at some point in his life, although the specifics evaded his memory.

The man tilted his head to one side then the other, sizing up his prey in a cold and callous way, and that was exactly what Evers felt like—prey. The man squeezed harder and began laughing. His grip was potent and Evers's arms began thrashing and reaching behind in an attempt to seize one or two fingers to try to unhinge the hold on his neck. A thousand judo and karate techniques ran through his mind all at once, but the pain in his torso was so great it rendered him immobile.

A succession of events happened in a matter of seconds. As Evers was looking into the man's eyes, the man spun Evers's body around then slammed his face into the wall. He tried to brace himself before his face made contact, but the man was just too strong. His face smashed through the drywall then right away slammed into a two by four header the drywall was mounted to.

Evers's cheek erupted in pain as blood poured over his face and down his shirt and jacket. His assailant began laughing, loudly as he picked him up further, preparing for another attack of sorts. Evers's body flew downward at an accelerated rate, his face zooming toward the hardwood floor. Again, Evers's reaction was slow and his face, ribs and knees slammed into the floor with such force that the building seemed to shake and vibrate.

The air rushed from his lungs leaving him gasping for oxygen. More laughter came from overhead as he felt the grip release from his neck. His knee felt broken and the lack of air in his lungs made escape all but an impossibility. Evers considered his options, but before he could decide on one he felt a heel hammering through a kidney.

Pain and agony sped through his renal system as blood spurted from his nose and mouth. He was certain that critical organs would begin shutting down soon; he had been the deliverer of such pain several times over the years and watched as grown men wept knowing that their time was at an end.

Evers ran his tongue over his lips and teeth. His lips were severely cut and three teeth broken. Inside his mouth he could feel the broken pieces rolling about and spat them on the floor. Suddenly, fire and pain erupted from his other kidney as he screamed in agony. Evers's head snapped around as he watched the man twist his knee into the small of his back then reach for a handful of his hair.

He pulled his hair back, stretching his neck to its absolute limits. Steely fingers wrapped around his jutted chin and gripped so tight that Evers thought his face would be crushed in an instant. His eyes started to roll to the back of his skull when he suddenly saw a pair of dark legs appear in front of him.

The form squatted down in front of him, and he immediately recognized the ebony face that smiled the most hideous smile he had ever seen.

"Ritah," he managed. "Help me."

"You killed me, white man, now I'm going to watch you die," she replied.

Ritah, her face as beautiful as he remembered, her smooth, black skin, long hair pulled tightly into a pony tail, and no makeup. She did not need face paint—that was something Evers always remembered about her.

She tilted her head back and laughed, his captor's laugh coinciding with hers in a sadistic duet. He felt a hot tear roll over his undamaged cheek and wondered briefly how battered he must look. Their laughter continued in a cacophony of hideous pitches and vales. Evers felt the man's grip tighten on his hair and chin.

"Wh-wh-who are you?" Evers grunted.

"A nightmare," the man whispered in his ear.

Evers heard a sudden and loud crack, pain radiating up and down his spine from the base of his skull all the way to his tailbone. He realized it was his own neck that had snapped, and for the final seconds of his life he thought about all the other people he had killed in a similar fashion.

Sweat covered his body and matted his hair as Evers sat up in his bed, his head snapping around so that his brain could process where he was, and more importantly that he was still alive. His chest heaved as he struggled to catch his breath. The dreams were coming to him more frequently than before, and the vivid nature of them made them seem so real.

He rubbed the back of his neck and winced. Evers threw his feet off the bed and walked to the bathroom and flipped on a light taking time to examine his neck for the source of pain he was feeling there. Two distinct finger marks lay on one side and a thumb print bruised the other.

"What in the fuck just happened?" he asked aloud.

His body began shaking, his nerves frayed. He grabbed a towel off the rack and dried himself, the shakes and sweat continuing despite wiping it off. Evers turned on the shower, the water cold, and got in. The sweat stopped but the shaking persisted, although he was not sure if it was because of the fear he felt upon waking, the marks on his neck, or the cold water pouring over his body. Most likely, he figured, it was a combination of the three.

He got out of the shower and gathered himself.

"It was a fucking dream. I don't know how those marks got there though. Maybe it was some strange form of dermographism that I had read about on a flight some time back. Weird marks that appear while people sleep. Yeah, that's probably what it was…my damned dreams are now causing bodily harm," he reasoned with himself.

Evers pulled himself together and got dressed. As he had grown accustomed to doing, he moved the memory of what just happened to the back of his mind and focused on the task at hand. His first stop was the hotel business center to check for messages on his secured email account.

As he had hoped, Buddy came through for him. He gave him the address of a local market where he would be able to acquire the .45 he had requested. The individual, Cathy, would also facilitate the purchase of anything else he might require during his stay. That made Evers smile.

He found the hotel concierge who called a cab. When the small white car pulled in front of the hotel, Evers jumped in and asked to be taken to the Brick Lane Market.

A heavy English accent replied, "Aye, it's about twenty miles away and in this traffic could take us a considerable amount of time to reach your destination."

Evers smiled at him and replied, "How long will it take us?"

"An hour, maybe an hour and a half. Traffic is heavy now."

"For an extra seventy-five pounds can you get me there any quicker?" Evers asked, a smirk on his face.

The cabbie licked his lips and turned to face Evers. A huge smile lit up his face. "Fasten your seatbelt, bloke, this could get a little hairy."

He punched the gas and the two sped off, the car swerving in and out of traffic, turning through residential areas until they arrived in the Paddington district. Not far from Buckingham Palace, the London Zoo, and the British Museum, traffic congestion brought their trip to a screeching halt. Evers watched as his driver considered his options, then suddenly the car made a sharp left turn, and they once again sped off on narrow roads and through moderately busy shopping districts, bypassing the main thoroughfares and arriving at the Brick Lane Market in less than forty-five minutes.

The cabbie once again turned and looked at Evers with a huge smile on his face, his five o'clock shadow heavy, but his eyes remained bright and cheerful.

Evers nodded at him and laughed as he handed him the promised money.

"I'm going to be just a little while here. There's more in it for you if you can wait and give me a ride back to the Marriott in, say, an hour?" Evers said.

"How much more, mate? There are people anxious to see our lovely city," the cabbie replied.

"An extra three hundred pounds plus the fare," Evers told him.

"Looks like I'm waiting on my new American friend," his cabbie stated.

The driver pulled a worn business card from a compartment in his dashboard and handed it to Evers. The name on it read James Donnington with a phone number just beneath it.

"I'm going to park, my friend, so give me a call when you are ready," James told him.

Evers nodded his head and replied, "I'll do that, James. And thanks."

"No worries," James said.

Evers began walking through the massive array of stalls and peddlers, many selling shoes, clothes, food, and items found at flea markets the world over. At one such stall he found a pair of deer skin work gloves and purchased them for four pounds. The vendor placed them in a small plastic bag and handed it to him. His eyes shifted left to right, on the lookout for anyone who might take an interest in him and for the specific stall Buddy had told him to locate.

After several minutes he found the stall he was looking for, a thin middle aged woman selling wooden crafts that appeared to be handmade. Evers looked over the assortment of clocks, funny signs to be hung in kitchens or on doors, and intricate airplane and car models that, Evers assessed, were detailed infinitesimally.

He picked up a model of a Porsche 944 and examined it, the stall owner not yet paying attention to him as she haggled with another patron. A few more moments passed as the clerk finished her sell. She turned to look at the intriguing man who was admiring the wooden car.

"That is a 2014 Porsche 944, a beautiful car. I spent a lot of time making sure every single detail of the actual car was transposed to this miniature. It would look fantastic on your desk or displayed upon your hearth," she told Evers.

"It is truly a work of art," Evers replied, his tone full of admiration as he continued to turn the car and look it over.

"Thank you," the woman said. "I'm asking one hundred pounds for it."

Evers put the car back on its display stand. "I'm interested and am hoping you might provide me with a discount if I make a couple of other purchases. We have a mutual friend who told me that you were willing to do so."

The woman's eyes narrowed as she looked Evers up and down. "Who is our mutual friend?"

"Oh, just a mean old American yank who talks funny," Evers said with a smile creeping over his face.

"My name is Cathy, and that old American yank sounds a lot like you," he chuckled.

"Perish the thought," Evers replied.

Cathy touched the shoulder of a young lady standing behind the table, obviously working with her and young enough to be her daughter Evers thought. She whispered something to the young lady who looked at Evers then nodded her head.

She turned and faced Evers, "Melinda will tend to our sales while you and I talk about bulk discounts."

Cathy motioned Evers to follow her to a seating area away from the throng of people. They found a bench suitably away from anyone who might overhear their discussion and sat down.

Evers got to the point. "I'm assuming our mutual friend told you of my need for a .45. I'm also in the market for a stun gun, low voltage, medium amperage should suffice."

"You know your electronics," Cathy replied as her eyes did a quick survey of the area. "I have the pistol you are requesting, but it will take me the better part of the afternoon to acquire the stun gun, as they are also illegal here on our beautiful island. I can call you when I get it. The combination of the two will be three thousand pounds. I'll throw the Porsche in for free," she smiled.

Evers laughed. "Thanks. I reckon it goes without saying that discretion is an absolute must," the smile falling from his face and his eyes hardening.

"I've worked in the realm of discretion my whole life, sir. I doubt our mutual friend would have sent you this way had he thought less of me," Cathy replied.

"That's probably true," Evers began, "but I just wanted to reinforce the need."

"Understood," said Cathy.

Evers gave her the number to the disposable phone he was carrying. "What time do you think we might be able to meet?"

"Ah, Americans are all so impatient. It's a shame some of our European genetic disposition did not stay with the seeds we left behind in The States," Cathy joked. "I suspect I will have the stunner no later than four o'clock. I shall call you as soon as I get my hands on it."

The two walked back to Cathy's stall where she reached under the table and produced a paper bag and handed it to Evers. Evers took a quick peek inside and saw the Colt Buddy had procured for him. Another pleasant surprise rolled around inside the bag: a sound suppressor for the pistol.

I love that man, Evers thought as he dropped the bag with the gloves inside the bag with the pistol.

He picked up the model Porsche and winked at Cathy as he dropped it in the bag. He smiled at Melinda, who was watching him closely, then turned in search of his cab driver.

Evers pulled his cell phone from his pants pocket along with the cabbie's business card and dialed the number. Within a few minutes John was there and Evers hopped inside heading back to the Marriott. On the ride back he pulled the small Porsche from the bag and examined it.

"Amazing," he murmured.

London, England
7:36 PM

Evers met Cathy at a pub in Kingston upon Thames where they both enjoyed a pint of beer and conducted their business. The stun gun was a Panther series, much higher voltage than Evers wanted, but Cathy assured him it was non-lethal. Evers got the distinct feeling that Cathy had spent time working in a covert position, possibly with one of the British MI functions, or as an independent contractor. Either way, he sensed the woman's pleasant demeanor could be easily thrown aside and a much darker individual revealed.

They finished their beers, Cathy paying the tab, which, he admitted to himself, made him more than a little uncomfortable. They shook hands and Evers made his way back to his hotel to finalize his plan.

Evers sat on the edge of his bed examining the Colt 1911 .45 caliber pistol. He broke it down and inspected each part for any signs of damage, wear, or tampering. Everything appeared to be in perfect working order. Deftly, he put the pistol back together and dry fired it, testing the trigger and hammer. It worked perfectly.

He laid the pistol next to him and pulled the Panther from the bag. In the hotel lobby he bought a battery and placed it inside the mechanism's handle. He depressed the trigger and watched as a bolt of electricity appeared between the two electrodes, the zapping sound like that of frying bacon. Evers put the stun gun down then picked up the city map he purchased upon landing at Heathrow.

The address he had for Trowton was close to London Bridge in a place called The Northern and Shell Building on Lower Thames Road. Apparently the building was one with several businesses on the lower floors, including numerous newspaper and media outlets, but a select few penthouse suites were built to accommodate the needs of London's uber-wealthy.

His research yielded a lot about traffic patterns and times the area was covered with tourists and business men and women. Most of the restaurants and pubs were further down Lower Thames, most likely as a result of the concentrated wealth in and around the building. Influential people could easily influence who and what was allowed in the neighborhood, Evers speculated.

Evers got up and changed clothes, putting on a jogging outfit he brought with him along with running shoes and a ball cap. The persona he would emit would be that of a businessman in London to take part in an important meeting, or perhaps he was serving as the liaison between a local company and one back in the States. All businessmen who worked in a stressful environment needed to blow off steam and stay in shape. In his case, he was just going out for an early evening run.

He stuffed the pistol in his waistband and pulled the oversized hoodie down so the bulge was hidden. Next, he placed the silencer in the hoodie's front pocket, which masked its shape. Finally, he shoved the small stun gun and gloves into his pants pocket.

Evers rode the elevator downstairs, walked outside, and stepped into the cool London night air. He began jogging parallel to Hatton Road before crossing over the street and passing the circularly built Holiday Inn. Continuing down the sidewalk he passed a few pedestrians and several cars driving to and leaving from Heathrow Airport, which proudly stood across the highway. Evers reached the Hotel Ibis, a gloriously adorned hotel and turned left on Nobel Drive.

From there he hailed a cab and got in. *Better to not be remembered being picked up in front of the hotel I've been staying in,* he thought.

He instructed the driver to drop him at the London Bridge Experience at 2-4 Tooley Street, a tourist drop-off point for those seeking more information about London and its darker history.

"Don't think it's open, mate," the cabbie offered.

"Yeah, I know. I just wanted to walk around over there while I have a little time away from my meetings this week," Evers lied.

The ride to Tooley Street was uneventful and the cabbie mostly quiet. He tried to engage Evers in conversation early in the ride, but Evers's mind was on the mission at hand. The driver picked up on his passenger's desired reticence quickly and chose to turn his radio up a little louder. A Justin Beiber song was playing and Evers rolled his eyes while the cabbie thumped the steering wheel in time with the music.

When they arrived on Tooley, the driver asked if Evers had a preference in where to be dropped. He saw a large white building with giant yellowish lettering over the entrance that read "St. Olaf House."

"There will be just fine," Evers pointed at the building.

"Ah, very good sir. A fine place St. Olaf's is. Some exceptional history that goes along with the building, originally built as The Hay's Wharf Company. Naturally, it stands where the former Church of St. Olave once stood, but I'm certain you'll get a chance to look around and learn more of its significant history here in London," the cabbie smiled.

Evers was always impressed with how much history cab drivers the world over knew about the city in which they transported people. It stood to reason that they would learn a significant amount about it, but sometimes the detail they shared was impressive. In this particular case, however, he was largely uninterested and merely shook his head during the man's mini-lecture.

He exited the car and stood long enough to watch the cab drive away. Several people were walking about enjoying the brisk evening air. Evers looked around and got his bearings, crossed the street and walked a couple of blocks until he found a sky-bridge that would take him to the foot of London Bridge. He entered the public entrance and walked up two flights of stairs, a glass door his only barrier to the bridge itself.

Several people were shuffling across the bridge on the pedestrian walkways, both coming and going. The River Thames's breadth was incredible, an expanse of river that served London since its settlement. Barges and ships moved along the waterway delivering and shipping goods in and out of Britain's largest city. Couples walked arm-in-arm and a steady flow of traffic in the bridge's middle provided an automated cross-stream that seemed to equal the waters below.

Evers kept his head low. He was aware of the innumerable cameras stationed about the city that constantly monitored its citizenry. A hand reached behind his neck and pulled up the hood on his sweatshirt as a measure of extra security against them. He stuffed his hands in the solo pocket on the front of his hoodie as he continued to scan his surroundings.

The walk across the bridge took about fifteen minutes. He controlled his gait so as not to bring attention to himself, keeping with the flow of foot traffic. Evers reached the other side, the chill of the night nipping at his nose and ears despite the hood pulled over his head.

Rather than turning right in search of Lower Thames Road, Evers elected to make a left so that he could check behind him for anyone that might be following. Since his encounter on his flight from Argentina, his suspicion level was running on maximum overdrive, and his recent nightmare and current surroundings created a strange sense of déjà vu, which created additional uneasiness.

He spent the next forty minutes traversing the area, making sudden stops and turns, dashes across the street and sudden one eighties in effort to draw anyone out who might be following him. No one appeared to give him a second glance when he made his turns and moves, which put his nerves slightly more at ease.

At last he came to Ten Lower Thames road and marveled at the building that stood before him. The glass pantheon housed those media gods so many entrusted with revealing facts about their government and local stars. The glass was smoked, darkened so as to reflect sun and city light from its surface. The upper reaches of the building revealed towers, staggered in differing heights, the apex formed at the building's corner and the Clarkson Tower adjacent to it. It was a marvelous structure, one fit for an extremely wealthy man.

He checked the front doors and noted the cameras above. His research had yielded information regarding the newspapers and other media outlets renting space there so he doubted that tenants would use the business front to access their living quarters. Evers saw an alley leading to the back of the apartment, the portion of the building that faced the river.

That feels right. If I were paying a substantial amount of money for a high rise apartment, I would want a view. And if I were a shipping mogul, I would most certainly want a view of the water, he thought.

Evers stooped to re-tie his shoe, taking the opportunity to look around. No one seemed out of place or eying him suspiciously. He stood and walked to the alley, turned left and made his way toward the back of the building as he searched for entrances.

He found a large set of double-glass doors with an awning above. Inside was another set of doors that appeared to be electronically controlled.

Probably card accessed only, he thought. *I guess I won't be walking in like I own the place.*

A panel with black buttons mounted next to the set of inside doors caught his attention. He drew the hoodie closer to mask his face from the camera as he walked inside the small vestibule. As he hoped, the panel contained a list of names next to each button. He found one name of particular interest: Trowton 932.

Evers acted like he was pressing one of the other buttons and awaiting a response just in case someone was monitoring the camera mounted in the corner of the vestibule. He waited twenty seconds before shrugging his shoulders, mocking someone who realized the people he was attempting to contact were not home, turned and exited back the way he came.

He continued walking down the alley, turning again at the rear of the building and saw what he was searching for—a service door that allowed employees to enter and leave without disturbing the tenants. The door was locked, but not electronically. It looked to be nothing more than a typical deadbolt. He scanned above and around the area and saw no cameras. A large grin appeared on his face.

Behind him was a large dumpster, a perfect place to hide until the night grew darker and the chances of anyone wandering to the rear of the building were considerably reduced. He made himself comfortable on the ground, staring out at the murky waters of the River Thames. The half-moon was low on the horizon and wispy clouds moved gently from the west. Brisk air blew across his face, but was made bearable by the hoodie and sweatpants he was wearing.

Evers pushed his legs straight out in front of him and began stretching to keep himself limber. Cold air and age had caused him to lose a step, although he was still quicker than most. Sitting behind a dumpster in the cool English air would cause him to become stiff, something he could ill afford this evening.

The hours passed and the night grew ever more still as traffic, both automotive and pedestrian, slowed to nothing. He kept a watch on the upstairs windows as lights went out. One by one their owners turned them off until there were none left illuminated.

Evers pulled the pistol from his waistband then reached for the silencer. The pistol's barrel had been retro-fitted for the suppressor and he screwed it until it was snug. He pulled the slide back and chambered a round from the magazine then walked to the service door. His eyes dashed left and right then up to the various windows, checking to make sure he was alone. He slid the deer skin gloves onto his hands.

No one was in his immediate view and he could not see anyone staring out of a window. He raised the pistol and shot three silent rounds beside the deadbolt into the door jamb destroying the wood around the lock.

Shooting a deadbolt with a pistol is a waste of time and only works in the movies, he thought.

He placed a shoulder against the door and pushed. It took some effort, but the wood began to give way to his pushing. As the wood splintered and cracked he eased off the pressure. Evers was afraid that a large piece of wood or a piece of the deadbolt may dislodge and fall to the ground if he exerted too much energy into the door.

A few seconds of moderate pushing and the frame gave one last resounding crack and the door opened. He took a second to breathe a sigh of relief that the door was not one that had to be pulled, rather than pushed from the outside. Evers stepped inside and closed the door behind him, giving his eyes a full minute to adjust to the dark.

Evers looked around and saw that he was in a kitchen galley. As with many corporations, full cafeterias were offered to employees, which included hot, freshly cooked meals each day. Straight ahead he saw a dim fluorescent light and walked to it.

He peered through a small window inside a galley door into the break room itself. Evers glanced around looking for cameras and did not see one. Through the double glass doors he saw an "emergency exit only" sign pointing to the left.

I bet that door leads into the apartment complex and is off limits to employees except during emergency situations, he thought.

A surveillance camera sat perched atop the wall leading to the emergency exit. Evers was able to see beyond the lobby to the security desk where two feet sat propped on its surface next to a small bank of monitors. He gave his watch a quick glance: 12:36 in the morning.

Evers would have to roll the dice and assume those feet propped up in such a manner most probably meant inattention and boredom. Although he could not see the person attached to them, he figured that person was busy looking at a smart phone, reading a book or magazine, or possibly catching a quick nap. He dropped his head, hoodie still covering his face, and ran as quietly as possible to the emergency door. The carpeted flooring made his approach almost silent.

He focused on his breathing for a few seconds as he faced the hallway from which he just ran, waiting to see if the security guard had seen any movement on a monitor. Seconds passed and he heard no sound coming from the direction of the security guard. He turned and focused his attention on the emergency exit, the next item of concern.

Evers searched the door frame looking for anything that resembled an alarm system. The last thing he needed now was to trigger a loud siren alerting security, the police, and the local fire department of his presence. He looked over the crash bar in the center of the door and saw no wiring on either end, nor could he find an electrical junction box mounted anywhere on the door frame itself.

The alarm system should be on this side of the door, as this way is a point of egress, rather than on the other side. An electrical junction box would also warn anyone against pushing against the crash bar and attempting to enter this area of the building. I suspect the management figured the warning sign would be enough to keep people from going through the door, he considered.

Gingerly, he pushed the crash bar and gritted his teeth as he did so. If he had to make a sudden exit he would continue on through the door and make a run for it once he got outside. The door opened as Evers pursed his lips, prepared for the worst.

He exhaled when no insanely loud alarm system blared. With one hand he slowed the door as it was pulled into place by the air-actuated closer. The latch caught quietly then he turned and hunted for the stairwell, wanting to avoid elevators and the cameras mounted inside them at all costs.

At the end of the hallway he found what he was searching for, opened the door and began the climb up nine flights of stairs. When he reached the top he mopped sweat from his head and eyes, caught his breath and stepped through the door. His eyes swept each direction then fell upon a placard showing apartments 900-950 to the left.

Evers looked for more cameras in the hallway before walking toward his target's apartment. None were present, and he assumed the rich and sometimes famous enjoyed more privacy than their poorer counterparts. He walked down the hallway focused on the right side where the even numbered apartments were.

Apartment 932 was little more than halfway down the hall and he turned to face the door, checking left and right before he stepped up to the door knob. The door was painted a semi-gloss white. No welcome mat or other adornment would tell a visitor who lived there, nor give any indication that anyone resided there at all.

He kept his head down in case someone was looking through the peephole while he worked. With a gloved hand he reached for the knob and gave it an attempted turn. Locked. Evers was not surprised to find the door in that condition, and for the second time that night, reached for the .45 and aimed at the right of the deadbolt.

Two rounds destroyed the wood around the lock. He bent down, still holding the pistol in case someone were to surprise him, and picked up the larger pieces of wood, shoving them in his pocket. *No sense leaving a trail that might catch a late tenant's attention.*

With his free hand he pushed the door open and peeked inside. As he had seen when he was stationed behind the dumpster, the apartment was completely dark. He stepped inside and closed the door, crouching against it to make himself a smaller target and to let his eyes once again adjust to the darkness.

While he squatted there he could hear the constant hum of something mechanical. The sound was coming from down the hall and to the right. Evers smiled, his good fortune still working in his favor.

The guy sleeps with a fan on like so many other people who need the air and constant sound, he thought.

Evers gave himself a full five minutes to allow his eyes to adjust to the dark before moving. He stuffed the pistol back into his waistband and reached for the stun gun from his pants pocket as he stalked in total silence toward the sound of the fan.

A fresh dump of adrenaline bombarded his stomach and was sent out through his body at the speed of light. Things began slowing down for him, and his pulse pounded inside his arms and legs. His hand tightened around the stunner as he pulled up short from the bedroom and took a deep breath. Controlling his respiratory system had become an important trait in his line of work, especially when dealing with the effects of adrenaline.

Evers followed the sound of the fan, turning a corner and keeping his back close to the wall. The bedroom was darker than the rest of the apartment, drawn blinds and dark curtains providing for a pitch black room. He could see the outline of a sleeping person on the bed and stepped forward.

He stopped short of placing the stun gun on the prone body and considered. *What if this isn't Trowton? I don't want to kill someone inadvertently. Fuck, why didn't I spend a little more time researching him and his residence?* Then he answered his own thought. *Well, his name was listed on the directory in the tenant entrance, but I don't know if he's got someone in the bed with him. Why didn't I think this shit through earlier?*

He reached out with a gloved hand and grabbed a shoulder and shook.

"Trowton, wake up," Evers said.

The person jumped and yelled, "Wha-a-a-t? Who the fu…"

With all the confirmation he needed, Evers jammed the stun gun into the man's ribcage and depressed the trigger. The familiar electric zapping commenced, albeit muffled as it was jammed into his tissue. His limbs and torso stiffened and convulsed as the voltage interrupted his body's own neuro-electrical system. The smell of cooking flesh filled the room.

Evers kept the trigger depressed a few seconds longer than necessary. Pain was generally a great compliance officer, and he wanted Trowton to remember the sensation for several more minutes after being released from its vicious grip.

He released the pressure on the stun gun and the current stopped. Trowton curled into the fetal position and held his burning side. Even in the dark Evers could see the grimace on his face. He depressed the trigger again, making the stun gun zap in the air, his own face slightly illuminated by the blue arc of the electrical current. Trowton looked up at him, fear and anger somehow merged in his own expression.

"I'm going to ask you a few questions, Simon and you're going to answer them honestly and without hesitation. If I even begin to think you aren't being honest with me, I'm going to jam this stun gun into your balls and fry them. Do I have your attention?" Evers asked, his voice deliberate and calm despite the rush of adrenaline still surging through him.

Trowton grunted then mustered, "Fuck you!"

Evers had to give the guy credit for his gumption. Most civilians could not handle tens of thousands of volts of electricity shutting down their own nervous system, nor could they take the smell of their own skin cooking.

Once again, he jammed the electrodes into Trowton. This time he punched him in the stomach with the device before triggering it. Air pushed from Trowton's lungs and before he could take a breath Evers pushed the button.

Trowton's body arched, his heals and head pushing into the mattress, his hips launched into the air. Electricity coursed over his body for several seconds before Evers stopped. Trowton's hands flew to his injured abdomen and rubbed; Evers heard him whimper.

Evers's head tilted to one side as he evaluated his victim. He punched Trowton in the face and when his hands flew to his cheek, Evers launched another punch directly into the man's stomach where the electrodes had brought so much pain seconds earlier.

Trowton's breathing was raspy and he struggled to fill his lungs with air.

"I'll ask again. Do I have your attention? If you cooperate, I won't shock or punch you again, but if you continue down the path you are currently traveling, this is going to be a miserable night," Evers stated.

Trowton stared in the direction of his assailant, the dark hiding his features, his outline barely visible against the dim light coming from his hallway. The pain left from the electricity and punches was severe and the man hovering over him did not sound like he was joking.

"What do you want?" Trowton struggled to ask.

"Why?" Evers asked.

"What the fuck do you mean, 'why'?" Trowton spewed.

Evers took his time responding, took a deep breath and replied, "Why did you do it? Why did you kill millions of innocent people? To what end does killing all those people serve you?"

Evers thought he heard the man try to laugh, the sound a little more than gruesome, and if a laugh could be considered condescending and sanctimonious the one he just heard fit those definitions. He frowned as his heart thudded away inside his chest and he pushed the stun gun into the man's neck.

Trowton convulsed and straightened, his eyes wide and teary as the electricity found its connection right next to his spinal column. Every muscle in his body contracted while Evers kept the pressure on the trigger. The smell of burning flesh reeked as only human skin can when burned.

"Last time I ask you a question without the appropriate response, Simon. Next, things will start getting nasty and not nearly as pleasant as our last few minutes together. So, I'm going to ask you one more time—why did you do it?" Evers asked, the intensity clear in his voice.

The injured man looked up at Evers, worry, hate, despair, and a little hope all on his face now. Evers understood each emotion the man was facing, but wanted to focus on the hope Trowton was feeling. His questions had to be such that the man did not feel he was releasing anything vital, only giving simple and broadly known information in exchange for time, or possibly for his release.

"It's simple," Trowton said, his breathing labored, "the world has too many people."

"What?" Evers asked, his voice nonplussed.

"That's right. Too many people are taking an irreparable toll on the planet. Using all its resources, polluting its air and water, overcrowding cities are causing racial tensions and hatred. The herd must be thinned," Trowton replied.

Evers stood there listening to him in sheer disbelief. He was not so naïve to think that type of ideology did not exist in the world, but to stare a man in the face that was largely responsible for acting on it was something entirely different.

"Soon the planet will no longer be able to sustain all its inhabitants, and future generations will be left with nothing, if people can even exist in such an environment," Trowton added.

Evers felt rage beginning to boil over in him, but forced himself to stand down as he continued his line of questions.

"Are you working alone?" Evers asked.

Trowton looked at him, fear and anxiety overtaking the previous emotions written on his face. He began panting then turned his head away from Evers, his eyes squeezed shut.

Evers hit him with the stun gun again, this time sticking the instrument of pain on the man's unsuspecting cheekbone. His mouth flew open, stuck in perpetual torment as electricity played havoc with the muscles in his jaw. For a moment, Evers thought his jaw would come unhinged.

He removed the stun gun from Trowton's face and gave the man a minute to compose himself. More sobbing and whimpering came from the man's mouth.

"It doesn't have to be this way, Simon. You could just tell me what I want to know then I'll leave," Evers said, his voice calm and reassuring.

"N-n-n-o-o-o you won't. I'll tell you what you need to hear then you'll kill me. I'm not fucking stupid!," Trowton screamed.

Evers dropped a hammer fist on top of his nose, a loud crack and explosion of blood following. He covered Trowton's mouth to mute the scream.

"Yelling and screaming is a sure way to upset me, Simon, and right now is not the time to do that," Evers's said.

Trowton blubbered and his eyes grew large when he saw his assaulter raise the hand brandishing the stun gun again. Blood was pouring into his throat from his broken nose, and he began coughing and sputtering. He turned his head and retched, blood and phlegm spilling onto his shoulder, arm, and sheets.

"Okay, okay. Just put that fucking zapper away," he pleaded.

Evers dropped his arm to his side but said nothing as he waited for Trowton to tell him with whom he was working. Several seconds passed without either man saying a word. Evers began getting impatient and raised the stun gun a couple of inches so his victim could see it.

"No more waiting, Simon. Tell me what I want to know or your life is over," Evers threatened and moved a half step closer to the man.

"Ab-Abaddon," he stammered. "His name is Abaddon. I swear that's all I know—his first name."

"Abaddon? Who is Abaddon?" Evers demanded.

"I don't know who he is, I just know he is one evil fucking man," Trowton implored.

Evers decided to back off his line of questioning about Abaddon and focus on the more important aspects of his interrogation.

"Tell me what's next," Evers said.

"What do you mean 'what's next'?" Trowton asked.

"Don't play stupid with me, Simon. You're already trying my patience. You know exactly what I'm asking you. What is the next target in your plans?" Evers asked coolly.

Trowton swallowed a mouth full of blood and gagged again. After another minute he managed to speak.

"I didn't have any more plans, but Abaddon demanded that I purchase a nuke and have it moved to the States," he said, staring at Evers.

Evers's mouth flew open in disbelief as he processed what he was hearing. His imagination flashed to countless casualties and incomprehensible damage. Innocent men, women, and children's bodies were littered about the ground, in houses, and in shopping centers. Buildings and homes were leveled and in his mind's eye he could see no signs of life, not even a squirrel scavenging for food.

The anger swelled inside him like water boiling over the top of a pot left on the stove for too long. He drilled another fist into the man's chest and felt a rib crack. Trowton gasped and convulsed.

"Where, motherfucker?! Where and when will the detonation take place?" Evers seethed.

Trowton rolled around and coughed, more blood flying from his mouth and broken nose. He turned to face Evers after the pain subsided and opened his mouth to speak.

"It will be detonated in three days…in New…" his voice trailed off.

"That will be quite enough, Simon," a sinister voice rang out somewhere in the darkness.

Evers spun around in search of the strange voice but could see nothing. He took a step away from Trowton's bed, felt something slam into the side of his head then everything went black.

London, England
3:19 AM

Evers opened his eyes, unsure of where he was. He could hear what sounded like feet shuffling on carpet or a rug but his vision was virtual blackness. His head felt like it had been split open with a dull axe and he assumed he was blinded by whatever or whoever had hit him.

Beneath his face he could feel carpet and knew he was correct in his assumption that feet were shuffling on it close by. He tried to recall what happened and where he was but his mind was still fuzzy. He could hear a conversation several feet away. It sounded as though it were coming from another room.

"You are weak, Simon. Weak in body, mind, and spirit. Your usefulness has almost outlived itself."

The sound of skin on skin rang out, and Evers could hear fresh sobs coming from a man. A thud resonated over the floor and Evers recognized the sound of a human body as it came in contact with hard wood.

Memories flooded his mind all at once and he realized where he was. He flipped his aching head over and could see light coming from under a door. Evers was relieved to know that he was not blind but had been looking at the underside of Trowton's bed. The lights in the room were still off, but apparently Simon had managed to get out of the bed, and whoever had hit him was still working him over in another room.

Evers pushed himself to his hands and knees and shook his head to clear the cobwebs. As soon as he did it, he regretted the motion. His stomach turned over two times and he felt warm acid flood his throat.

That's just great. I have a concussion and I'm stuck in an apartment with a guy I was about to kill. And who the hell hit me in the head, he wondered?

Evers felt another torrent of vomit stir in his belly, but he managed to suppress it. He pushed up hard enough to reach the top of the bed and pulled himself until he was able to stand. His butt flopped on the mattress and he closed his eyes until the newest bout of dizziness passed.

Outside he could hear the sound of heels falling upon the hardwood floor that he heard Simon fall to earlier. The steps stopped and he could hear Trowton breathing and blubbering then start to cry.

"Shut up, Simon. I cannot stand to hear a grown man grovel, and believe me when I tell you I've heard many do just that. It never ends well for a groveling man when in my presence," the deep voice said.

Something tickled the back of Evers's mind when he heard the man speak. The sound of his voice, the way it carried, the deepness of it, and the power it held over its listeners was one that he could not quite recall, but thought he had heard at some previous time. It had an evil, ethereal quality to it, one that sent a shiver down Evers's back.

In the few moments he sat on the bed his stomach settled and the thumping on the side of his head lessened considerably. He attempted to stand, pausing long enough to assure he would not get dizzy and fall flat on his face. His legs felt wobbly for a couple of seconds then they steadied.

For the first time he felt the .45 still tucked in his waistband; obviously his captor had not frisked him, or left him for dead after the slug to his head. The stun gun was missing, probably picked up by the man who hit him or resting somewhere on the carpet. He reached under his hoodie and drew the pistol, the silencer still screwed into the barrel.

Evers reached for the door knob and pulled gently. Light crept in from the hallway and the conversation from beyond became much clearer. The evil voice was speaking again as Evers listened intently.

"What were you thinking, Simon? Did you believe telling Mr. Evers what you knew would save your pathetic life? You have no idea how angry that makes me," he hissed.

More footsteps fell on the hardwood followed by a dull thump. Trowton grunted and the sobbing got louder. Evers realized the man had kicked him once again. Another thought flashed through his brain as well. *He knows my fucking name. How does he know who I am?*

"H-h-h-e said he wouldn't kill me if I told him what he wanted. He was beating me and hitting me with that fucking stun gun, Abaddon," Trowton screeched.

"Don't use my name like we are familiar, Simon. And you thought he would let you live after telling him what he wanted to know? Do you have any idea who that man is? He's a killer. Mr. Evers is a killer of killers, and he came to assassinate you.

"But you thought you could escape death by telling the specifics of our plan. What did you think was going to happen when I found out you relayed them to someone else, Simon? Did you believe I would take it kindly and just smile at you, or perhaps you thought I would simply pat you on the back and tell you I understand the duress you've been under," Abaddon growled.

Trowton whimpered but did not reply. Evers heard another stomp then a muffled scream. It appeared that Abaddon was a formidable interrogator himself. Evers gave him props for being so cold blooded.

"My fucking hand! You broke my hand!" Trowton wailed.

Evers stepped out of the bedroom, the gun leveled on Abaddon who was wholly focused on beating the downed man. Trowton turned his head in Evers's direction and his eyes grew large and his mouth flew open. Abaddon turned slowly to face Evers and smiled. Despite having the firearm trained on the man, Evers shivered again, the man's evil grin.

Abaddon's eyes met Evers. "Why, William, it's been a long time since last we encountered one another. I'm happy to see you well and want to apologize for the strike to your head earlier tonight."

"What do you mean 'it's been a long time since last we encountered one an…'" Evers could not finish his sentence, the words stuck to the roof of his mouth.

All at once, everything hit Evers's mind like a massive boulder sent smashing down a mountain's face until it ricocheted and crashed into his chest, squeezing the last ounce of life from his body. Abaddon's voice echoed in his head and a portrait of the man's evil grin stuck to the inside of his skull like rotten mud to the side of a rusted car.

"Yes, you remember don't you, William? Our first encounter in Uganda when you interrupted an important discussion with one of my servants. I had to admit being very upset when you and that absolute trash of a friend of yours, Mr. Smith, eliminated my young protégé. For years, I have wanted to exact revenge for ruining my plans, first on you then on Mr. Smith. It would appear that my revenge will soon be carried out, and the greatest part of it is that I get to watch you die a slow death, all the while knowing that Mr. Smith will be dead in a short time.

"That nasty, vile disease he has. How do you suppose he came by that, young William?" he asked, the hideous smile growing larger and revealing pointed teeth.

"He has cancer, you sick bastard. I hardly believe that will serve as your revenge," replied Evers.

"Interesting that he just recently revealed his cancer, isn't it, William?" Abaddon asked.

"So what? What does his telling me have to do with your revenge, you weird fuck?" Evers demanded.

Abaddon's smile widened, which hardly seemed possible given the width in which it was already spread.

"Perhaps nothing, but dead is dead, huh? Anyway, I am very happy that you are here, although I admit some disdain about Daniel's misgivings in New York. Good help is so hard to find these days," Abaddon replied smoothly.

"You sent him to follow me? But how did you know where to find me?" Evers asked, his voice confused but stern.

"William, William—do you not yet understand that I know *everything*?" Abaddon laughed.

His question made Evers nervous. There was something about his tone and lack of fear of having a fully loaded .45 pointed at his head that made a cold chill run up his spine again. Evers trained his pistol on Trowton as Abaddon watched, interest apparent in his eyes.

Abaddon turned away from Evers and began pacing, his hands opened and crossed behind his back like a professor lecturing a university class on quantum physics. Evers thought if the man had been wearing a pair of squared glasses that rested on the end of his nose the look would be complete.

He walked to the kitchen table and sat down then turned and looked at Evers using his chin to point at a chair across from him.

"Come sit, William. All this blatant hostility tires me, as I'm sure it does you. You may not realize it, but you are at a significant disadvantage right now, so you may as well relax for a few moments."

Evers felt a bizarre pull in his mind to do as he was told, the tug subtle but purposeful. He walked to the table and took a seat across from the man who willed him into doing what he was told. One part of his mind screamed to stay where he was, while the other told him it was okay. He kept the pistol drawn and above the table top in case he felt the need to use it.

"I've watched you for a long time, William and understand the battles you deal with in your own mind. We share some similar traits, you and I, in that we have both been betrayed by those we felt would be there for us. You feel as though your country has turned on you and given you nothing in return for your years of sacrifice and service, while I have been exiled by the one individual who promised me nothing but love and affection," Abaddon shared.

"I don't think my country turned on me. My government, maybe, but not my country," Evers replied.

"Be that as it may, I see little difference between elected officials and those who put them in positions of power," his response curt.

"Most people have no idea what goes on behind the scenes. If they did, they would behave differently. Governments suppress the truth in hopes of remaining in power. So, like I said, my country didn't turn its back on me," Evers stated.

"Ah, to the point, William. I've always admired that about you," Abaddon replied.

"Wait, what did you just say?" Evers asked. "What do you mean you've *always* admired that about me? You don't know me!"

"I've watched you for a long time, William…a very long time. Look at me and remember," Abaddon demanded!

Right then it hit Evers like a sucker punch. His recent dream and the man who grabbed him by the neck—Abaddon. The black shadows that crept past him in his nightmares just before the anxiety would fill his mind, or the increasing sense of paranoia he felt even when he was alone suddenly made sense. Evil was real, not some conjured tool used to scare people into submission.

But could this man be that evil? Did this man have some strange metaphysical power that enabled him to get inside his brain and stick there like some sort of disgusting bloodsucking organism?

And abruptly Evers snapped out of his trance. His own self-worth flooded back into him as his eyes narrowed and he glared at Abaddon. Whatever strange hold the man had held over him was gone and Evers raised the pistol and pointed it at the man's head.

From the corner of his eye Evers saw movement. Trowton pushed himself to his feet and lunged at the man who had beaten and shocked him so severely. In an instant, Evers made a decision and swung his gun wielding arm around to the Englishman.

He squeezed two rounds off in a nano-second, both slamming into the man's chest. Trowton dropped in a heap on the floor, holding his chest and sobbing. A few final breaths escaped his lips then there was nothing, just stillness.

A roar exploded all around Evers, a vocalization like none he had ever heard. The sound was primal, guttural and seemed as though it was emitted from a sub-woofer. The floor beneath his feet began vibrating and for an instant he thought the roar of anguish would bring the ceiling crashing down upon them all.

"Nooooooo! Why did you slay him?" Abaddon hissed.

In a mili-second he was staring up at the top of the table. Abaddon, lifted the heavy piece of maple and slammed it down in a single movement, faster than anything Evers had seen. The back of his head hit the hardwood floor and he saw stars. The previous blow he received to his head, coupled with the new knock he just received, made his stomach lurch.

Evers rolled from under the table still clutching the .45. He started to push himself up when a heavy shoe stomped on his hand. Pain and fire shot up his hand and into his arm, all of it radiating in one massive globule until it reached his elbow. In an instant he knew his hand was broken as the pistol lay directly in front of him, unclutched by his destroyed hand.

He rolled in an attempt to grab the Colt with his good hand, but Abaddon was too quick and kicked it away before he could reach it. The man placed another foot on Evers's neck and began pushing downward. Evers forced his chin toward his chest in a vain attempt to keep his airway opened.

"All of my plans, the time I've spent putting things into motion, and you destroyed them with that gun of yours, Mr. Evers," Abaddon yelled!

Evers tried to reply but could not as the force on his trachea was too much.

"I know what you are thinking, William. Why not do it myself, right? Well, that's not how this works," he seethed and pressed harder on Evers's throat, the man's weight and strength much more than his outward appearance would suggest.

A fresh dump of adrenaline hit Evers's gut as the twinkling lights of oxygen deprivation began dancing in his eyes. His years on the judo and karate floors told him he had seconds remaining before he lost consciousness. With his good hand he reached up and grasped Abaddon's pants, the leg that was pressing against his throat.

Everything happened quickly as Evers spun his hips, placing the shin of one leg behind Abaddon's other calf. Evers's free leg swept over the man's hips then with every ounce of remaining energy he pulled with both his hand and leg. Abaddon's balance was ruined and he came tumbling down on his back releasing his crushing hold on Evers's neck and windpipe.

Evers rolled on top of Abaddon, smashing his good fist into the man's face. Abaddon arched his back and pushed Evers away with amazing strength and control, throwing him to the left. Evers landed on his belly and felt something push into his ribs. The pain was immense but his brain immediately understood the outline of what his ribs had fallen on.

He scooped the pistol from under him, rolled to one knee and leveled it at Abaddon's head. His breathing was troubled, having just regained much of his breath after the man had nearly collapsed his throat, and the energy spent getting Abaddon off him was tremendous. Yet years of dealing with exhaustion and adrenaline created for him a certain dynamic that most would lack in times of crisis: a steady hand.

The pistol did not waiver, his sites settled directly on Abaddon's forehead. His eyes darted around the apartment, the destruction incredible. In the distance he could hear sirens approaching. Abaddon smiled his greasy smile.

"Did you honestly believe you could rid yourself of me, William? Even if you pull that trigger, I will still find you. That's right, son, I will seek you out and eventually claim you just like I will soon claim Mr. Smith," Abaddon said in a calm voice.

Evers nodded as he stared his target in the face. "If you are who I think you are then you may claim me one day, but it won't be this day. And don't call me son, I hate that shit."

He squeezed three consecutive rounds into the man's face, the silencer on the weapon offering a pfffft as each round launched from its end. Each bullet landed within millimeters of each other. Abaddon did not have time to react to the attack, his head snapping backwards and his body falling in a heap a few feet from Trowton's lifeless body.

In one deft motion Evers stood and pushed the pistol into his waistband. He walked into the bedroom and picked up the stun gun, stuffing it into a pocket. With his good hand he grabbed a sheet off the bed and walked back to the dining area, pausing long enough to flip the table over so he could wipe down any finger prints he may have left behind. He did the same to the chair he had sat in then tried to recall anything else that he touched in the apartment.

Doorknob, he thought. He walked to the front of the apartment stopping long enough to look one last time at the scene. The two men lay motionless. He walked quietly into the hallway searching for tenants awakened by the fight the three men had. Obviously, someone had called the police as the sirens continued to grow louder, but no one lurked in the hallway for fear of dealing with whatever was happening in their neighbor's apartment.

He pulled the hoodie over his face and ran to the stairwell, exiting the way he entered the building.

Heathrow Airport
1:42PM

Evers sat in the leather-bound seat of the Airbus A380, the largest commercial aircraft in the world. As with most planes, the Air France jetliner was jammed with passengers heading to other places. The airlines were sure to utilize every free inch with a place for another paying passenger to sit.

His escape from London was not as difficult as he thought it would be. He walked over London Bridge after getting out of the Northern and Shell Building stopping long enough to ditch the pistol and silencer over the side and into the murky waters below. He reached the other side of the bridge and hopped on a bus that took him close to his hotel near Heathrow International.

Once he was inside his room, he showered, changed clothes and wrapped the jogging suit and shoes in one of the plastic laundry bags the hotel provided. Downstairs, he asked the concierge to call a cab for him then rode to the airport where he caught the first flight to New York's LaGuardia airport. While he was at the airport, he stuffed the laundry bag in one of the restroom trash cans then covered it with several wet paper towels. He was certain that the people responsible for cleaning out the trash cans would not rummage through it to find his clothes, and they would soon be in a heap in some landfill outside of London proper.

Through the window he watched as a landscape of cloud cover stretched beneath the passenger jet. The old lady seated next to him snored loudly, her eye mask blotting out any daylight that might to keep her awake. He smirked at the sight of her drooling on her own shoulder before turning his attention to his conversation with Trowton and Abaddon.

Before they were interrupted by Abaddon, Trowton explained that a nuclear warhead was being transferred to the United States. When he pressed him on the nuke's whereabouts, the man had managed "New..." before Abaddon interceded.

Despite Trowton's inability to complete sentence, the target was obvious — New York City. Less apparent would be the bomb's location and detonation target, although a blast anywhere in the New York City metropolitan area would be catastrophic.

There were several ports of entry up and down the East Coast. Would Trowton have the bomb moved to a smaller, less frequented port then moved into position for detonation later on, or would he have it moved directly to New York? Both options offered legitimate possibilities, and his mind bounced between each of them.

The problem with having the warhead shipped to a smaller port then transferred to New York was one of simple logistics. There were too many factors and too many unknowns for Trowton to take those kinds of risks. Although he was a very rich and influential man, wealth could only buy so many illegal activities before someone with a moral compass pointed true north would blow the whistle.

Evers continued to think through the problem, "Trowton told me Abaddon forced him to purchase the nuke and have it shipped to the States. That could only mean that he used his personal influence as a shipping mogul to move the bomb over international waters and into a port local to the City."

He let his head tilt back on the seat rest and listened to his neighbor snore. Somewhere behind him he could hear a baby cry and its mother try to quiet it. Flight attendants were focused on serving food and drinks. Evers did everything he could to take his mind off the nuclear warhead that sat somewhere around New York City, but it was all in vain.

He willed the plane to fly faster, to get him into LaGuardia so he could find the bomb. But what would he do if and when he found it? It was not like he could ask for it to be hauled to the local nuclear deactivation guy on Fifth Avenue.

Evers sighed and ran his fingers through his hair as the beginnings of a headache began creeping into his head. He could feel his pulse pounding in his temples and in his neck. With his arms folded, he leaned forward and rested his head on the back of the seatback directly in front of him. Evers sat like that for two full minutes, breathing in and out, doing everything in his power to stop pounding in his head from getting worse.

On one shoulder he felt someone tapping. He turned his head to find the little snoring lady staring up at him with sleepy brown eyes. Her face bore the wrinkles awarded to those who dared to defy the grave for several decades, but something in face looked kind and tender, and Evers tamped down the sense of annoyance that was quickly churning in his stomach.

"You look really tired, young man. Would you care to use this?" she asked as she held up her eye mask.

Evers felt a weary smile slide across his face as he replied, "You know, that's the nicest thing anyone has offered me in a long, long time, but I don't think you want to give up your eye mask to a total stranger and risk losing some sleep."

"Don't worry about it, son. There'll be plenty of time for me to sleep when I die. Right now it looks like you are on the verge of collapse and need sleep much more than I do, so take this mask and don't make me ask again," she commanded.

Evers barked a laugh, much louder than he intended. Several people sitting around him looked his way to see what was so funny.

"Well, I could hardly say no to that, could I?" he asked.

"No you couldn't," she responded as she handed over the mask.

He slipped the mask over his eyes and slept, mercifully, for four hours.

New York, New York
6:12 PM

Evers awoke as the plane touched down on the runway. He pulled the mask from his face and smiled as he handed it back to the lady. Before exiting the aircraft she touched his shoulder again.

"You should take care of yourself. It's not healthy allowing yourself to go so long without rest," she lectured.

"Yes ma'am, you are right. I'll work on getting more sleep. Thank you again for allowing me to use that mask. I think I'll invest in one the next time I have to travel internationally," Evers said.

She continued, rather loudly Evers thought, "I bet you don't have a wife or girlfriend either. A good woman wouldn't let her man feel and look like you do. You're a good looking man and deserve a good woman."

Evers felt his face heating up as several passengers chuckled and giggled; he cut his eyes at the man sitting adjacent to him across the aisle. The man dropped his eyes and stopped laughing.

"As a matter of fact, I met someone not too long ago, but she lives in another country. I'm kind of hoping to see her again soon," he stated a little too defensively.

"Well, you need to. And find yourself a good American girl. I've never understood you men who feel like you have to cross international waters to find a woman. Makes no sense to me!" she finished.

For a second time, Evers laughed. "Well, sometimes I'm away from home for long periods, so I'm not so certain that an American girl would put up with that."

"What do you do for work?" she asked.

"Me? Oh, nothing special...I just fly around the world saving humanity from total destruction," he said with a big grin on his face.

"I see," she began, "you're like Superman. Do you have a cape under that jacket you're wearing?"

Evers chuckled as he stood. People began filing down the narrow aisle and he thankful his conversation with the little old lady was over.

"You have a great stay here in New York, ma'am."

Evers grabbed his bag from the overhead bin and walked up the ramp into a dank, dirty terminal that LaGuardia International Airport was known for. He turned on his phone and saw that he had three new voicemails.

"I'll check those later," he mumbled to himself.

He found an empty seat away from prying eyes and began searching for shipping ports around the New York City area. There were no fewer than six major shipping ports in close proximity to Manhattan, two of which were within easy striking distance of the southern portion of the island.

Evers studied the map more closely and researched each of the shipping locations. In the Newark Bay area, directly adjacent to Newark's Liberty International Airport were three massive ports. He had seen the impressive cranes that loaded and unloaded vessels both from the air and from the New Jersey Turnpike on numerous occasions.

It was no secret that the Mafia continued its strong hold on shipping and waste management in the New York metropolitan area. They paid off politicians and Port Authority agents to sneak drugs and weapons into the surrounding communities, so it was reasonable that with his connections, both legal and illegal, Trowton would move the weapon into one of the larger ports for easy concealment until it was time to transfer it a closer port for detonation. The GCT Bayonne Terminal was located just south of the Holland Tunnel and the Red Hook Container Terminal was on the Brooklyn side — both would be ideal launching points for the bomb.

That path seemed the most logical, even though he knew he was rolling the dice when making his assumption. If he began alerting the authorities, it would not take them long to link him to Vasquez's murder, which could potentially lead them to Buddy and somehow to the Agency. He doubted the Agency left any sort of document trail, but a lot of the pencil pushers in Washington were sloppy even though they worked on the Farm, so he could not rule out the possibility.

Evers knew he would have to go this one alone, at least for now. Locating the bomb was priority number one; he would have to think about next steps when the time was right. He gathered his belongings and walked to the Hertz rental car counter where he paid cash for a navy blue Impala.

He found his way to the east side's FDR Drive before turning west on east fifty-seventh. Dodging cabs and pedestrians as he closed in on upper Midtown was a game he hated, but it was necessary to save time and to avoid the always congested and massive George Washington Bridge.

Eventually, he arrived on the west side's Henry Hudson Parkway, the dark waters of the Hudson directly in front of him, and in the distance the tops of shipping booms on the New Jersey shoreline. Evers continued south on the Hudson Parkway until he saw the exit for the Holland Tunnel.

His car entered the labyrinth of the tunnel, far below the murky waters of the Hudson River, and pushed westward to New Jersey. After several minutes of driving, lights from the Garden State peeked through the opening directly in front of him.

The Impala merged into New Jersey traffic, the rough streets of Elizabeth and Newark daring Evers to enter and navigate the terrain. Planes took off and landed at Liberty International and the new MetLife Stadium stood proudly in an otherwise impoverished and blighted area.

Just to the south of him the bright lights of the Port of New York and New Jersey. Each of the terminals were run by the local Port Authority with auditing authority by the various government agencies, most especially the Department of Homeland Security, which, Evers knew, was sorely understaffed and busy with other problems at the moment. In addition to inspecting shipping container bills of lading, and the periodic container for contraband, the Port Authority also ran the massive subway and Greyhound bus terminal in New York City. Their hands were more than full.

Evers eased the rental car to the security gate with no clear plan in place. A very large black man filled out his security guard outfit like someone who lived eight hours a day in a gym. He was focused on a small television in the guard shack and did not look up until Evers pulled even with his window.

"Yes sir, may I help you?" the guard asked, his deep baritone voice echoing inside the small shack.

"Do you have a supervisor or manager on site this time of night?" Evers inquired.

"There's one night shift supervisor, sir. What agency are you with?" he asked as he reached for a clipboard. His movements were rehearsed and sure.

"Well," Evers began, "I'm not exactly with an agency. I would just like to speak with the night shift supervisor if that's okay."

The guard frowned suspiciously at Evers. "He's a busy man. You need to come back tomorrow when the other management is here."

Evers stared at the man, "Can't do that, my friend. I need to talk to him right now. Tell him it's an emergency."

"Man, if you don't tell me what's up, I'm going to call the fucking police. I ain't got time for this shit, 'cause the muthafucking Yankees is playing," the guard replied.

Evers considered his next response and how the guard might take it. Slowly, he put his hand on the door handle in case he needed to jump out of the car and deal with the NFL defensive tackle protégé seated in the shack to his immediate left.

"Alright man, look. What I'm going to tell you is real. I'm not drunk, and I'm not on drugs. You understand?" Evers asked.

The guard continued to stare at him suspiciously.

Evers took a deep breath then exhaled. "Somewhere in this goddam yard there's a bomb. Not just any bomb, do you hear me? There's a nuclear warhead that's set to detonate in a couple of days.

"Your next question will be, 'why don't we call the cops.' Well, how do you think the eleven million people living in and around the New York metro area will react when news leaks out about an undiscovered nuclear bomb set to destroy the entire fucking metropolitan area?" Evers said.

The guard continued to stare at him, his features shifting from disbelief to utter terror.

Evers continued, "Look my man, I'm not asking you to do anything illegal, immoral, or against the rules. I'm only asking that you request the night shift supervisor to come up here and speak with me. You can search me and my car — I have nothing to hide. This is all legit."

The guard asked, "How do you know there's a bomb here?"

Evers, almost exasperated, yelled, "Because I killed the motherfucker yesterday after he told me his plan! Now get the fucking supervisor up here!"

After several long, agonizing seconds the guard picked up his radio and called," Hey Brad, I need you to come to the shack for a minute. There's some guy up here that is saying there's a damned emergency and he needs to talk to you. I think this is for real, bro."

"Darius, I ain't got time for no shit. In the first place, I'm already at least twenty containers behind, and on top of that, do have the proper shipping marks for the split load scheduled for tomorrow. Tell that guy to come back tomorrow," came the reply on the other end.

"Man, I told him that. This looks serious. Can you come up here right now?" the guard asked.

Evers eyed him carefully, "Thank you, Darius. You have no idea how serious this shit really is."

Darius's hand shook as he placed the radio back on its cradle. "Should be a minute or two before Brad gets up here."

Evers nodded his understanding then gazed at the hundreds of containers that lined the incredible expanse of concrete. He wondered how the workers kept all of them straight and in order, although he knew computers played a significant role in helping with that, just like in other industries.

Five minutes later an electric cart pulled up to the guard shack. A thirty-something man wearing a green hard hat jumped off the bright yellow vehicle and looked at Evers for a few long seconds before turning his attention to Darius.

"What's up man? Who is this guy?" Brad questioned.

"Dude, you need to hear what he has to say and decide fo' yo'self," Darius responded.

Brad turned his attention to Evers. "How can I help you?"

Evers took another deep breath, hopeful that he could make some headway with Brad.

"Look, this is going to sound crazy, I know, but I have reason to believe that there may be a nuclear warhead stored in one of the containers at this port. The bomb is scheduled to detonate in two days, and I need to know for sure if it's here," Evers stated.

Brad shook his head and rolled his eyes. "Look man, I really don't have time for this shit, okay? I have a stack of paperwork as tall as the Statue of Liberty to review and file before my shift ends. My admin called in sick tonight, so it's just me taking care of all this stuff.

"Anyway, DHS spot checks shipments all the time, and we carefully review all of the bills of lading and shipping marks as they enter the country. Hell, we have to be extremely careful, or the port could be shut down and all us out of a job.

"What I'm saying is, the chances of a nuclear bomb being in any of these containers is as likely as me getting a shot to play second base for the Yankees," he finished.

Evers fought to control his temper and stuffed his hands in his pockets to keep from strangling Brad. He took a couple of short breaths through his nose and exhaled.

"I understand your doubt, Brad, but you have to trust me on this one. Have you been following the news lately? Do you know anything about the Ebola and SARS outbreaks around the world, or the nuclear attacks in France and India? How about the mass graves they're still upturning in Argentina? Have you heard about any of these things?" Evers demanded.

"Sure, man. What's that got to do with our shipping yard though?" he asked, his accent suddenly thicker and more Jersey-esque.

"This sounds crazy, I know, but each of those events are linked to one another. There has been a plot to attack people globally, and next on the list is New York City and north Jersey. Time isn't something I have a lot of Brad, so if you don't believe me I'll leave. You need to understand that when I get out of here, I'm not coming back, and you'll be left wondering if what I said was real or bullshit," Evers stated.

The three men stood frozen with eyes fixed on each other. Evers saw a bead of sweat form on Brad's forehead, while Darius rubbed his hands together nervously.

Brad stammered, "I-I-I need to call my supervisor."

"There's no time, Brad. Now or never, bro," Evers replied.

Darius turned his attention to Brad. "What's it going to hurt, man? I ain't going to tell anyone you let the guy in, if that's what you're worried about, brother. Let him do his thing then we call all breathe a little easier."

Brad looked Darius in the eye then slowly nodded his approval. "Alright, man, but you better not be trying to dick me over. I'll kick your ass if I lose my job."

Evers had to smile at Brad's hubris. The poor guy had no idea who he was threatening. For warriors, threats meant little. The two men headed toward the shipping yard office, Brad leading the way. Darius returned to the guard shack, his expression one of worry and dread.

As they entered the shipping office, Brad turned to Evers. "Okay, I'm going to need a little more information than you just telling me there's a fucking bomb in one of these hundreds of containers. Do you have any idea where the container originated?"

Evers sighed, "Not really, but I've got a pretty good idea that we could use a little deductive reasoning and narrow our search."

Brad replied, "I'm listening."

"Okay, from what I've gathered, the warhead was moved quickly, which means European origination, no further than the most eastern point of the Mediterranean Sea," Evers surmised.

"Have you considered Africa?" Brad asked.

"Yes. There are too many people in Africa who would love to get their hands on a nuclear warhead. It's highly doubtful that one purchased anywhere over there would have made it beyond the reach of local pirates or dictators.

"The safest bet would be either European, former Soviet Bloc, or a Middle Eastern country with easy access through the Mediterranean. I'm guessing it would have arrived here no less than a week ago. The person who shipped it here wouldn't want it left unattended for long, nor left with the prospect of some Homeland security agent stumbling upon it," Evers finished.

"Well, that's a start," Brad said as he began typing furiously on his desktop computer.

He looked at his monitor, the glow from it lighting his face in an eerie, ethereal way. Evers watched as numbers and verbiage populated the screen, but he struggled to make sense of it. A few minutes passed then Brad spun in his chair and faced him.

"Eighteen containers were received from outbound ports in the Mediterranean over the past week," he said.

"Okay," Evers began, "at least our search is narrowed. Help me understand what I'm looking at on your computer."

"This is a detailed list of incoming shipments. The first column of numbers are the shipping marks, or unique numbers assigned to each shipment. The second column lists the BOL, or bill of lading, that is assigned to each load on a given container. If multiple products are riding on the same vessel, the BOL is specific to a certain product from a particular supplier. This is how manufacturers track items in the event of product recalls.

"Next on the document is the manufacturer or shipper name. Essentially, this is the company responsible for setting up the shipment. After that is the port of origination, or shipping port, and the date the load left the dock," Brad explained.

"All of that makes perfect sense. Do you mind if I look over the list?" Evers asked.

"Help yourself. I'm going to get some coffee. Would you care for any?" Brad responded.

"I would love a cup of coffee. Strong and black," said Evers.

Brad turned and walked toward the back of the office as Evers slid into his seat and began scrolling through the electronic document. Two of the eighteen shipments originated from ports in Italy, three from Greece, and several others from neighboring countries. One container was received from Cyprus.

Evers rubbed his chin, his eyes narrowed in thought. Behind him he could hear Brad walking in his direction. The man was carrying two cups of coffee, the steam rolling over each.

"I don't see anything listed from any seaport out of North Africa. Is that a fair assessment?" Evers asked.

Brad leaned over Evers's shoulder and reviewed the document carefully. "Yep, I don't see anything from Morocco, Saudi Arabia, or Egypt. We don't import from Libya, so there's nothing to worry about there."

"You received two containers from Turkey. Let's mark them as a possibility," Evers stated. He wrote down the shipping mark and BOL information.

Evers spun on his chair and asked, "What do you know about shipments from Cyprus?"

Brad handed him his cup of coffee as he responded, "What do you mean?"

"Do you receive shipments from Cyprus very often? Do you have any idea what is generally shipped from their ports?" Evers inquired.

"Rarely. In fact, I don't remember the last time anything shipped here from Cyprus," Brad replied, concern growing in his voice. "Would anyone have access to a nuke on Cyprus, man?"

Evers continued to scroll up and down as he replied to Brad, "Bad people can get nasty things anywhere in the world, but I'm not inclined to believe that the shipment originated in Cyprus if it really has our little surprise on it. You said the BOL was a way for a receiver to track down the shipment, whether it originated in another country, through a broker, through a different port...whatever."

Brad nodded his agreement. "That's right, but what does that have to do with this load?"

"The guy who procured the nuke was a smart man, and I doubt he would have his name associated with a shipment like this. He would most likely ship from one port, have it moved to another, have additional paperwork created for the shipment then moved to its final destination point. It's called layering, Brad, and it's how people who work in the shadows do business," Evers stated tersely.

"What do you mean the guy who procured the nuke *was* a smart man?" Brad asked, the worry apparent on his face.

"Because I killed the evil sonofabitch," Evers replied without hesitation.

Brad stood there holding his coffee, his hand shaking and his jaw slack.

"Careful there Brad, I would hate for your to catch a fly in that mouth," Evers smirked.

"Wh-wh-wh-wh-what do you do for a living, mister? You fucking killed a man?" Brad managed.

Evers spun around in his chair to face Brad. "You can think of me as Superman, Brad. I fly around the world and save it from assholes intent on doing bad things to innocent people. And yes, I fucking killed a man. In fact, I've killed a lot of men. If we don't stop dicking around here, a lot more people are going to die, including us, so I need you to remain focused. Do you understand?"

Brad nodded again, but didn't respond verbally.

Back on track, Evers said, "I need you to take the information from the Cyprian load and trace it backwards. Find out everything you can about what's in that container, and be quick about it."

The two men traded places silently, Brad's fingers flying across the keyboard entering information, reading it then entering more. After five minutes he turned to face Evers who was watching him with great interest.

"It looks like the shipment BOL's all originated in Tunis, Algeria and moved to the small port in Cyprus. According to the paperwork, nothing was unloaded or loaded. We call that cross-port docking," Brad stated.

"Just as I suspected. It's well known that the arms trade in Algeria fuels its economy and keeps its government afloat. I wouldn't be surprised to learn that a nuke was moved through the country. Can you locate the container in the yard? We'll need to search it," Evers said.

"Look man, I helped with the research, but if we break the seal on that container, I will be unemployed," Brad said.

"If you don't break that seal, Brad, being unemployed will be the least of your worries. Now, let's find the container and worry about the aftermath later," Evers replied, his voice emphatic.

He swallowed hard then got up and began walking, Evers in tow, toward the yards and the miles of stacked shipping containers. The two men zig-zagged between rows of containers then stopped. Brad stared up at the top of a stack and pointed to the container that lay two-deep.

"The second from the top is the container from Cyprus. I'll have to hop in the crane and de-stack them," he said as he walked toward one of the massive loading booms.

Evers watched as the man hopped atop the stack of containers, connected the harness to the crane hook then expertly picked them up and placed them on the ground. He waited until Brad returned before moving to the one he was anxious to open.

Each container had side entry point, as well as the larger loading point on top. Brad took a deep break then broke the seal on the smaller walk-through door. He produced a flashlight from his back pocket and looked inside, Evers standing directly adjacent to him. Inside were columns of boxes neatly stacked.

The labels on the cardboard boxes identified the items clothing to be sold in the United States of America. Without hesitation, Evers walked to a stack, pulled and ink pen from his pocket and stabbed it into a box. He tore downward creating a huge gash then dropped the pen and began ripping the case open.

Inside the box was nothing but paper and other stuffing material. He turned and looked at Brad.

"Open the top and let's get these boxes out of here. I believe we've found what we were looking for," Evers said.

Brad did not hesitate. He ran to the crane and positioned the boom over the top of the container. After climbing down from the crane and on top of the large, steel box, he repeated the same steps from earlier before he lowered the two to the ground.

Back inside the crane, he lifted one door open then went through the same exercise until the second lay against the compartment side. He and Evers climbed ladders that were affixed to the sides and peered inside. With one hand, Brad swatted at a box near him and watched it fly effortlessly, confirming what the two men already knew — the boxes on the container were empty.

The two men worked feverishly, pitching boxes over the edge until they were forced to climb over the sides and begin throwing boxes out the side door. Evers kicked and pushed boxes, while Brad worked with a little more care, although later he would be hard pressed to explain why.

Twenty minutes passed when Evers heard Brad scream out a line of expletives any military man would be proud to vocalize.

"What's wrong?" Evers asked over the den of empty boxes.

"I just slammed my shin into a large wooden crate and ripped my goddam pants!" Brad replied.

Evers made his way to Brad's voice and stared down at what he knew was inside the wooden box.

"Get a crowbar or something to open this thing, and do it fast," Evers ordered.

Brad hobbled off and returned with a large black crowbar. He handed it to Evers who immediately went to work prying the lid away from the body of the box. For several minutes he worked the end of the bar into the gap of the box, lifting and prying as he did so. Finally, the lid popped open revealing a body of packing material.

The two men tore frantically at it, slinging the material over the ground as they dug toward the bottom. Evers hand hit something metallic and he brushed away the remaining packing material to reveal what he knew was there.

A large electronic display showed a numerical setting that he was unfamiliar with, but he realized it was most likely a strange algorithm developed to count down the time remaining until it was to be detonated. The immediate problem was that he had no idea how long it would be until it exploded taking half of New Jersey and most of New York City with it.

Brad stumbled backward and asked weakly, "Is that what I think it is?"

Evers did not respond, he just nodded his head.

"What do we do now?" Brad asked.

Evers mopped his sweaty forehead with the sleeve of his shirt. He had been face-to-face with some very strange people and things in his lifetime, but he never found himself staring at a fully armed, and extremely large, nuclear warhead—until now.

He considered his options and quickly realized there was only one. From his front pocket he pulled the small satellite phone he carried for emergencies, powered it up, and found one of the very few numbers he kept in his digital black book.

The phone rang twice on the other end before the familiar gravelly voice picked up.

"Hey, mijo, how are you making it?" Buddy asked.

"We've got a big fucking problem here, man," Evers replied.

Buddy laughed, "We've always got a big fucking problem, Buck, that's why we get paid the big bucks."

"Not this time, Buddy. This is way over my pay grade. You want me to chase down voodoo witch doctors, okay. Need me to track down ex-spooks searching for ancient jewelry that will turn loose a crazed army on the world, no problem. Seek out a shipping mogul intent on de-populating the world, got it. But disarming a fucking nuclear warhead ain't in my career wheel, my friend."

Buddy sat quiet for several seconds, for so long in fact, Evers thought he had hung up. Suddenly, he heard Buddy take a deep breath then engage in a long, drawn out coughing fit.

"A nuke, huh? Where are you?"

"New Jersey. The Port Authority shipping yards directly across from Manhattan," Evers stated.

More silence on the other end.

"Let me make a phone call," Buddy said.

"Make it fast," Evers said as he clicked off.

New Jersey Port Authority Shipping Yards
11:08 PM

The two men waited with as much patience as two people sitting next to a nuclear warhead could muster. Evers checked his phone every few seconds to see if Buddy had texted or called, while Brad worked on picking up the empty boxes they had thrown all over the place after opening the container.

"Are you sure we shouldn't call someone else?" Brad asked.

Evers eyed him momentarily before responding. "Who are you going to call, the local police, feds, or maybe the nuclear bomb disposal unit? What will you tell them? How will you handle all the media attention you will get approximately five minutes after you hang up the phone? You'll have local and national news stations up your ass in no time flat, be fired for breaking into that container without notifying you bosses, and be the subject of a shitload of public scrutiny.

"You and your family will be subjected to the worst kind of humiliation you've ever faced, and the chances are better than average that you won't be able to find employment beyond flipping a burger at a local fast food restaurant. So, you go ahead and make that call, Brad," Evers quipped.

The night shift shipping supervisor said nothing and returned his attention to the empty boxes. He stacked them neatly outside the container housing the bomb as though they might provide a buffer in the event of an explosion. Evers wanted to laugh, but stifled it.

In less than an hour the familiar sound of helicopter blades washing through the sky came closer and closer. At first, the two men assumed them to belong to an emergency med-flight, or some local tourist ride that often flies around New York City and the Statue of Liberty, but as the sound soon turned to something much louder, they looked up to see several military choppers hovering overhead. Several men, all dressed in black, fast-roped into the shipping yards. One of the first men to touchdown, a large black man that looked like he should be playing outside linebacker for the Giants, made his way to Evers.

"Mr. Evers, I'm Special Agent Tim Harlass. I understand we have a situation on our hands here?"

Evers stood and addressed the physical specimen of a man. "You could say that Agent Harlass."

Evers showed the man the crate as more and more men encircled the container. Each of them looked deadly serious while holding fully automatic rifles. He watched as one of the men escorted Brad toward the office.

Harlass examined the crate then spoke into a lapel mic. Bring ten units inside the container to remove this crate. Place it outside so it can be moved.

Within seconds then men appeared and gingerly lifted the crate and its contents and carried it outside. Harlass barked commands loudly over the sound of the chopper blades.

Evers watched the men work as one secured the crate lid back onto the crate itself then wrapped several around it before finally hooking it another strap hanging from one of the helicopters. The rigging was smaller, but similar to what Brad had used on the crane earlier that night.

Harlass gave a signal and the chopper carrying the nuke headed south, disappearing in the night sky. Another helicopter landed a hundred yards away as Harlass tuned to face Evers.

"I know who you are, Mr. Evers. I don't necessarily agree with the federal government paying citizens to perform jobs like the one you just completed, but I have to admit a certain level of admiration," Harlass said as he stuck out a hand.

Evers laughed and said, "I do what I can, sir."

He took the man's giant hand and shook it. "What about the guys who work here? Both are afraid they're going to lose their jobs."

"They are both being de-briefed as we speak. Both will be instructed not to breathe a word of what they saw here tonight for fear of reprisal. Additionally, their bosses will never know this container, or what was inside it, was ever here. We'll take care of all the details," Harlass finished.

Evers thanked the man and turned to leave as Harlass called out, "Can I give you a lift somewhere, Bill?"

He turned around with a smile on his face and replied, "No sir. I'm going to drive to the nearest liquor store, buy a bottle of something, and lock myself in a hotel room until I'm shitfaced drunk."

Harlass laughed then retreated to the waiting helicopter.

Oxford, Alabama
9:31 AM

Evers sat on his porch staring over the small lake that stretched two full miles beyond his property. He smoked one of the Cohibas Buddy had given him several months prior, lost in his own thoughts. Not at any time in his life did he imagine that he would enjoy smoking a cigar. Perhaps his old mentor was rubbing off on him after all.

After arriving home he slept for two straight days, waking long enough to use the bathroom or grab a quick bite to eat. He was happy that he could not remember any of his dreams, although he was sure of a few haunting occurrences. Over the lake he watched as a white heron swept low, its wings expanded, in search of food.

He grabbed his phone and flipped through his electronic address book, found Buddy's name and pressed the virtual call button. He listened to the ringing on the other end until the familiar voice answered.

"Hello," Buddy answered.

Evers thought he sounded weaker than he had the last time they spoke.

"Hey," Evers replied.

"Well, I'll be damned. I was wondering if I was ever going to hear from you, Buck," Buddy laughed.

Evers heard him cover his phone and cough several times. For a few seconds he thought about the conversation he had with Abaddon then pushed the memory from his mind.

"I guess the jet lag caught up with me. I've been sleeping for a couple of days," Evers replied. "How are you doing?"

Buddy responded, "Me? I'm right as the rain, Buck. Never better."

Evers heard him cough again.

"Yeah," was all Evers could muster.

"I'm not sure if you've had a chance to check your account, but Big Brother has taken care of our financial needs, Buck. I put a couple extra dollars in there too. I hope you don't mind," Buddy said. Evers thought he heard a smile creep into his voice.

Evers chuckled, "Buddy, I don't want any of your money. We pulled this thing off together, just like we always have."

It was Buddy's turn to offer a, "Yeah."

There was a few seconds of uncomfortable silence then Buddy asked for details about the mission. Evers shared everything except his conversation about Buddy's cancer with Abaddon. He shuddered as he mentioned the man's name.

"What happened to that guy, Buck?" Buddy asked.

"What do you mean, Buddy? I'm sure you've read reports and articles about the two bodies found in Trowton's apartment," Evers replied.

Another few seconds of silence passed between the two men. Evers heard Buddy clear his throat, an impulsive response many had when they became uncomfortable.

"Buck, they only found one body in that apartment and it belonged to Trowton. There was no sign of anyone else according to the reports I've read that were shared by my contact at the Agency," Buddy said.

Evers was momentarily dumbstruck. Abaddon's evil grin and the way he temporarily had control over him rushed through his mind. Finally, he was able to speak.

"I don't know what that means, Buddy, but there's something else you should know about him. His voice..." Evers took a deep breath before continuing, "...it was the same one we heard in the jungle when that old boy stopped to chant. You remember?"

Buddy exhaled, "Yeah, I remember, Buck, but I doubt that was the same voice."

Evers replied, "He brought it up, man. Recalled it as well as the two of us. And his eyes, Buddy...when they locked on mine, I felt drawn to him. Do you think..."

"Stop, Billy, don't say it, in fact don't even think it. That weird juju has a way of sticking with you if submit to it. Remember, there is power in names and visions, so let's keep all this between us, just like before. I don't think I need to remind you that there are things much worse than death. No one else need know anything about this guy," Buddy demanded.

Buddy cleared his throat then continued, "Buck, you said you felt drawn to him, yet you were able to break from his spell. Why do you think that is?"

"Not sure, it was like I was in a trance, forced to listen to him until his thoughts were complete," Evers replied.

"What if he couldn't *make* you do anything, only suggest and try to bend your will through the power of suggestion?" Buddy asked.

"I'm not sure where you're going with this," Evers responded.

"Free will, Buck. Without free will we're all just robots, but our ability to decide what to do is what makes us so valuable," Buddy reasoned.

"Valuable to whom?" Evers pressed.

"That's a great question," Young Buck.

The two finished their call and hung up. Evers sat for a few more minutes considering his next call. He listened as the cicadas buzzed and birds sang their songs to anyone willing to listen. For a couple of hours that morning he searched the internet in search of a particular phone number. When he found it, he wrote it down and stuffed it in his pocket.

Evers punched the international number into his cell and waited while the long distance ringing began.

"Hola," Emilia's sweet voice rang out.

Evers paused for a few seconds to smile.

"Hey, it's me," he said.

"Randy," she screamed, her voice excited!

He winced at the fake name he had given her. Evers spent time explaining that he was there conducting some very sensitive business and had told her that name to keep them both safe. For some time she was upset, but Evers could sense that she was calming after several minutes. When the timing was right, he asked the question that had driven him to call.

"Listen, Emilia, I'd love to make that lie up to you. What do you think about coming to the States for a month or so? I would really enjoy showing you around," he said nervously.

She hesitated before answering. "You promise no more lying, Bill?"

"Yeah, I, um, I promise no more lying, but if there's something I can't talk about, I hope you will understand," he compromised.

"Then I would love to come see you," she replied.

He checked his off-shore account and almost fell out of his seat. Buddy had deposited the entire half million dollars in his account. Evers knew refusing the money would only make him more stubborn, so he sent him an encrypted email thanking him. A couple hours later he received a reply. *Don't go getting all gay on me.* Evers erupted with laughter.

Evers purchased a plane ticket and flew her into Birmingham the next day. They spent weeks traveling the United States, Evers taking her to some of his favorite places and suffering through the usual touristy things like New York City and Los Angeles.

As with any romance there were arguments and disagreements, but for the most part the two enjoyed each other's company, finishing their last week in St. Augustine, Florida, touring the Castillo de San Marcos and The Old City. Evers could not remember the last time he had been that happy, or slept without nightmares.

About the Author

Howard Upton spent his professional years in the corporate world, but has always considered himself a writer and storyteller first and foremost. An avid outdoorsman, traditional martial artist, back packer, motorcyclist and global traveler, Howard has been blessed to observe, firsthand, areas of the world about which he writes.

He currently resides in Alabama. When he isn't writing, Howard enjoys planning his next adventure with his beautiful wife, Cathy. Howard's eclectic knowledge in martial arts, military science, international geography, history, and conspiracy theories combine to give him the perfect background for writing Bill Evers' adventures.

Howard Upton can be reached at: www.howardupton.com Inquiries and feedback are welcome.

If you like action and adventure, and enjoyed *Occam's Razor*, you should also consider purchasing a copy of Howard Upton's highly acclaimed first novel, *Of Blood and Stone*. *Of Blood and Stone* is an action-packed adventure filled with martial arts, covert operations, conspiracy theory, fantasy, and magic. It has been called a whole new genre by Upton's fans. Order your copy today and find out what all the excitement is about. Available on Amazon or from the author's website: www.howardupton.com. Signed copies are available from the author.